WAVING, DROWNING

WAVING, DROWNING

ADRIAN LACEY

EST. 2019

BLKDOG

www.blkdogpublishing.com

Life can only be understood backwards, but it must be lived forwards.

Søren Kierkegaard

To my encouraging English teacher par excellence Gill Newman (née Hollingshead)

Sorry my homework's late

Author's note

Along with plenty of entertainment in *Waving, Drowning* I should point out there are references to suicide, attempted suicide, and severe mental illness. However, I've always striven to come from a life-affirming place of suicide prevention, with the narrative implicitly suggesting approaches to better mental health, of which the humour is a part.

Part One

Adrian Lacey

1

New York, New York ...
Ed Sullivan Theater, Manhattan – 28 December 1999

The modern world began when McCartney screamed his way out of the chorus and into the guitar solo of 'Can't Buy Me Love'. That's a fact, by the way – not an opinion. Non-negotiable.

Sorry.

The recording was all but finished – bar the screaming and guitar break – when The Beatles came here, to New York City's Studio 50 in February '64. They'd landed at JFK on the 7th, started rehearsals on the 8th, then did their big TV stint – *The Ed Sullivan Show* – the following day. (Not for nothing is this venerable venue now called the Ed Sullivan Theater.)

More screams:

Those offered up by teenage fans on the night seeing the Fab Four perform here in the flesh for the first time. And another scream, the one from my mother willing me into the world on the other side of the Atlantic, on February 10th at around 01.10am London time. I calculate it was part way through 'She Loves You'. Or, given my arrival wasn't instant, it might have straddled the ad for Anacin pain relief. Appropriately.

And, barely twelve weeks before, did I kick against the wall of my mother's womb when her adrenaline surged on hearing the news of JFK's shooting? Did I offer up a silent scream?

In the midst of life we are in death ...

'You gonna stand there all day, buddy?'

A gruff, chunky electrician was not treading softly on my dreams.

'Excuse me,' I said, über-English, moving to one side.

'It's just – I gotta job to do.' He had a pole to bash the lights into submission above the centre of the stage. 'Up on fifty-three,' he hollered to his mate on the panel, his accent suggesting New Jersey roots to my alien ear. The spotlight above his head obeyed, rising a few feet before his 'Whoah!' halted it.

Other sounds added to the mix: wooden panels for the set being sawn, camera operators swapping notes loudly to get above the din, a scaffold pole dropped with a clang. And then a boom as the PA was turned on and thrummed into life. I started pacing down the fire lane on the studio's perimeter, away from the stage, hoping for a quieter life.

'Nate – do you have another hilarious script for me?' For a moment, I couldn't place the voice. Then, through a gap in the black drapes defining her six-foot- square lair, I saw Penny the prompter operator. She was bearing a mock don't-get-mad-at-me look, all blonde ringlets and bangles.

'Do I write any other sort?' I shot back. I walked into the gloom of her grotto. The mini-TV screens by her cast a bluish pall on her bright features. 'And all my words are served up with cutting-edge technology, Penny,' I said, flourishing a floppy disk.

'It's Jenni,' the other twin corrected me. Yes, there are two prompter operators who are identical twins, Jenni and Penny. And, no, I'm not making it up. When I say identical, I mean really identical. Swapping-their-different-coloured-specs-over-would-fool-me kind of identical. Doesn't help I suffer from mild prosopagnosia – from the Greek *prosopon* and *agnosia* – literally 'face ignorance', or face blindness. Proof God has a sense of humour, as do the twins' parents for naming them that way.

Two earnest graduate types with headsets and foppish hairdos walked by, their speed as committed as their fringes. I caught the end of a transmission from one of them: 'Yes, he's here.'

Jenni inserted the disk into the reader, next to a sticker saying 'Y2K compliant'. The legend on the screen changed from 'Ricky Ryan's Friday Fandango' to 'Do you want to upload a script?' She clicked on 'Yes' and, without missing a beat, said, 'Louise wants to see you.'

'Ah.' Lovely Louise. But that could be good news, or bad news. 'Do I go to her, or she to me?' I asked.

'Here's your answer,' said Jenni, pointing over my shoulder. I spun round to see Louise approaching, dodging two hairy guys carrying two hairy pot plants.

Louise's mixed-race roots gave her a shower of funky beige curls. As she stepped in and out of the shadows her complexion kept you guessing about her genes. But her accent was one hundred per cent young London. 'Hi, Nate. How's the jet lag?' she asked.

'Mmm. Let's just say I left my body clock at Heathrow.' She might have discerned this from my stoop and lazy drawl. 'You?'

'Same. Nothing a knock-out Bourbon won't sort tonight.' She laughed lightly and played with her silk scarf. 'I'm afraid this won't help you sleep, though.' She offered me an A4 file labelled 'Draft Script'.

'Oh God.' Bad news. I propped myself up theatrically on the mini TVs. Both women smiled indulgently. 'Go on,' I said.

'It's Ricky. He's – he's not happy with the 'Millennial Quiz' script.'

And that last sentence would work as well ending on the word 'happy'. Ricky Ryan, Irish-born star of the show, was possessed of a monstrous ego, and had long since not merely kissed, but swallowed the Blarney Stone whole. A radio radical tamed for TV, he had a type-A personality: he was an Arsehole. But he was my arsehole. So to speak.

Regarding the quiz script, was Ricky 'fixable' or 'lost cause' not happy? I wondered. 'To business,' I said breezily, hoping I'd kept my nerves from my voice.

Earlier that morning I'd tried to get back to sleep, knowing there was a long day's rehearsal for the millennial show yawning ahead of me. It wasn't happening; my biorhythms clung to London time.

I got up and tried to avoid my reflection in the mirror but found it worse to half see a shadowy figure on the edge of my vision. So I looked straight at my reversed self. My dark hair's dodged the greying bullet – so far. My schnozz is larger than I might like, but on the whole I'm symmetrical – the measure of healthy genes, they say – side parting aside. I claim to be five feet ten, but that might be optimistic. My former slight build has evolved into slim to medium. Shadows have formed under my brown eyes but I put that down to temporary tiredness. My verdict is 'not bad', physically, considering I'm halfway through my three score and ten.

I get out my laptop and put it on the teak desk that's at right angles to my hotel room's window. 55th Street bustles below to my left. I power up and wait. A police siren wails on 3rd Avenue, then another. Car horns puncture my hearing like needles breaking skin.

Unquiet city.

The marble-tiled hotel reception belied this room's sparseness. The morning's sharp sun throws oblique shadows of fire escapes on to the buildings opposite.

A radio near me carries the music of a New York phone-in: smoothly carved vowels of a local woman intoning the struggles of her urban life, the host goading and chiding.

'Why can't you raise your daughter yourself?'

'I just can't, sir.'

'That's no answer, ma'am. I think our listeners are owed more detail, Miss ...'

'Mrs Shorter.'

'That child needs a mother – you're depriving her of that.'

'I gotta work. I can't afford childcare. I can't leave her on her own.'

'Stop being a victim, Miss – Mrs Shorter. You'll be blaming Clinton next. Thank the Lord he's near the end ...'

Enough Judgment Day, however cool the accents.

Click.

Satisfying silence. Then the sounds of the street percolate up again.

The Windows 95 logo appears. I defocus for a moment, mesmerised by the jingle and the sky-blue background. I open a file on my desktop:

Film script 1

OPENING TITLES
EXTERIOR SCHOOL – DAY
HIGH-ANGLE   WIDE   SHOT   –
MONOCHROME

We see the front of a Victorian GIRLS' SCHOOL. The camera cranes up as the front doors are flung open, and a large group of GIRLS, casting age twelve, pours out. They look eager and wide-eyed, fanning out through the school gates towards the pavement outside, each looking ahead of themselves, smiling. There is one exception: a girl who looks more hesitant, and who looks straight into the lens for a moment. Then she runs to catch up with the others.

2

Meetings: the practical alternative to work
Ham Yard, West End, London – three weeks earlier

I sometimes say the stories behind the scenes in TV are much more interesting than the ones we put on-air. But, midway through another endless pre-production meeting in London, that doesn't sound so smart. Even the meeting room's mustard-infused walls, a few shades duller than they started out, seem to have attention deficit. An advent calendar, with four doors open, adds Christmas drear.

It is a truth universally acknowledged that the more laughs are required of a TV show, the more tears are shed in the making of it. The star of the show, Ricky Ryan, is deep in thought, resting his chin on his interlocked fingers, his elbows placed on the scuffed white trestle table obscuring his long legs. His unkempt wholemeal-coloured hair and slightly wild beard are at odds with his neatly coiffured public image. A subtle black onyx piercing in his left ear, a gold Rolex watch, and the crisp cut of his mud-brown pinstripe jacket hint at stature.

'So let me get this straight.' Ricky mimes holding a bowl in one hand, the other hand points at it from above. 'The nuts sit in there, is it? Then there's a static flash when the punter puts their hand in?'

'That's about the size of it,' said Roger. Years of fielding questions from TV stars had torn him in two directions: he displayed limitless reserves of patience and kindness, yet behind his rheumy eyes you could see he was constantly scraping the bottomless barrel of despair.

Ricky's still quizzical expression suggested, sadly for Roger, he would need more of the former while adding to the latter. 'So, what's to stop me getting an electric shock?'

If anyone thought from Ricky's soft, England-diffused Cork accent they'd be getting an easy ride, now was the time to reconsider. Irishness aside, something about his height, wide mouth, and pronounced cheekbones always reminded me of Abraham Lincoln. But neither Abe nor Ricky was a pushover.

Roger knew the limits to his knowledge, another of the fruits of his decades as a director-producer in Light Entertainment. 'Terry – can we help Ricky here?'

'Surely.' Affectionately known as Terry the Techie, he was in his element now as the solutions man. 'Don't worry, Ricky – we'll stand you on some insulating material. You'll be fine.'

At the point where it was clear from Ricky's forehead it wouldn't be fine, I started doodling. After a while my eyes panned up from my spiral-bound pad and met Louise's gaze opposite. We both tried to express our exasperation in subtle eyebrow raising. As Roger's right-hand woman, as well as sitting on his right as production assistants do in studio galleries, Louise was also fluent in discretion.

I should, of course, have been thinking about material to accompany this section of the *Millennial Special*, but (a) I was losing the will to live, and (b) gags about nuts tend to write themselves.

'Any more for any more?' enquired Roger, looking around the room at the respective craft heads. Either they had no questions or no desire to prolong the agony. The meeting was adjourned with a click of ballpoints retracting and electronic organisers snapping shut. A collective shuffling of papers merged with some repartee about resiting the meeting on the fourth floor. Regulars here at Television Towers would know that held the promise of a lunchtime lager.

Louise caught my eye again, but this time it was less subtle. 'I forgot to mention – someone's on your case,' she said, brandishing a Post-It note with some details scribbled on it. 'They e-mailed the show. A woman called Jane?'

I indicated with pursed lips and a shake of the head it wasn't ringing any bells.

'She said it's something to do with a show about genealogy.'

I took the note and stuck it to my pad. Already my freelance-writer machinery had kicked in. I'm ashamed to say I mentally drafted a joke about a dog weeing up a family tree.

One reason I don't work in news.

3

'Millennial Quiz'
Ed Sullivan Theater, Manhattan – 28 December 1999

'Would you ever give me a bit more applause on that round?'

The sound department obliged.

'Then some tension-builder ...' Pulsing, sustained synth music began under Ricky's words, then faded out. 'But then you've got me saying, "Stick or twist". Come on, now. Too bleedin' obvious.' Ricky looked out from the stage to where I sat a few rows from the front in the stalls, lit only by half-powered lanterns with orange gels. 'Nate?' His brown suit trousers with white pinstripes were no more casual than his work ethic. He'd cast the jacket to one side and rolled up the sleeves of his black shirt, but even that was more about industriousness than standing at ease.

I stood to attention, narrowly missing a swooping camera crane. 'How about ...' I was literally thinking on my feet. '...Twist or ... Shout?'

Ricky looked impassive.

'Beatles reference – as we're in the Ed Sullivan?'

'Jeez – yeah, I know that. It's just: what's it got to do with the quiz?'

Never work with A-listers if you want a quiet life. I took a gulp of air and said, 'It means if the comper wants to go into the next round, they say Twist. And if they don't, they have to shout ... [Christ, what do they shout?] ... er ...: SHOUT!'

The sound mixer played a musical explosion. Oh, the power – for a few seconds.

Then the tension as the reverb died: was it going to satisfy Ricky? I'd seen him bawl out young researchers till they were in tears, male and female. Roger had described Ricky as 'a bomb waiting to go off'. Shame Roger couldn't defuse it.

Tick, tick ...

'Mmmm ... I can see that,' said Ricky after a while. Phew. And relax.

'Happy, Ricky?' enquired Steve the floor manager, his American tones – despite his living in London – finally sounding at home here. 'Happy' is a relative term in TV – or a euphemism. A small tilt of Ricky's head assented.

'That's lunch, studio.' Steve spoke loudly through chewing gum, in the process parting company with saliva. His ponytail had outlived its usefulness, like many of his follicles. His untucked shirt suggested he was bucking decades of received wisdom that in vain did you try to look cool in plaid. 'Back at 2.05, ladies and gentlemen.'

I made good my escape for lunch. Turning left out of the theatre I started pounding the mean streets of Broadway, looking for a deli without too much of a queue.

'Nate – not so fast, bro.' That Cork accent and false bonhomie. Bugger.

'How's it going?' I asked, redundantly.

'It's certainly going. Too feckin' quickly. D'you think we'll get through it all this afternoon?' Ricky projected his voice over the lunchtime traffic.

'You mean there's a choice ...?' I began. Then, remembering I had no interest in panicking him, I added: 'Joking. Of course we will. Look – we laid the foundations well in London. This should be a breeze. We've got a good show.' I could feel my nose growing by the second.

'Jacqui's worried,' offered Ricky. 'And that worries me.'

Jacqui, Jacqui ... I struggled to remember any Jacquis on the production team, then recalled she was his latest squeeze. Latest of a large field. And, boy, has he played the field.

'It's touching she cares – but it's almost worse for her 'cos there's nothing she can do.' I was a sophomore in sincerity. 'At least we can polish our shoes – and our lines.' I flicked my eyes right to see how I was going down. Equivocally, would be one word for it.

An outsize truck blasted its two-tone horn at some perceived motoring slight. Contraflow passers-by broke us up every now and then. Under a black winter coat flapping open, Ricky's three-piece brown pinstriped suit looked alien on Broadway in daylight. In fact, it would have looked alien anywhere except, perhaps, at an alien convention.

'Will this do?' I said, about to open the door for Ricky on an Italian-run deli: Franco Furters on West 54th Street. His lips puckered in disapproval.

'We don't want to mix with the fan base,' he said. There was a moment when I thought this was irony, but it soon passed. He seemed to have forgotten he was in a land of wannabes where he had no profile. 'How about Hotel Chantelle further down? Much more exclusive.'

I could only hope he was paying.

4

Radio daze
Dunstable, Bedfordshire – August 1984

'This is better than sex, isn't it?' Ricky whizzed the tape back and forth like a man possessed. Flashes of white flew past the heads where he'd made incisions into the oxide and removed the unwanted sound. He'd grafted the remaining bits of the quarter-inch tape together, making new neighbours.

'Sex is what I have when I'm not getting enough radio,' I responded. It's a mystery I can't sustain relationships. Except with broadcasting.

Ricky lit a cigarette, took a drag, then started spooling. Fag in mouth, he wedged some of his generous crop of hair behind his ear. ('Art-school' hair I called it in the 1980s, to his obvious pleasure, especially when I said he was the follicle double for Roland Orzabal of Tears for Fears.) He pushed the tape against the playback head while rewinding, and a chorus of Minnie Mouse squeaks gave clues to where he was in the recording. When we heard a big backwards music number, he slammed the brakes on.

'That was it, Paddy! I just heard the words, "Paul's dead",' I said hilariously. 'Play from there.'

A little explanation. Paddy is Ricky's real name. He's only Patrick to his ma, but I usually address him in person as Paddy. When he's performing, or at least working, I'll call him Ricky here and in front of fans or TV folk, otherwise he's my old school chum, Paddy Ryan. Excuse any grey areas. It's the summer of 1984 and he's just changed his name professionally to Ricky Ryan at my suggestion. I like the alliteration and the trochaic pulse (the stress on the first syllables: RICK-y RY-an). He likes 'not sounding too Irish'.

A fanfare blared from the studio speakers. My recorded voice then intoned excitedly: 'Ladies and gents. We give you ... the Beds Bros.'

'Not the brothers in bed,' said a recorded Ricky.

'Ooh, matron!'

'No, it's the Bedfordshire Brothers.'

'P'raps we should spell it out. B-E-D-F-O—'

'Or we could get on with the show.'

'Ricky's the dunce at the table ...'

'...Dunstable. And Nate's got his lute on.'

'...Luton.'

Cue the sound of a lute.

What seemed like the big time to me after hospital radio looking back seems hopelessly parochial. The county of Bedfordshire, with its twin towns of Luton and Dunstable, barely an hour out of London to the north west, might as well have been stuck in the Dark Ages compared to the UK capital – or the Big Apple.

'Dun-da-da-Dun-da-daa-de-daa-dang-Luton-Luton-Luton ...!' Ricky burst manically from the tape, singing his localised, bastardised take on 'Blue Moon'. It could barely be contained by the speakers, especially with the big dollop of reverb on top. True, we had the volume cranked up to eleven.

Ricky moved into MC mode, with his polished Irish brogue. 'Ladies and genteelfolk, can you cope with our soap that brings hope to the Pope ...?'

'...And his antelope ...'

'Uh?'

'At Whipsnade Zoo,' I explained. 'Up the road from here.'

'Aaah!'

Cue donkey braying. We couldn't find an antelope sound effect. Nor would we have recognised one if we'd heard it.

'Ee-aww. Ee-aww. Ee-aww,' mimicked Ricky.

'Ee-ye are aww-ful. But I like you.'

'So to continue our soap: an everyday story of commuter folk.' Ricky had switched on a calm, voice-overy voice – more anglicised. 'We find the beloved brothers on the Bedfordshire Boneshaker, the 7.35 to London St. Pancras – known lovingly as the BedPan line ...'

'Diddle-de-dum, diddle-dee-dee ...'

'Fuck's sakes, Nathan.' The oath snapped me out of this taped trance.

I swallowed my defensiveness. 'Easy, Paddy ...'

'What are we – some prime-time Saturday-night schmaltz-fest?' Paddy's eyes, alive before, were now fierce.

I stopped myself from saying, 'It's only entertainment'. That would have been kerosene to his flame. There's no 'only' in entertainment. To its driven practitioners it's as serious as brain surgery, rocket science, and geopolitics combined.

Paddy was burning with ambition in those days, like a lightning bolt in search of a steeple. But that was the point: it almost didn't matter where it discharged. He wanted to be a kids' TV star, an illusionist, a lead guitarist, a front-man rock god, a movie star – any and every kind of performing high achiever.

Non-believers thought I clung to his coat-tails for advancement, hitching a ride with a high-flier. They weren't seeing what I was seeing, though – an endearing line in self-deprecation, even pathological self-doubt, only on show to his inner circle, and usually only after a few jars. That take-no-prisoners self-confidence was an act in the early days. Fake it till you ... fake it some more. Plus, dammit, he had – has – a level of skill and perfectionism I felt at home with. He stretched my horizons: without him, would I have left my myopic home town for the bright city lights? Would I have found myself working in the Ed Sullivan Theater where the Fabs had trod? Would my words have gone multinational?

There was a nagging voice within, though, questioning why either of us would need the approval of strangers to be able to live with ourselves. What's that phrase: Adored by millions, known to no one. Is that a tragic life, a Faustian bargain where the price is too high?

I have a confession: when I'm not at work, and when no one's looking, I dabble in the great thinkers. Philosophers. You know, the kind of people who aren't content without asking themselves a question they can't answer. It's the best antidote I know to mainstream TV. So to weigh in with philosopher Rousseau, isn't the task to live authentically? But he didn't allow for the fact that someone like Paddy seems to be at his happiest when he's being *in*authentic – the act fits like a glove. That would have given Heidegger a right old headache, too. He went nuts for authenticity.

But he never had to face the burning question like I did: where does Paddy end and Ricky begin?

5

Lunch
Hotel Chantelle, Manhattan – 28 December 1999

A grand piano playing at lunchtime – that's a measure of opulence in my book. Sun glared through the faux-Georgian windows, catching the audaciously low-hanging crystal chandeliers. Waiting staff sporting starchy white shirts and fawn-coloured aprons were attentive to the point of obsession, setting my teeth on edge. It felt like one false move, one missed bow, or misaligned garnish, or reversed cutlery would cause an explosion – of the customer, the waiter, the chandelier, or all three.

'I'll have the *foix gras en croute* followed by the *cassoulet Toulousain* and a bottle of the *Georges Vigouroux Gouleyant Malbec.*' Paddy's alien look was now, perhaps counter-intuitively, more at home.

'Sir?' A petite fair-skinned waitress with a hazelnut ponytail turned to me, a hint of fear in her intense gaze. Or were her eyes reflecting back my fear?

'Er – the vegetarian. The roulade. And we'll share the wine. Won't we?' Paddy exhaled. 'And – and some tap water – *eau de*, er, *robinet.* Ple – *si vous plait.*'

'Of course.' She scooped up the menus under her arm and sashayed off, the full-length apron hiding the mechanics, as if she was on wheels.

'I'll cut to the chase, Nate.' Paddy pivoted towards me on his elbows, lowering his voice. 'Jacqui's concerned—'

'You said. I know.'

'No – you don't know.' Paddy leaned in and lowered his voice. 'She's concerned I'm leaning a bit too much on the old powder.'

I guessed he wasn't referring to make-up. Slap. But I wanted to clarify. I moved in, in a mirror image of Paddy's manoeuvre and mouthed, 'Coke?'

'Of course, dammit.'

'Ah – I see.' A treacherous thought flew through my head: What's it got to do with me? But it didn't touch the sides, as I realised with a leaden heart Paddy's powder problem had everything to do with me.

The pianist struck up, somewhat incongruously, with 'Embraceable You'. The song belonged to this city via the Gershwins; it even belonged to this part of the city through its Broadway heritage. But it didn't belong to a conversation between two TV workers about cocaine hydrochloride.

'It's like this, Nat.' Paddy would revert to a childhood variant on my name at times of stress. 'We had a bad meeting. Roger, Colin. Me.' Colin Ward-Clemens was the exec producer (over director-producer Roger) who rarely sullied his shoes on the studio floor. He had an air of Sandhurst about him: officer class, white gloves (metaphorical), stiff back, and an even stiffer upper lip. Little wonder he'd acquired the name The Colonel, although he was the only one who didn't know. Elvis fans got the reference, but it felt, if anything, that as a label it was too kind. The King's manager, Tom Parker, had only killed one performer, whereas our Colonel was rumoured to have ended the careers, if not the lives, of half a dozen. And he could sniff status, or its lack, at fifty paces.

I swallowed the question, Why wasn't I invited? because the answer would have been both obvious and humbling: it was a political summit, not a creative one.

'They're sweatin' a bit,' Paddy went on. 'Well – a lot. They don't think we've got a show to justify the time slot. Or the occasion. Or the money.' Paddy's eyes became two tunnels of anxiety. He excused himself and headed to the restroom.

I hadn't seen that look of fear on him since one summer holiday together on the outskirts of Cork, a place called Knocknaheeny. We were eight or nine. It was in a meadow on the edge of his home town. We'd been playing in the stream there when a couple of older lads blocked our route back to the village and started to taunt him. He stood out then as now, though not for all the same reasons: tall for his age, yes, but then also a specs wearer; moving awkwardly; shy. The bullies threw pebbles at him – small ones at first, but when he deflected those, or they pinged off his lank form, the missiles got bigger. I positioned myself on the far side of him from the other boys and tugged his arm, shouting, 'Run!' I was going to steer us in a big loop through the woods and back to Paddy's home.

It worked for a while as he ran with me, and I could hear the boys deliberating over which stones to throw, giving us an advantage. But then Paddy caught his foot on a rock further up by the stream, went flying, and slid down the bank into the water. He lost control, spun round and fell backwards, and it was then I saw that hollowed-out look in his eyes, the dread I imagined in an instant was his contemplation of making contact with the gravel base of the stream. I was too far away to catch his arm a second time and found myself pointlessly shouting, 'Look out!'

A splash and a short, sharp scream marked the collision of bone and stone.

I ran the few feet down the bank as Paddy lay still in the water. I shouted his name then found his shoulder through the stirred-up silt. 'Come on!' I said, energetically, roughly pushing him to rouse him.

I could see a fresh, vivid red mix with the brown of the stream's bed.

'Paddy – Jesus, get up!'

The cheerful babble of the brook jarred against the loneliness of the moment.

I saw bubbles leak from Paddy's nostrils. Even the sound of the current seemed to fade to silence before he blew a big puff of water from his mouth and, with effort, brought his head forwards out of the stream to sit up in it. After a moment he started sobbing uncontrollably. My hands felt lost in the air, then landed gently, one on each shoulder as I knelt by him. 'It's OK,' I said quietly.

I'd lost all awareness of the older boys but here they were suddenly, looking down on us from the bank. They'd caught up. I could see their hands full of stones, and the pockets in their shorts bulging, and they were panting. The darker haired one was about to take aim when he registered Paddy's tears. 'Christ – are you alright there, fellah?' he asked.

It was as if someone else had been hurling stones and insults. Where do these people get off?

Paddy – the grown-up, not the kid – returned to the table, just as the wine arrived. 'So what's our game plan then, Natey-boy?'

'The good news is we're a monopoly provider – there's no rival show all wound up and ready to play. And they're not going to put out blank screens on the eve of the millennium.'

'But they could make life difficult for us,' the Lincoln lookalike countered. 'Squeeze our time, reduce the promotion today. Tomorrow. The Big Day.' He shifted in his chair with barely concealed rage. 'They could kinda disown us. The bastards.'

'Steady, Eddy. This lady wants you to taste the wine.' The waitress had quietly returned and smiled as Paddy sipped the Malbec and nodded to her. 'What did The Colonel think was lacking?' I asked, dangerously. The waitress filled my glass, then Paddy's.

'You name it, Nate: dynamism, star names ... and laughs.'

Oh. For a moment I thought I wasn't implicated. 'Look, Paddy – we just need to zhuzh it up a bit. Starrier names are going to be hard to come by at this notice. But we can up the dynamics.'

'And the laughs?' asked Paddy, running his tongue around his gums.

'They shall surely follow ...' I promised.

Bullshit baffles brains.

6

jane.butterworth@altavista.com – 1999.12.13

Hi Nathan -

Thanks for letting me have your e-mail address via Louise. I'm a producer on a new US genealogy-based TV show called *Roots & Offshoots* (working title). We're trying to meet the insataible [I shan't highlight every typo of Jane's; life's too short. So for the sake of veracity I'll leave them uncorrected hereon in.] American demand for knowledge about our European ancestry.

You've been recommended to me as someone who could help with the London end of our operations. I know your big in TV entertainment and we need someone who can serve a mainstream audience but who also has an attention to detail. And is London, England based.

Would you be interested in getting on board? i do hope so.

Sincerely yours -

Jane Butterworth (Ms)

nathan.daniels@connectright.co.uk – 14.12.1999

Dear Jane -

Thank you for your e-mail.

Sounds like a project which could catch on.

But I don't really think it's me, to be honest.

Flattered by your approach. Wishing you well in your work.

Best wishes –

Nathan Daniels (Mr)

7

Relocation, dislocation
September 1982

The trees, sporting the last of a late-summer lushness, fizz by in a Monet blur. My lap belt grips my thighs too tightly. I'm travelling sideways on a blood-red ambulance bench, destination unknown. Winding country roads carry some echoes of memory; an early school trip, perhaps? My head throbs through a sedated muzziness. I feel like a baby trying to make sense of the passing colour wash, without experience or context. I am strangely free, yet strapped in. I feel sick.

How long to go?

8

Show rehearsal day one
Ed Sullivan Theater – 28 December 1999

TV studios have a weird kind of chemical smell about them. In my years in the biz, I've never quite worked out what it is. The paint for the sets? The floor cleaner? Some kind of singeing of the dust on scorching hot lights? Or the general dreary odour of a culture gone sour?

It felt like 'all of the above' hit me as Ricky and I returned from lunch. Or at least, I returned to the studio after lunch. Ricky did the celebrity sleight of hand that is the disappearing act. He might be in the gallery, or talking to make-up, or in his dressing room. The uncertainty principle for celebs suggests the more you can pin down where Ricky is, the more uncertain it is what he's doing there.

There's a school of thought that says the sense of smell is more acute when under the influence, and I was certainly that. I never quite learn that a drink in the daytime murders productivity in the afternoon. It wasn't that clear in any case what I was meant to be doing. I mean, I knew I had to bash some words around to plug the gaps in the transitions between items for the *Millennial Special*. But, true to Ricky's confessional about top-brass worries, there was a growing sense of feelings running high, and the show was becoming a moveable feast. It wasn't simply nailing jelly to the wall; it was like nailing jelly to more jelly.

'Positions, cameras.' Steve was still chewing gum. But was it the same pre-lunch gum? Something about his bearing with his script folder and his lean into his right leg as he stood, whether habitual or to avoid some pain today, made me doubt he'd taken a break.

Time for what's known in the trade as a 'stagger-through'. It's a term which dispels expectations of a steady slide through the script, as if in a frictionless universe. Rather, it's the stop-start mechanical act of getting the metalwork in the right place to get the right shots.

Here's the scene set in this two-hander: an English male has temporarily moved in with a female native New Yorker – in much the same way the Ricky Ryan circus has moved into town for a few days – and he's getting to know her ways, and other local customs. The *Millennial Special* is being beamed back to Blighty, where we're expecting to mop up ninety-five per cent of our audience. Only a small viewing crowd is anticipated to see the show via PBS (the Public Broadcasting Service) in the States and NYTV in New York. But why would we tell the Brits that? We're in the perception game, and my brief is to make the UK audience think it's a 50:50 production.

Immoral?

I don't think so – nobody's lying or forcing anyone to believe anything they don't want to. The bigger juggling act is with the audience in the room on the night: we've encouraged the production team and tech crew to bring British friends and relatives to pack the theatre audience. Likewise, Ricky's fan base has been alerted, and there's quite a few who'll stand the air fare of hundreds of dollars to go transatlantic for the privilege. You might think that's screwy – but we forget at our peril 'fan' is short for 'fanatic'. Plus, we didn't want to shut the doors to the locals – you need a reservoir of them on standby in case of British no-shows.

Net result is the material has to keep both sides of the pond on board. Cue references to English breakfast tea, pastrami on rye, NYPD hats against British bobbies' helmets, etc., etc.

'Opening positions for the loft-apartment sketch please!!' Steve could bawl for Brooklyn. The twenty-something actors took their places: Rich plays Tom, a super-English posh guy, sporting neatly combed hair with a side parting. He parked himself just outside the 'door' to the 'apartment'. Confusingly, the piece of set with the door built into it is called a 'flat', because it is flat; it's nothing to do with apartments. Sophia, playing Lucy, took up her position within the set of the apartment, sitting on the settee reading a magazine, her long, dark hair cascading down her back.

Steve simultaneously scythed through the air with his right hand and bellowed, 'Action!'

DOORBELL rings

LUCY jumps up from the sofa where she's been reading a magazine. She's chewing gum. She opens the DOOR to TOM.

...Or, at least, she would have done if it *had* opened.

'Can somebody help, please?' asked Sophia, of no one in particular.

Individuals in TV often get referred to by their department name. So Steve called out: 'Design? We have a door malfunction.' His chewing became more vigorous. Sophia mimicked it, when he wasn't looking.

Rich played peekaboo with Sophia, looking round the side of the flat with the door in it, breaking the fourth wall. Actors' prerogative, in rehearsal at least.

A production operative armed with industrial-strength oil and some fierce-looking tools runs on set and works his magic. 'Sorted,' he says, retreating into the shadows.

'From the top again, please folks.' Steve turned his script back one page.

Sophia becomes Lucy once again on the sofa, chewing gum and reading. She jumps up at the ring of the bell.

She opens the DOOR to TOM.

TOM
You must be ...
LUCY
Lucy. You're here for the accommodations?
TOM
No. Just one. One room. In your flat.
LUCY
Flat? Oh, you mean apartment.
TOM
Er, apartment?

'Hang on. Sorry, I've gone wrong', says Rich, looking slightly sheepish.

Steve sidles over with the script and diplomatically shows Rich the line. It transpires it's Sophia who's stumbled, and Steve moves to the other side of the flat (that is, the piece of set with the door in it) to show Sophia the line. Sotto voce he says to her, 'Your line is just "flat".'

'Yeah – give it more energy!' Rich can't resist saying. Adding, in mock New York-ese: 'You're flatlining!' It was good to have actors bring my lines to life and even augment them with an ad lib. Though nobody likes a smart-arse. Something in Rich's cheekiness and disposition suggests he and Sophia maybe taking their work home with them. Or to a local hotel.

The stagger-through staggers on, till we get to a bit about refreshment.

'From shot 22,' steered Steve, projecting to cast and crew. 'Lucy's, "Would you like ...?", after a pause.'

They sit at each end of the sofa. There's an awkward pause.

LUCY
Would you like a cup of coffee?
TOM
Do you have tea? That would be nice.
LUCY

(mimicking him)
'Nice'. Hot tea? Cold milk?
TOM
Hot tea, cold milk.

Rich giggles. 'You've stolen my line!' he says to Sophia.

She looks mortified for a moment (is she still acting?), then says, 'I'm so sorry.'

'It's okay, darling,' Rich reassures her.

Steve interjects with his trusty script in its tatty red folder. Lucy quietly repeats to herself, 'Cold tea. Hot milk. Cold tea, hot milk ...'

'Red lorry, yellow lorry ...' adds Rich, helpfully.

'Positions please.' Steve calls order. 'Same again: from, "Would you like ...?" And action!'

LUCY
Would you like a cup of coffee?
TOM
Do you have tea? That would be nice.
LUCY
(mimicking him)
'Nice'. Cold tea? Hot milk?
TOM
Hot tea, cold milk.
LUCY
Which?
TOM
Both. Please. Sorry.
LUCY
(She gets up to move to the kitchen area)
You guys! Something to eat?

At which point camera 2 collides with camera 3 in a scramble for shots. While the production pauses and the camera operators sort it out among themselves, the right-hand sound-boom operator – the action is sufficiently wide to need two booms to cover it – leans down to have a word about a shadow with the lighting director.

'Okay, guys?' Steve tries to ascertain; part enquiry, part encouragement to move things along.

Finally they get to end this sketch on more of the transatlantic tongue conflict where I began it: with a classic mismatch. Lucy is in the kitchen with a quandary.

> LUCY
> I'm clean out of most food.
> (Looks in the fridge)
> Wait – I could do you a salad?
> TOM
> Mmm. Tea and salad. A great British delicacy.
> LUCY
> (Missing Tom's irony)
> Really? That's lucky. Tomato or potato?
> (She pronounces them 'tuh-MAY-toh, puh-TAY-toh.')
> TOM
> Tomato ('tom-AAH-toh'), potato ('puh-TAA-toh') ..?
> LUCY
> Whatever. Are you English all so indecisive?
> TOM
> Let's call the whole thing off ...
> LUCY
> Excuse me?
> (Tom does a big theatrical wink into the camera in close-up.)

'Applause, applause, applause,' booms Steve, using a TV convention of audience reaction triplets, in the place of the crowd who'll only be there on the night.

9

Fab idea
Ham Yard, West End, London – 9 March 1999

Another day, another ideas meeting in London during early pre-production. On the agenda: what to have as the final musical number to go out on? There was a feeling that 'Millennium' by Robbie Williams was, perhaps, too obvious, although almost no one wanted to completely dismiss it; we kept it in our back pocket. Similarly, Prince's '1999' wasn't the most creative idea, and it had the disadvantage of looking back, not forward. But no one had the heart – or the bottle – to bin it altogether.

'What about something spacey from Bowie?' Not the daftest outpouring in, let's face it, a strong field from my tragically incompetent script editor, Edwin – rechristened Script Ed by me. But he lost credibility for mispronouncing 'Bowie' as if it rhymed with 'now-ee'. The verdict overall was that 'Space Oddity' or 'Life on Mars', while classics in their own right, as part of the *Millennial Special* would resemble an outmoded vision of the future, like the controls on the original Starship Enterprise resembling a vision mixer from 1973.

I had to pick my moment to boldly launch my pitch – late enough for the ideas flow from the others to dry up, but not so late that my colleagues underwent a second wind. Leaving a gap in the conversation as long as I dared, I decided it was now or never. And *I* was going to be the second wind.

'I think we're missing a trick here,' I began. 'On the *Fandango* we aspire to the best in popular culture, the highest production standards to connect with the largest audience. The Benthamite broadcasting ethic, you could call it: the greatest entertainment for the greatest number! We want to be the talk of the town, to infuriate broadsheets, to spark conversations at bus stops and in pubs and clubs. And in that we're heirs to the cultural estate of an ensemble from a city which has otherwise been in decline since the war. Like the stage being set for the spread of Christianity with the expansion of the Roman Empire, everything came together for this outfit.'

There was a cough somewhere in the room, and a bit of shuffling as one or two listeners shifted their weight from one cheek to another.

I started pacing round the long, pine-effect table, trying to not have the life sucked out of me by the puce paintwork. Along my journey I tried to catch the eye of Roger the director, Louise, Steve the production-and-floor manager, Script Ed, Terry the Techie, Colin the Colonel, and Estelle his PA. Ricky had deemed himself above these meetings now and, realistically, Colin was showing less interest in what I said than in his leather elbow patches.

I developed my theme. 'A rival TV channel started a poll to determine the UK public's *Music of the Millennium* a few weeks ago. We won't get those results for a bit, but we do have last year's results for the top 100 albums. The top 10 included a smattering of the usual recent rock suspects like Radiohead, Nirvana, Oasis. Radiohead even got two entries. But one band from an earlier era had no fewer than three entries.'

'Maths aside your point, Nate, is ...?' Things are bad if even sweet Roger's having to ask.

'The point is the group that dominates the albums in the nation's affections is the group we should feature in our finale: The Beatles.' I felt awkward standing up, so pulled out my chair from under the table, and slunk into rejoining the others.

Steve, the only American in the London-based team, piped up with his rich, confident baritone. 'It may have escaped your attention that The Beatles aren't currently touring.'

I expected flak, but didn't expect it from him and his acerbic tongue. 'I'm aware of that, and there are different ways we could go with it.'

Terry offered, 'There's The Threetles.'

'Indeed there are,' I acknowledged. 'The three survivors: Paul, George, and Ringo.'

'You can forget that for starters.' Who else but the man with dollar signs tattooed on his eyelids? The Colonel. 'A budgetary no-no from the outset.'

'Chances are they're already booked or want to be with their families for the millennium, in any case.' Louise had found a way into the conversation, tacking diplomatically between me and the Colonel.

'Ah, yes – Threetles Not For Sale.' I felt smug but my audience looked baffled, with the exception of fellow Fabs fan Terry.

'*Beatles For Sale* was an early album,' he said, helpfully. The silence was merciless.

Louise was probably right about the surviving former Beatles and commitments, so I couldn't contradict her. Quite apart from fancying her. She wore a beige checked chemise with a wet-look indigo belt, and it was the first time I saw her with glasses. Large round frames picked up on the blueness of her belt but shifted it up a few megahertz, making it brighter.

'Shame we can't afford the real deal – they might have found the Ed Sullivan a temptation too far, especially for the millennium,' I said. 'Lest we forget, it's where they broke America that fateful night in '64. The night I was born.'

'That Nateful night,' Louise chipped in. God, I loved her for that – though I instantly resented her for getting there first.

'Nice.' I went on, 'I was hoping the combination of the Theater with the mammoth event might be irresistible to McCartney and Co. Just as well there are other ways to skin the Fabs cat.'

'A troupe dancing to a Beatles track?' Terry was trying at least, even if it was a non-starter.

I observed the rules of the brainstorm and didn't pour cold water on Techie Terry's terpsichorean twattery.

The Colonel observed no such niceties. 'You can almost never clear The Beatles for TV use, unless they're making it themselves. About themselves.'

Roger rose above his torpor and offered, 'That surely only leaves one Beatly option. If you can't get the real musos playing, and you can't play the real recording, what about a tribute act?'

My initial thought was that was a bit Fourth Division. Fortunately, brainstorm ethics controlled my tongue. Then I thought we could put a different spin on it.

'Roger, Roger. You might have something there,' I said, my brain heading down what can only be described as a tributary.

10

Dressing down from the Colonel
Ed Sullivan Theater, Manhattan – 28 December 1999

I was up before the beak.

Colin had taken exception to the sketch.

'What the bloody hell do you think you're playing at? Your little playlet might have worked its magic in the '50s, but it's useless for the new millennium. Christ.' The Colonel paced anxiously around his desk. He had a printout of my not-so-bon mots which he cuffed dismissively with the back of his hand. 'You do know you can fly to the States from England, don't you?' he said, waving the script in my face as he passed. 'I mean, these days it's not three weeks on a bloody slow boat from Southampton.'

Stress makes you do daft things, and I started to mouth the word, 'Yes', till I twigged his question was rhetorical. Script Ed was sitting slightly sheepishly on a puce-coloured sofa, identical to the one I was on. The sofas were planted opposite each other at the feet of Colin's outsize cherry wood desk. Script Ed was put on earth to squeeze all humour out of my jokes, though he saw his role as refining them. His long face accentuated his humourlessness, which you would have thought would be a career-limiting condition in comedy, but perhaps it was his avuncular style which earned colleagues' trust – undeservedly. He was no more threatening than his Marks and Sparks jumpers. A proper script editor knows where the gags are buried and teases them out if they're too throwaway. Script Ed has developed the art of burying my perfectly good gags. And, as part of the production team, he'll always happily side with them against me; he knows which side his bread's buttered.

Red braces fell out of favour in the Eighties, but Colin missed the memo. Furthermore, he didn't appreciate they should on no account be worn with a checked shirt. The ensemble was strobing before my eyes, not helped by the dressing down I was getting. 'Do you know anyone in the real world? Anyone? There's a show called *Friends*. British viewers love it, though it's American. Brits don't seem to be ignorant of the US vernacular. Just you.'

Script Ed shifted slightly uneasily on his sofa, but he wasn't about to leap to my defence.

I was a five-year-old again, being lectured by my infant-school headmistress, Miss Dyeball, on not running through the car park next to the playground. (The complication was that there were two school buildings, one old, one new, and between the two was a church with its car park behind.) I tried to pre-empt the punishment, then as now, by being submissive. 'I'm sorry Miss Dyeball ... I'm sorry, Colin – I thought there was still mileage in the two cultures, common language ...'

My innards had turned to jelly in 1969, and the dial had barely shifted in 1999. My dream of personal progress had died a death. A Dyeball death.

The car park next to the Victorian school building was home to a grand old black limo. At the age of five, I told Mummy I thought it was fabulous. She told me years later she hadn't had the heart then to let me know it was a hearse, or what it was for. And, more years later, I found out it had been owned by the neighbouring non-conformist church I became a member of in my teens. It might have been funereal black, but now it makes me think of Lennon's psychedelic Rolls-Royce. Both cars had a hippy ethic to them. The church youth group seemed to have first dibs on the use of the hearse, and I imagine a certain smugness among them they could subvert the original purpose of the vehicle. It had ceased being a conveyance for old diseased, deceased bodies; in their hands it had become a youthful transport of delight.

'My point is, the whole premise of this, this ... thing ...' Colin waved the script with disdain, 'is suspect. The characters don't understand each other, but the reality is in Britain, American culture is king. Doesn't matter how many Lewinskys queue up to suck Clinton's cock, millions of Brits still want to wear baseball caps.' Script Ed squirmed at the mention of the president's member but still stayed schtum. The Colonel threw the script at me, mumbling something about it not being worth shredding.

Fair to say a rewrite was a no-brainer.

11

jane.butterworth@altavista.com – 1999.12.16

Hi again Nathan -

Sorry to trouble you a second time. I do take No for an answer. Sometimes. But now isn't one of those times.

You see, you've been recommended and I am programed to go with recommendations. As opposed to licking my figner [give me strength] and holding it to the wind.

So I'm hoping you'll reconsider your possible involvement in *Roots & Offshoots*. In fact, I think we should talk. Real soon.

Have my cell number: 617-555-0132. I don't know if you need the 001.

I should say we're Boston based. Boston, Mass that is. We're five hours behind you in London.

Here's hoping..!

Sincerely - Jane

12

OD
August 1982

It's a beautiful summer's day. The net curtain in the dining room is gently caressing my face as the breeze moves it. I'm coming round, but from what I don't know. For some reason I'm on the dining table. Time has clearly gone backwards and landed me here. There's a man in uniform in a dining chair opposite, appears to be talking to someone, and there's someone standing to his left, near to the window, with their arms folded.

I realise after a while the guy in the chair is talking to me.

'What have you taken?' he asks.

I fixate on the silver badge on the pocket of his white shirt. He has a solemn, straight black tie. Is he in the funeral trade? The badge is catching the light. He's quite short with rotund ruddy features, and grey, thinning hair.

When I process his question, I decide it's of no consequence. 'It doesn't matter – they were all placebos.'

Nothing seems real. Except perhaps the net curtain as it touches me. I'm hovering in the middle of time. It could go forward, it could go back.

'It *does* matter,' he quietly insists. 'They weren't placebos. I need the name.' Something about his worried expression cuts through the fog. Perhaps I should trust him more than I do myself.

Somehow, I end up on a stretcher wheeled on to the ambulance. The portly ambulance man, as I've now realised he is, is next to me, leafing through a book of drugs, trying to find a match for the bottle in his hand as the driver pulls away. Ambulance man curses under his breath as he can't find a reference to the right medication. He explains to the person who was standing next to him in the dining room, now with us in the back of the van, they struggle to get issued with up-to-date books, so they don't have details of the latest pills. 'How do they expect us to do our bloody jobs?'

I realise the person with him is my dad.

I have a soft cream blanket immediately on top of me, and a blood-red one on top of that. I'm interested in all the switches and gear around me, but it doesn't make much sense. None of it does.

I like the feeling of being chauffeured while lying down, though. I start to fly.

The siren ricochets off the narrow railway bridge – we must have turned right out of my road – but the pitch doesn't go down like a normal siren does in the street as it passes you. Strange.

We don't stop until we pull into the hospital. There's a team there already, as if they were expecting us.

I have a hard-on under the blanket. A nurse blows a kiss. God bless her for all time – whichever direction it's heading in.

The shiny russet tiles on the walls of the hospital remind me of school. I'm wheeled into a side room with an aluminium machine in the corner, like they were going to do some dentistry on me. Suddenly a middle-aged man climbs on to me and pins me down, all four limbs on my four limbs, arm to arm, leg to leg. What the fuck ...?

The nurse is now an accessory to this crime and operates the machine of torture. She approaches me with a red rubber tube which she pushes past my tongue into my oesophagus. The rubber is rough, like it's perishing. I wonder how many other gullets it's been forced down. I hope it's been washed since it was last used.

I try to fight this alien invasion but the guy on top of me is using his weight to make my attempts at writhing useless. I try to tell them to stop but the bastards have stolen my speech. The machine makes a sickly sucking noise. Just as time went into reverse, so now does the eating process.

Bye-bye, breakfast.

I'm wheeled out through the anteroom and feel that, along with stealing my food, they've now stolen the first fifteen years of my life. Gone. The nurse wheeling me into position in what looks like a children's ward asks how I am. I tell her about the lost time, and she repeats it back mechanically, 'You feel like you've lost your first fifteen years, do you?' Perhaps she's not shocked because they're stealing people's lives every day.

I'm moved into a bed which is against a wall. It's pointing towards a colour TV facing out from a pillar.

I ask the nurse what day it is. She says it's Thursday. August 26th.

At last, time has stabilised.

It's Boxing Day.

13

Show rehearsal day one – evening meal
Arturo's Restaurant, Manhattan – 28 December 1999

Raucous laughter. The clatter of stainless steel on bone china. A five-piece band working its way through the Great American Songbook. Decompressing at the end of the first day of rehearsal.

'...And he said, "The difference between them is Lonny is the shit, Johnny is shit and Donny *is* a shit!"'

A crescendo of perfectly timed laughter for Ricky. Set up, build, false end, frustrated hopes, and – bang! – the punchline from beyond the boundary. Plus a tag as a second chorus. Consummate. Thus the defamation of two-thirds of that much-loved triple act the Booze Brothers. Ker-ching.

Based on an original idea by me, but no writing credit. His Master's Voice. Suck it up, English boy.

Ricky leans back in his chair as the laughter's long tail sounds, the reward written over his face. A quick look and a half wink to me so swift it looks like a twitch. I affect a micro-nod from the other side of the virgin-white tablecloth. Perhaps that was my credit after all.

Jacqui leans into Ricky's ear, her laughter lines darkening as she says something shielded by her left hand. No quarter for lip readers. A cloud scuds across Ricky's face for a second then clears; it's all smiles again. She runs her hand briskly up and down her partner's forearm, pushing up against his loosened cuff.

'Shouldn't you be tweaking a script or two?' Louise next to me seems concerned.

'Dear Louise. I'd swear you were put on earth to spoil my fun ...'

'Nate ...'

'...But that would imply I'm having some fun in the first place.' I swill my wine. 'My kid sister on my case.'

'Jesus, Nate. God forbid anyone should ever give a toss about you. I'm beginning to see your wife's point of view.'

Ouch.

Louise reset her spine. 'You use words as a shield, Nate. A beautiful, shiny shield. But from what?' She tapped her fork on her plate.

Bugger. Having hidden my dark family secrets from her it transpires I'm transparent. I think she senses I'm two gags short of a script. 'Sorry Louise – did I miss the bit where you and I got married?'

'Make your bloody mind up, Nate. Am I your sister or your fucking wife?'

Background noise was no match for this large verbal arrow. Louise blushed. To our right Roger caught my eye, then immediately looked away.

'I'm sorry,' Louise said with a slight catch in her throat. 'I don't know why, but you make me care about you. It's a weakness.' She managed a shallow laugh through a sniff. Gently I put a knuckle under her nearer eye to diffuse a tear. She blew her nose on her napkin. Classy. 'Alright, if you don't feel like working tonight, at least don't punish yourself with an extra-late night. You'll feel fresher in the morning. You could do an hour on the laptop first thing, then we have breakfast together.'

'I see visions of hash browns ...' I could feel the catchlight return to my eye.

'That's my boy! I gotta go. Some of us know our limits.'

We did the charade where she makes as if she would walk through the city back to the hotel alone. 'Wait for me, Louise. I need protection on the mean streets of Manhattan.'

14

Largactil chaser
Psychiatric Unit, Watford General Hospital – August 1982

Arms rise up. The chlorpromazine clench.

'C-c-ca ...' The sentence freezes on my tongue but continues in my head: Can you tell everyone I'm going sane?

Dark room.

Mattress on floor.

'So as I say, "OOijofislkdlknokonnbronnijogige ..."'
No response.

Ah. I'm on my own.

Sleep. Rest. Oblivion, please God.

Shards of neon slice through the suicide slats. The Overnight Shift plays with his pager outside my door.

To continue: "Hoigwewejn dv0zvnf ..." Stir. Sit up. Lie down.

Nobody in here but me.

More of same.

Stir. Speak. Repeat. No reply.

Repetition is Hell. Repetition is Hell. *Repetition is Hell.*

I feel dreadful. I must be dreadful. If I'm dreadful I must make myself feel dreadful. There is no hope. There is no help. The constant refrain. World without end. Amen.

I've screwed up terribly. I must have to be in here. Here's your proof.

I won't see the age of twenty. Like other mass-produced items I have built-in obsolescence.

This is the People's Dispensary for Sick Animals.

* *

The three laws of depression:

    1. Yours is the worst depression there's ever been.

    2. You can't see an end to your depression.

    3. All thoughts that you were ever not depressed are illusory.

15

Bedding in
Napsbury Hospital, London Colney – October 1982

A few of us new ones have to go to get our chests X-rayed. It's in a separate building. To get to it, we have to walk through the soft rain across a courtyard. The leaves are turning orange, red, brown.

I stand in front of the machine. I know I'll have the last laugh when they look at my X-ray and see the dove of the Holy Spirit in my lungs.

* * * * * * * * * * * * *

We're walking through a wide tunnel with ruddy, shiny tiles on the walls. It curves to the left and goes slightly uphill the way we're going, back to the ward. It's as if they forgot to build the railway track for this underground line. The nurse beside me seems Italian; he's certainly very dark-haired. I wonder if this is now the limit of the world – just this building. I ask him, 'How big is the world?' He says, 'So many questions, my friend,' with a big smile. I don't think he knows it's a serious question.

I'm wearing a badge on my brown V-necked jumper. It's a miniature cymbal, as if from a drum kit. It's also a symbol.

If I run fast enough at the window, I can break through it and fly to freedom. Fly down into the courtyard then scarper.

I've only got the length of my room, just a few feet, to get up enough speed to shatter the window. It's a short runway to take off from.

I have to do it at night, under cover of darkness.

Here goes ...

One, two, three, four strides – I bang my nose on the window. It's Perspex. Why would they have plastic, not glass? Madness. This place is mad.

My nose throbs a bit, but no pain, no gain.

Another attempt.

And another.

Another.

Busting for a pee now. There's a wooden box under the window with holes in it. In this magical place, that must be the right device. It's practically willing me to use it. I piss into a piss hole.

I turn in for the night. Plenty more chances to escape another night. I've done some good groundwork.

I close my eyes and hear a train skulk through the night. God is trying to heal me through the sound of a train. In my mind's eye, I see it as one of those fancy tilting trains leaning into a curve. Then silence, rest.

I wake with a start. A strange face at my window, sliced into horizontal strips. The person looks left and right and straight at me. Then the strips of face disappear. The horizontal slats now let through bland light from the ward outside.

My father tells me the hospital is near the site of an annual pilgrimage. I think it's not just near, it *is* the site – I've seen a parade of people at night come to witness me, the first Christian martyr to survive here. They look in those slats and shine a light on me so they can check for relics. They march slowly past, showing reverence for me. They check to see I'm alive. Actually, I'm not sure I am, because why would those uniformed pilgrims keep coming if I was?

I call someone's bluff one night. I bring the sheet over my head and keep still as a corpse, holding my breath or taking in the tiniest bubble of air without disturbing the sheet. Ha! The pilgrim nurse is fooled and stands at the window for ages, shining her lantern, the lady with the lamp, looking for signs of life.

16

Show rehearsal day two – morning
Ed Sullivan Theater, Manhattan – 29 December 1999

More bashing of lights, more wheeling on of props, more organised chaos. Day two of rehearsals in the Ed Sullivan Theater.

The hash browns were sitting a little uncomfortably with too much black coffee swishing around them in my stomach. I sat in the stalls, praying I wouldn't be called on to move. I looked busy with my laptop. I *was* busy with my laptop.

Ricky was wearing dark glasses, that old cliché of TV artists who are not only famous, but who have to be seen to be famous. As an ophthalmic device it's a disaster: when they take the shades off for transmission their pupils are more open than they would have been otherwise.

'Positions for the "Millennial Quiz", please, folks!' Steve seemed different today – a bit brighter. Couldn't help speculating why. Good meal after work last night? Pay rise? Great sex? My guess is he's gay, but discreet. Perhaps he's buoyed by a combination of the above.

It was only when I'd got to the diner, I remembered Louise had tasked me to write for an hour before breakfast. Jeepers. How could I forget? Getting ready to leave had been a tortuous affair. Raiding the minibar for whisky last night added an extra layer of grogginess to my waking up. With my intolerance of alcohol, the miniature felt like a magnum.

Through my waking mental fog I'd recited my secular creed to try and jump-start my brain:

- I don't believe in the Father

- I don't believe in the Son

- I don't believe in the Holy Ghost

- But I believe in Love — or at least, positive forces with a life-affirming effect — benign at worst

- I believe in Me

- I believe I'm going to feel better later

- I believe that once I get started it's going to get easier

- I believe I really need to my arse out of bed pretty pronto

Shower. Dress. Scoot.

Amazingly, I'd beaten Louise to the diner. With the manic whir of food and drink desires being met around me I asked myself, What I was going to tell her as to why the writing hour hadn't happened? Extenuating circumstances? Hotel dog ate my homework? The problem with telling porkies to Louise is her role on the show means she's across how much I've written – she's got access to High Command who keep tabs on these things. So a flat-out lie is pretty useless.

The reality is, I thought, I'm screwed.

My best hope in the short-term as she arrived at the diner was deflection, distraction – and a charm offensive.

'How was Macy's?' I stood, as my dad insisted I always should, when a lady enters the room, as if Louise was the only person here.

'I bought a handbag for my niece. Not sure the floral design will cut it with a teenager.' She produced the box it was in, bearing a photo of its lotus-leaf motif.

I plumped for a low-risk compliment. 'That's cute. She'll like that.'

A waitress in traditional diner garb swooped like a bird of prey from nowhere. 'May I take your order?' Her smile seemed wider than her face.

'Could we have a moment longer, please?' asked Louise.

In desperation I corrected her. 'Actually – can we make a start on coffee at least?'

'Sure.'

I play a game with myself trying to catch the moment where the mask slips on an NY smile. Our waitress puts on a pretty good act, leaving the decay till she'd left the stage.

'So, Nate ...' Oh God, here we go. Another mask slips. 'How's the writing? Or rewriting?' Louise has a professional and personal interest in the answer. I'm not always sure which comes first.

'Well ... I've got ideas to zhuzh up the loft-apartment sketch.'

Louise didn't need to say, Go on. Her eyes, her silence, and my need to self-justify did it for her. She's always generous in the provision of rope.

'I've got to crank up the end a bit. Er – a lot.'

'Nate – you do know I've got to get it to Sophia and Rich by mid-afternoon? At the latest. Preferably lunchtime. They've got to learn their lines. It's not just about you, you know.'

'Chill, Louise, it'll be fine.'

Coffee arrived briskly. I poured for Louise first, then for my own, longing palate.

Our waitress came back, notebook and pen poised. There was to be no third go at this.

Louise efficiently dived in: 'Pastrami on rye, two eggs over easy, grilled mixed veg please.'

Match that. 'Mixed grill. Veggie grill, that is. And hash browns. Please.'

'Hash browns are inclusive, sir.' Did I detect a slight tetchiness? 'Coming right up.' The bird of prey soared and disappeared.

'Nate? Earth to Nate – can you hear me? Have you got something for me?' It was Jenni the prompter, speaking to me in the stalls. Another woman on my case. I wasn't sure if I'd been lost in deep contemplation or daydreaming. Either way I came round with a start.

'Blimey – you're efficient!' I sat bolt upright.

'Trying to get ahead with the script upload. There's a quick pause now before we dive into another long chunk of rehearsal.'

I'd lost track of the schedule. 'Can I give it to you in instalments – like Charles Dickens?' I knew the answer before I'd finished the question.

'Er – no.' And we said together, as it was a well-worn phrase between us: '*It doesn't work like that.*' That's how I knew it was Jenni; her sister embarrassingly didn't pick up on that phrase when I used it before, confusing the twins. Jenni now wore a beneficent expression, but it was not to be mistaken for tolerance. The blonde highlights in her hair caught the house lights over the audience seating.

'Can I find you as soon as it's done?' I asked. 'I've got my foot on the gas – honest.'

Jenni anchored some of her shoulder-length hair behind her right ear. Was that a passive-aggressive move, or did I misread it because I was on the back foot?

'I guess that'll have to be okay, Nate. Soon as you can though. Please.' Politesse was an afterthought, as was her wan smile. And both were in down payment for future good conduct.

17

As if by fire
Napsbury Hospital, London Colney – October 1982

Grandad2 (who looks like my grandad, my mum's dad, who died the year before) is playing the piano in the lounge of the hospital. They say he played before the Queen. I said, 'Before the Queen what?'

The Falklands fleet is coming home to Portsmouth on the TV. The Queen – she gets about – wears powder blue, as far away from blood red on the rainbow as possible. Grandad2 provides the soundtrack, like in the early days of the silent movies. 'Show Me the Way to Go Home'.

Everyone's saluting, serried ranks, blah blah blah. Her Majesty's Ship is *Invincible*, though some of the frigates weren't.

Grandad Junior (who looks like Grandad2's son) rattles in. He speaks of himself in the third person. 'He's been told you're to take the orders for tea.'

'He's been told by whom?' I enquire.

'By The Domestic.'

The Domestic is, of course, Mama Mia. She wears an orange overall and an occasional smile. She hit five feet and couldn't grow any taller, so she grew wider. That's not being nasty, it's just a fact.

Lines are etched in her face, partly of pain, but also of smiles. She speaks in a bouncy Italian, as if from an operetta.

I visit her in the kitchen.

'You take-a da numbers for tea-a, huh?' she confirms.

'Si. I take-a de Holy Orders, Mama Mia.' I clicked my heels obediently. Das Boot. Das Boot of Italy.

I borrow a spiral pad and a pen from the charge nurse.

I must get everyone's tea tastes correct.

Back in the lounge I say: 'I'm taking-a de orders for-a da tea now. For Mama Mia. Whadda you want?'

First it's Grandad2 at the piano. He doesn't miss a beat on the keyboard as he asks for two sugars, quite milky, not too strong on the tea side. (Tea side. Isn't that in the north-east?)

The Artist (who's 'four times better than Van Gogh') wants strong tea – no sugar.

Polythene Pam – a large lady who wears a plastic overall when she's doing pottery – wants coffee. Gesù Cristo!

Sue, who's petite with tight chestnut curls and a furrowed forehead, wants strong tea – bag in longer, but just a dash of milk. One and a half sugars.

And so on.

I walk down the Royal Mile from the lounge back to the kitchen, passing my room – number twelve – on the left. (Well appointed, with a view of the railway. On a clear day you can see the M1.)

I show the list to Mama Mia. She nods sharply. I place it by the hob.

Back in the lounge, I watch SS *Canberra* pulling into Portsmouth. I need the loo. From outside the toilets the charge nurse asks if I'm OK. I say I'm in my anal stage.

I look down at the lino in the stall. A universe of multicoloured specks and speckles on a black background – the great void of space. 'What is man that thou art mindful of him?' The Bible's psalmist is with me, even at stool.

Having cleansed my soul – our soul, arsehole – I return to the kitchen, where Mama Mia is filling the teapot with boiling water. She's thrown in teabags without number, and now was adding sugar and milk straight into the pot.

'Mama Mia – stop!' I interrupted. 'They all want their teas differently. Including Pam who wants coffee. That's very different.'

She gave a shrug. 'They can-a come in here – make-a their own, uh?' Another shrug. I wasn't going to win this one. 'You deliver these teas now, yes?'

'Si, Mama Mia, si.' I took the first tray and headed back to the lounge.

HMS *Hermes* was just pulling into Portsmouth as I delivered the first set of teas.

I was handing them out with apologies they weren't quite right – they wouldn't be here if they were – when there was a commotion from down the Royal Mile.

'FUOCO! FUOCO!'

I thought Mama Mia was swearing.

I ran to the kitchen where it was bedlam.

'The list,' said Mama Mia. 'She go up in-a flames!' She flapped around, distressed, then disappeared.

My lovingly crafted tea list was cinders by the hob. A tea towel by the cooker had caught light, and now a hand towel it was draped over was being licked by the flames.

Two nurses rushed in, looking fearful. One said to the other, 'That's a 999.'

'Yeah, I'll smash the glass and phone 'em,' said her colleague. 'You get the extinguisher – quick.'

I needed my fire jacket – and fast.

I rushed back to the lounge, shouting, 'Fire, fire!' and from the armchair grabbed my red jacket (made authentic with scorch marks on the sleeves) and ran, sirens blaring NEE-NAH NEE-NAH to the kitchen.

The room was empty, with not even a gas ring alight.

Only the sound of a distant piano disturbed the air.

18

jane.butterworth@altavista.com – 1999.12.17

Hi Nate—

Hope you're doing ok.

I know you're busy, but I'm busy too - if that's any consolatoin! [No comment - about her claim or the typos.] It's just I could really do with your help on this.

I've had to be a bit opaque with the details of the show I'm working on – production sensitivity, privacy issues, NDAs, yatter, yatter – but it is involves members of your family.

I'm attaching some photos of some of them. Hope you don't mind Could you help me with the relationships? Specifically, would you identify your cousin (if that's who it is - in the T shirt?) and are the other 2 your parents? Thanks -

Jane

19

Birth of the Fabs
Psychiatric Unit, Watford General Hospital – November 1982

We are to cook a meal together – four of us who eat at the same table: me, Sue, Reagan, and Polythene Pam.

Jock said so. The Scottish charge nurse. 'Make sure Nathan pulls his weight, eh?' he said in his bluff Glaswegian tones to the others. 'And stop him talking rubbish and shave off his bloody bum fluff on his chinny-chin-chin while you're at it!'

'Aye, aye, Captain,' said Pam. She had this habit of not being able to look at the person she was talking to. So for a moment I thought I was the captain. Pam made showbiz wigs in the West End. When she was well.

'Where's all the ingredients?' asked Sue.

'Usual place, darlin'. Guess where?' teased Jock.

'The kitchen?' Reagan (who didn't look like Reagan) offered. The likeness might not have been there, but he did carry a dark cloak of fear about him, despite his smile.

'I can see why you're a world leader, mate. According to your man Nate, here. Anyway, yous are on your own the noo.' Jock liked 'cranking up the Glezger', as he put it, becoming more Scottish than Scottish. 'Steady with the knives, uh? I'm away to sort out the bogs. Non-stop glamour, this job.' His last words faded away as he did, down the corridor. 'Busy, busy!'

We relocated to the kitchen. Polythene Pam was in command mode. 'Right – who wants to do what? Sue: you wanna chop?'

'Chop Suey,' I said.

'No – it's ratatouille,' Sue corrected.

'Point taken. At least it rhymes. I'll catch the rat. There should be one in here.'

'How about you lay up?' Pam seemed rather weary of me. But because of her looking problem, she looked over my shoulder, so it didn't feel so bad. 'And Paul [she seemed to not know he was Reagan] – could you butter some bread, please?'

Reagan did that thing he did – be shruggy and grunty. He was short and white-haired with a boxy head and a stubby nose. He shuffled to the cupboard and started taking out side plates in slow-mo. His light-blue cable-knit sweater sported some battery-acid stains.

'Let's have some music.' Pam clicked on the little paint-spattered radio and Carly Simon sang out her pain to a boppy backbeat. It was the song 'Why'. Yeah – why?

Sue tried to cut courgettes in time but couldn't keep up. She did a twisted smile under her deeply furrowed brow. 'My son likes this one', she said, and immediately burst into tears. Pam moved over and Sue buried her head in the nook between Pam's chin and above her voluminous breasts. It left part of Pam's animal-print blouse damp, making an extra dark patch over the orange and black paw prints.

Carly's pain carried on. Verse-chorus-verse-chorus.

'Where's the cutlery?' said I to whoever would listen.

'In the cutlery drawer,' said Sue, pulling back from Pam. Her eyes were wet.

'Where's the cutlery drawer?' I asked.

'It's where you get the teaspoons when you make the tea, Nate.' Pam seemed irritated again, but sometimes you have to ask the obvious. It's how progress works. Every question leads to another and to another. Used to drive my mum mad, but you've still got to ask. Healthy inquisitiveness. Like my maths course. Analysis. Convergent series. Ask enough questions and you get closer and closer to the answer.

It worked for Socrates – until the end. 'I know that I know nothing.'

Later when we sat down to eat, I asked Sue why she'd cried.

'Because that bastard shrink won't let me see my son. My beautiful little Simon. With his perfect blond hair and his perfect blue eyes. Mr Hendry, the shit. Goes home to his wife and kids every day. How does he sleep?'

'I've heard he sleeps with his mistress on the way home,' piped up Pam. 'Money he's on, he can afford to run two women!' Sue's face lit up in laughter for the first time this evening.

'This is good ratatat-tat, girls,' Reagan passed judgment, as only the leader of the free world could.

'Ratatouille,' corrected Sue. 'But thanks.'

'Thanks,' echoed Pam.

'I hereby declare ...' I began portentously, 'us – Sue, Reagan, me, and Polythene Pam – the Fab Four. And, lo, that's what we are!'

'Are we fabulous?' Sue asked.

'Compared with the others, yes,' I explained. 'The dregs of humanity. They're the Dregs. We're the Fabs.'

'To the Fabs!' endorsed Pam, offering her tumbler of grape juice to anyone who would clink her.

20

Therapy part one: catch-up
Thornton Heath, south London – 7 September 1999

'How has this week been?' Mary played the intensity of the therapist to perfection. This was no prelude to small talk. Her dark eyes distracted me for a moment, then called me back to focus.

'You know ... Okay – you don't know. Feeling wretched but working round it. Or trying to. Things are wobbly with Samantha – that's not helping.'

'Wobbly? Could you unpack that a bit?'

Touchez. I'd left my flank exposed there. Mary was conventional in her approach to the role, but didn't always dress to her trade's stereotype. She wore grey combat pants, crossing her legs just above her dark trainers. Her couture was topped off by a dark green sweatshirt with pink gems in concentric circles.

'It's the death of a marriage by a thousand cuts. Attrition. But being ground down makes finding the energy to call it a day harder. Like light trying to leave a black hole.'

Mary nodded just enough to acknowledge what I'd said. 'That's quite a stark image, Nate. And, of course, the black hole is black precisely because light can never leave it.'

Blimey – I sound even bleaker than I feel when I'm quoted back. We both seemed absorbed in the image for a moment. Mary's eyes carried their own gravitational field. I defied the pull and looked away.

We were upstairs in her family home, in an elegant room at the back set aside for this confidential work.

'I used to think a relationship was science,' I offered into the void. 'Do the right things, tick the boxes, give and it shall be given unto you. Now it seems more of an art. An art I don't have. And it's a bit late to acquire it, isn't it?'

Mary uncrossed her legs. 'You're asking me to sit in judgment.'

Schoolboy error, asking a therapist a question.

'Maybe keeping the relationship alive is an art, but ending it is science,' I mooted. 'There's a simple law: by the time you're thinking of going into counselling together – and we are – it's too late.'

'It needn't be too late. Who floated the idea of counselling first – you or Samantha?'

I exhaled more loudly than I meant to. 'Might have been a rare example of us being in sync. Think it came with us waving the white flag over having kids. Having them naturally, anyway. Neither of us has the stomach for UVF.'

'UVF? You mean IVF?'

'Bloody hell – yes. Not to be confused with the Ulster Volunteer Force. Crikey! Freud would have a field day.'

Mary couldn't disguise a little giggle. She had said in one of our first sessions that this was a place to be taken seriously, but not necessarily to always be serious.

I took a moment. 'Maybe it was the image of the white flag – made me think of the Troubles.' I felt I was walking on the line between tragedy and farce. 'I literally saw the flag as blood-soaked as I said it.'

'But attrition, as you put it, can still be very wounding. We need to look after ourselves when we're going through the wars.' Mary looked at me with that tunnel vision. 'What's your refuge when it's tough?'

I took an uncommon interest in her rubber plant while I thought. 'If I can't stand the heat I go into grizzly bear mode. Head for the cave. Fantasise about escape.' What I didn't say was how I fantasised about escaping with Mary.

'That can certainly seem very appealing.' Wow! Was she mind-reading? So, it's reciprocated? Countertransference *is* a thing.

Hang on ... She only said fantasising can *seem* appealing. Calm down. Get a grip.

I have to draw myself out of this. I look at the print of a lone poppy in a frame over Mary's right shoulder. The beech surround and the white mount complement the apricot of the walls. Nothing thrown away.

A recent memory came back to me. 'I was working on my laptop the other day,' I began, 'On my – our – balcony. It was a warm evening – I'd angled myself towards the sun setting over the river. I was lost in thought – scripting away – when I heard what I thought was a radio. A solo female voice singing what sounded like an aria. A famous one. Then I twigged it was 'Time to Say Goodbye', a pop hit masquerading as opera. A moment later I connected it with a young woman walking a dog in the park opposite. She was wearing headphones – you know, those chunky ones that are in vogue. She was singing along, presumably to the full orchestra in her head. My heart lifted for a second, then almost immediately sank again.' I was silenced by the remembrance of this falling away.

'Why do you think you had this dual reaction?' Mary's eyes were locked on to mine.

'I think it was the innocence that was so moving. Then the deflation of innocence lost. The singer was so carefree – not worrying about what any passer-by might think. Sam and I had that in the early days. So absorbed in each other the world may as well not exist.'

'That's a characteristic of falling in love, of course. And it feels wonderful. Thank goodness we have that capacity. But if you analyse it, the "head over heels" thing is nothing but a set of elaborate illusions.'

I snapped. 'Aren't you meant to be cheering me up? Not snuffing out my one bit of hope. That there might be something better the other side of this?'

'It's not wrong to hope, Nate. But I'd be setting you up for a fall if I didn't prepare you for the more difficult feelings the other side of the dizzy ones – for what's been called "the death of love". That's regardless of whether things are repairable with Samantha or not.' Mary sat with perfect comportment – she must have gone to a school where they balance books on their heads. She seems to have dyed her hair dark. I tried to remember what it looked like naturally.

'I can't lie: I prefer illusions to the truth. The painful truth.' I felt a freedom in saying this. 'I read somewhere people who are materially better off have a lower resistance to PTSD. They're least likely to see it coming down the track. They think it's going to hit the other poor sod who's already down on their luck.'

'Certainly, trauma is no respecter of persons. It can hit anyone.'

'I have a horrible feeling we're a species of malcontents which will keep you lot in work forever, no matter what "progress" we make.' Mary seemed to wince at my branding her and her peers 'you lot'. 'Now we live longer lives and have higher expectations we've got more room for disappointments.' God – I'm sounding like Woody Allen's darker period; *Interiors*, not the early, funny movies.

'Go on.'

'Well – I remember the joy of getting a dishwasher. See, I can set the threshold that low. It could get mugs cleaner than an hour's scrubbing I could do manually. I thought I'd hit on the New Jerusalem – this liberating machine revolutionised my life.'

'I feel a "but" coming ...' Mary wasn't short on wit. She could keep a gentle hand on the tiller. Wish it was my tiller.

'Two weeks later I resented the bloody thing for not loading and emptying itself.'

Mary dropped the mask of impartiality and smiled, fetchingly wrinkling her nose. Ker-bam! Then she settled back into professional mode. 'Surely your sense of humour can dig you out of depression?'

'Up to a point. But if I'm on my own, the jokes don't move me. No audience, no laugh – no therapeutic effect. Plus, I can see the punchlines coming a mile off.'

21

Film script 1 – scene 1

INT. HOUSE – DAY

We see the BOY climb the stairs, eyes downcast. He looks resigned, as if on a mission. As he approaches the top stair the Steadicam, shooting from camera left side of the staircase [i.e. from the left of the viewer's perspective], on the first-floor landing, pivots left with him. We follow him into the bedroom. His body obscures all but the feet of a body on the bed. We hear the boy's rapid, shallow breathing, in time with his shoulders rising and falling.

22

Show rehearsal day two – delivery
Ed Sullivan Theater, Manhattan – 29 December 1999

Delivering the sketch to Penny should have been a weight off my shoulders, but I was disappointed to find it wasn't. The load lingered as it does when I finally post my tax return; I'm usually so hard up against the deadline I wonder if I'm going to get fined, and the disappointment I feel in myself having procrastinated so long lags in my muscles, and the relief is slight.

Penny – I knew it was her because I'd called her Jenni and she'd corrected me – saved the script from my floppy disk to the prompter in the twins' bunker on the edge of the studio floor. For a moment my heart palpitated when I saw the time on her PC as 20.07. Then I remembered the studio computer systems were working on UK time, so we had one point of reference for our more important, larger audience.

Next I had to take the disk to Louise upstairs in the gallery so she could save it on a separate production network. My timing in escaping the studio was spot on: I could see from four different camera angles Ricky was having one of his 'stop the world I want to get off' moments. And, lo, the world of rehearsal, at least, did indeed duly stop.

This meant Louise, freed from her immediate tasks in the gallery, could at least acknowledge my digital gift with a grateful smile. She'd spun round in her chair next to Roger, who was lost in annotating the yellow pages of his script. 'Thanks – wicked!' she said. Was that a subtle look at her watch as she took the disk? Her upbeat reaction was the reward I now realised I was seeking all along. From sister to wife to approving parent in a matter of hours! I could feel her relief spread through me like warm honey. I finally clocked the large bow on the front of her fawn chiffon blouse. Semiotic subtext: 'I'm a professional with close attention to detail; access behind the bow is strictly on merit.'

TV's stop-start operations were once explained to me like this: it's as if you're a load of frozen peas in the freezer one moment, then you're chucked into boiling water the next. As Steve bellowed, 'Shot 50 please studio', from the control room's speakers, Louise climbed this 120-degree temperature gradient in the time it took her to rotate back away from me in her chair, expertly finding shot 50 in her script. Simultaneously she executed a half-wave in my direction with a quick mirror-signal-manoeuvre look over her shoulder as she said on talkback – the communication system mostly for studio operatives – '50 on 2 – 3 next', i.e., 'shot 50 on camera 2 – camera 3 next'. It was a compromise between, 'Thanks again for the script,' and, 'Sod off – can't you see I'm busy?'

I looked at my watch: 3.12pm local time. Neither best case nor worst case. But surely time for a wander.

The trick was to navigate a route out of the building with the lowest likelihood of bumping into Ricky. Okay, so he was tied up in the studio, but he might suddenly storm out. I ad-libbed my escape in a way which avoided direct access to the studio, and also bypassed the corridor leading to Star Dressing Room One, his domain. Not as easy as it might have been, as I wanted to get to my dressing room round the corner to pick up my CD player, a disc, and cans (headphones). I wired myself for sound in my dressing room, but left the cans draped round my neck. Anyone witnessing my exit from the room would have wondered who this strange figure was peering out the door, looking right then left, then creeping as flush as possible along the wall to the right. At the end of that corridor, I looked right to Ricky's room then turned left to the nearest staircase, and on to the stage door.

Breaking free from the theatre I turned left, walking north up Broadway, crossing over 57th and 58th Streets. The afternoon traffic was carried south by its own dynamic, as if it would take plunging into the Hudson several miles away to finally stop it. Pedestrians welcomed the warmth exuding from the shops as they opened the doors to enter. Those leaving paused to do up coats against the December cold. I skirt anticlockwise round the right side of St Columbus Circle and hit the south-west corner of Central Park.

The park occupies a contradiction: an oasis of relative calm within a bustling city. Kate in the 1980s Big Apple sitcom *Kate & Allie* observed there weren't enough tranqs to go round. And, yes, the show was recorded at the Ed Sullivan Theater. The park's green space is a repository for misfits, horse and traps, and Lycra-clad joggers. Director Jonathan Miller once said on Clive James' TV chat show that he looked at joggers and imagined the Grim Reaper a few paces behind them, saying in a spectral voice from under his monastic hoodie, 'I can keep up with you.'

The Grim Reaper's spared Miller and James, but John Lennon wasn't so lucky. I instinctively walked in the direction of the Strawberry Fields memorial, opposite the Dakota Building where John lived and, eventually, died. The apartment block was apparently so named because in 1880, when construction began, it was considered as remote from central Manhattan as Dakota Territory is in the mid-west. Hard to conceive of such remoteness with the traffic weaving its way on Central Park West ahead of me, as I settled by the Imagine mosaic. I donned my headphones. I purposely avoided choosing a Beatles disc; I thought that might be a bit too much in this setting. Instead, I chose a Bach organ work: Sonata No. 2. I put the disc in the machine and hit play. The busy musical ornamentation seems to match the bustle I could see ahead of me; a bold statement in a self-confident city. Behind me, twenty-somethings whizz by on rollerblades, young parents wheel buggies with their kids in, older people support each other at a gentle pace. A weak winter sun casts broken shadows. As the energetic organ movement ends, my thoughts turned to the waste of a life just reborn at forty. Lennon was, like his song, starting over.

I thought of him, shot over the road twenty years before, fighting for his life. Four bullets from that murderous bastard that doesn't deserve a name, more blood loss with every beat of John's heart. In those frantic, dying moments did he think of his mother and her early death, catapulted by a car after she left the house of her sister Mimi? Or did he think of his Aunt Mimi who raised him after his mother gave him up? Or of Yoko or Cynthia or Julian or Sean? Was there time and consciousness to think of his remarkable journey from the back streets of Liverpool to cracking America with the help of the rest of the quartet and a guy who, like McCartney, was of Irish descent: Ed Sullivan? Could John think of anything at all, other than struggling for his next breath?

I had heard the news on the radio while I'd been getting ready to leave for school. 'John Lennon has been shot dead in New York ...' I did a double take and rushed to the radio. I remember wondering earlier in 1980 which Beatle would die first and I now felt guilty for even thinking it, as if I was complicit in John's death. But I had lost my mother the year before, and the world seemed consumed by grief. *Media vita in morte sumus.* That phrase again: in the midst of life we are in death. Except there didn't seem to be much life to be in the midst of.

23

OTT OTs
Psychiatric Unit, Watford General Hospital – November 1982

'Throw all your bad stuff into this pile, everyone.' We all flicked our hands into an invisible pile of doo-doo in the centre of the room. It was as if the lunatics had taken over the asylum. Two earnest occupational therapists – or 'occupational hazards' as Polythene Pam called them – were miming ridding themselves of all the sickly, treacly nastiness on to this quasi-pyre. And we were daft enough to follow suit. Not just the Fabs, but a dozen others. Dregs.

I daren't look at Pam. If she starts to go Sue will, too, then it'll be my turn. Not sure what Reagan's breaking point is, but everyone's got their limits.

Organic material notionally got rid of, we sat down and Tweedledum – or was it Tweedledee? – called the meeting to order with a little breathing exercise.

'Look as far out the window as you can,' said the one with no make-up and a dowdy grey top with an even greyer waistcoat. I was expecting to see a pocket watch on a chain in her hand next. I could see no further than the nurses' accommodation opposite. We were in a therapeutic block, a square grey 1970s riposte to the red-bricked Edwardian sanatorium I'd come back from a few weeks before.

'Then look at something in the middle distance. Name it quietly to yourself. Love it. Nurture it.'

Before I could work out how to love a red Ford Escort parked on a double yellow, we were returning to ourselves.

'Say your name lovingly to yourself ...'

'Doris,' said a patient in her sixties to my right.

'...Under your breath ...'

'Doris,' the white-haired woman now whispered.

'...Silently.'

Doris, you-know-who mouthed.

It was Tweedledee's turn. 'Pottery. That's the life skill today.'

'Cos we all need to know how to make pots to get through life, don't we? Polythene Pam thumped my thigh. Must have been thinking out loud again. Doris disease.

'Does anyone know what we normally use to make pots?' Tweedledee raised her eyebrows in that over-enthused way taught at good schools to motivate the lower orders. She managed to maintain a controlled smile during the long silence.

'Our hands?' offered Charlie, a well-meaning train driver who'd suffered a points failure. His face had more lines than Clapham Junction.

'That wasn't quite what I was thinking, Charlie. What *material* do we use?' I took in her grey turtle neck under a black cardi.

'Clay,' said Reagan.

'Yes, Paul – clay.'

Charlie was an artist, alright. Did beautiful drawings of steam locos – down to the spokes on the wheels.

'So, we're going to mould our clay, then put it in the kiln. We'll then glaze our pots and fire them a second time. Now I've been saying "pots", but in fact they don't have to be pots at all. The task today is to make yourself in clay a gift – anything you want. Literally. So, if you'd like a partner, make them in clay.' For the first time in this session there was a ripple of laughter. 'If you'd like a motorbike, mould one in clay. Just a gift to yourself – a guitar, new TV, whatever. I can't guarantee you'll get the real thing, but at least you'll have something – something solid – to remind you of what you'd like. So let's share out the clay and get moulding ...!'

Suddenly, Tweedledee wasn't so boring.

The Fab Four had a confab over what we'd make. Sue wanted to make an effigy of her son, her 'beautiful boy'. Pam wanted to make the bust of Jane Fonda wearing one of her – Pam's – wigs. Reagan wanted a Ford Mustang. 'The Sixties classic, not the Seventies retread,' he insisted. And I – what did I want? World peace and an end to hunger? On a good day. But that would be hard even on those days to mould in clay. A grand piano (not to scale)? A tasty hi-fi? For sure – some day. But today I made myself an effigy: a little model of my mum, a happy, early-summer version of her in a swimsuit, lying down by the unseen waves, head supported by one hand, smiling, not a care in the world. To make up for the one stolen from me on 26 November 1979 when she died.

24

Day two rehearsal – Daemon & Fiske
Ed Sullivan Theater, Manhattan – 29 December 1999

Daemon and Fiske, two male trampoline artists with a twist – 'a postmodern Laurel and Hardy', according to their publicity – shambled on set, carrying a decade's worth of injuries which, we were assured, would vanish on the night. That's not all that would vanish. For rehearsal they wore workmanlike overalls in a colour euphemistically called 'television white'. This is what normal folk outside this industry would call 'grey'. Reason being the broadcast system can't cope with pure white as it burns out on camera, losing all detail and making everything else look dull.

Daemon was, given his name, suitably scary-looking, even without make-up. He was lithe – scrawny, even – with a shiny, shaved dome, and piercing blue eyes. His partner was almost his physical anti-matter opposite; amazing they didn't explode on contact with each other, which was frequent. Fiske had a long, mousy-brown mane tamed by a bobble, and a highly developed physique borne, I'm sure, of many hours spent in the gym. He was a good few inches taller than his partner – maybe six-two, six-three?

From this act, according to their business blurb, we were promised 'high-octane twists and turns, plus conjuring with clubs and words', the latter naturally making my ears prick up.

Roger had, I gathered from those rambling London groupthinks, tried to steer the double act to be a little more mainstream than was their wont; in the nightclubs they could get quite political and a little obscure, chucking in references to Derrida, Barthes and Foucault, along with samples of the wartime speeches of Churchill at ear-bleeding volume. Apparently in one meeting the Colonel had asked, 'Can't they get on with jumping on the fucking trampoline and stop titting on about politics and post-structuralism?'

It seems the answer was 'yes'. Up to a point.

Once Messrs Randy Daemon and Bob Fiske had run the physical side of their routine for the cameras, they jumped off the trampoline and faced each other, standing on the adjacent electric-blue rubber mat, in an intense eyeball-to-eyeball. By a sleight of hand – or foot – the shorter one smoothly found a box on the mat the exact height of the differential between the two showmen. The camera supervisor on the crane framed a tight two shot – close enough to see the beads of fresh sweat trickle down the performers' profiles – and alternately Randy and Bob rapped in their all-American accents:

> 'For Mike and All Angels
>> '*And angles*
> 'Of dangles
>> '*Pentangles*
> 'And strangers
>> '*And dangers*
> 'And juggling
>> '*And cuddling*
> 'Befuddling
>> '*And muddling*
> 'Confusing
>> '*Contusing*
> 'Contorting
>> '*Retorting*
> 'Cavorting
>> '*And snorting ..!'*

'Whoah, whoah, whoah,' said Roger on talkback from the gallery. 'This is them being more mainstream, is it?

Steve, love, we can't go with this. They've gone from St Michael and the heavenly host – assuming they're not talking about Marks and Sparks – to a bloody coke-snorting reference in half a dozen lines. Er – pun not intentional. 'Struth.'

It took something for our eternally laid-back director to utter an oath – even a mild one. Now Steve on the studio floor had to translate this to the artistes in a way simultaneously diplomatic for them but robust enough for Roger. The sound mixer joined in the diplomacy by knocking back their radio mics and substituting a general wash of indistinct studio noise. Listening in the prompter den on a spare pair of cans Penny supplied I could hear Louise say to Roger next to her, sotto voce, 'This wasn't agreed.'

'Damn right it wasn't,' Roger concurred. 'We can have a bit of patter, but we can't have this.'

In a tea break Roger quietly approached me to rewrite the post-tumble dialogue. Bashing words together held no terrors for me, of course, but squaring up to the lads and representing to them the faceless corporation which was clipping their creative wings was different.

I thought at least Roger would join us to explain the situation and, yes, do the dirty work for me, but oh no; *I* was to do the dirty work for *him*. He'd do no more than alert the guys – and even then via production assistant Louise, his human shield – that I was coming down to the green room for a chat.

Après-Rog, *le deluge*, I thought.

I won't get into the origins of the term 'green room' – there are 150 different theories doing the rounds. Suffice to say, in the day it's a refuge for the artists away from the studio. A refuge I was about to violate.

As I approached the door I tried to slow and deepen my breath. '...And relax.' Icy calm. *One-elephant-two-elephant-* ...

But before I could open the door, it swiftly swung open in front of me, making me step back. Out stormed Bob

Fiske, virtually spitting over his shoulder, 'Sell your fucking soul if you want to, but you won't get much for it, dude.' The ponytail bobbed on the backbeat of Fiske's footsteps down the corridor away from me, but then swished around in an abrupt about-turn. Its owner, who'd clearly thought of a footnote, headed back and bawled into the green room's near-empty space, 'Thirty pieces of silver don't go far in this godforsaken town!' He stormed off again as before, this time compounding the effect by casting curses not quite under his breath.

Gingerly I entered the green room. With Fiske's partner looking vulnerable at the apex of a corner sofa, I thought I'd play the Englishman card. I aimed for understatement to the small figure now in sweatshirt and jeans. 'I'm sorry. Your partner seems a little put out.'

'Don't worry, mate – we get on each other's tits the whole time.' His working-class London patois, once I got past the surprise factor, put me immediately at ease.

'You're a London geezer!' I said, stating the bleedin' obvious. I can't have been the first person to clock the difference between his conversational and on-stage accents.

'Yeah. What a con, eh?!' He winked like a dodgy barrow boy. 'Have a beer, mate.' Using his toe, he hooked open a low-level fridge close to where he sat and tilted his head to indicate, 'Help yourself'.

Like a fictional TV cop, I don't normally drink on duty, but the task in hand required a bit of trust and rapport building, so I leant in and grabbed a lager.

'A little bird tells me you're on a mission, Nate.' I was taken aback at being known by name – I'm not even credited on the show as a writer for fear of stealing glory from Ricky; I'm merely a 'programme associate', so people barely connect me to a role.

'I've been given a little task, yes,' I said, sheepishly. I sat down at one end of the L-shaped sofa and mimed a bottle-opener's action. Daemon took the beer to a flight case in the corner of the green room, and with a swift move banged down on the bottle-top against the metal edging of the case.

'In one!' he rang out, triumphantly, handing me the opened bottle and settling back into his cosy corner.

I continued: 'The network's a bit jumpy about religious references banging up against coke-snorting.' Feeling uncomfortable about taking glass to my front teeth I now mimed pouring the liquid into a glass.

Without skipping a beat Randy did a backward flip over the sofa, grabbed a glass from a neighbouring table, spun it around three times in the air, kicked it with his left leg, caught it in his right hand and threw it to me.

'Who said anything about coke?' Daemon continued, as if nothing had happened. 'Anyone with a nose can snort. If you wanna change the words you'll be pushing at an open door with me. That was Dicksplash's idea – and, yes, he called it a 'cocaine rap' – ha ha – with a silent 'w'. I said it'd get blue-pencilled. Buggerlugs thought he'd get it through on the nod. I'm a bit embarrassed by it, to be honest, so if you can think of anything a bit more bouncy, be my guest. Long as we can square it with the tall guy.'

Daemon had taken up a super-relaxed posture on the sofa. He was ridiculously bendy and now reminded me of a lizard at repose.

On a pincer movement to bond with him and to satisfy my curiosity I had to delve more into the act. 'So, tell me, what's with all the Derrida? The fancy post-structuralism? Weaving philosophy into a physical act?'

'Management wanted it. What do they call it? Differentiation, USP, brand values ... all that word wank. Bob gets off on it, but it leaves me cold. I just want to do a turn and fuck off, but you can't do that these days. Marketing suits found we had a student following so they wanted us to play to that. S'pose it gives us an air of danger, but I get enough danger from triple backward flips twenty-feet up – you know what I mean?' He guffawed at this. I laughed along then took a swig.

I was hatching a plan. Was there some triangulation I could do between the two guys, equidistant, which would please them both? 'So if I could find a form of words – something fun with a rhyme and a rhythm, nothing too serious – you'd be cool with that?' '*Cool*? Hark at me, getting down with the kids.

'Sure. Sound.'

The door swung open and Fiske walked back in.

Daemon slid off the sofa. 'I'm dying for a ciggie, so see you round,' he said and skedaddled.

I stood up and offered a hand to the taller partner. 'Mr Fiske.'

He took my hand in a way that suggested it wasn't his style. 'Please – call me Bob.' I heard a Scandi edge to his accent that had been absent in his earlier rage.

'You know what this is about, Bob? It puts me in a slightly awkward position ...'

'Yes, I know. But it is only words, isn't it?' I was convinced he was Swedish. 'No point worrying ourselves and getting an ulster.'

25

A kind of community
**Psychiatric Unit, Watford General Hospital – December
1982**

So here we all are again. Another day, another community
meeting. So-called. Weirdest use of the word 'community'
I've ever come across. A bunch of fruit bats crammed
together in a cage – the only thing we have in common is what
we don't have in common with normal people. We don't see
the world the way they do. And we can't make it work for us
the way they do.

Take Janet. Yesterday, me and Sue were sent on a
mission, mid-meeting, by one of the two shrinks here, Dr
Samuels. He asked us to coax her down from her room
upstairs.

Janet's middle-aged with shoulder-length greying
hair, and wears multi-coloured polyester tops and furry tweed
skirts. Every phrase from her takes a sad arc downwards. Dr
Samuels was talking to me the other day then drifted off and
said to himself, 'So many disturbed women.' He must be
including Janet. He sounded despairing. God help us if he
despairs. Aren't we meant to look to him to cure us?

Anyway, when me and Sue went into Janet's room
she was writhing between her clinical white sheets. 'I want to
be beaten up,' she said with that upside-down-smile tone.
What do you say to someone who says that? Especially since
our job wasn't to talk to her but to get her downstairs.

Sue said, 'We're not going to do that, Janet. Come
and join us. You'll feel better for it.' I couldn't tell if she
meant it, but after a while the writhing stopped and Janet

walked with us, achingly slowly, down the stairs, as if she'd already been beaten up.

'Where are you, Janet?' asked Dr Samuels. All three of us joined the thirty or so forming an untidy oval with their chairs in the meeting room. I'd learned 'Where are you?' wasn't a geography question. Janet thought for a moment – or perhaps this was the Largactil lag, a tranq-induced delay to normal speech.

'My hubby says, "Play with my balls",' she eventually offered, to the sound of the odd gasp in the group. She then moved to the middle of the oval, raised her skirt and shat on the floor.

And this is community.

A nurse hurries to get some kitchen roll.

Dr Samuels asks us how we feel that Janet's always 'acting out'? He adds, 'And now she shits on the group.'

There is someone with community spirit, though. A forty-something patient called Angela takes the roll off the nurse and clears up after Janet. Perhaps that means she can't be in the Dregs after all. As she's wiping in a very determined way she says, 'This is what I've always done for the family.'

26

'The Bass Player and the Blonde'
Soho, London – December 1977

A few weeks after a TV producer has scouted my dad's commercial art studio as a possible location for a drama, they're shooting there in Carlisle Street, off Soho Square. The film crew – and it really is on celluloid as there's no video recording outside of studios at this time – are shooting the exterior scene of an ITV drama, *The Bass Player and the Blonde*. It's a freezing-cold Saturday, but this is a captivating world of lights and actors and cameras and sound gear, plus pecking orders and giving orders. The technicians and artists arrive en masse like travelling show people.

There are trompe l'oeils: a set-up filmed with a car further up the road, closer to the square, is picked up again outside my father's workplace near Carlisle Street's cul-de-sac, perhaps to create the illusion the street is longer than it really is. Once they're shooting immediately outside number seven, the car is stationary. For the shot, though, to make it look as though the car has just pulled up, a couple of scenic guys press down hard on the car's suspension, giving the effect of bouncing after braking.

As well as Dad having to be there to open up, Mum's come along too; she's as intrigued as me. Perhaps it reminds her of that shot taken outside her school in the Powell and Pressburger film *I Know Where I'm Going*, of her pouring out of the gates at speed with her mates.

The crew in Soho are a cast of characters, never mind the actors. One man I now at this distance in time assume to have been gay, and possibly working in the wardrobe department, if that's not terrible stereotyping, says loudly to some colleagues nestled around him, 'This coat's really warm. Cop a feel of my lining.' He opens his jacket to reveal a rich cream fleece on the inside. A woman by him responds without hesitation, 'We'd all like to feel your lining, love,' and she makes great play of running her hands over it. Much laughter follows. In my sheltered world of homework and holy communion this exchange is novel and transgressive. Yet in my recollection there's real love between these colleagues. It's as if they've all run away to the circus together.

A few weeks before, a little over half a mile away at All Soul's Langham Place, I've been with a very different crowd. A preacher is quoting St Paul from one of his epistles saying that homosexuals cannot enter the Kingdom of Heaven. Protestors have gatecrashed this so-called 'Festival of Light' service, and as this homophobic verse is read out, one of them says loudly, 'Superstitious nonsense'. As another protestor takes to the pulpit and starts to speak, the mic is turned off. At this point I'm on the wrong side of history. Our pastor that weekend interprets this disruption as the worldly manifestation of a 'battle in the heavenlies'.

I want to put my imprint on *The Bass Player* in some way, and all I can think is to approach the camera from a discreet distance near Soho Square. Not quite a style icon, I'm probably wearing an undistinguished grey duffle coat and, so I can pick myself out in the back of shot (assuming I get to see the final product), I produce a conspicuously white handkerchief from my pocket, and make as if to blow my nose. The crisp, wintry air seizes on my exhalation, creating condensation. It mimics smoke or steam and pleases me as it increases my chances of being seen. I'm a stone's throw away from an office on the square proper bearing the unassuming initials MPL. The clue is that Dad's reported occasionally having seen Paul McCartney around. Later, I discern and decode he's likely to have been in the area for a meeting at his company, McCartney Publishing Ltd. It's headquartered here in London and on 54th Street, New York City. And George Harrison's Hari Krishna friends are just around the corner as well. Connections to two out of four Beatles off one London square ain't bad.

Later a slimmed-down crew moves into my dad's studio. It's an L-shaped open-plan office in which Dad enjoys his dream: a north-facing light. They're filming the reverse angle, looking over the actor's shoulder as he bawls down to a character by the car a floor below. Later, the actor's name acquires significance for me: it's Edward Woodward.

Between takes I get into a conversation with the camera assistant and express an interest in going into his trade. He suggests that, rather than approach his employer, a branch of ITV, I should join the BBC, the main industry trainer. The broadcasting bug had bitten.

When cast and crew have left town, my parents and I go for a meal at a local Angus Steak House.

I remember little of the meal, but a sticker on a road sign on Oxford Street made a lasting impression on me. It contained a very familiar design, and an unfamiliar word. On the horizontal part of a London Transport roundel was the label 'Lesbian Line', a reference, I later realised, to a phone helpline. And ten years after homosexual acts between some men had been legalised, what was the sticker's pay-off for their female counterparts? 'We're not underground any more'.

27

jane.butterworth@altavista.com – 1999.12.28

Hey Nate -

Hope your doing ok. I know you're busy, but I'm busy too -
if that's any consolation. I could really do with your help on
this.

I've had to be a bit opaque with the details of the show I'm
working on -production sensitivity, privacy, NDAs, yatter,
yatter -- but it invovles members of your family.

I'm attaching photos of some of them. Hope you don't
mind. Could you help me with the relationships?

Specificaly, would you identify your cousin (if that's who it is
in the T shirt) and are the other 2 your parents?

Thanks

Jane

nathan.daniels@connectright.co.uk – 28.12.1999

Jane -

For the love of God I CANNOT help you with this damned project.

I have neither the time nor inclination, and above all I have no interest in helping you out. Brutal, but true.

Frankly I've gone beyond wishing you well to wishing you further.

I don't want to get into threatening injunctions, but this really has to be our last communication. Cease and fricking desist. Anything further from you will be an invitation to instruct my lawyers.

Yours finally -

N.

28

Rehearsal day two – Ricky's dressing room
Ed Sullivan Theater, Manhattan – 29 December 1999

Paddy's legs seemed even longer than usual as he propped his feet up on the glass coffee table, his chair tilted back precariously against the basin in his dressing room. His pink-and-green check shirt combined with black jeans were calibrated to be 'smart enough for rehearsals', as he would say. My blue jeans and grey hoodie were a couple of social notches down from that. The room had a Scandinavian pine theme with some Sixties chic in the orange and green soft furnishings.

'Ach – the loneliness of the corporate clown.' Paddy's facial expression hovered between an ironic take on the smiley Ricky his viewers would recognise, and a more distant, defocussed stare. 'A clown with a frown.'

'A clown's life's no sadder than his scribbler's,' I mused, to zero reaction.

I love and hate downtime in TV. Time to think. Too much time to think. The sketch set was being struck and we had an outsized tea break to talk turkey. Or we could talk American: verbal detours and evasions.

I thought I'd take a risk. 'How's the battle with the powder?'

'What battle? I want a lift, I do a line – no battle.' He sniffed; I wasn't sure whether it was a joke. 'I'm sick of the battle metaphor. It's the same with cancer. "He fought a long battle with cancer." No, he didn't. You might as well fight a battle with the colour of your eyes. If I'm felled by the Big C, be it known I made no effort to fight it off. When they air my obit the newscaster will say afterwards, "Ricky Ryan, who died as he lived – a coward."'

'But that's Jacqui's worry, right?'

'What – that I'll die of cowardice?'

'Nah – another big C. Jacqui's worried you're not putting the fight in against coke.' I hoped invoking his girlfriend's name might be a canny move; to stop it from being my nag.

'So now you're an agent of Jacqui's, is it? Stasi 2.0.' Bang went my theory. 'You'd deny me my one pleasure ...?'

'It's not your one pleasure. And you raised it with me – just yesterday – so you must be worried.'

'Wish I hadn't mentioned it now,' Paddy said mournfully. Then, slapping his thighs, he moved up a gear. 'Change the subject. Nothin' to see here.' He landed his chair on all four feet and paced around the dressing room like he was beating the parish bounds. 'It's not easy having the Colonel breathing down me neck. He was on the warpath again today.'

'Sorry to hear. What did he want?'

'Blood. As per. Frettin' about the big show, of course. He was poring over the ratings from the last quarter. A certain "decline over time" as he put it.'

'What did you say?'

'What could I say? "That's the past, Colin", I says. "Tomorrow is unwritten. Past performance is no guarantee of future failure."'

I sat forward. 'You really said that?'

'Course I bloody didn't. But I wanted to. The Colonel doesn't do irony, remember? Nate, this celebrity thing's not all it's cracked up to be. If fame's the answer, it must be a stupid feckin' question.' Having completed a circuit, he reached into his black holdall on the coffee table and drew out a packet of fags. He slumped into a swivel chair, lit up and puffed vigorously.

I bit my lip; you pick your battles.

As a plume of smoke floated up, he went on, 'I mean – if I'd known when we were messing around with tapes twenty years ago this would be the high point of my career ...' He spun distractedly with his hands out, palms up, like he was pleading with some unseen god and/or TV executive. 'Playing petty politics with Colin the Colonel, getting it in the ear from my latest belle, sitting on a cack-coloured seat talking to you ...'

'Gee, thanks.'

'Don't take this the wrong way, but there's a whole load of ball-ache you'd think you'd get past if you put the hours in. And it just seems to get worse.'

'Well, don't take *this* the wrong way but – Paddy, what did you expect? What would ever be enough? You have a beautiful house in leafiest Berkshire, a spare one over the Irish Sea, a stunning girlfriend, a garage full of cars, a swanky home studio ... Plus, no one gets to avoid politics – not even the most powerful people in the world.'

'That's because they're politicians, Nate.'

'Ah – fair point.' Damn. Move on. 'So would you feel any better if your seat was upholstered with ermine?'

'You know I'm allergic to stoats.'

'I was being figurative. The point is there's no ceiling on what the human heart can desire. The trick is to find contentment. What did Nietzsche say about embracing fate? "One wants nothing to be different ... in all eternity." Acceptance is key.'

'Oh yeah – your friend Nietzsche,' Paddy screwed up his face. 'That dude whose name's an anagram of Nazi shit. Or something.'

'Blame his sister for that lie. He wasn't a nationalist – she was. She misrepresented him.'

'Okay – how about this, then: his philosophy turned him mad? That's a great sell.'

'Disputed. I reckon he was bipolar. With the odd psychotic ep.'

'Sounds familiar.' Paddy flicked a look to me and drew deeply on his fag. Then he spun another circuit in his chair and breathed out through his nostrils, like a car with two exhausts. 'Doesn't sound like the path to happiness.'

'Let's try a different angle, then. Think of your parents and mine. When I was born in '64 my folks could only afford to heat one room in our bungalow. In February! They kept me by the fire in the lounge to stop me from turning blue.'

'What's this: your sob story – sorry – life story, Nate?'

I was on my feet by now. I realised I was pointing my finger at Paddy. 'Then your folks – scrimping and saving so you could go to drama school. Sacrifice is an old-fashioned word, but it meant something to them. And it meant you didn't have to do back-breaking work like your dad.'

'Christ, Nate! You clearly missed your vocation as the village priest. Or being on *Mastermind*. Specialist subject: smugness.'

'Much easier to take the piss than see what our folks really went through.'

'Yeah, well reality's a bit of a downer. Congratulations Nathan me ol' chum – you've made me want to do a line more than ever. So if you'll excuse me ...' He walked across the dressing room to the safe, punched in a few numbers then produced a mirror, a razor blade, a straw, and a small, sealed plastic bag.

'You're not going to do that in front of me? In broad daylight?' I nearly laughed the words out. We'd always had an understanding we'd speak in euphemisms and I'd absent myself if he was going to partake. Don't ask, don't tell. But now this: brazen.

As he poured some of the powder with care on to the little oblong mirror Paddy said, 'The great thing about coke is – it dulls the sound of nagging.' As he reached for the blade, I grabbed his wrist.

'Fuck's sake, Paddy. No!' I whipped away what was left of the drug, and we tussled over the blade in a frantic arm wrestle.

Forearms flew in a random dance of bones.

'Jesus, Nate,' Paddy spat. 'Give me the goddam sharp!'

He made one last desperate tug on my left arm holding the blade, and in the struggle I caught his right cheek with it.

Silence, bar our stressy breathing.

Then I watched in horror as two diagonal lines of blood oozed into view above Paddy's designer stubble.

This was the face that was going to be on transatlantic TV on New Year's Eve.

Paddy looked at me with pure contempt. He grabbed a towel from the sink and dabbed the wound.

There was a knock at the door. I looked in panic from Paddy to the little mirror with the powder on it, and back to Paddy.

'Who is it?' he asked, calmly buying time as he put the mirror and its layer of coke in the bin. A white cloud drifted up as if they'd elected a new pope.

'Jenna. Floor assistant.'

'Oh, come in,' said Paddy nonchalantly. If there's one thing prime-time presenters can do it's ad lib. I couldn't bear to turn around to the door behind me. But I saw Jenna appear in the main mirror. Her glossy dark hair was immaculate, but for where it had been disturbed by her headphones.

'They're ready for you, Ric—. Jeez – what have you done to your face?'

Paddy held the towel against his cheek like a comfort blanket, but the incision was still visible underneath. 'Oh, it's nothing.' He lowered the towel, revealing the red shadow on the white cloth. 'I cut myself shaving, is all.'

Satisfied, or at least deferential, Jenna and clipboard backed out the door saying, 'See you on set in five.'

'Sure,' Paddy confirmed.

I only found my voice as the door clunked shut. 'I'm so sorry, Padd—'

'That's okay, Nate – a bit of the other kind of powder should sort it. A dab of make-up.' His sing-song tone seemed at odds with the scene.

'So ... we're alright?'

'Sure. Everything'll be fine.' Paddy had switched to blotting the cut with a tissue from a box on the side. 'Now you're off the show.'

'What?' My heart rate, which had just recovered, shot up again.

'I said, "You're off the show." Goodbye, Nate.'

Part Two

Adrian Lacey

29

Walking the streets
Manhattan – 29 December 1999

New York City is not a place you go to feel tall. From the top of the many skyscrapers, I am a tiny dot. But close up I'm a tiny dot now, too.

Another failed-to-be in a land of wannabes.

Another dreamer's dreams dashed in a land of delusions.

Another workless bum trudging the streets.

In a daze I head for Central Park again on foot, but I can't face Strawberry Fields feeling like this. Instead I head right and drop down to 65th Street Transverse which cuts across the park. Skeletal trees frame the road alongside evergreens. I am going where the mood takes me. The sky's indifferent in its distance. For a moment you could forget the rampant consumerism cutting its own throat above the cutting.

Past the park I trudge past block after block of anonymous buildings, traffic, people. Then one building catches my eye: the Beekman Theatre. I feel that I know it like an old friend, but it takes a moment to make the link: Woody Allen's *Annie Hall*. Woody's character Alvy Singer's waiting for Annie to arrive for their first date to see a movie here – about where I'm standing. Comedian Alvy gets recognised by some not-very-bright dude and denies himself thrice, sort of. Like a 1970s Judas trying to avoid autograph hunters.

I mourn the passage of time.

If I'd only been here twenty-two years earlier I could have casually bumped into Allen while he was filming *Annie*. But then I would have been just another autograph hunter. And what do you say to someone whose work you revere, however flawed they might be? Did David ask for Goliath's autograph?

I take a moment to drink in the frontage of this classic cinema; the Beekman name is in cursive script but, curiously, its italics slant to the left, not the right. Designed, perhaps, by a fellow left-hander?

I mourn also for the loss of a dream, long since conceded: I'd wanted to be the New Woody – a stand-up for sophisticates of the late-boomer generation, a writer for the age of aspiration. And where was I? I couldn't even cling on by my fingernails to a gag-writing gig. I was sliding down the side of the ship, nails scraping and screeching as in a hack cartoon, putting your teeth on edge.

I stand looking at the canopy, the cinema's overhang where the expectant crowds will gather later. I have my back to the road. An elderly woman appears over my right shoulder. She clocks me being lost in thought at this Mecca to cinema.

Gathering her beige mac eccentrically about herself and wriggling her shoulders inside of it, as if to make it fit better, she asks, 'You an art-house lover?' I can't place her accent; it seems sixty per cent American.

What can I say? The truth might kill the conversation immediately, and I could do with the company. 'I ... dip a toe in.' I deflect. 'What's your favourite movie you've seen here?'

'You know *Day for Night?*' she asks. She gives a little chuckle. I think she senses I'm out of my depth, but she wasn't going to leave me dangling. 'Truffaut. '73. Not his best artistically, but I can't help liking the in-jokes. He's a director struggling to complete his film against the odds.'

'You don't have to be a director to identify with that.' I was looking for common ground. We briefly bond over unspecified shared struggles.

'My husband loved this place. He was a poet. Not big time – but he was big time to me. He was a bank manager by day.' She had a faraway look in her eye.

'What sort of things did he write about?'

'Oh – nature. Birds, rivers, the sea – you know.'

She adjusted her see-through rain hood against the non-existent rain.

Quick: which art-house director was into nature? I've got a vague recollection from the 1980s. Ah yes, the one Tarkovsky film I've seen. 'So perhaps he liked *The Sacrifice*? Did he see it here?'

'Sure – we both saw it. The last film we saw together.'

'And Tarkovsky's last film, too.' Wow. Jammy. I was trying to better myself in the '80s. Maybe '85, '86? I was feeling uncultured; I'd heard of Tarkovsky but knew nothing of his work, then I saw *The Sacrifice* advertised. To secure my place in Pseud's Corner I had to see it in Knightsbridge. Truth is, I remember more about the decor than about the movie: warm light-beige notes throughout, including soft material on the walls, and sumptuous seats you could lose yourself in. And I did – lose myself. For an hour or two. I awoke for the climactic house-fire scene at the end, but even in my dozy state everything was moving too slowly on screen. The camera panned restlessly from side to side following these floundering souls, and all I could think was, They should phone the ruddy fire brigade. But for some reason there was an ambulance there. I was sure there was some heavy symbolism going on, but I wasn't sure what it symbolised.

'You saw it?' The lady had edged in, a little needily.

'Sort of – well, yes. Not really my *tasse de thé*, as we say in Britain.' My listener smiled. 'Like I don't quite dig his aesthetic.' Christ – what's possessed my tongue? 'I prefer kinetics to, er, static imagery.' Kinetics? I suppose that meant car chases.

'Todd loved it. I guess the poet in him embraced it. The fire as an image for our self-destructive spirits. Or our creative muses. Both/and. Either/or.'

'And you?' I looked into her eyes, still bright blue for all the years. 'What did you make of it?'

She paused. A sharp intake of breath – and out again. 'A whole heap of horseshit.'

We laughed. A deep belly laugh. She pushed her horn-rimmed glasses to the top of her slightly crooked nose. I noticed her long-established laughter lines splaying out from the edges of her eyes.

'We rowed about it for days. When we weren't sitting there sulking. Perhaps it became symbolic for us – the unbridgeable divide. I was close to torching everything we owned – till I realised that would be doing Tarkovsky's work for him. So we sued for peace, me and Todd.'

'Not you and Tarkovsky?'

'Uh-uh. An uneasy truce, perhaps. But it was as well my husband and I made up. He died at the end of that year.' She seemed to fold slightly at the waist. 'I remember thinking Todd outlived Tarkovsky by ten days and, being desperate, I felt it was a crumb of comfort.' She looked away. A street light caught a tear in her eye. I wasn't sure if it was grief or the chilly December air. She straightened herself up and returned her gaze to me. 'I guess, looking back, the Beekman was more for Todd than for me. But we liked being together, especially after the children left. So I tagged along.' She suddenly collected herself and became more animated again. 'Anyhow, I gotta scoot. Friends over for tea, then off to MOMA. For the Keith Haring exhibition.'

'Bit more relatable than Tarkovsky, eh?'

'Don't you let Todd hear you say that.' She cast an eye skywards, and I wasn't sure how literal she was being. 'I'm Elsa, by the way.' She offered a hand encrusted with jewels.

'Nathan. Nate.' We shook hands.

'Oh – take my card, Nate. Here.' She fumbled in a messy canary yellow handbag. I put the card straight into my pocket without looking. Elsa voiced her goodbyes and nice-to-meet-yous and walked off in a Midtown direction on Second Avenue.

I was already feeling the loss of her company.

I felt that awful void that descends on being alone once again, the low, thick fug, a pea-souper of despair, and I remembered the loss of my job. Elsa seemed to have found a way of avoiding the void. Why is it one soul can scoop themselves up and move on, while another is stuck swimming in sadness?

I walked on to keep myself occupied, but whereas distraction works with young children, an adult's self-awareness gives the game away; I knew I was trying to distract myself, so I couldn't.

But I decided to suspend disbelief and give distractions one last go.

I resolved to visit all the New York locations for *Annie Hall*. It seemed doable, maybe over a couple of days. It could be inspirational. I could get inside my favourite film and really inhabit it.

But immediately, the voices.

What do I hope to achieve by this? Is it some thinly veiled attempt at self-flagellation, of beating myself up for not being Woody Allen? Or a mad ego trip of kidding myself I'm his equal?

It would take some planning. I decide to prep it in a bar somewhere. I start off in a south-westerly direction. In spite of myself, I eventually wind up in O'Riordan's Irish Pub. I feel like an extra in a more-Irish-than-Irish movie. Overcompensation for its not being in Ireland is the name of the game. Waiters are the giveaway; don't remember seeing those in Dublin.

This dislocated theme park gets me down. It fails the Heidegger authenticity test.

But I could murder a Guinness.

30

Film script 1 – scene 2

> INT. HALL – DAY
> GRAINY, SEPIA SUPER-8 EFFECT
> The doorbell rings. We see the boy answer it in LONG SHOT. He opens the door to reveal the neighbour DOREEN.
> DOREEN
> Oh lovey – I'm so sorry. Andrew said about your mum. Where is she?
> BOY
> Upstairs. In bed. On the bed.
>
> Doreen heads towards the camera then disappears camera R out of shot.
> CUT TO: POV BOY as Doreen climbs the stairs ahead of him. We see the woman on the bed beyond her.
> DOREEN
> (As if addressing the woman)
> Barbara. Barbara. Can you hear me? It's Doreen.
>
> Doreen turns to camera, as if addressing the boy.
> DOREEN
> (cont'd - straight down the lens)
> Have you called an ambulance?

BOY
Yes.
DOREEN
Get your shoes on then, luvvie. We'll go to the hospital together.

FADE TO BLACK

31

O'Riordan's Irish Pub
Lower Manhattan – 29 December 1999

I stare at the sawdust on the floor. I wonder at the effort that's gone into this self-consciously self-denying oddity, like ripping your own jeans or setting fire to your hair. Let's turn the colour down on our TVs to make them monochrome, and enjoy the snap, crackle, and pop of vinyl we've been so cruelly denied with CDs. Jeepers.

The clientele is no better. Throwbacks to a more unruly age of bad teeth, bad breath, and bad behaviour. Oh, and the exception to that, women are a novelty here, only admitted thirty years ago on legal sufferance. Three decades of regret in some backwater of this bar, no doubt. There's a clear fear of evolution, of change. And so this place has become a metaphor for getting stuck; a comfortable rut. Some corner of a foreign field that is forever fantasy Ireland.

Framed pictures cram the walls as if in fear of letting any surface breathe, uncovered.

So unconvincing is this Irish mirage, it doesn't even sell Guinness. The choice is fizzy light ale or fizzy dark ale. I plump for dark. Expectations lowered, I'm still disappointed by the malt-and-hops-by-numbers taste.

Standing room only at this hour with the millennium approaching. Not the refuge I'd hoped for in my naivety. The sensory assault extends to my ears.

'First time here?' A bespectacled, bald, fifty-something man adds to the noise. Where the baldness runs out, he's white-haired round the edges.

Do I look like I need company? Maybe I do. 'Is it obvious I'm a stranger?' I'd moved in closer to his ear to get above the noise. I feigned what I hoped resembled a smile, but it was probably a chimp-like rictus.

He wore a green and red stripy rugby shirt with its white collar turned up. He mirrored my action by moving in. 'You were taking in all the sights very deliberately. I'm Peter, by the way.' He offered his hand, which I took with what I intended to be little hesitation, although it felt like I'd stared at his fingers for too long, as if trying to understand this strange white-man's ritual.

As I took another insipid sip my elbows were bumped by passers-by. The shock was passed on to my glass and its contents. I tried to appear more understanding of the jostlers than I felt.

We shook hands. 'Nathan.' I didn't feel like giving him the familiar version of my name, or any embellishment.

'What do you do, Nathan?' Straight in there. Pure Big Apple.

Yes – what do I do? I wander aimlessly about the streets licking my work wounds, bumping into the odd unsolicited stranger. Sometimes literally. And I go to a bar for reasons I now forget. 'I'm a writer. TV. An electronic wordsmith.' I hoped my lumpen phraseology would ward off further questions. No such luck.

'Fascinating. A writer of dramas? Documentaries?'

'Lower life forms. Entertainment shows. Writing links, sketches, and penning gags, mostly.'

'Ahh – but still a skill, no?'

'Of a sort.' It was all a bit academic now I was workless. 'And you? Your calling card, Peter?'

'I'm an academic.' Oh brilliant. That really is a bit academic. 'Philosophy, with a side order of English lit. At Columbia.'

My highly tuned intellect took a sudden interest in the pipe emanating from the nearby boiler. Or furnace. A defence against actual thinking, no doubt.

Quick: what do I know about Columbia Uni? 'Ah – yes. Your official Columbia Blue on approved logos is Pantone 290.' Another sip. 'Don't ask.'

'As an academic, I have to ask! Why would you have such a bizarrely niche morsel of knowledge about my employer? And what is Pantone 290?'

'It's a specific shade of blue. And I won't say printer's ink flows through my veins, but my double helix is in Dingbats.'

'Blimey, as you Brits say.'

'I'm the son of a commercial artist,' I fleshed out. 'I was baptised in a font. Helvetica twelve-point bold italics. It's my birthright. And – and we don't, by the way. Say "Blimey" – except in self-parody.' I took a swig to swell the swagger.

'Admonishment taken.' Peter looked reflective as he swirled his pint. His lack of hair played to the egghead stereotype and made the creases in his forehead more prominent. Wiry rogue eyebrows, some white, some darker, added to the impression content was more important than presentation to him. The mental cogs were clearly turning. Was he warming to a joust? Or just bemused? Alienated, even? He was hard to read early on, and with my low tolerance of booze my chances of doing so fell with every mouthful. Perhaps he thought I was a tit.

I lowered my risen shoulders. 'So is this some kind of postmodern joke – a philosopher walks into a bar?'

Peter laughed. 'There are funnier jokes, for sure. But maybe your question implies my sort don't belong here?'

'Not necessarily.' I hedged. 'I mean, it's holiday time ...' Peter reminded me of someone, but I couldn't pin down who.

'Of course.'

'Though ... you never stop thinking?'

'Nobody does! I try not to think too much – least of all during vacations. The semester finished a fortnight ago, so my brain's kinda off duty. But whenever I come here, it's to switch off, to disengage from being "my sort". And to enjoy some stout and company. Not necessarily in that order!'

He seemed charming. It unnerved me I couldn't find a catch.

Peter went on, 'But I'm interested in you and your use of language in your work.'

Oh God. How long could I sustain the myth that I was in work? 'Go on ...'

'You must have to choose your words with precision?' As he looked to the wooden slats on the ceiling for inspiration I saw the smudges on his lenses. 'You're creating pictures with words, but they have to be the words that connect with a mass audience, right?'

'Yes – they have to be in common currency. But you're also trying to surprise and, well, stretch the meanings of words. Muck about with them a bit. A colleague once said, "I bet your parents didn't give you toys to play with as a child. They gave you the English language."'

'Ha! Play is an important part of our development. But I guess to have fun with words is part of your job.'

Some busty beauties at the bar distracted me for a moment. How this place ever wanted to exclude females beats me. 'I'm not the only one needing to be careful with words, though, Peter. Didn't Orwell say people need to write clearly to think clearly?'

'Something like that, certainly. "Or someone will do their thinking for them." Sure, my profession needs precision to do its work properly. But there's one imperative you have that my tribe doesn't – laughter.' No shortage of empathy here.

'That's true – though I'm afraid it's a bit more formulaic than it might appear. $a + b + c = laughter$. Often there's a straight line between a and b, but c is the quirky outlier that gets the guffaw – if you get the rhythm right. You're cantering your audience to the cliff edge and pulling them back at the last minute. And your reward for saving their skins is the chuckle.'

'It's a fascinating psychology. And I envy you the dynamism of your trade. I pursue mine in sedentary lecture theatres – yours gets the adrenaline flowing under the bright lights.'

Crikey – someone envying me. Not sure if that's humbling or flattering. Or plain daft. And from a top-tier academic, as well. 'Didn't yer man Wittgenstein have something to say about words and their relation to the world? My memory's sketchy from a TV philosophy show years ago. Bryan Magee, bless him. Words had to express something in the world for the sentences to be meaningful, according to Wittgenstein – isn't that right?'

'You're making me work now, Nathan!'

'Sorry. As we Brits do say. Rather a lot ...'

'That was his earlier position – the picture theory of language. But in his later period Wittgenstein said we need to be sure we're speaking the same language – the same *kind* of language – for successful communication. So if I say, "I like the look of your drink", you'll need to know whether I literally mean I like how it looks, or I might be speaking more figuratively – perhaps I like the idea of a drink. Or the look of your drink stimulates memories of having enjoyed one before – and I may get one myself. Or I might steal yours!' He play-acted going to grab it; I wrapped both hands around it and swivelled to my left in a mock show of protection. 'It's okay, Nathan – I have my own drink.' As he turned to the bar momentarily I spotted some breakaway hairs starting a trek down his neck. It looked like compensation for their colleagues giving up on top.

Peter turned back and swigged from his pint.

I said, 'Please, call me Nate. And I think my job is to piss off Wittgenstein – well, all students of his school. Because I get laughs from those very misunderstandings. Take the "my dog's got no nose" gag. The teller and the listener can happily and accurately try to picture a noseless dog – like a car with a sawn-off bonnet – sorry, hood, as you'd say. But then the gag does a handbrake turn and the humour centres on the wordplay of, "How does it smell?" "Terrible", where enquiring after the dog's sense of smell is deliberately confused with the dog being malodorous.'

'Yeah – that misunderstanding would have given Wittgenstein kittens, as you might say. In America he may have had a cow.'

'So many animals, so little time.'

A philosopher who 'speaks human' (as well as bovine, feline...) and is playful. And who likes going to a bar to switch off. That's quite something, I mused as I left later. But who did he remind me of?

I should probably have got his business card, too.

32

Rhythm of Life
An embryo-eye's view

A central pulse beats steady. All systems go.
My world a growing crimson window of brightness
Like a paisley pattern, the embryo a seahorse swirl.
Am I a king or a scullery maid? Am I a boy or girl?

Gas! GAS! The cuckoo compound binds to my air line
Pulse goes mad and overloads
Panic spreads with threat to nascent life
Gasp! Gasp! Kick and fury, dragged from hell's flameless
                        kitchen

Calm restored and life affirmed
Bright white sheets cocoon the cocooner
Basso presence anchors the trio
Pulse, pulse, three hearts beat as one.

33

Therapy part two – Sam leaves
Thornton Heath, south London – 21 September 1999

Silence.

After a while Mary says, 'Is it about Sam?'

More silence. Then I realised I was responsible for the silence – and I was paying for it. 'Yup – gone. She's gone.'

'I'm so sorry.' Mary looked earnest, clasping her hands together.

I made some noise I didn't recognise, halfway between a 'thanks'-type acknowledgment and an 'it happens' acceptance. There was a third element, a guttural, primal pain, but that was a sleeping leviathan best left alone – assuming Mary didn't poke it with a stick.

'How did you find out?' The furrowed brow facing me oozed concern. I literally took it at face value.

'A note. A brief note. A touch of the "Dear Johns" – only more curt. Sam's not one to waste paper. Or ink.'

'What's the main feeling you're left with?' My inquisitor spared me the old counselling cliché, How does that make you feel? – just.

'You probably want me to say "rage".'

'I want you to tell the truth,' Mary said bluntly. 'As you experience it.' She looked like she might be suppressing her own rage – with me. Her hair is dyed jet black. Think I preferred it greyer.

'I feel hollowness right now. Coming back to an empty home. The silence seems louder than someone pottering about.'

Mary's eyes locked on to me like a heat-seeking missile. 'What do you fill that silence with, Nate?'

I paused to think – then realised the irony of leaving a silence between us. Mary might think I was taking the piss.

'I ... I start a not-very-constructive inner monologue. Sorry.' I knew the apology was redundant but given it feels like a teacher-pupil relationship with a therapist – or should that be parent-child? – I knew I'd disappointed and done wrong.

Mary chose not to pursue this line. A subtle widening of her eyes said, Tell me more. She and I had developed our own shorthand like a long-married couple. Ironically.

'I'm thinking anything from, How dare she? to, What did I do wrong? I'm all over the place. And I don't know what the hell I'm going to do.'

'Confusion's normal, early on. I think you know that. You've just got to allow that natural process to breathe. As to the future, it really is a case of "one day at a time". Longer term, I suggest trying not to become a refugee from intimacy.' Mary shifted in her chair. I became fixated by a mark on the wall over her shoulder as I mulled on that last phrase. She moved her neck forward subtly to get my attention again. 'Are you looking after yourself, Nate? The basics: eating, sleeping ...?'

'What do you think?' I broke my rule of not asking a therapist a question. And I probably sounded too angry – or sarcastic. But I couldn't apologise a second time.

Mary wasn't deflected. 'We need to still look after ourselves in difficult periods. It's important not to let depression triggers take over. Easier to arrest a slide now than when it's got too much momentum.'

She'd been privy to the slide with Sam for the last year or so. She had me charting how I reacted to different situations emotionally using the 'thought records' she gave me. It was a standard part of the cognitive behavioural therapy (CBT) we were working with. I documented stressful situations which gave rise to negative thoughts and, according to CBT doctrine, ultimately these feed depression. The theory is that by challenging the negative thoughts you can reduce depression. So, using a thought record, this is how I logged Sam's leaving and its immediate emotional effect on me:

Situation	Feelings	Evidence for	Evidence against	Feelings now (% change)
Sam walking out on me	Very depressing – it must be my fault, something wrong with me	The note she left saying she could no longer tolerate my moods	I'd had depression long before I met her, so she'd chosen to be with me despite my moods	Slightly better (10–20%??)

It's a strange business, talking about a failing marriage to a third party without the other spouse there. Like a weird ménage à trois, but without the fun.

Sam was having all the fun. By day, a much-loved infant-school teacher (you should see the cards from the kids at Christmas), but by evening a distracted, restless soul, emotionally absent and, at other times, physically absent too. The dates for frequent so-called 'parents' evenings' didn't quite marry up (pardon the pun) with her diary. Or, at least, the version of her diary she gave me. The credibility gap was brushed away by Sam with a 'Well, we have to be flexible for different parents' needs,' an over-polished non-apology.

The chief suspects for the presumed infidelity were as follows:

Daniels' Hall of Infamy

Job/name	Evidence for	Evidence against	Chance of guilt
1. Deputy Head, Colin Mathers	Overeager to be nice to me at functions; culturally sophisticated	Fondness for wearing tweed	50%
2. Fellow form teacher, Stephen Powers	Has the motive and the opportunity – flirtatious manner	Church warden and five children of his own	30%
3. Head, Chris Cox	Spends a lot of time with Sam; in a position of power over her	Female. Admittedly gay – but Sam not thought to be	20% (possible experimentation?)

34

Bed of sorrow
Northwick Park Hospital, London – 10 October 1996

My father lying-in-state. No – in a state. He hasn't spent a day in hospital as an inpatient in my life. So it comes as a shock to see him unconscious, catheterised, cables trailing from electrodes on his exposed chest. The same hospital where Mum's parents were treated. NHS but cutting-edge in the 1970s. Despite the stark, brutalist concrete, it was the height of tech spec to us. It had continuously moving doorless lifts for staff which intrigued me as a child. I'm guessing those perma-restless lifts haven't survived evolving health, safety, and energy concerns. Visiting Grandad when the hospital was new, Dad leaned into his father-in-law and joked, 'Are you sure they're not charging you extra to go private here?'

And now, Dad's on the receiving end of its care. No joke.

'How are you, Dad?' I ask, with no hope of acknowledgment or reply. I've been encouraged 'to keep it positive' by the gerontologist, despite Dad appearing to be out for the count. This consultant has asked me if his new patient was 'the life and soul of the party'? If so, they have good connections with a specialist neurology hospital in central London. They can do ops returning people close to their former vivacity. I'm appalled when my mouth, despairing of two years of decline, says he's not life or soul, he's taken a deep dive. Such treachery from a son. And towards such a loving father who endured the torture of my mother's early death. Shame on me.

After never being able to see a likeness, can I finally see myself in him? Something in the cheek bones, somewhat deep-set eyes, and slightly sallow skin. And that skin occludes his eyes, hiding our shared brown irises. He held on to his hair colour later than most, but at the last his dark hair has thinned and greyed. In recent months he's succumbed to the comb-over.

They've given him his own room. If he was conscious, I could have reprised his joke about whether he was going to be charged extra for going private. But I'm not sure he can hear anything, and even if he could, I have my own quiet theory about why he's been given a side room, and it doesn't lead anywhere good.

He's been unconscious for over twelve hours. I got here as soon as I could. A neighbour called the ambulance. The consultant got my father a brain scan yesterday evening. Diagnosis: Dad's had a stroke. But he'd been weakened by Parkinson's already for what seems like an age; even before this shock the disease had robbed him of his sparky wit and catchlight.

'He's a very sick man.' A charge nurse in crisp white uniform with a blue belt at the waist looks at my father as he struggles to breathe. She's at the end of his bed as she utters this solemn judgment. Her tone and simple, slow delivery imply there's no return from this.

Later, a young consultant, his auburn curls a bit anarchic against his smart white coat, engages me in a chat in a nearby corridor. Autumnal afternoon sun is streaking through the window behind him, giving him a saintly reflected glow and the hint of a halo. We have an oddly circular conversation about me being given some choice over my father's care, especially where medication for his lung condition is concerned, although the young doctor makes it clear my decision can be overridden at any time. 'It's typical for an elderly unconscious patient to get a lung infection as they're not moving,' he says; would I like my father to be treated for it? The consultant's eyes seem to be pleading. But

I'm at a loss: why *wouldn't* I want Dad to be given relief from the infection?

After a couple of conversational circuits, it becomes obvious that such treatment would extend Dad's life, but not his quality of life. I finally agree to go where I'm being led and sanction Dr Daniels – no relation – not to treat the lung condition. I feel surprisingly light and guilt-free, even though I think I can hear Dad's laboured breathing twenty feet away. I also feel sorry for the consultant, doubtless young enough for the word 'empowerment' to have been used in his training in the context of people like me, the next of kin. More bizarrely I feel sorry for him in that he doesn't seem to have gone through the loss of someone close to him, otherwise he wouldn't be tiptoeing his way around death with me, an old hand at mortality.

Sam arrives from work and after she says something perfunctory to her father-in-law, we go to the canteen to eat; she says she's starving. But I realise for me it's a pretext for getting away from the difficult sights and sounds of the side room; I offer no resistance. We return, a bit sheepishly, and I briefly tell Dad where we've been and that we'll be with him for a bit longer.

We hang around for about an hour, then I make the thoroughly non-medical calculation that he'll survive the night, based on his breathing, a hunch, and wishful thinking. The following morning I phone ahead, asking the charge nurse if there's any change in his condition. She replies in the same code I've used with her. Decoded, I gather I shouldn't delay getting in.

Sam goes to work and will join me later. I check in with the nurse's station on arrival at the ward, and they wave me through to Dad's side room. They have no real news to impart; he was the same overnight. When I arrive at his bedside I realise how successfully I've cut myself off from his suffering overnight, but here it is again, writ large: the noisy struggle for breath, the beeping machine. I've been told there are a number of levels of consciousness for a patient in his condition, and that I could see if he could squeeze my finger when asked, to indicate a higher level of consciousness. For whatever reason, I don't do it; maybe I don't want to know if he's at that greater end of awareness. That would mean he would be more alive to pain and to his situation. It would also mean I would find it even harder to switch off from his suffering. I'm tired of dressing up my self-interest as compassion.

I've brought in with me a small radio cassette player to distract Dad if he can hear it. I plug it in, in the socket next to the monitor. The radio's too unpredictable to leave on the whole time and would carry too much speech, so I quickly bought a compilation of British orchestral music on my way into the hospital in the rush hour. It's got some of his favourite composers on it – Vaughan Williams, Elgar, Bridge, Delius. I hit play and it burbles away in the background.

Speaking over his laboured breathing, I give Dad an update of what's happened since I was here the previous evening. I was about to tell him of the struggle Sam and I had to get home on the tube when I recalled the gerontologist had counselled me to sound cheery. I carried on reliving the previous evening, trying to make household chores sound as upbeat as possible, then I explain to my unconscious father I'm going to get a coffee.

The route to the canteen leads via an elevated walkway. Alternating with the windows looking out on dour concrete and the hospital's service roads are a sequence of abstract paintings nestling at the orange-brown end of the colour spectrum, all by the same artist and all apparently from the same series. With a hint of Rothko there's such energy in the brushwork, and they seem to make a positive statement amidst all the suffering on this site. The pictures suggest shadowy outlines of buildings, maybe of a religious nature, but they're too impressionistic to be tied to any particular beliefs. For me they've captured a spirit and an optimism which is, for this moment, attractive. I make a mental note to try and buy one if they're for sale.

While I was sitting with a coffee my phone vibrated in my pocket, in defiance of signs telling me to turn the device off 'as it could interfere with our equipment'. A voice in my ear says, 'Could you come back quickly please, Mr Daniels?' It sounded like the sister who'd made the pronouncement yesterday about how ill Dad was. 'Your father's having more trouble with his breathing.'

I abandoned my drink after a last gulp then, blinded by nerves, couldn't see where to leave the canteen. I asked a stethoscoped gent and he pointed to the now-obvious green exit sign. In a moment I was back in the walkway passing a blur of orange, and then a group of white coats laughing loudly, then into the lift, down to Machin Ward, the geriatric ward. I could still sense the institutional smell of stewed vegetables in the air. Nurses at their station reacted because of the urgency of my steps. They relaxed as they recognised me. I strode on to Dad's side room.

The young consultant was just leaving as I arrived, and we exchanged weak smiles. Two nurses were adjusting equipment and then quietly slipped away. Dad's breathing was louder, which I'd braced myself for. I thought of Sam. A quick check of the time – 3.30pm – placed her at work. I messaged her to, 'Get to hosp asap. Dad not good. x'

He'd never wanted to stop working. While he could lose momentum when the pipeline of jobs dried up, essentially he loved his trade as a graphic designer. Provided he could have some classical music on and be supplied the occasional cup of tea, he could go for hours without a break, even at weekends. For him the ideal way to die, I'm pretty sure, was to finish a job, clean his tools for one last time, retire to his favourite armchair and drift away to the sounds of Elgar's *The Dream of Gerontius.*

But here he was, back on earth, with a mortal's struggle for air – and no music. While I'd been away the tape machine had been unplugged in favour of some medical equipment needed temporarily. I plugged the little Philips machine back in and hit play where the tape had got to: Delius's 'In a Summer Garden'. I anxiously observe Dad's struggle for breath. At school they taught us about air pressure, and that you only have to make space for air in your lungs for them to fill. Very little effort seemed to be needed. But Dad here appears to be sucking air in, hard work that's costing him his remaining energy. His head is on its side, so I'm viewing him in profile. A nurse walks in as some foul-looking brown fluid is coming from Dad's nose and mouth. She discreetly puts a new piece of white paper towel on top of his pillow. The subtle choreography of the nurses to be present then absent on cue quietly impresses me.

I look at my father's left arm resting on top of his blanket to allow the tube coming out of it a free passage to the IV drip next to him. I think of how his arms have held me, shielded me from harm – and even mimed punching me. It was a game we used to play when I was four or so. I probably landed real punches on him then without making the slightest impression. He would play-act boxing with me while I ineffectually hit his chest for a few seconds, then the physical joke was we would cuddle for a few seconds before beginning the boxing again. I wonder now if there was some symbolism going on, the outward expression of ambivalence we felt towards each other, or am I overthinking?

It's certainly true to say in the cuddling phase as I placed my head against Dad's chest, the reassuring slow, steady ker-thud of his heart was my anchor in a choppy world. Easy to put an adult spin on perceptions now as I watch my father dying, but with my mum's mercurial temperament, I was so lucky to have Dad's counterbalance: he was even-tempered, with a low centre of gravity. But as I grew up that could lead to despair at his undemonstrativeness. Was it a response to the anguish Mum put him through: to withdraw, hurt? So English. So male.

So me, now.

The gasps are getting louder. Is this the death rattle they talk about? I want to believe he's got the lowest level of consciousness, to be as distant from this pain as possible. Or maybe he's looking down on himself from above, on this scene, with me by his side. Maybe while I observe this wrecked body, in his mind he's walking towards a light, as people coming back from near-death experiences report. But who is the 'he' in that sentence? Does it even exist any more?

I lay my hand softly on his head, the first time in two days I've felt able to do that. And now, inconsistently, I hope his consciousness is high enough for him to feel my touch. I want to say 'I love you' and to thank him for everything, but the words don't convert from thoughts to vibrations in the air. I smile recalling this; he'd understand. I'm truly made in his mould.

The breathing stops for several seconds; is that it? I'm then startled by one huge noise, all the louder to make up, it seems, for the extended pause. More akin to a snore than a standard breath. Is this his last joke – to draw me in, make me think it's all over, then upset expectations? Set-up – build – punchline ...

It's his last breath but not his last joke.

As the noise of breathing finally departs the room, bubbling up to take its place is the tape machine playing 'Rule Britannia'. A suitably jingoistic send-off for the man who fought for King and country. Well, not so much fought as coordinated munitions supplies at the Royal Ordnance in Bicester, Oxfordshire. He was a counter, not a fighter.

> *Farewell, but not for ever! brother dear,*
> *Be brave and patient on thy bed of sorrow;*
> *Swiftly shall pass thy night of trial here,*
> *And I will come and wake thee on the morrow.*

Dream of Gerontius – St John Henry Newman

35

Production line
Napsbury Hospital, London Colney – October 1982

'If you carry on like this, you'll kill yourself.'

The nurse looks serious, but I can't control my seized-up muscles. Fingers clenched like claws, feet curled away from me like I'm a monkey gripping a bough. But the drugs, not me, are running the show. I feel I'm in a different room to my normal number twelve. Am I in an examination room or have I just been moved to another room while mine's repaired or cleaned?

Perhaps it's like the time they tried to throw me by turning everything round the other way in the bathroom. Taps one end a couple of days ago, taps t'other end yesterday. Only continuity was the nurse. (Smiling John. Very sweet, but is he gay?) Or when they drove me to that gym. Minibus bumping over sleeping policemen, but an impossible gap between front and back wheels. First time bump ... gap ... too long a wheelbase then second bump like the minibus is stretched. Cried out with eyes closed. Made no sense, but that's how they get you – if you can make sense of it, you're mad. If you don't spot the bathroom changeround you're bonkers and they've got you.

Minibus arrives at the gym, and they put a football in front of you and it's another test. The Dregs are there with you ambling around and your job – you work out – is to corral them into teams. No other bugger was going to do it. Test of my macho mettle. Ended up playing on me own. Not a team player.

Get back to Funny Farm and I'm taken to the Rubber Room. They think I can't work it out. There's no rubber in it, so it must have been a padded cell – a bloody big one. It's a euphonium or a euphemism, the term 'Rubber Room'. It's some kind of meeting room. Brilliant white walls. Arches. Minimal furniture and fittings. It's used for work, give the Dregs something to do, make them some pocket money. There's half a dozen of us working here. Except it's not very efficient. You're given a wodge of coloured pens – felt tips – and you have to put them in a box, Nurse John leading the exercise. He's in civvies: white shirt, checked light-brown trousers. Professional looking, without going OTT. They don't let 'em wear white coats in case we think we're nuts. As if.

He shows us the form: yellow pens in this white plastic section – part of the moulding which fits in the cardboard box – blues in this section, and so on. But I work out we can go faster if we each specialise in a colour. My favourite is purple, same as my mum. So I say to John, Why don't we each have a colour and pass one box at a time along the line, and everyone puts in their colour when the box gets to them. Holy Joe, the believer, puts in green, Grandad Junior red, I add purple and so on. A production line Henry Ford'd be proud of. Yes, more alienating 'cos you don't get to finish the product but needs must in a capitalist world. I congratulate myself. John smiles, gay or not.

After finishing a few boxes, he takes me to one side and says he's just got to do a bit of artwork on me. As a thank you for my ideas, increasing productivity. I smell a rat but sit there as he takes a felt pen to my face and draws away. I can feel the skin round my mouth stretching as he fills in details, though I don't know what he's doing. The others look on, smiling. John's got an even cheekier grin than usual.

He looks a bit more intense as he colours in – I can feel the cross-hatching, as my dad calls it. The Dregs seem to be willing him on. Finally, Nurse John finds a mirror and shows it to me. Thanks to him I have Noel Edmonds-style topiary: a sketchy golden-brown, down-turned built-in tache and beard, a lookalike or facial hairalike of my radio hero. But I can't laugh 'cos it's too close to the bone. Edmonds is going to pick me up one night, a Ford taxi like he was picked up from the Donkey Derby where I met him for five glorious seconds as an eleven-year-old. Long enough to get an autograph. Still got the programme he signed. I'm going to get picked up and taken to Broadcasting House with him. Then it won't be such a joke for John to make at my expense.

But John originally *was* Noel Edmonds, light-entertainment TV star. He denies it but he is, or was. It's all part of the game. You wouldn't think a TV personality could be a mental nurse, but anything's possible in here. The other night all the top radio DJs were going to do a gig. At the nuthouse. I knew it. I could *sense* it. They've got a big hall here so it's perfectly possible. I was so sure I told a visitor – Dominika – to come back that evening for it. She laughed but she won't be laughing when it happens.

36

Two cities
Streets of Manhattan – 29 December 1999

I find myself walking past Grand Central Station. I think I got deflected from the more direct route, which would have meant turning for Lexington Avenue via E 42nd Street, because I didn't realise it was at a lower level than Park Avenue. I approach the terminal's three suitably grand arches on the 42nd Street side, each separated by fluted double columns; you could be forgiven for thinking the railways were built by the ancient Greeks.

But maybe the railway should be given this elevated pantheon-style status. America long ago ceded the primacy of the train to the automobile and covered large swathes of the nation in tarmac. It suited the rampant turbocharged individualism of this nation's psyche; even the term 'railroad' sounds like capitulation to the car. Compare the stereotypes of the two modes of transports' fans: petrolheads the go-getting, swashbuckling, leather-jacketed *Top Gear*-watching adventurers; versus the guys who stand at the end of a platform with spiral-bound notebooks, biros, and dodgy glasses held together by Elastoplast.

Focussing ever more resources on individual transport is fine while you can afford it; great till the individual is needy. When hard times hit, suddenly the collectivism of public transport – sharing an affordable space and spreading the load – doesn't look so terrible. Those pillars seem earned to me right now.

I go around the station on the right-hand section of Park Ave, which splits just past 42nd Street. I feel a sudden pang of homesickness, prompted by being a stranger in a strange land, and being spewed out of the mouth of the television machine. Showbiz is bipolar: you're on-air or off-air, hero or zero, working or resting, waving or drowning, a hit or a shit. And right now I'm on the brown end of the spectrum.

I close in on Midtown Manhattan. A man with a grey blanket over his shoulder approaches me. His brow is furrowed and he's chewing. Tufts of hair look like the remains of dreadlocks which have been cut down to stumps. He wears a tatty light-green jumper with loose threads, like untamed wires on a guitar neck. His rich dark skin looks weathered and etched, the lines somehow deeper than they should be. I feel he's mid-thirties like me, but the street, or whatever life's dealt him, has put years on him. 'Money for a room for the night, sir?' he drawls.

The deference kills me. I reach for a ten-dollar bill in my wallet. It's something, yet nothing. 'Here.'

'Why thank you, sir. It's just I – my girlfriend was murdered and the Feds won't let me back in my flat. It's all taped off ...'

I have no idea, and no way of checking, if that's true, or if it's a cover story for addiction. But equally I have no stomach for interrogating him. I couldn't cope with looking into those tragic eyes and seeing an infinity of need. I belatedly realise his blanket started out white, not grey.

We were speaking at the foot of the J.P. Morgan building.

I walk on, having wished him better days in the new millennium. I don't look back. I can't carry his burden and mine. McCartney sang how no one got saved in 'Eleanor Rigby'. My mum wondered what it meant that Eleanor had a facial expression in a jar. I told her it was something to do with loneliness.

A few minutes further up St Bartholomew's church looks confident nestling among towers and banks. I reflect on meeting Blanket Man, and how Jesus promised, 'Ye have the poor always with you.' The only promise he kept.

A bus horn blasts me out of my trance. I look round as revellers scatter from the driver's path. He doesn't look like someone you'd play chicken with.

37

Next door
Oxhey, Hertfordshire – 15 August 1975

Selica is our pretty next-door neighbour. She's 'with it' as my dad, who isn't, would say. Her bell bottoms have bell bottoms. She cut into her flared black trousers to insert an extra triangle of material, with colours and swirls. When she's dressing up, she sometimes wears a black choker with a jewel which goes over her throat. Her husband, Marcus, is a travel courier. I'm not sure what that means but he's away a lot. They're both South African and have olivey skin with dark hair, but Marcus's is a bit curly and Selica's is straight, down to her shoulders. They have two children, Anthea (five) and Bethany (three), who have mousey-brown hair. They are cute, and sometimes I babysit for them. I'm eleven.

They have a cat called Fred. He's pale ginger, as if someone's turned up the brightness on our cat Sandy, who's a deep ginger. Selica said before they moved next door to us (a couple of years ago) she used to have Czechoslovakian neighbours who couldn't believe you could give a cat such a short name as Fred. So they called him Freduçska.

Selica likes music. She has the latest Bread album with the song 'Guitar Man' on it. She's also played me The Beatles' *Abbey Road* album. She says they keep having to make more copies, even though the LP's from ages ago – five or six years ago – because it's so good. She has a posh stereo cassette player in her lounge, which also has a bar and howdy cowboy swing doors into it – and she plays me side two, starting with 'Here Comes the Sun'. That's amazing enough, but then comes the song 'Because'. I truly think it's the most beautiful song I've ever heard. The singing is magnificent, even though it hangs in a funny way at the end. The group blends together in such a gorgeous way it makes me want to cry, like the words of the song seem to say. There's a strange keyboard going through a lot of it, but somehow it all works.

Selica has dark brown eyes and is slim. When I grow up, if I have a daughter, I'm going to call her Selica. Then her name will begin and end with 's'.

I don't know if I should tell you, but a few weeks ago I was playing with my Irish friend Paddy at my house and I was telling him about pretty Selica and the drinks bar and the howdy doors and he wanted to see it all. Selica and her family had gone back to South Africa for three weeks, and me and my parents were keeping an eye on the house. I had to feed Fred every day and water the plants every few days. It was the end of the summer holidays, just before Paddy and I started different secondary schools in very different places. He was moving with his family back to Ireland.

Paddy and I do lots together; for instance, recently we've been trying to dig our way to Australia – or at least, dig an adventure room in my garden, and see how deep we can get. We talk about The Men (secret creatures only we can see which hide under stones) and this year we've been learning Morse code. Paddy can blink it with his eyes and I can decode it.

Paddy stood beside me as I knocked on our neighbour's front door, just in case they'd come back from their break early. When there was silence, we went through the back door, which I had the key for. I felt bad but I had to tell Paddy to take his shoes off, like we all did. The combined kitchen and dining room were spotless and flashy compared to our house. There was a split-level cooker my Mum envied, stainless-steel everything, and even a clock on the oven. Plus there was a lamp over the table you could adjust the height of by pulling it up or down. And a snazzy Trimphone in cream on a teak sideboard. Paddy was impressed.

Then, past the howdy doors, he saw the bar against the long wall of the lounge.

'Let's have a drink, Nat.' Paddy ran his hand along the copper counter. The bar was in an S-shape on the right side of the lounge as you left the kitchen. There was a light grey stoney wall between you and the drinks. There were a few upside-down bottles on the wall.

'We can't have a drink, Paddy – we haven't got permission.' I looked at my Timex watch. 'Plus, it's only eleven in the morning!'

'Sod permission, Nat.' Paddy's dad liked saying sod this and sod that. 'Let's have some fun before school starts up again. Decent!'

And before I knew it, he'd hoicked himself over the bar, taken a tea towel from near the mini sink in the corner, put it over his forearm and said, in a pretend posh English accent, 'Can I take your order, sir?'

Again I protested, but then I thought of the drink Marcus had given me which I liked most and said, 'I'll have a Cinzano please, barman.' Paddy poured twice the amount I've ever had, then he found a cocktail stick and a glacé cherry and a light green parasol and put those in too. 'Crikey,' I said. I couldn't drink all that, but I wasn't going to let him know. I sat down opposite him on a bar stool which had a brown suede cushion and chrome legs. 'And what are you having?'

He was still playing all posh. 'Well normally I wouldn't drink on duty, sir, but if you're sure you don't mind, I'll ... I'd love a Babycham.' With that he opened a small bottle of the stuff and poured it into one of those glasses with a stalk which looks like it's been squashed till it's wide and shallow.

We did that clinking thing with our glasses and tipped our heads back. Paddy started singing the conga song with all those da-da-daas in it, and then he led me upstairs. He opened the first door he came to and it was the loo. Paddy said, 'Release the bog roll!' and he tugged on the toilet roll then he started wrapping it round me. It was apricot colour – the soft sort. Paddy stuffed it into the neck of my jumper, like the ruff I wear as a choirboy.

I suggested we left the room. I was pleased he went along with my idea, but then he couldn't resist going into Selica and Marcus's bedroom. I tried to protest, but he wouldn't listen.

'And what have we here, then?' Paddy said, like a TV cop, as he opened the brown-painted door. There was an old-style metal-framed double bed with a white continental quilt on it. The built-in wardrobes at the end of the bed were white, too, with mirrors on the tall, thin doors. The cream carpet was soft on my feet, the deepest I'd walked on in my life, like wading barefoot through long, comfy grass.

Paddy moved to the drawers in front of the big mirror. He opened a drawer and pulled out some dark men's socks. 'Bo-ring,' he said. From the next drawer down he produced a couple of white handkerchiefs like a magician drawing them out of a hat. Then he opened the next drawer down and giggled, saying, 'You gotta see this, Nat.' I moved closer and in front of me he slowly drew out a pair of black lacy knickers – Selica's.

'Paddy – you're a bad boy,' I said. That didn't stop him slowly drawing out a tan-coloured bra and some red panties, too. He draped the bra over the middle of his head with one strap trailing down his nose, the other going down his back. And the bosomy bits were on his head, like he was half-boy, half-camel. He blew on the strap sitting on his nose so it rose, then it fell when he stopped puffing.

He opened one of the tall wardrobe doors and revealed some of Marcus's suits and shirts. 'Very swish,' he said, running his hand along the edge of the clothes. He took out a suit at random, a dark blue one with fine white pinstripes. With it still on its hanger, he held it up to shoulder height and, looking in the door's mirror, said, 'I could see myself in this.' He took off his jeans and started to put on the suit trousers.

And then the doorbell rang.

'Christ,' said Paddy and froze.

'Blimey. What are we going to do?' I could hear my pulse thumping in my ears.

'Keep our voices down for starters, that's what.' The bell rang again. 'Oh, God. Well, I can't open the door like this.' He looked down at the trouser legs on the furry carpet. 'You do something.'

'Maybe they'll go away.'

Then there was a knocking on the glass panel of the front door.

'Doesn't sound like it, Nat. But you're allowed to be in here. In the house, anyway. Just don't let the buggers upstairs to see me.'

Reluctantly I took one step at a time down to the open-plan lounge. I saw two shadowy figures through the thin pane of frosted glass that ran to one side of the front door.

My heart was working hard like a high-revving engine. I took a deep breath, raising my shoulders to make more space, and opened the door.

Two smiling faces, one male, one female, greeted me. The man held a copy of *The Watchtower* towards me. Phew. Jehovah's Witnesses, not killers.

'Hello,' said the man. 'I'm Joseph and this is Julia.' At the mention of her name, the woman smiled even more, which I didn't think was possible. She had a smart, dark-red handbag looping from her forearm. 'Are Mummy or Daddy in?' Joseph asked.

'Er – no,' I said. Even though I was telling the truth, it sounded like I was lying. I didn't know if he was trying to catch me out. My parents could be in, but not in this house.

Joseph and Julia were both getting on a bit – in their thirties or even forties. Joseph had a wave of Brylcreemed black hair with bits of grey in it. He was saying something about the Lord, but I was looking at the front cover of the magazine he was clutching. It looked like a disaster movie. It was hand-painted in an old-fashioned style, like something from the 1950s. There was a big mushroom cloud with flashes of red and orange at the bottom, where there were also buildings at funny angles with people hanging out of them looking horrified. It reminded me of the poster for the film *The Towering Inferno*. Diagonally sprawled across the picture in big painted white letters was the word 'Armageddon', and underneath it the question: 'Are you ready?'

It didn't seem to fit with Julia and Joseph's smiles. I caught the tail end of what Joseph was saying: '...And so nobody knows why we die. It's a mystery. But we know we don't have to. And the main thing is to be prepared for what's coming later this year.'

I didn't want to admit I hadn't been listening to what was coming later this year – I had enough to worry about going to secondary school. It was a bit depressing to think there might be mushroom clouds as well as uniform and bullies to think about.

I began to feel they weren't going to go away unless I bought a copy of the magazine. I had to explain I didn't have any money on me.

They seemed to accept me not being able to afford a copy of *The Watchtower*, and both said goodbye politely. They turned and started to walk down the path, but then Joseph stopped, thought for a moment, and turned back to me. He hesitated again, then said, 'Excuse me for asking, but is there a reason you've got toilet roll around your neck?'

Without thinking I said, 'It's a religious thing,' and slammed the door shut.

'Jeepers,' I said to myself, my back leaning against the door as if I thought they might return. I pulled the loo roll from out of my jumper.

I climbed back up the staircase from the open-plan lounge, turning left then left at the dog leg, and called out to Paddy, 'Jehovah's Witnesses. Got rid of 'em. Easy-peasy.'

I walked the last few steps up and returned to the main bedroom. And there was the sight before me: Paddy wearing an Afghan coat over Selica's white and lime big-patterned dress. It had a line of large black buttons down the front. He also had on her beige wet-look boots, which went virtually to the top of his legs, and a wide-brimmed floppy straw hat. He wore her big round sunglasses, and had even put on some deep red lipstick, a bit messily. The coat flared out around where his hands were on his hips.

I couldn't help laughing but Pads just stared back at me, stony-faced. And then I realised the hem of the dress was rising and rising. I now had an awkward after-smile expression, and I felt the tension burning into the back of my jaw. I could feel my lips starting to quiver. And as the hem of the dress rose I could see Paddy was wearing Selica's black lacy knickers. With one hand he held the hem up and with the other he undid a few buttons, revealing the tan-coloured bra around his chest. A hint of white cloth above it showed he'd stuffed it with a couple of Marcus's hankies. Part of me still found this funny, but I didn't dare laugh this time. In any case, part of me found it very weird, especially with Paddy's expression. And then it got weirder: the hand holding up the hem pulled the knickers to one side to show his willy. It was hard. And the other hand moved from the buttons to his face. He rested his index finger on his mouth as if to say, 'Shhh'. And I've never mentioned it to anyone, including Paddy, from that day onwards.

38

St Peter's gate
Midtown Manhattan – 29 December 1999

I look at my watch; no more than four hours have passed since the dressing-room altercation with Paddy. Four hours without work. Redundant.

As I cross 54th Street at 3rd Avenue I'm passed by a stretch limo with gaudy signwriting whoring itself for 'parties and private affairs'. Consumer capitalism in crisis made flesh. Or made metal. Who needs to have a party on the move? What kind of person is afraid of inviting friends to a static address? Why would you hire a post-modern charabanc with the turning circle of an oil tanker when you could hail a cab? The party in progress seems to cock a snook at me as they roar over the junction, all pompous prom outfits and extreme wining and dining. A heavy thump of R&B accompanies, that form with a borrowed, confusing name: I hear the rhythm, but I don't hear authentic blues in it. The song is 'Say My Name', the perfect anthem for these narcissistic passengers.

I walk past block after block of anonymous monoliths, home to the titans of turbo-capitalism. In a city that lives on its nerves these are the synapses, but feelings are dulled in this fag-end of the millennium, commerce is in suspended animation, inebriation being the go-to state to survive the party to end all parties, laying the ground for the first great hangover of the new millennium. Any illumination in buildings here is liable to be for security purposes and the occasional office party. I strain my neck looking for signs of life way above street level. Building ever higher in this high-rise metropolis looks like corporate confidence, but it might conceal the opposite. With Manhattan land at a premium, you could view low-rise as more confident; more affluent.

I've been schlepping up Park Avenue for too long. Have I overshot my hotel? That's the problem with numbered streets – they don't enter my memory. I take a right into 54th Street. This must be where it is. A rash of stars and stripes on the other side of the road isn't much of a clue; I could be anywhere in this benighted city where the locals rally around the flag, or any other cloned city across the land. Last refuge of scoundrels.

A bistro to the left, more corporate America to the right. But no hotel. I keep going for a block, till I'm faced with another crossroads. I feel queasy deciding which way to turn. Then I'm captivated by the sight opposite: a modern church nestling among the stilts of a vast corporate skyscraper. God meets mammon.

I cross over Lexington Avenue to get closer. The angular planes of this twentieth-century church at street level assault me, topped off by the sheer chutzpah of the vast office block above, caught as if stepping over this sacred space on its way to somewhere more trendy.

Would Jesus see the corporate banks of 'Lex' as the 'whited sepulchres' he spoke about in the gospel – the lawyers and Pharisees who were beautiful on the outside but contained the bones of the dead within? Would he leaf through the banks' glossy literature and see the porcelain-capped smiles of the bankers for their clients, provided the clients met a minimum-wealth threshold? Perhaps those bankers' teeth are the whited sepulchres themselves: a ceramic cover for the pestiferous filed-off rump of a tooth below, a bright headstone marking the burial ground of a bacteria-riddled corpse. Would Christ turn over the bankers' tables in rage at how they'd commodified every aspect of life, cradle to grave, leaving nothing pure, nothing to chance, nothing holy? Or would he despair, trudging through the streets, head bowed like he was crucified again, the world on his shoulders, spirit broken, and cause lost?

I get closer to the church. From one angle it looks like a pyramid made of grey breeze blocks cut in two, off-centre, top to bottom. It's as if a narrow column of glass has been inserted in the gap between the two uneven halves. I cross the road when the early-evening traffic allows and press my nose to the glass. Beneath me the house lights reveal a sacred space, empty but for a lone female figure tending to some flowers. She's arranging white orchids fleshed out by sprigs of fern on the plinth by the central white altar. Moving unselfconsciously, absorbed in her task, she's the calm at the centre of the city storm. She's black and has perfect comportment, exuding pride in her posture: this is a vital, not a lowly task. Occasionally she stands back from her creation, views it from the aisle, and seems to be checking its symmetry. Serried pews in light-coloured wood have clean, Scandinavian lines. The white walls open out the space, while the ceiling feels disproportionately tall at its highest point. The height must remind worshippers of their inconsequence; when seated, their heads would reach perhaps a thirtieth of the way to the top. Even in such a radically designed building there has to be a nod to the infinite.

I was wondering where the flower woman had gone when she appeared at my left shoulder.

'I was beckoning you in, but you couldn't see me!' She let out a hearty staccato laugh. Her accent seemed a blend of Caribbean and native New Yorker. 'Well ...?' She tilted her head slightly, holding my gaze.

'Oh my God ... er, gosh. I was lost in thought. How rude of me. Sorry.'

'No matter. Come.' She touched my elbow, and I followed her.

We went through what felt like a side entrance, but since this building didn't follow the Victorian norms I was used to – west doors, naves, porticos, and all – it was impossible to say which entrance was the main one. The glass door closed behind us and Midtown Manhattan's cacophony faded away.

'You must be English?' she queried, turning back to me as she led me into the main space.

'Is it obvious?' I teased.

'We just met and you said sorry.'

'Brits have a lot to apologise for.'

'This is a place for forgiveness.' I wasn't sure how tongue-in-cheek she was being. She walked towards the altar and absent-mindedly rubbed the vase she'd been working on with the chamois in her hand. 'Do you want the tour?'

'Sure.' Now I was sounding North American.

'This is where we worship – the sanctuary. We're all on the same level here.' Ah, the symbolism. And I'm always struck by how modern believers can talk so casually about 'worship'. Sounds medieval.

'I'm Brigitte, by the way.' She offered her hand.

'Nate.' We shook.

Brigitte pointed out the main features of this area; she talked about its minimalism, and the practicality of its design. 'Everything is modular so we can move things around, depending on what we want to use it for.'

The pews were so sharp-edged and basic that from above, with their regimented right angles, they looked like unused staples. I smiled as I realised the diamond shapes overlaid on their cushions' pink, red, and orange grids resemble those on London's tube trains.

When she saw my interest, Brigitte pointed out how the sanctuary was frequently used for concerts. 'We're big into music here. And we have two organs and five pianos.'

'That seems greedy,' I jested, testing Brigitte's tolerance.

'Not at all, Nate! We cater for different audiences and different groups using the building. We have a special side chapel, too.'

'That I must see.'

She led me through a side door to the small Nevelson Chapel. 'It's named after the Russian-American sculptor Louise Nevelson. Her work was commissioned for this area.' The initial sense on walking into this side room was of more white walls, in keeping with the sanctuary we'd just left. But when Brigitte raised the light level I could see textures, white-on-white: what looked like sanitised disposable objects, shapes hinting at fish forms and cutlery and crockery. Some objects fell inside white boxy frames, similar to shelves for books or trinkets, others broke out of them and dangled from them. These were modernist bas-reliefs, not fully 3-D, yet not flat either. I counted up to four layers in some areas.

And those staples again. Wooden pews in a light pine with a simple rectangular frame, all horizontal and vertical planes as before, except they were arranged more closely here. And far fewer of them: ten or twelve. And no London Underground cushion patterns. Instead, a calming pastel cappuccino shade for the soft back-and-thigh support.

Something was dislocating me in this chapel, though. As I said to Brigitte, 'In a city of full-fat consumption, it's odd there are no brand names here? I mean, among all these objects.' I knew it sounded dumb as soon as it left my mouth. What was I expecting: Warhol's 'Campbell's Soup Cans'?

'This is a place for reflection, Nate. So you leave your ego – and your brand loyalties – at the door!'

'Okay.' I was humbled. And yet ... 'If egos are banned, how come Nevelson gets a namecheck?'

'I wasn't here when this chapel was dedicated in 1977. But I imagine our predecessors were pretty proud of snaring Louise – one of America's leading sculptors of this century. And it might have seemed too traditional, too anti-modernist to do the obvious – say, to go with the normal run of a Lady Chapel or St John the Baptist's Chapel. To be precise, the full name of this area is Louise Nevelson's Chapel of the Good Shepherd. We don't worship Nevelson here any more than you would worship John the Baptist in a chapel named after him. But we do respect her.' Brigitte's arms, which had been drawing great arcs in this space, fell by her sides. 'Do you like this area, Nate?'

Brigitte caught me off guard as I'd got used to asking the questions. I soaked up the atmosphere and after a pause said, 'Yes. Yes, I do. Above all, it's peaceful. No mean feat in the city that never sleeps.'

Brigitte smiled. For the first time I took in the visual gag of her wearing a floral blouse while being a flower arranger. Rich reds and greens with flashes of gold, a tropical riot of large-patterned colour. And a hint of a gold filling revealed on one side of her mouth.

There was more gold, or gold leaf as she told me, on the wall behind the altar table, the one exception to Nevelson's sparse, bleached look. It was all the more arresting for being juxtaposed with white. The table was, of course, simplicity itself, as if it had mutated from a pew. It bore a white cloth, perfectly sized not just to cover the top surface but also to run down each side, effectively covering the vertical supports.

'Are you uncomfortable, Brigitte, is this church uncomfortable with its wealth? In some parts of the world, it would be thought of as obscene. You could worship God in a tin shack and give the money to the poor.'

Brigitte took a deep breath before answering. 'I don't know if you're aware of the story but on this site the previous St Peter's was a nineteenth-century building.' Then she seemed to add in brackets, 'You may know many believers understand the word "church" to mean the people, rather than the building.' I nodded. 'Well Citicorp - the bank - approached church management about wanting to build a large HQ on this site at the beginning of the Seventies, and St Peter's said, "You can do that if you make a new building for us here." Which, of course, is what happened. Wise elders made sure St Peter's wasn't at the wrong end of the deal, so to speak. I don't think the bank would have put up with a decrepit building over their foundations. Citicorp is wealthy and there is money in this city for sure. I think believers would find it hard to understand why among the wealth they were obliged to go without. Though that's not to dismiss or trivialise poverty, of course. I spent part of my childhood in Jamaica and the reality of poverty there is very ugly. And it leads to people doing ugly things.' She looked down, pursed her lips, then looked back at me. I had a foot in two camps – radical redistribution and tolerance. Tolerance of inequality. I was falling for this place and so ended up absorbing its contradictions.

I realised I'd got this far without even knowing what denomination this church was. The symbolism was Protestant, not Catholic, but beyond that I had to rely on Brigitte for the detail. 'We're Lutheran evangelicals,' she explained.

'That sounds like a contradiction in terms to me. I associate Lutherans with hard work and evangelicals with being saved by their faith, not what they do. Where does that leave you?!'

Brigitte shot me a twenty-four-carat beatific smile. 'I'm not a great denominationalist. You may tell that from the fact you raised the issue, not me. But I like to think we tap into the best of both worlds. It took a lot of hard work getting this building together, but we also thank God for his grace in giving us the gift of this place and the setting, and the circumstances which have enabled it to flourish. Hard work alone would have meant we could never relax, never settle into this gift. I'm thankful for small – and large – mercies.'

She gave me a whistle-stop tour of the Scandi and Germanic roots of the church, and I was reminded of the pay-off of that great Irish yarn-spinner Dave Allen: 'May your God go with you.' Danes, Germans, Swedes, and more made sure their God went with them, even as they boarded the boats that brought them to the New World. Their convictions still hold up the rafters here at St Peter's as surely as their faith seemed woven into their DNA.

I headed down a wormhole to do with my loss of faith.

'Is there something wrong, Nate?' Brigitte looked concerned.

'Oh, nothing. Nothing.' I hooked a thumb inside my jeans pocket. The fingers tapped to their own beat on the outside. The hand freed itself to motion a no-through road. 'Don't mind me. I'm a bit down in the mouth at the moment. Work's gone belly-up.'

'I'm sorry to hear that. This is always a place of refuge if you need when we're open in the day. And we have people on the end of a phone at other times.' No chance to save souls left unturned.

'Thanks, Brigitte – and thanks for the tour. Enlightening. I wish you well. But I'd better get on.'

39

Lobby fodder
Next-to-Lex Hotel, Manhattan – 29 December 1999

'What do you mean there's no room in the name of Daniels? I was in it last night. My key worked this morning – room 512. And now it doesn't.'

'I'm sorry, sir. I can only go on our list and there's nothing here in that name.' The woman on reception ran her pen up and down the printout on an outsize pad in front of her. Her dark ponytail swished in sympathy as she tried to reconcile two different documents.

'What about Nate? Nathan? I even get Nathaniel sometimes.'

She wore a gold badge reading 'Ms. Solinski' with the catch-all title 'Administrator' beneath. 'Nothing of any of those names I'm afraid, sir.' Her forehead was furrowed.

'I need to see the manager, then.' I heard a sigh behind me. 'Urgently.'

'Sir, I am the duty manager.' Her white bib on a jade skirt suit looked professional but wasn't going to buy me off. There was a constant flow of resident traffic; people returning from work summoning a lift, others emerging from either of the lifts dressed for the evening's entertainment.

'Surely someone knows something about this. Is there a proper manager I can talk to?' I felt my throat tighten.

'Sir: I've just started my shift. I can at least talk to the colleague who was on duty before me, if he's still—'

'Could you?' I cut in before she could rethink.

'It might take a moment.' Another sigh from behind.

'I'm not going anywhere.' Sometimes I don't know whether I'm being sarcastic or ironic, or merely matter-of-fact.

Ms Solinski abandoned the desk and headed to her left through the side door which bore the foreboding words 'Staff Only'. Through the glass pane in the door, fitted with a wire mesh that reminded me of graph paper, I could see the duty manager in discussion with a sharp-suited twenty-something with jet-black, brushed-back hair. He was expansive with his arm movements, but he shrugged and shook his head too much for my liking. He had his back to me. He turned around and I saw his designer stubble and slightly drawn look as he led Ms Solinski through the door.

'Hi, sir. I'm Jack.' He smoothed down his stubble, though it looked perfectly tamed to me. Ms Solinski stood to his side, her gaze locked on him. 'It seems you haven't been told, and I'm sorry for that. We had a cancellation from Ryan On-Air Productions. "Room no longer required".'

'No longer required? Jesus – nice of you to check with me. It very much is required, thank you. Without it, I don't have anywhere to sleep tonight and I'm 3,000 miles from home.'

'Sir, we have to go with the choice of the bill payer ...'

'Choice? And if the bill payer said, "Kill all the firstborn in New York" you'd go with that, would you?'

'Sir, we assumed you'd be going back early ...'

'Assumed? Then you can bloody well un-assume it.' More sighs from behind. A shortcut formed in my mind. 'Let me rebook my room and I can charge it back to the TV people.'

'That's not an option. We're now full tonight – we relet the room. We're very busy with the new millennium coming ...'

'Relet my room? Christ on a bike. Would you like the clothes off my back, too? Talking of which, where the hell's my stuff? Or have you pawned it all off?' A forty-something woman wearing a black fascinator and a beige fake-fur wrap glared from the lift area. I was beyond caring. I wasn't going to be here much longer.

Jack went sotto, probably in overcompensation. He leaned closer over the desk. I could see the fine stitching in his pinstripes, magnolia among the charcoal of his waistcoat. His synthetic aftershave hung in the air. 'Sir, could you please sit over there ...' – he motioned behind me to the low-slung cream sofas – 'and I'll get your property momentarily.'

The fight had gone out of me, and reality was dawning. I slunk away from the desk, clocking the source of the heavy sighs behind me: a sweaty man in his fifties with too much head for the amount of dyed hair he was combing over it. I lowered myself onto one of the sofas, its chrome frame optimistically shiny, betrayed by the tired plasticky cushions within.

The activity in the hotel lobby mimicked the busyness outside in miniature. I defocussed, and suitcases carried by the clientele became boxy buses vying for road space. A super-keen young man stood behind a lectern with a landline phone and a clipboard on it, and appeared to be taking orders for cabs, a lot of them bound for JFK Airport. He paused at the end of each transaction for a tip. America's legendary customer service comes at a price.

The fascinator woman headed out the door, and I found myself wondering why an immaculately turned-out lady would be in a modest place like this. A family fortune frittered away on booze or gambling? Or was she visiting a down-at-heel friend? Down at her heel, and leading her by eighteen inches, was a white toy dog with bright bulgy eyes and a small tartan winter coat. The little pooch seemed to greet the world with such hope, partly borne out of ignorance that it was only ever half a second away from being crushed under someone's foot.

'Sir, your luggage.' Jack was back again, placing my two black expander cases at the end of the sofa by me. He smoothed his chia-seed stubble once more. And he disappeared as he'd appeared: in an instant.

I headed out into the street trailing my suitcases.

40

Green Line to Godshill
Early August 1978

We'd taken the 708 Green Line bus to East Grinstead in Sussex, a supposedly express service with limited stops. Mum was sitting next to me, and we were each sitting in what, years before as a five-year-old, I'd called a 'king seat'. I meant it was like a throne; to me it was the height of luxury, height being the operative word. We were on what looked like a standard bus back then, but it had seats with a much higher back than normal. Instead of stopping half-way up the back, this was more like a coach seat with a built-in headrest. I reminded Mum now – some nine years later – of that phrase 'king seat' and she smiled. She was well.

I was feeling much more adult now, and we were going on an adventure. There was a degree of spontaneity about it; no need to book our places in advance and no plans for when we reached our destination. We picked up the bus – confusingly, as this was a longer express route, it was a coach – by the steps up to the Baptist church where I had been plunged into water at the foot of the pulpit earlier that year.

I had hoped undergoing baptism by total immersion would indeed be a rebirth, a blank page. A new start. Instead, the old anxieties, my demons, followed me into the pool and out again. They were waterproof. I felt a fraud; the person eating sandwiches with the others who'd just been immersed – a record fourteen of us took the plunge in a single service – was a hollow shell; I was a body munching and chewing, notionally there, but not really present. And it was my fault.

I had to think whether my mother was at my baptism. In my memory she was barely there, like a figure half smudged from a photograph. Yet the date in the Bible I was given 'on the occasion of your baptism' (part of a beautiful inscription by my father, urging me to 'support the weak, honour the afflicted ...') was the year before her death, so she must have been there. Like my simulacrum eating sandwiches after the soaking that day Mum, too, was a hollow shell. The month of the baptism, written in my dad's florid script, is key though: December. My mother's condition was cruelly chained to the calendar. She said she would wake on a day in late August feeling odd, and then the blanket of deep depression would descend. She wouldn't emerge from that crippling dark tunnel until the following spring – March at the earliest.

But here she was beside me on the bus, laughing and joking, solid as she could be, eagerly anticipating our arrival. Her brunette curls were as lively as her bright blue eyes. Her lines betrayed she'd been through the wars, both external and internal, but her happiness in the moment overwrote those pained shadows. And it was no coincidence it was summer. We were gifted a warm, sunny day, late-20s Celsius with a light breeze and the subtlest of watercolour strokes of high, white cloud. There is, perhaps, a coincidence that it all started – my beginnings, or the beginning of my beginnings – on a bus. Dad recalled later how one of his first dates with Mum began with a bus ride (neither of them drove) and in that carefree way of new couples they spoke their own cute language. He said they'd landed on the phrase 'silly-billy bus'. I cringed on hearing that in my late teens, but with the greater passage of years now I'm left reflecting on how lucky I was to have had a father who was always ready to open his heart to reveal that kind of detail.

The bus ride with Mum went by in a blur of chatter and sunlight, broken only by the heavy foliage and occasional tall building. I pointed out cars and their number plates, both of which intrigued me, and which got fancier the closer we got to the wealth of the West End. Dropping down from central London, places sounded ever more glamorous to me at that age, such as Brixton, Norbury, Croydon, and Purley. And then we started to see Godshill mentioned on road signs, and Mum and I remembered that was where our former neighbour Selica moved to when she split up with Marcus to live with Ron. She'd told us she and Ron were going to run a hotel in Godshill but we hadn't heard anything from them once they'd left my village of Oxhey three or four years before, an aeon in my young lifetime.

The more we talked about Selica and Ron, the more curious we got as to how their post-Oxhey lives had worked out. We were especially fascinated by the idea of the hotel: how big was it? How did they run it – on their own, or with extra staff? Had they had a child together? As Purley led to Whyteleafe, and Whyteleafe gave way to Caterham, we hatched a plan to get off the 708 early to try and hunt them down. We were undaunted by not having an address, the name of the hotel or a phone number for them; the curiosity cut through all of that. By the time we left Caterham we'd resolved to get off at the next town: Godshill.

We asked the driver to drop us at the first stop in the town; Mum thought we might get lucky and land right by Selica's hotel or, if we didn't, it wasn't such a huge place and so we shouldn't be too far out. The bus pulled in by the village green, bordered by a couple of restaurants, a hair salon, and a pub: the White Hart. An ornate sign on the green by the duck pond the other side of the road completed the chocolate-box effect. It was almost trying a bit too hard, as if this was England, Hollywood-style.

The next task was to find the hotel. I suggested we try asking at the pub, but Mum was funny about a woman going without a partner into licensed premises, plus she felt she couldn't take me in. She said the hair salon would be ideal as they were likely to be local women there, both the hairdressers and their customers, but as we were heading there we saw an elderly couple approach the bus stop where we'd been dropped moments before. They were wearing light grey macs, their concession to the heat, with a checked scarf and a tweed cap for the gent, and a light brown felt hat for the lady.

'Excuse me – do you know where the hotel is?' When she was well Mum had a warm, smiley style that won people over.

'Let me see, love,' said the lady. 'That depends which hotel you mean.' Nightmare – there was more than one. She looked to the man I assumed was her husband. 'She probably means the young couple, Edgar, doesn't she?' Selica would now have been early thirties, more than twice my age then. 'I mean the inn here isn't really geared up for proper guests.'

'Reckon she means The Whyte Harte Hotel ...' Edgar looked to my mother with a slightly pained expression. 'I'm afraid they're right the other end of the village – bit of a walk.'

'Thanks, duck.'

I squirmed at Mum's use of this familiar term. She'd used it years before in talking to a boy in infants' school who was bullying me, and I squirmed then. Even as a five-year-old I instinctively felt it undermined her defence of me. Years later, though, a psychotherapist seized on that moment as a useful image for having an advocate in my mother, now the bully was on the inside.

The walk to the hotel was bathed in sunlight. I remember passing a parade of small shops opposite the green, but I know I would have been more taken by the parade of cars passing us. This was Ford Granada country to me, home turf for the middle class tank for middle-ranking executives that – horror of horrors – was now only made in Germany. I was more attuned to cars' continual design upgrades – 'revised rear light clusters' were a favourite – than to the incidental beauty of water and recreational features that were the embodiment of fierce civic pride. The clue is in the title, after all – this was God's own town, Godshill in Surrey, and that set a high bar for the residents to maintain.

I vividly remember this being the stretch of the journey in which my mother told me that, putting her dark moods through autumn to spring to one side (as if she or anyone could), she wasn't subject to the day-to-day mood swings of normal folk. At the time that seemed a reasonable trade-off. The next year I was forced to see it was an unconscionably high price to pay for making hay while the sun shone.

The Whyte Hart Hotel's brickwork was perhaps unsurprisingly white; the most eye-catching feature for me as a fourteen-year-old was the ivy growing along one side of the L-shaped inter-war building. The foliage was threatening to cover the wrought ironwork of the venue's name. The hotel was on two levels.

I honestly don't remember either of us ringing the bell, or who came to door, or their reaction. My mind for someone reason cuts, like an economically paced drama, to all of us sitting together: Ron on my left, then Selica opposite me, and Mum on the right. We were at a round metal garden table in the property's back garden. There was some sort of partial cover, maybe an overhang for a barbecue. The colours in recollection are a little too vivid, as if my mind has taken a Polaroid with its exaggerated blues and greens, but with a hint of sepia from the passage of the years.

The gathering in Godshill was very relaxed, and we were made to feel welcome, even though as an adult I now realise that, having arrived uninvited, we probably disrupted their routine. And in answer to one of our questions about the newish hoteliers, Ron spoke about how hard it was to make sure all the food stayed hot as it was plated up by him and his wife (they'd married two years previously), before it was served to the residents. So, while they didn't have staff for cooking, they brought in cleaners as needed, and they had a receptionist-administrator full-time.

Another answer to Mum's and my curiosity arrived with Anthea, Selica's eldest child: she was wheeling in front of herself her half-sister, a flame-haired eighteen-month-old called Charlotte. Together with Bethany, who joined us shortly afterwards, Selica was now clearly working her way through the alphabet. Mum cooed over the littlest girl, who seemed to have absorbed something of Ron's Celtic features and less of his wife's swarthiness. Selica reintroduced us to the older girls. 'Do you remember our neighbours Barbara and Stan – and Nathan here?' I was deeply saddened Anthea and Bethany needed the prompt, especially as I'd babysat for them both numerous times. My throat burned; I wasn't used to being forgotten. Together with seeing Charlotte, it was my first conscious awakening to how people can become obsolescent, and of how friends' or former friends' lives can diverge.

41

jane.butterworth@altavista.com – 1999.12.29

Hi Nate
Sorry not to have heard from you since my last message - hope you're good?

Pressure's being piled on me to nail down certain facts for this doggone TV show.

In addition to the photos (i mentioned before) I'd apprecaite you identifying, a little potted history of your life, particularly your early life, would be fantastic.

Thanks in advance - hope your millenial show's going well!

Sincerely yours -

Jane

nathan.daniels@connectright.co.uk – 29.12.1999

Dear Jane,

There's no pain-free way to say this, but I really can't help. And I'd appreciate it if you accepted that as fact rather than twist the thumbscrews.

There are plenty of talented people out there with far more exotic lives than mine who will make for fascinating TV.

I hope you find them. And obliterate me from your records.

Yours –

Nate

42

Millie part one
1975–88

Millie and I first met when we started secondary school. She had wavy blonde hair, a bright smile, and a rare quality of complexion: where most people's flesh has a natural sheen due to the skin's oiliness (before any face powder goes on), Millie's skin was stunning in its lack of reflectiveness. It was no less healthy for it. More peach than nectarine.

There was a certain rivalry between us from the off which felt awkward. That's not how it should be between the sexes, even at age eleven. If boy–girl don't get on so be it, but to feel in competition for the same space is odd.

In adolescence we moved closer to each other through a shared faith. At one point we'd take it in turns to lead school prayer meetings for the self-selecting few, while the whirr of hundreds of kids on their lunch break continued outside. After leaving school Millie was directionless for a while ('A year out was a year lost', she said later), until hitting on biology as a focus. For a time she seemed to soar in her studies. She faltered, though, in her final exams. She retreated at that time to the safety of her long-term boyfriend, Tom. I saw her once in that time and regretted it; it felt like an intrusion on their tight bond. I also witnessed ugly flashes of anger in her I hadn't seen before.

I remember seeing Millie and Tom as a couple for the first time. We were all teenagers, taking advantage of the settled snow in a local park, which had a sharp incline down to the path running by the canal. A selection of fellow teenage friends from the local church were alternately sledging down the hill and walking back up, laughing and joking. After a few loops of this budget slalom, I saw Millie and Tom hold hands as they headed back up the hill. At fourteen-, fifteen-years-old, to me they were now grown-ups. Star-cross'd lovers.

The park was picture-postcard perfect. A canopy of mature evergreens, as if Christmas trees were growing in the wild, were made more beautiful by nature's rare icing: this was the first snow in years. But I hold this beauty, made more fleeting and fragile by the early fading light, in hindsight; it would have been of little consolation to me at the time. I just felt the biting cold. I was fourteen and my mother was still alive, but depression for me, never mind for her – deep melancholy with periods of extreme withdrawal – was already becoming a ride I couldn't get off; lonely tobogganing where the only way was down. The crisp, sunset-kissed snowscape was at odds with the dead weight of my internal world, like a TV show where the sound doesn't match the pictures.

When I moved into showbiz in the mid-Eighties I didn't see so much of Millie but, when we did manage to meet, she'd call me Natebiz. She'd sing out, 'There's no business like Nate-business!' at the top of her lungs, Ethel Merman-like, even in a crowded café. *Especially* in a crowded café. It was highly affectionate, a nod to my having broken out on my own, getting a break in a ruthlessly competitive world. Putting the past behind me.

For she knew how bad the past had been.

Millie had come to visit me on the locked psychiatric ward one autumn evening in 1982. She rocked up, all sunny smiles, hoop earrings, gypsy chic couture and 'Great to see you, Nate – great!' And in this most godforsaken of places. Abandon hope all ye. And, inevitably, the sun spilled over and others caught the rays. There was this one nurse, a handsome Asian guy, mid- to late-twenties, who took a shine to her. He can't have had much work to do that night, or if he did, he dodged it – for a while at least. He joined me and Millie at the table in the visiting area. I called it the Royal Mile as it reminded my fevered brain of the main thoroughfare in

Edinburgh, which I'd visited as a child on a family holiday. That night in the hospital I had a pound note in my back pocket from an earlier visit. Literally pocket money, for sweets and other sundries. I got through more sweets in that period as a nineteen-year-old than in an equivalent time as a five-year-old. Classic comfort eating, but madman style.

The nurse – I think he was called Sunil – did the old brainteaser of the missing money. I've heard it several times since. You know, the one where three friends eat out for a tenner each, then the waiter realises it should have only been £25.00, not £30.00 in total. He gives them each a quid back, but pockets £2.00 from the £5.00 going spare. So they've paid 3 x £9.00 = £27.00. Plus the waiter's two quid makes £29.00. So where's the missing pound?

In a rare moment's lucidity, I drew the pound from my pocket and said, 'It's here!' to no one's apparent interest. I thought it was clever, me doing that, but there's no accounting for folk. I think Sunil and Millie were probably too wrapped up in each other, enjoying the flirting. Plus, now I think of it, I was stealing Sunil's punchline.

The flirtatiousness was brazen. Millie was on the other side of me from Sunil. An awkward triad at a rickety table in the visiting area. Sunil said to me, 'She's beautiful, Nate – why don't you go out with her?' His head panned between us.

'Because I'm as nutty as a fruitcake and locked in here, and she's getting on with her life,' I might have said. But didn't.

And with that he used his body to block her from me and made as if they were having the most enormous, passionate kiss, his head moving slowly from side to side like a drugged pendulum. To this day, nearly twenty years on, five per cent of me could believe it was a real French kiss. The other ninety-five per cent assumes he must have winked at her as he turned from me and done something like pursing his lips without making contact with Millie's matte skin. Oh to have Sunil's confidence with a woman you've just met.

What's certainly true is she was fully compliant in this act, and made no attempt to bust his bubble, then or later. She never felt the need to set the record straight, Tom or no Tom. Perhaps it was in a period of fallow with Tom. Five years after that hand-holding in the snowy park they were still an item, if a little on-off.

During that hospital visit Millie, who was studying in London, told me how the previous day she'd been walking along the South Bank, admiring the late-afternoon reflections on the Thames. I felt the pang of separation from the city of my birth like the loss of a friend. I pictured the concatenation of lights along the edge of the river outside the Royal Festival Hall, and the stunning view of the City looking east over Waterloo Bridge. And here I was, detained at the NHS's pleasure.

Cut to: being in digs with Paddy in south-west London, at a time when he was commuting between radio gigs in the UK and Irish capitals. Millie came to stay with us before going round the world. This was her real, deferred gap year, a punctuation mark between being a working biologist and doing an MSc in genetics. I was an immature gag writer and there was Millie on the threshold of a real grown-up job, a career of consequence. She came to Paddy's and my place bearing gifts: a couple of saucepans. She didn't want to part with them but had to slim down her belongings, having given notice on the flat she shared with Tom in Camberwell. (He would have to make his own arrangements while she was away.) She moved a few boxes of belongings back into her parents' place but said she couldn't stretch their generosity any further.

Paddy, in town for his weekend radio spot, was on form when Millie stayed over. Of course he was: a fly to a honeypot. He made great comedy capital out of the saucepans, ending up wearing one as a hat with the handle sticking out to the side. He mock-staggered around the kitchen, apparently blinded by the pan over his eyes, bumping into walls and the door jamb. Emboldened by

Millie's laughter (and my occasional grudging titter) he swivelled the handle to the front and repeated, 'Destroy, destroy!' in the manner of a Doctor Who Dalek. He then ventured beyond the bounds of our modest ground-floor conversion to demonstrate how Daleks can't climb stairs. And, yes, cheap red wine was flowing like the bloody Ganges. With every sip I headed in the opposite emotional direction to the other two, they to ever greater bacchanalian highs and closer to each other, I to light-starved depths and greater isolation.

Daleks might not mount steps, but Paddy seemed to have no problem mounting Millie. As the *Chateau de Plonk* insinuated its way into every dark, despondent alley of my bloodstream, I could hear my newly coupled friends flex each other into ecstatic escape from this dour part of the capital, even as a black cab swished through the night rain outside my window. While the joint moans of abandonment crescendoed through the thin partition between our rooms, I felt my system gather to expunge the unwelcome toxins from my body. Waves of black-red puke spasmed out of my mouth on to the mottled acrylic carpet to the soundtrack of 'Yes, Christ, yes!' and, 'Fuck, yes!'

43

Millie's visit
Napsbury Hospital, London Colney – October 1982

I've got a letter from Millie. It's in multi colours. I told her how I keep thinking of things in different colours. Blues, greens, reds – and black, if that's a colour. It makes things clearer somehow. Her letter fell into a pattern, like that – BGRB – whoops – those Bs mean different things. Try BlGRBl. Bugger. Both blue and black are Bl. Blu could be blue and Bla can be black. But 'blu' is nearly all of 'blue'. And they've both got 'l' in, so that cancels out. Can Bu mean blue and Ba mean black? So Millie wrote in BuGRBa, BuGRBa etc and I got used to it. But then she went BuGRBu as a joke just to fool me!

She wrote it in a way that didn't make me feel silly reading it. Dad used to think presenters on children's TV talk down to you. I don't think so. Or I didn't. But Millie didn't talk down to me in the letter. I'll keep it forever. If I ever get out of here it'll remind me of her visit.

She arrived in her little Austin 1100. Navy blue. I saw it through the window, outside this stately home. I waited minutes for her to walk up the windy staircase and to knock on the glass with the wires in it. I said to the nurse we had a visitor but he wouldn't believe me. He's the same nurse who doesn't believe I'm Jesus or that the entire band of Radio 1 DJs are performing in the Big Hall tonight, or that God the Father, my father, will be returning to Earth to visit soon. What can you do? A prophet is accepted anywhere but in his own country.

Anyway, I persuaded another nurse – the Asian guy Selin – to go to the ward's door and, lo, there Millie was. 'See,' I want to say to the other nurse, but the moment's gone. Millie was all eager and friendly and called me 'Nate the Great'. Selin invited her over to the table on the Royal Mile and we sat and chatted for a bit. Mama Mia was making tea, so we had some. Millie pulled a face at all the sugar in it.

I sat opposite Millie then Selin pulled up a chair. He turned it around and sat on it back to front between me and Millie. He rested his elbows on the frame of the chair and then asked me why I wasn't going out with Millie. 'She's beautiful,' he said and I could tell he meant it. He then seemed to kiss her, turning his back to me. His head moved from side to side like it was a real deep snog, but I don't think it was. He'd get arrested for that, wouldn't he? But then again ...

At one point Selin was talking Millie through a puzzle. Something about a restaurant and three guys and a waiter – I didn't pay much attention. But at the end he asked, 'So where's the missing pound?' And – Bingo! – by chance I had a pound note in my back pocket. So I drew it out and held it so both of them could see it and I said, 'It's here!' Neither of them seemed interested. Millie was frowning – she was concentrating on trying to solve the puzzle. Selin was concentrating on Millie.

Selin then got called away by his boss and Millie told me how she'd been walking along the Thames the weekend before. She talked about passing the Festival Hall and the National Theatre, and looking over to parliament and Charing Cross station, and I felt a weight on my lungs and sighed.

Millie left for London soon after, but she left me some chocolates she'd bought near the South Bank. Of course, as usual, I dipped them in milk.

44

Leaving the hotel
Next-to-Lex Hotel, Manhattan – 29 December 1999

I walked away from the hotel, luggage, and all, with what I hoped looked to Jack like a purposeful gait. The truth was I didn't have a clue where I was going, or if there would be a bed there when I arrived. Maybe I needed a halfway house to gather my thoughts and plan. With money tight I couldn't appear in a hotel bar with all these belongings and not check in. Perhaps the answer was to go somewhere where a transient population breeze through without much curiosity about anyone else. So I headed back in the direction of Grand Central.

On arrival at the terminus I looked at myself: my suitcases were a bit battered and I could have done with a shave and a smarten up. The hotel personnel had cleared my room and so had packed for me, not as a favour but out of commercial necessity: freeing up my room for the next occupant. I thought I'd take the moment to open my suitcases to straighten things out in a quieter part of the station concourse. While I was separating clean and dirty clothes I found out this was not the time to look even slightly vagrant-like in this city. Two uniformed NYPD officers approached me. One took the lead.

'You know our mayor's tightening up on guys like you?' The cop adopted a power pose, legs astride. His mate was looking distractedly up at the roof, no doubt appreciating the Beaux Arts detail.

I put on my best British cut-glass accent as a defence. 'No, I wasn't aware of this. Sorry, officer.'

'Yeah, well, we had an office worker attacked by a hobo.'

'*Mighta* been a hobo,' said cop number two, checking his watch, his lips now making an O-shape, as if he was about to whistle.

'Like I say,' said cop number one, 'Giuliani wants to crack down on that kinda thing. People are calling for violent crazies off our streets.'

'The headlines are calling for it.' Cop two looked in the middle distance and ran his fingers down his jaw line, as if checking it was still intact.

'Streets are for walking, not sleeping.' Bad Cop continued undaunted. 'Railroad stations are for travelling, not dossing down. You got some place to stay?'

'Sure. Yes. Of course I have. Sir.' I sounded like an arsehole. It's more their prerogative to call me sir. I doth protest too much. I started to fabricate an address in my head, and mimed searching for something in my pockets.

They say that someone lying gives too much detail. I relaxed a bit. It didn't look like Bad Cop needed to hear the actual address. But something gave me pause.

'Get on your way then. And I don't want to see you here again. Else we might have to give you some encouragement to move on.' The first cop himself moved on, not looking back.

'Take it easy, fellah.' Good Cop gave his valedictory as a parting gift. He smiled as he left.

I'd felt an alien object in my pocket as I'd mimed looking there. Its edge had caught me between two fingers and given me a paper cut. For a writer, that's an industrial injury. I pulled the artefact out to look at it: it was the business card for Elsa Myeroff – the lady I'd met outside the Beekman Theatre or, as I thought of it, the Woody Allen/*Annie Hall* cinema. Before I could digest the card's details, I realised I'd left two suitcases open on the ground, with the threat of my room for the night being a police cell. I hurriedly tidied my belongings, kneeling on the shiny floor. Station announcements bounced off the marble walls with booming promises of transit to places that sounded impossibly romantic: Port Jervis, Spring Valley, Poughkeepsie, White Plains, and Wassaic.

So how did this Elsa woman, lover of art-house cinema (minus Tarkovsky), describe herself on the cream laid card? In brown embossed lettering – Tempus Sans typeface, if I'm not mistaken, giving it a rustic look – it said simply 'gallerist'. And beneath that, her phone number. I dialled it on my mobile.

No luck at first, till I remembered I had to dial the country code, 001. Then the ringing tone, a comforting one-note melody from a myriad of US sitcoms, chimed in my ear above the din of holiday displacement. But every repetition of the refrain made my heart sink further. She wasn't in and didn't have an answering machine. Or even if she did have, what could I leave as a message? Or she was in and had caller display and didn't pick up to strangers and strange numbers. Or she was out and had left the answering machine switched—

'Hello?' said a distant, uncertain female voice. What if she lived with her sister and this was her. Could I tell the difference?

'Er – hi. This is Nathan. Nate. Beekman Theatre? We met there. Tarkovsky horseshit? Or are you your sister ...?' I finally hit on the right word. 'I mean, is that Elsa?'

'I'm certainly not my own sister. I have a sister for that. But I do answer to Elsa. Are you in trouble, Nate? It's kinda noisy there.'

'No – I'm fine. I-I often ring art-loving widows from station payphones. It's a fetish.' A laugh down the line. 'OK – when I say "fine" I may not have factored in losing my job, my wife, my hotel room – and my sense of purpose.'

'Oh dear.'

'Plus, I nearly got arrested for exposing my dirty laundry in a public place. Grand Central – where I am now.'

'Too bad.' Fortunately, my grasp of American English allowed for this being a phrase of concern, not sarcasm. 'Would you like to come here for dinner?'

Blimey. Did I sound that desperate? 'Of course, I'd love that,' said a voice that sounded like mine, only more spontaneous.

45

Millie part two
1989-92

Millie's Tom was drawn to performance and definitely had something of the showman in him, even at school. I remember my father approaching him to compliment him on a production when he was in his teens. It was Wilde's *The Importance of Being Earnest.* Tom played Ernest, and just 'had it', whatever 'it' is. He could be quite insular at times, and didn't always hold himself well, but on-stage he burst into life, upright and proud. Of course, I was envious of the attention Dad gave him, even as I stood at Dad's shoulder; me, the mean spirit.

After leaving school Tom followed his passion and went to drama school. It was a minor one on the fringes of London, but he seemed to fit in. I largely lost touch with him, even as I saw Millie more through our continuing connections in the capital, but reports coming back via her were positive. Though as a glowing coal soon loses its lustre if it falls out of the grate, Tom lost his mojo when he left drama school. He drifted, as Millie had done. Maybe they somehow set each other off. Tom started to doubt his talent and got into a tailspin of diminishing confidence and ever-decreasing auditions for less and less significant roles.

Then as Millie found her feet in her studies it began to get lopsided. She could see herself becoming the one thing she didn't want to be: a working woman supporting a struggling actor. Hence taking her pleasures where she could find them; virtue isn't its own reward. When someone as confident, outgoing, and fun as Paddy crossed her path, who could blame her for going along for the ride, especially as she was about to be out of the country for a year, crucially, without Tom? She called it her 'World Tour'.

So it came as a surprise when word filtered back after a few months that Tom had not only joined Millie in Thailand, but that he'd also proposed to her on a tuk-tuk weaving its way through the Bangkok rush hour. He was still enough of an actor for the odd theatrical gesture.

Back in England, they both threw themselves headlong into wedding plans. It was not an understated wedding: magicians (two working their way around the tables), musicians (a tea-dance band in the afternoon morphed into a hot-rocking covers band by night) and a comedian (like the band, it was temperate stuff in the afternoon, becoming more risqué in the evening). Everyone seemed to have as much fun as is possible on someone else's tab. Nearly everyone.

In the gaps between acts, though, and in the cracks between distractions, I caught Millie a couple of times looking pensive; 'miles away', as my mother would have said. That smooth skin had acquired some faint lines, especially on her year away. And she was more attractive as a result. But something in her eyes, focussed on an infinity beyond the windows she was staring through, seemed fearful. I tried to fill in the holes in my understanding in later conversations with her. Months afterwards she confessed in a private chat to concerns about Tom and her being sufficient for each other. For life. If she was looking to me for reassurance, I wasn't the best person to provide it. 'It's a big ask,' I said non-committally, borrowing a new phrase Millie had brought back from Australia.

46

Dinner with Elsa part one
Central Park South, Manhattan – 29 December 1999

The smartly uniformed concierge took the view 'any friend of Elsa Meyeroff is a friend of mine', and waved me on through to the lobby. 'Elevators to the left, sir,' he said from behind the glass.

I was the only one in the lift, and I was still trailing two suitcases on wheels for company. The door pinged open after a few accelerated seconds. I was facing ceiling-to-floor bronze-smoked mirrors and outsized rubber plants. Dark marks on the mirror looked like incongruous dirt for a moment, until I made out the tinted '11' on the glass surface. I found Elsa's apartment numbered 1106 and pressed the doorbell. A classy chime rang out in the marbled walkway as I stood back, nearly bumping into a woman with a fur drape and a canary-coloured coat breezing behind me. I mumbled an awkward apology.

I nearly did my party piece of putting my eye close to the peephole so that Elsa, on checking my identity, might be greeted by a giant eye. But that was a trick for mates of decades' standing, not second-time acquaintances. Besides which my magnified eye, bloodshot and tired-looking, might have given too much away. I stood passively at a non-threatening distance until I heard the lock being turned.

The dark-stained walnut door swung inwards on the diminutive Elsa. She smiled brightly, pulling focus to her brick-red lipstick. When she blinked, her metallic emerald eye shade shimmered in the light. She wore off-white face powder with a dab of rouge on her cheeks. 'I nearly sent out a search party, Nate,' she said, laughing and beckoning me in.

'Yeah – but they charge by the hour in New York. Extra for the millennium'. I took in her stylish, predominantly beige decor. So this was life south of Central Park. Through the lounge window were the needlepoint lights of other high-rises. 'Sorry I'm later than advertised. I had a bit of a contretemps with the geography.'

'Never mind directions, Nate, are you moving in?' Elsa eyed my luggage. She wheeled it into a generous storage cupboard.

'It's a nice cupboard, but I'd miss the view.' Relax, I told myself. You're off duty. Cooking odours mixed with Elsa's floral perfume. 'What's for dinns?'

'Dinns? Ah, dinner. Fennel and potato gratin. Hopefully it's a safe option. Do sit down.'

'That sounds more than safe,' I said, moving from the kitchen to the adjacent open-plan lounge area, where I collapsed on to the white leather sofa. And then immediately sprang up. 'Ooh, I forgot. I've got some vino for you.' I popped back to the cupboard and, unzipping the large front pocket of the smaller suitcase, produced a green bottle of Pino Grigio which I took to Elsa in the kitchen.

The wine looked inadequate to the setting but Elsa disguised any disappointment. 'That's very sweet of you. Do you want we should have this or a G & T or—?'

No contest. 'G & T. Please. I hope I haven't upset any plans?'

'Well, I was due to go on holiday with my sister ...'

'Really?'

Elsa smiled.

'Oh, bugger – you're referring to our phone call, aren't you?'

Her smile grew in affirmation. It's not only pros who do comedy callbacks.

'Your sister's not here then?' I asked.

'No. She's in Europe – she won't make it for dinner.' I registered Elsa's heavy-duty oatmeal dress and chunky beads for the first time.

'Amazing place you have here.'

'Thank you. I moved in ten years ago. I couldn't keep the family home going after Todd died. My husband, remember? And did I tell you we had kids?'

I nodded, although I couldn't remember.

'They'd left already,' she continued. 'So it made sense to ... What do they say now? Downsize.'

I spotted what appeared to be a rushed drawing of a centaur, framed and hung near a cork board by the oven. 'This is intriguing ...' I said, pointing to the black-ink-on-white picture.

'It's a Picasso.'

'You're kidding. Not an original?'

'No – and no. My son has the original – he had a print made for me. Long story but his wife – a waitress in Vauvenargues in France when she was younger – was given a napkin drawn on by the neighbour opposite the hotel she worked at.' Elsa was cutting slices of lime. There was a waft of Mozart in the air. 'And that neighbour was Picasso. His chateau was – is – opposite the Hotel Sainte Victoire.'

Elsa's French pronunciation was spot on – not like the stab-in-the-dark of your average American. I commented on it.

'There's a reason for that – *je suis Parisienne*. I'm a French import!' She laughed and handed me a gin and tonic, coughing unbecomingly.

'To the Statue of Liberty!' I said.

'*A Statue de la Liberté!*' She recovered from the cough. We clinked.

After the food, wine, and coffee, out came the cognac. Amadeus had given way to the Jacques Louissier Trio with some jazzed-up Bach. The view from the window on to the adjacent towers was too good to be true, like a backcloth from *Friends*.

After hearing how Elsa owned a gallery on 57th Street specialising in European postmodern art, and how I'd had a past in radio, we'd run out of small talk. 'So – tell me, Nate.' Elsa swirled her brandy glass and leaned in, elbows on the table. 'What went wrong with your job and with the hotel?' She lit up a Gauloise without asking.

'The two are related.' My turn to cough. 'I write for an entertainment TV show. I *wrote* for a TV show. I had a run-in with the presenter, Ricky, er, Paddy. His stage name is Ricky, but I know him as Paddy – an old friend. Or maybe I should say he *was* an old friend. Strictly, er – what's French for "*entre nous*"?' Elsa laughed, needing no further explanation. 'Anyway, between ourselves, he's developed *un penchant pour la poudre blanche.* He's a bit fond of the white powder. Coke. I tried to stop him, but it led to tears – and my dismissal. My hotel room came through the TV company, so no job – no room.'

'*Quel dommage.*' A variation on her previous 'too bad'. 'So what are you going to do?'

'Apart from leaning on the kindness of strangers?' Elsa's eyeshadow glistened under the dimmed lights. 'I don't know. My flight back to London's not due till after the show – January 2nd. Anything can happen in the next half week. One thing's for sure: I'm out of contract for the millennial show.'

If Elsa was mourning the literary landmark for which I should have been responsible, she hid it well. I don't think *Ricky Ryan's Millennial Fandango* was going to be big in the salons of New York or Paris. I'd already found out over the exquisite gratin – complete with double cream, shallots, nutmeg and kosher salt – her tastes were more Sartrean. The place mats we put our plates and the serving bowls on carried images from the front covers of Sartre's major works. Elsa's platter was on '*Les Mouches*' (*The Flies*), mine was on '*Le Mur*' (*The Wall*), and the glass bowl of French beans was sitting on '*L'Être et le Néant*' (*Being and Nothingness*).

When I asked where *'Nausea'* was I was met with a steely stare.

'One shouldn't encourage sickness at the dinner table,' Elsa said reasonably. After a while she added, *à propos* of our previous topic, 'You could stay here for a few days.'

While not exactly a bombshell, this could be a game changer. I said, ' *Vous êtes très gentille*, Elsa.' Not too bad – but too kind. Elsa batted it away with an 'it's nothing' – '*de rien'* – dismissive movement of her hand. 'And please call me "*tu*", not "*vous*".'

The moment was slightly marred by my choking on her cigarette smoke.

Nausea, indeed.

47

Millie part three
1996

Millie was overjoyed to be pregnant. She rang round the whole of the gang, or rather gangs: ex-school, church, her science crowd, old mates, new mates, old neighbours. And of course the news spread supersonically among her family. One or two early adopters even spread the word via a text message. Perhaps texting's going to be the twenty-first-century version of lighting a beacon on a hill. Don't even get me started on the abuse of the word 'text'.

Similarly, copies of the first ultrasound were widely distributed by printout and fax, accompanied by Millie's exclamation, 'My life's been turned up side [sic] down by something the size of a bloody BROAD BEAN!!!' A technophile friend of Millie's found an arcane way of attaching a scratchy monochrome picture – maybe a scan of a fax – to an e-mail.

Regular updates were, of course, obligatory. Opting out was not an option. ('Week 12: we've done THE shop! Bibs, gloves, crib, buggy ...!!' etc., etc.) I tried to share in her joy, but my demons were in the ascendant at that time. I worried for the unborn child's health and for the 'thousand natural shocks that flesh is heir to', the poor mite's sad inheritance. It would at least have a head start in a caring mum like Millie.

I was particularly close to the information stream – as some wag called it, baby-dot-com – because I was married to Millie's best friend, Sam, at that time. Millie's impending motherhood couldn't but throw our childlessness into sharp relief. It became yet another source of frustration, and fanned the flames of countless rows into the night. It was as if Sam was plotting a graph – profits in Tom and Millie confidently rising, with a pivot point of even better performance from the date when the pregnancy was announced. And the shares and business confidence in us were trailing off below. How Sam thought rowing about it and treating marriage like a competition was going to improve things beat me. And I'd been clear when I first started going out with her that I hadn't really wanted kids. Not that I didn't like them – if anything, I liked them too much; as I said to Mary, my therapist, I couldn't respect any child that had me for a father. Mary didn't appreciate my Marxist humour – Groucho, not Karl. 'Ouch,' she said, after a pause.

But maybe, hypocritically, I'd made my own profit-and-loss analysis of having children already. Perhaps I'd calculated that bringing a new consciousness into such a damaged world was never going to give rise to a sufficient return on investment. I saw friends drift into parenthood and heard horror stories of broken nights, mental and physical ill health, stress without end and strains on marriages, and decided it was not for me. That this branch of the Daniels family tree was going to end in a stub didn't mean the tree would die. I once asked Mum if, like loads of other species, humans were going to become extinct. She smiled a knowing smile and said, 'I don't think so, love.'

It didn't have to be this way, though. I once bumped into a woman I'd been in the psychiatric unit with years before – she'd had severe mental illness, bulimia, all sorts – and yet she now had in tow two bouncing boys who would know nothing more of that episode from their prehistory than she chose to tell them. Maybe my mistake was in trying to apply logic to something which isn't logical. Depression is a pair of dark glasses, and sufferers see through a glass, darkly.

Millie's ultrasound scans at ten and then twenty weeks seemed to go well. For a moment, I thought it might be Selica scanning her as it was at the same obstetrics unit, till my befuddled brain recalled Selica had left health and hospitals for a different kind of hospitality. I saw Millie shortly after the second scan and she seemed to be one of those women who blooms in pregnancy: her face looked more vital, she was very smiley, even by her own standards, and she was looking to the future with Tom and the child, seemingly with confidence. If there was such a thing as natural, unforced optimism, this was it.

We met one day in Cambridge; I can't quite remember why. I have a feeling she was still working then and had a conference she was speaking at, at the university. Something about practical genetics (sounded to me like a contradiction in terms). For me it was possibly a bit of a jolly between jobs, between series of Ricky's show.

Millie told me that day about her status woes. As we sat on the banks of the Cam on a glorious August afternoon, watching the lazy punting through the willows, which were alive with delicate goldfinch song, she talked about snide remarks she'd endured growing up. I'd never heard her say before about getting grief over having been brought up on a council estate. I asked her point-blank – not normally my style – about whether, after all her achievements, she could now see the funny side of it? Or did it still wound her? She surprised me by saying the latter. That was the one cloud scudding across the blue sky of our conversation. It was swiftly followed by a kick from the baby which was weeks from joining us. I said whatever happened the bairn would be a punter, and Millie's laugh was back.

And that was the last time I saw her well.

48

Dinner with Elsa part two
Central Park South, Manhattan – 29 December 1999

We'd moved to the L-shaped sofa by the picture windows. Elsa was on one branch, with me on the other, next to the built-in smoked glass table where the sofa's two sections met. Elsa looked haunted as she related her wartime trauma.

'July 1942 in Paris was not a time and place to be Jewish. My parents were rounded up on the Thursday, the 16th. *"La Rafle de Vel' d'Hiv"* – the round-up was named after the velodrome where it happened. Mama and Papa had made arrangements for me and my sister to be looked after by our neighbours.' Elsa drew on another Gauloise, her hand shaking.

I leaned in. 'How old were you?'

'I was ten. My sister was twelve. Severine. We had a brother who wasn't so lucky. Francis was fifteen. They came back for him. His screams still visit my dreams, from time to time ...'

What could I say? 'I'm so sorry.' What could anyone say?

She continued, 'Years later I spoke to a police officer who was involved.'

'German police? Gestapo?'

'No, French. *"La PP"* – *Préfecture de police*. The Paris branch. It was what you might call an "inside job". I'd found the records and traced a name. He was a young officer starting out in 1942. I spoke to him just before he retired in the Eighties. I don't know how he slept. I couldn't – for years.'

I sat back for a moment.

Exhaling the last of that cigarette she added, 'I'm not sure if it was ironic that we were German – the Meyeroffs. A Yiddish name. Foreign Jews – that is, non-French Jews – were rounded up, while French Jews were mostly spared. We were *les déchets* – the dregs. My family didn't flee far enough in '33, the year after I was born. I don't blame my father – he had limited means. And France had seemed safer. Who could see into the future? My parents and Francis died at Auschwitz.'

Through one of the picture windows a helicopter hovered between two skyscrapers a couple of blocks away, like a curious dragon fly.

'How have you lived with it?' I couldn't decide if that was a sensible or a dumb question, but I had to say something. Her anguished expression on mentioning the camp demanded a response.

'I met Todd shortly after the war and our reaction was to get married and start a family quickly. Almost without thinking!' At last, a brightening of her features. 'To do anything else would have been to let those bastard Nazis kill another generation. The only answer to death is life. It's the one defence we have.'

I was now cross-legged on the sofa. The helicopter moved off.

'So – are you taking up my offer of refuge or not? L'Hôtel Elsa. It's time-limited.' Her eyes sparkled.

Whether through inertia, or lack of alternatives, or for the love of a freebie, I said, 'Yes – of course.'

I enjoyed the fade to black.

49

Millie part four
1996-97

Far from there being a great crescendo to her due date for giving birth Millie fell entirely off the radar, to the point of being uncontactable. Phone calls went unanswered, answerphone messages ignored, e-mails bounced back with an automatic reply like 'the recipient's inbox is full'. I tried different routes: Tom, normally a cheery interlocutor, went silent. Our mutual social network, whose nodes usually sparked in all directions, couldn't help with Millie or Tom; everything was quiet. Any grapevine had withered.

And then it came out that Millie had had puerperal (or post-partum) psychosis. I had to look it up – the prefix, at least; I was no stranger to psychosis. Apparently, it could kick in days or weeks after giving birth. It was a kind of birth-induced madness (not that official sources used the M-word). Some sources suggested it could even be a reaction to the mother missing being pregnant. It was hard to know what to believe on this info infant the Internet. But I didn't feel too inclined to believe what we were gleaning in dusty leather-bound volumes at the reference library either. I do know she was so unlucky to get it – a one-in-a-thousand chance. Fate can be cruel.

Facts, which felt like borderline rumours, dripped out frustratingly slowly, as if it was restricted information from a war zone. Millie was in a mother and baby unit – the baby was fine (phew) – Millie needed constant supervision – she was struggling to bond with the child – it was a boy, Felix –

no time frame for her to leave hospital – it was a progressive, safe environment, etc., etc.

Winter '96 came and went. Trees blossomed, but it seemed an academic, automatic process, not a sign of new life. Days got longer and warmer, but there were still only scant details about Millie. Until one day in August '97, a message on the answerphone: an invite for me and Sam to join the extended family and friends for a celebration of Felix's first birthday. A kind of deferred christening. It was to be held at a community hall near to Millie and Tom's home in Luton in Bedfordshire.

The day went by in a whir of bunting, cork-poppings, smiles, laughter, finger food, team washings-up, celebratory music on the PA, conversational subgroups forming, decaying, and re-forming, and the click near my ear of my camera shutter, as I indulged my passion for black-and-white portraits. And, at the centre of it all, the couple I'd first seen holding hands that snowy December twenty years before, climbing back up the hill to sledge some more. Here they were, proud as punch as the parents of not-so-new arrival Felix: Millie and Tom. Everyone there, barring any children, must have known the peculiar circumstances of the birth and what followed, but it was an unspoken rule to do no more than whisper about such things away from the couple's ears. The determination was not to spoil the day for them at any cost. They had suffered enough.

When the late summer's night fell with a hint of approaching autumn in the air, I was one of the stragglers. Millie, Tom, Sam, and I resolved to meet up again soon, but with less of the freneticism. The hook was to look at the photos once developed. I promised Millie and Tom copies of the 'good 'uns'. In the event Sam opted out of the intensity of this meeting with the struggles we were going through. But I honoured the commitment to see Millie and Co. and so, come September, I took a bottle of red and some flowers, and a plaything for Felix, and caught the train north out of London to Luton. It was just like the old days.

And nothing like the old days.

It was mostly pleasant and lovely to see them again, especially away from the sideshows of fizzing party energy. But further cracks were appearing. They accepted without question the apology from Sam I conveyed for her not making it. They probably didn't have the spare capacity to query it. Without the distractions of a large group, it was more tangible the couple had been through the wars. I had steeled myself for Millie to look spent, and she most certainly did, but I hadn't prepared myself for the effects on Tom. It wasn't so much how he looked but that he had acquired a tic of running his hands repeatedly through his auburn hair. Felix seemed oblivious and cooed on demand, performing for my camera. But there was an unspoken hollowness between all of us. And to cap it, there was open fractiousness within the couple. Filling in the gaps, it transpired that Millie had taken it on herself to set up an organisation for women like her who'd been through or were in puerperal psychosis. She was on the phone as I arrived, and I worked out it was to a talk radio station that was wanting to interview her the next day. Tom, normally the model of diplomacy, lost it while she took the call, saying she couldn't do it, she had too much on. He didn't care that the producer on the other end would hear his interjections. In fact, it seemed pretty clear he wanted them to. My heart was heavy for both of them. They'd always presented a united front; this was a mark of serious decay. Marriage is to dating as governing is to campaigning: all kinds of bright futures can be promised in glossy handouts, but ultimately realpolitik kicks in. And the couple had been so unlucky in the shift from one state to the other.

Felix liked my gift – a small furry toy based on an indeterminate-looking animal. Tom named it Hartley, I assumed after the TV puppet, Hartley Hare. Felix was as fascinated with that as he was with my face; I suppose I represented a strange intrusion, a new fizzog to process, but at least I was a stranger bearing a gift for this child barely out of babyhood. In fact, as the couple explained after Felix had been put to bed, things had been so fraught at the time around his birth they said they couldn't remember which date was his birthday.

And that's where there was a discontinuity in what had happened; things not stacking up. Millie's psychosis followed the birth, yet the couple stopped responding to my attempts at contact weeks before the due date – and Felix's wasn't a premature birth. I didn't want to probe too much in our first small-scale meet for months, but the timeline was a blur and raised more questions than it answered. For the purposes of that evening it didn't matter what order things had happened in but, in the light of subsequent events, and as I chewed over it on restless nights, it mattered more as I tried to make sense of things.

A subsequent meeting, just me and Millie, had been more upsetting still. Further tantalising bits of the jigsaw came from mutual friends beforehand, to the effect Millie 'wasn't herself', that 'she wasn't quite there'. But once in her presence or, rather, her partial absence, I realised how euphemistic those nuggets were. As we sat over a drink in her local pub there was a rage behind those unfocussed eyes, and she was obsessing over negative details, things whispered behind hands, people letting her down, rumours and betrayals disturbing her peace. There was no leavening of the faintest flicker of a smile for the entire evening.

And then the kicker.

With minimal expression she looked at or more through me and said, 'I can't forgive myself for killing my baby.'

50

Waking at Elsa's
Central Park South, Manhattan – 30 December 1999

I thought I'd woken up in a hotel. Maybe that was Elsa's wit in coining the term 'L'Hôtel Elsa', or her professional-grade hospitality, or the first stirrings of my waking mind. It could also have been the quality of the crisp white Egyptian cotton sheets.

I took a sip of water from the small tumbler by the bed. Its heavy base exuded quality, including the stylish bubble within it. The closed burgundy velvet curtains were too heavy to allow through any clues about the time of day. But I had a pain in my lower back which hinted I'd been lying down too long.

Elsa, in beige blouse with a striped cravat like an outsized school tie, breezed in with a fierce face and said loudly, 'You are sleeping like a baby. It is eight o'clock already. You will get nothing done all day. Alley-oop!' and she threw back the duvet, revealing me in T-shirt and briefs. She clapped her hands, adding, 'Chop-chop!' A rude awakening.

Why the sudden change? I rewound last night's events. I remember agreeing to stay over. Before we headed up to the next floor of her apartment she poured me a glass of water, so that checks out with the evidence. I remember also some good-natured but encoded discussion about the allocation of rooms. Ah, and then there was the memorable phrase, 'Strictly a knickers-on experience.' I recall seeing Elsa remove that metallic eye shadow at her built-in dressing table. Next thing she was in a nightdress, and I experienced the now foreign feeling of another's body heat and animal closeness, and we were cuddling into oblivion, submerged in warm sheets and a thick duvet. So I'm not sure what my crime is. Sloth? But we hadn't discussed a time to get up. And what the bloody hell am I supposed to be rushing up for? I'm hardly heading to the Manhattan job centre where they ask, 'Sir, what are your skills?' 'I write gags for downmarket TV shows. Do you have anything?'

From the kitchen I got a waft of warm pastry and the pungent promise of fresh coffee. That would be something to get up for. A Schubert string quartet wafts up the stairs, too. Or is it Schumann? They're filed next to each other in my brain. But then there's an unmusical vibrating sound I can't place. Distant drilling? Or a rodent in the bedside table? Both seemed unlikely. It happens again and I'm on the case. It's coming from my jeans folded on the back of a chair. I draw my lozenge-shaped phone from the pocket. I've received a text (so-called):

Hi Nate Where r u? I'm worried abt u. Pls ring. Lou x

I will get back. But first I have a date downstairs with a croissant and coffee. I think she'd understand.

51

Millie part five
Leighton Buzzard, Bedfordshire – September 1997

On the eve of Millie's funeral, I started obsessing about what I would wear. I knew it was daft even as I chewed over the options: should I go strictly formal and trad, with a plain black tie and starched white shirt, or should I reflect a little of her informality, say a subtle pattern in the shirt, black leather jacket, dark boots with a bit of a heel (even a Cuban heel?) – and maybe no tie at all? No, that might upset her mother. Maybe some halfway point: a charcoal flax jacket (there was a late-summer warmth in the air), a dark tie with a hint of a woven-in curlicue when it catches the light ...

I caught myself in the wardrobe mirror as I reached inside yet again and thought, 'You dick.'

Ah, the auld enemy. The self-critic. Driver of so much misery since teendom. Doesn't help to be born three quarters English and a quarter Scot. Built-in aggro. A product of the union trying to hold himself together. I searched inside for a kinder voice. I looked up again at my reflection and there behind me to my left was Millie. Well, a photo of Millie, sitting on a chest of drawers. She smiled from the past, with her shoulder-length wavy blonde locks, small black-gemmed earrings, grey knee-length skirt and black leather waistcoat over a dark blouse, head tilted forgivingly. She'd just been given a professional award. I'd forgotten that stunning matte skin. And my kinder inner voice was indivisible from her voice. I imagined her saying softly, warmly, 'Come as you are. It's not about clothes, is it? And it's not about you. It's about me. I'm really going to miss you,

Nate.' And her voice, and my memory of her voice, melted away.

I had an early night and took comfort in a montage of dreams.

At the church I was okay. Sort of. I sat near some old school friends and we talked in straight lines: expressing our shock, concern for Tom and Felix and the wider family, acknowledging it would take time to heal. I kept it together as the coffin arrived on four sombre shoulders; I could even cope as Tom, head bowed so his hair, slightly tousled, fell forward and obscured his face, but couldn't obscure the shaking of his shoulders at cross-rhythms with the mournful organ. But it took one look at the order of service in front of me, headed by 'Millicent "Millie" Carroll', to make me lose it. It wasn't the name, it was the sum which followed: 1964 – 1997. Too short an interval to do her justice, to be called a life, too much pain within those thirty-three years, especially at the end. And what of Felix at home during the funeral, absorbed in play with the childminder, who'll spend the rest of his life trying to make sense of his mother's absence? In the short term, before the memory fades, he'll miss her voice, her smell, her touch. Longer term those things must pass into a more shadowy place, all the more powerful for being hidden. How can he not someday wonder why his mother couldn't be a perfectly flawed Mum, instead of punishing herself for failing to reach an impossible ideal?

As the vicar intones platitudes betraying his lack of personal knowledge of 'the deceased' I kept replaying my last conversation with Millie, looking for clues. Looking for exoneration, if I'm honest. Absolution. Big clue: the fierceness of her gaze, the intensity of her delivery. No light. Why didn't I respond to that – raise the alarm? She was slipping away before my eyes; I've seen that look before. What's that quote? 'For the triumph of evil it is only necessary that good men do nothing.' And how 'good' is the man or woman who does nothing anyway?

'Please turn in your psalters to Psalm number twenty-three ...'

We can all wash our hands and pass people over to 'the professionals', but you can't pass over culpability. You can't outsource your conscience. Is hand-wringing any better than handwashing? Either way a good friend dies. And that night she talked of having 'killed her child' – did I do enough to say an abortion must have been the lesser of two evils, to make clear she shouldn't carry that awful burden alone? It takes two to conceive, after all, and the time just wasn't right for her. She was only young. And what gets lost in the binary, shouty debate ('pro-life' versus ... versus what – 'anti-life'?) is that there's a woman saying goodbye to a part of herself, a part she needs to mourn. She doesn't go skipping and dancing into it. As Millie said to me once, there's no automatic right to counselling after a termination. I didn't realise then she was speaking from experience. She'd been hungry for help, a context for her pain.

'Don't tell Tom,' she'd begged me at our last drink together. 'Or Paddy.'

'The Lord is my shepherd ...' A weak, reedy organ strikes up, and the congregation attempts to sing through tears.

But that may not have been the burden that broke her back anyway. That wretched psychosis, an unseen disease of the dendrons, has a hell of a lot to answer for, upsetting that delicate balance in the brain we want to take for granted but know deep down we can't afford to. Yeah, do I ever know that. Seems her equilibrium was knocked out of kilter and never recovered. Mum said a woman is at the mercy of her hormones.

'I shall not want ...'

And what is this mad male drive for the procreative act, paired with a morbid fear of fertility? How fucked up is that? I'm in the dock on this, too – yea, even nice-guy Nate.

'He leadeth me by still waters ...'

As Dad said after Mum had killed herself, 'I feel guilty I don't feel guilty.' That really is a life sentence; those left behind yearning to pick up the tab for the fallen. And the 'pro-lifers' in denial the main alternative to legal abortion is illegal abortion. Or, as my mother tried when carrying me, a surfeit of town gas. She was going for the double. Whoever thought it was a civilised thing to pump poison – carbon monoxide, for God's sake – into people's homes? She was snatched from the jaws of death – and me, too, by extension – by my father arriving home early by chance. But Sylvia Plath and thousands more weren't so lucky.

'Yea, though I walk through the valley of the shadow of death ...'

I don't know how Millie took her life, and I don't want to know. In the jigsaw of information I was slowly assembling there were murmurs of an earlier attempt. A husband arriving again on the scene by chance. Someone – don't know who, names and faces are now merging – conjured up a hideous picture of Millie staggering around the garage, her face bloodied and bruised as she bumped, drugged, into breeze blocks. And Tom dragging her like a limp puppet to the roadside ready to meet the ambulance. And rumours of her coming round and even then putting up resistance against her saviours. An overwhelming desire for numbness, relief from the pain of consciousness.

'...thou anointest my head with oil ...'

And after the service chatting to a friend of a friend about showbiz, about the pop acts he touts about the world, an inexhaustible supply of product – or, as you might call them, people – he throws at the wall to see what'll stick. So engrossed in the conversation was I that I missed Millie's burial, the final obscenity, missed seeing her coffin lowered with that fake grass carpet covering up the rough muddy edges of the gravedigger's work, and the vicar's sprinkling of soil *...ashes to ashes ...* and the plaque with her name and that ugly sum *...dust to dust ...* the subtraction making thirty-three years, too few to call a full life, too many to dismiss as,

'We'll never know what she could have become'. The cruelty of knowing what she *had* become, the further potential she had, the blossoming and the withering.

Or did I engross myself in that pop trivia conversation deliberately to avoid seeing Millie's coffin swallowed up by the ground? My denial of death? And is there any macabre comedy to be dragged from my screw-up? As with Dad dying to the sounds of 'Rule Britannia', could I imagine Millie laughing about me being late to her burial? Perhaps she'd call me 'the late Nate'. Or is that itself obscene? The point is we can all have the Millie we want now; she's not a living person, she's a collection of memories we pull out of a mental drawer at will. Another cruelty: she doesn't get to choose which version of her we cleave to.

Cedar trees dapple the September sunlight, speckling the mourners on their slow march from the graveside. I attach myself to the middle of the group then go at their pace, as if I was with them all along. Thirty, forty feet away, a tall figure wearing dark glasses and a black pinstripe suit gets into a swish car. It roars into life and vanishes before I process it's driven by Paddy.

Tom, last to leave the grave, approaches me on the cemetery's main roadway, arms outstretched. Tears striate down his cheeks. He doesn't so much hug me as collapse on to me; I've never seen grief so total. I literally had to be strong for him to stop him from falling. It's tempting to think this is a metaphor for what's to follow, but I know in this moment I'll never see him again.

Except I do see him one more time, but through the eye of a lens and the window of a screen. A couple of years later, flicking on late-night TV, I chance on a rare production of *After the Fall* by Arthur Miller. And there he is, Tom in the lead as Quentin, a lawyer evaluating his life and choices, asking himself why his marriages failed, and most poignantly agonising over the suicide of Maggie, widely – though wrongly – thought to be based on Miller's former wife Marilyn Monroe. Tom poured heart and soul into the role, and it doesn't take a genius to work out the wellspring he was drawing on for his authenticity: the dénouement felt like a howl of pain for Millie. Some rocky road Tom had been on since my dad complimented him after that school play.

I never felt as good a friend to Millie as she seemed to think I was. Though how does one measure these things? And who's qualified to play point scorer? It could be the self-critic talking again, the enemy within. At first I was bruised not to be let into the loop when it all started going wrong around Felix's birth. At times I nursed a god-like delusion I could save Millie, brandishing the badge of having entered the kingdom of madness myself; I felt I could meet her there and talk her out of it. At other times I surrendered to utter despair: her illness was too big for any of us.

Millie very nearly met my mum. I'd gravitated to Millie's kindly listening ear when I was fifteen. I wanted to open up to her about thoughts and feelings that were already slipping out of my control. We'd arranged to meet one inhospitable Sunday in February 1979. I'd planned to go with Millie on a local walk; not quite the literary blasted heath of my imaginings, but it might have involved the odd field and stile up the road from me on the outskirts of London. I told my mother adding, perhaps unnecessarily, it wasn't a romantic adventure. She said she understood: she'd had platonic friends at my age. But with a couple of days to go, without giving a reason, Millie cried off. Maybe she had a real hot date, maybe she had family commitments, or was behind with her homework. Maybe she realised she didn't want to listen to a whinge-fest from me on a windswept moor, or by a busy A-road, after all. Whatever it was, it deprived Mum and Millie of an encounter. After the funeral, for a second I fantasise their meeting could have sparked a *Sliding Doors* chain of events that gave them each a happier outcome. It's sad beyond belief how they were united in their tragic exits.

So goodbye Millie, flawed angel. Rest well.

Age shall not weary your perfect skin.

52

Breakfast at Elsa's
Central Park South, Manhattan – 30 December 1999

You can't knock a culture – even a foreign culture transplanted to New York City – that prizes pastries with chocolate and jam as the way to start the day. That and lashings of fresh coffee. May healthy eating never impinge on the French *petit déjeuner*! But my enjoyment of breakfast was severely crimped by Elsa having the right hump with me.

'You sit there looking at that phone thing, not a care in the world, being ... What's that phrase? "Away with the fairies". It must be a lovely life.'

I slammed my coffee down, spilling some of it. '*Mais oui*, Elsa – what could be finer? Marriage gone south, Mum topped herself, one of my best friends ditto, spell in the loony bin, and now I've lost my job and I'm having to rely on the kindness of a stranger ... who isn't very bloody kind.'

Across the small round kitchen table Elsa's espresso cup landed with a double clink on its saucer. I looked across and saw her hand shaking. I remembered the Vel' d'Hiv' round-up, Paris '42.

'Jeez – I-I'm sorry, Elsa,' I said. 'I've had a picnic compared to you. I never wanted to be one of those whiny showbiz types. And I've become one of those whiny showbiz types.'

She didn't acknowledge. Instead, her look became more focussed, more quizzical. 'Your mother improved herself? And your friend. Surely that's a good thing?' Elsa affected a Gallic shrug.

Baffled for a moment I chewed over a croissant, wiping a blob of strawberry jam from my lips with a gold-edged napkin. 'They topped themselves – they took their own lives ...'

'Ahh ... Over here it means to improve on your personal best.' Elsa lit another ciggie. We both stared at each other, stony-faced. Then the wrinkles round Elsa's eyes started splaying out and she couldn't suppress a laugh. This triggered a cough. I had to laugh, too. I laughed at her laugh, then I laughed at her cough. As her first wave of laughter subsided, she found my laugh infectious and that started more hacking, and that prompted a second wave of the giggles for me. Finally, as her laughter and coughing fit subsided, she said, 'My turn to apologise, Nathan.' She dabbed a tear with her napkin.

Taking her cue, I dabbed my eyes too, succeeding only in filling them with croissant crumbs which then triggered more tears. As I laughed at this latest absurdity I said, 'You can't beat starting the day with a good joke about suicide.'

'Oh, Nate. You should join me for breakfast every day to cheer me up – it's the worst part of my day.'

'Worst? What could be finer than a continental breakfast?' I was doing a Gallic shrug now.

'Worst for feeling, I mean. Dragging myself up from the sludge of sleep. Or no sleep.' She stubbed out the cigarette, exhaling the last of the blue exhaust. I suppressed a cough. 'But croissants are compensation. Best meal of the day.'

'Mornings are the best of times, the worst of times,' I offered.

Elsa's eyes glinted. '*A Tale of Two Cities* – *Paris et Londres.*'

'Or Paris and New York for you.' Bzzzzz ... My phone vibrated loudly with the kitchen table as a soundboard. 'What the Dickens? Excuse me.' I took the phone with me, walking from the kitchen area to the lounge.

I assumed Louise couldn't wait for my call. I was rehearsing what I'd say to her, when I saw it wasn't her name in the display. I took the call.

'Nate.' A male voice. Not just any male voice: Paddy's.

'H-hullo?' Bloody hell. An olive branch?

'I've been thinking. Do you remember when we used to skim stones in the local wood? Knocknaheeny – back in the old country?'

'Y-ess,' I said cautiously. 'Summertimes.'

'Uh-huh. And do you remember The Men?' He put a familiar lilt on the last two words.

'I do ... remember The Men.' I deliberately tried not to echo back the lilt. Now was not the time to be chummy; we were two scorpions circling each other, sussing the other out. The Men were characters of our own making, the product of idle boys' minds in the summer holidays in Ireland. They supposedly lived under the stones we skimmed. They could get disturbed when we lifted their homes up.

'Well ... they've been visiting me of late. The Men.' Was he for real? 'I mean, not often. And they're usually harmless.' Oh God; he wasn't joking. This was not good news. 'I just thought I'd check whether they're visiting you, Nate?'

'Er – not to date, no.' One-elephant-two-elephant ...

'OK. That's all for now. Go well, Nate.'

'Yes. And ... and you.' I hung up.

Usually harmless?

Shit.

53

Call to Louise
Clock Diner, Manhattan – 30 December 1999

Last time I was in an NY diner I was with Louise. This time I had to content myself with talking to her on a scratchy mobile line – excuse me, cell phone. I struggled to hear her above the clatter of plates and orders being shouted behind the chrome counter fifteen feet away.

'Ricky's going loopy, Script Ed ditto – he's stepped in for you and remembered he's forgotten how to write. I'm not sleeping, the band have turned up but their gear's in Wisconsin, the Colonel's having kittens, Daemon and Fiske have had another hissy fit, and the unions are raising merry hell about the hours.'

'So, situation normal then?' I nodded to the waitress she could take my plate. The residue of smeared brown sauce and egg yolk looked like a Jackson Pollock. 'At times like this I remind myself "it's only TV".'

'Grrrrr ...'

'I'm getting interference on the line.' I tapped repeatedly on the mouthpiece. 'Sounds like you're at a zoo.'

'I *am* at a zoo.'

'Zoo-Lou? You're a born worrier. Er, warrior.'

'Very good. In the hands of a pro that could be turned into a joke.' How I'd missed the Ice Queen. 'And I'm guessing you're not in a monastery either?'

'Not so fast. I'm taking Holy Communion right now. Breaking bread and consecrating the coffee. "This is the blood of Nate – thanks be to Bob". Bob Hope and Glory, patron saint of gag writers.' The air was heavy with the sound of Louise not laughing. 'Stop me if this gets out of hand ...'

'Think that ship has sailed, don't you, Nathaniel Daniel? Look – I'll cut to the chase. The clock's ticking. All the other writers Ricky will work with are already committed for the big night.' Gee, thanks. 'We've got to get you and him talking again. To get you back in the fold. Or whatever bloody pigpen image you want.'

'Funnily enough, that ship – or floating zoo, ark, the Ark Royal – has sailed too, Louise. Well, it's moored alongside ...'

'Spit it out, man.' Fate's a cruel mistress, but Louise is crueller. Cruella.

'I spoke to Ricky this morning.' I remembered The Men. 'A version of him, anyway.'

'Really? He didn't mention it.' Funny, that. 'So, you can pick up where you left off.'

'Me assaulting him, you mean?'

Louise sighed. 'Just talk. Eat humble pie. And Ed'll liaise with the two of you. Thanks to Ed's incompetence, Ricky knows he needs you.'

That and all the other writers being busy. 'Where am I going to stay? I've been walking the streets.' Sounded far more dramatic than, 'I've just stopped over with a wealthy widow near Central Park. Oh, and by the way, we slept together.'

'Don't worry about accommodation, Nate – I'll get on to the hotel. A bit of TV booking power works wonders. They'll be falling at our feet. Especially if you work in a favourable reference to them in the script ...!' Mmm. The muscle of mass media, the ultimate aphrodisiac. Then Louise sounded suddenly more sombre. 'I meant to ask – have you heard about George?'

'George who?'

'George Harrison,' said Louise, matter of factly. 'Stabbed. This morning.'

'What? Fuck? Where? How bad? All he needs after the cancer.' My heart was suddenly pumping harder.

'I think he was at home. In England. London, maybe. Some knife-wielding nutter.'

'Fighting for his life? Dying? How bad? Jesus, how bad?'

'Still "with us". Maybe not "with it". Hanging on. I think.'

The opposite of karma.

Harrison's life seems to flash before my eyes, from being the kid in the quartet – fourteen to Lennon's seventeen – to being the architect of 'Something', with its sublime guitar solo, at the age of twenty-six. Possibly my favourite Beatles song (sorry, Paul). And now George is 'hanging on' at fifty-six.

The tinselly 'Happy New Year 2000' decorations suddenly seemed obscene. They framed the window next to me. Who could be happy while George was suffering?

'George ... keep hanging on, mate,' I said absent-mindedly, staring out at the busy sidewalk. The city stops for no one.

'I'm sorry, Nate. Oh, and one more thing.' Louise had moved to a Columbo moment. 'That nice Jane woman who's making the genealogy show called again – says her e-mails are bouncing back. So I gave her your number. Hope that's okay?' Butter wouldn't melt.

Bollocks. On top of everything. I'll never get rid of Jane now, I thought. And bouncing back e-mails, my arse.

'Of course it's okay,' my mouth uttered, my brain's natural censor having overloaded.

54

The Long One
Napsbury Hospital, London Colney – October 1982

The medley from side two of *Abbey Road* is playing in the Quiet Room at the end of the Royal Mile, by the locked entrance. There's a mislabelling if ever there was – the Quiet Room's got a radio in it. Mental. DJ Paul Burnett says before playing The Beatles what the purpose of Radio 1 is – to play pop music for people across the country like he's a man on a mission. And what a mission. Could there be anything more important?

Another resident there isn't getting it. He keeps talking and talking about getting out of here by eating his way through the walls. He thinks I should join him eating the walls too – we'd get out in half the time. I tell him he's nuts but my dad's there too and he asks me to rein it in. The Wall Eater's only an actor, though, so what does it matter? Also, I don't want him to talk through 'Golden Slumbers', one of the best songs in the world. And Ringo's the best drummer in the world so I'm looking forward to his solo bit, too.

The music reminds me of Selica, who moved away from being our neighbour to run a hotel in God's Hill. She first played me *Abbey Road*. But I don't think she's running this place. The hotel I'm in now is for mad residents, a ship of fools – a floating hotel? Makes you wonder why I'm here. I think it's for insight. I'm here to help the others, free them from their chains.

You see, I'm going sane. They can sense I can see through all the showbiz nonsense here. For instance, I told them I knew the medical consultants here were referred to as 'Mr'. You start as a Mr (if you're a bloke), and then you study for seven years and become a Dr. And then you study a bit more and you become a Mr again. So one minute I see a man's in a white coat in the boss nurse's office. The next time I see him he's in civvies standing on the table changing a lightbulb (OK – he's got a pager on, so that proves he's important). He's gone from mister to doctor to mister again. Case proven.

'Hospital' is an anagram of 'i asp hotel'. Nearly. The 'i' is the ego-less self (that's why it's lower case, not a capital), 'asp' represents the serpent, the tempter in the Garden of Eden, and the hotel comes out of 'hospital'. Back at the general hospital they're putting up a new building just for me. It helps that my dad is God. I'm a member of the God is Dad movement. I told one of the other residents here that I'm the Son of God and she said she was the Queen of Sheba. It's amazing who you meet in these places. As long as your mind is open.

And the i pops up everywhere. BMW 320i. Golf GTi. Secrets of the i-Ching. 'The i ascending on a slow last thermal breath'.

Proof if proof were needy.

55

Incoming
Clock Diner, Manhattan – 30 December 1999

Meanwhile, back in the busy diner. The call I dreaded.

As a freelance in the small world of TV you're genetically modified to bite your tongue, keep people on board, keep your thoughts to yourself and so stay solvent (dressing-room fights with old mates excepted). So the impulse to 'let Jane have it' must be quashed at every turn. And with Louise as the go-between, it's even more important.

What if I need this Jane person further down the line?

What if she's a conduit to useful people in the trade?

What if, God help us, I'm interested in my genealogy after all?

I've got incoming: an unrecognised number. With an 001 code. Am I being charged over the odds for this?

Stranger in a strange land.

'Hello?' I looked at my watch without taking in the time.

'Jane here,' intoned an all-American voice. Lower register for a female – probably alto. 'Is that Nate?'

'Guilty as charged.' Errrgh. The original comic voice reduced to cloying cliché.

'Hi. I don't know if Louise warned you I—'
'She did.'
'Well—'
'I thought I'd made it clear—'
'I know. You did.'
'So there's nothing to discuss, Jane.'

'That's, like, where it gets a bit complicated.'

I took a swig of coffee.

'Does the name April mean anything to you, Nate?'

'Other than being a girl's name from the same stable as May and June – no.' A fertile quarter for female monikers, now I think of it. Why's no one called February or July?

Jane cleared her throat. 'It's my name, actually.'

'Good. And Jane's a stage name, no doubt. I'm very pleased for you. Now we've established that ...'

'Not a stage name, no. No ... It's the name my parents ... my adoptive parents ... gave me. My original name was April McEvoy.'

A distant penny dropped through time, decades, its journey accompanied by a discordant orchestra, like an out-take from 'A Day in the Life'.

A drop of water held in suspension on the end of a tap.

A word that fails to leave my tongue.

'The i ascending on a slow last thermal breath'

'McEvoy April STs Pots T-rolls Advocaat Walnut Whip Angel Delight.'

'McEvoy April'

Mum's maiden name – McEvoy

A voice through the floor

My bedroom over the phone

A call to the Samaritans

Me in and out of consciousness

Gotta sleep. School tomorrow

Suicide slats

'I have a lovely son. I had a child out of marriage. A baby girl'

Dream state

'I can't forgive myself for what I've done'

– Mum's mysterious confessional.

Must have dreamt it

Can't have dreamt it

I'm on the phone to Jane. April. Live. In real time.

Now.

I think I can guess her next line
'I'm your half—'
'Yes. I know.'

Adrian Lacey

Part Three

Adrian Lacey

56

A foreign country
Outside Clock Diner, Manhattan – 30 December 1999

They say Russia is the only country where the past keeps changing. Walking the streets of New York I was an honorary Russian. Shops and offices and traffic and high-rises were the same. But everything had changed utterly.

I emerge from the diner dazed. Wheels spin with their own urgency, the city thrives on its neurotic energy, but I am numb within. The Christmas-tree lights living on borrowed time to see in the new millennium are bathetic. A truck unloads on E 83rd like a clanging cymbal, disgorging its contents till it's empty; passers-by pass by.

'Hey! Dude – you forgot your luggage.' A guy with a white apron from his waist was wheeling my two suitcases.

I thanked him perfunctorily; he loitered on the busy street corner long enough to confuse me, not long enough for me to realise he was expecting a tip.

'Why the secrecy?' I'd asked Jane.

'The charity helping me find you recommended it. For the first approaches. They've seen so many skeletons fall out of family cupboards. And the upset that follows.'

I feel my phone go; there's no chance of hearing it above the New York din so it has to be on vibrate. It's Louise. 'I've got some good news and some bad news about the hotel,' she says.

Was April born in April? Or is that too obvious? Did Mum give her away freely or was she coerced?

'Don't you want to know what the news is, Nate?'

A truck horn blared. It took me a moment to connect it to my missteps. I waved a meek apology to the driver riding high over the city.

'Are you okay, Nate?'

'I need to sit somewhere. I'm waiting for a camera crew to film my reaction. To prove it's all a set-up. *Surprise, Surprise*-like.'

'Nate – you're not making any sense. And it's too noisy where you are. Why don't you meet me at the hotel in an hour or so? Say 12.30? They're cool with you leaving luggage any time.'

Cool? Cool-cool-cool. Cooler. Coolest. Coola. Coolam. Coolae. Coolam. Coolae. Coolas. Coolarum. Coolis. Cull cool.

'Nate? 12.30 – okay?'

So I'm not an only child. Both parents – three parents? – took that secret to their grave. Weird shit. I'm not who I thought I was. I won't be who I used to be.

'Jesus, Nate – I'll take that as a yes. I'll text you so you've got no excuse. If you don't show, we're going to have to dig deeper into Script Ed's contacts. I've been fighting for you, Nate – don't let me down.'

'Yeah – sure, Lou. I'm, like, cool with that.'

'Don't take the piss, Nate. See you later.' She hung up.

I remember joking in primary school with Paddy about each of us finding out we had long-lost brothers. (For some reason the idea of a 'long-lost sister' didn't have any resonance with us.) I felt giddy imagining it back then, the same feeling I had when trying to imagine infinity or eternal life. Or an expanding universe. Paddy's mum, Rena, was young enough to have more children, and indeed did provide him with a younger brother, on top of the older one he already had. My mum was that much older than Rena and, although it was theoretically just possible, I felt it was practically unlikely she'd have another and, sure enough, it never happened.

Except it was sort of happening now – in reverse. Almost as if I'd become my own long-lost brother, a newly mysterious figure, playing to a script I didn't even know I'd signed up to. I could finally be my own man, yet all along I've been fashioned from a playbook written by somebody else.

So surely April's the missing link: she's the reason Mum died. Mystery solved. Case proven. 'I can't forgive myself for what I've done.' Look no further ...?

And what was Dad's part in this? Mystery man masterminding the cover-up? An *ingénu?* Or Thane of the Third Way, a Tony Blair-like compromiser, somewhere between the two? Might have to get used to not knowing, to the limits of knowledge. But that's infuriating. I have to know. Can't be complete without knowing. Drive meself barmy trying to find out. But worth it. Know or die trying. Know or try dying.

57

Warm reception
Next-to-Lex Hotel, Manhattan – 30 December 1999

Same old hotel reception, yet seen with new eyes. Old Jack, new Jack – same waistcoat and emerald shirt. I try and block my trailing luggage from him with my approaching body. A man has his pride. Don't want to return with my tail between my legs. But I'm here and not-here. April fallout. Must focus. And, forgive my hormones, Louise is very definitely here, sitting twenty feet away, side-on, on a white sofa looking ravishing with a beige silk scarf, white blouse, porridge-effect skirt, and black boots. She's lost in thought. How could I not have noticed her ski-slope nose?

'Aren't you cold?' I say, approaching her, noting her lack of jacket. I'm bringing with me the time-lag chill from outside. 'It's December, remember?'

And then the most amazing thing. Louise stood up, spun around and gave me an enormous hug, combined with a kiss on my right cheek. It felt weirdly damp, but not from her lips. I realised her tears had found my cheek bone.

'Thank God you're okay, Nate. Sorry.' She was apologising for the rasp as she blew her nose to clear the tears. Idealising someone works best at a distance. She scrunched the tissue in her hand.

I locked on to those hazel eyes. 'It wasn't quite the north face of the Eiger. But I'm glad purdah's over.'

'It's the stress of the whole bloody show. Boy, will I be glad when this millennium's over.'

'Yeah – it's not been my favourite. Let's hope the next one's better.'

Louise smiled and managed a noise not unlike laughter, but you could hear the tears. 'Aren't you curious about the good news/bad news? To do with this place?' She blew her nose again.

'Uh?'

'Over the phone. I said I've got some good news and—'

'Oh, yeah. I was a little ... distracted.' I didn't want to frighten her off with my mad family's skeletons. I could barely explain them to myself, let alone her.

'That traffic noise didn't help.'

'Ah. So what's the deal? I have to polish Jack's shoes?'

'It's worse than that.' Louise rolled the tissue in her hand. 'The good news is you don't have to sleep under the stars. The bad news is, with the holiday season gone bonkers there were no rooms available. Anywhere. Let's get the lift up and I'll explain.'

Didn't sound like the bad news could be that bad. Could it?

58

Rover's return
Ed Sullivan Theater, Manhattan – 30 December 1999

'Tell Ricky that's not going to work. The rhythm's all wrong – it won't get the laugh.'

The way Script Ed looked at me – round the gold frame of his mid-Eighties glasses – I could tell he wasn't going to tell Ricky, the rhythm wouldn't be right, and it wouldn't get a laugh. Five minutes back with this chump and already I feel my skills are 'surplus to requirements'. How quickly they forget.

'You see,' says oh-so-reasonable Ed, mind reader to the trade, 'I know what Ricky'll say: "Nate don't know the half of it. It's not him staring down the bottle – I'm the one looking into the lens. I have to carry the show."'

'Kindly tell Ricky my words have to carry his ego,' I said with all the compassion I could muster, knowing full well Ed wouldn't pass it on. It was great to be back.

'Oh – and I haven't told you about the Colonel.' Script Ed raised his trousers over his stomach, but they quickly recoiled. 'You know the network's taken back half an hour of the show? We're off at 12.30, not 1.'

'No way ...?' Theft of airtime when a show's in rehearsal is unheard of. Except, it seems, when there are three zeros on the end of the year.

'So the Colonel's out on manoeuvres, spitting blood.' Script Ed ran his hand all over his face, as if he'd forgotten he was missing a flannel. 'And it's not phoney blood, that Kensington Gore telly stuff – it's the real thing.'

Ed's one of those people who says 'there was literally steam coming out me ears' and thinks he means it.

'I'm not surprised the Colonel's mithered.' I'd fallen prey to Script Ed's supposedly Yorkshire patois. And I wasn't surprised about the Colonel's reaction. In military terms, having your TV programme castrated by thirty minutes is like losing the Battle of the Bulge.

I could see from his eyeline I'd lost Script Ed's attention. Turns out the male gaze had fallen on Jenni, who was carrying a sheaf of notes ready to escape her clutches.

'Let me help you with those, Penny,' said Ed. Bugger. Penny didn't correct him. I was sure it was Jenni. How did he do that?

Penny smiled an indulgent smile. 'Thanks, Ed.' To her he was a harmless old uncle, a non-threatening fifty-something. To him she was a potential bit on the side, squirrelled away for another day when the missus was playing bowls.

'What's with all the paper, love?' asked Script Ed. 'I thought computers were meant to do away with all that?' Ed pushed his glasses up his nose. They'd slid down in the sweat of desire.

'They haven't invented the device that can read scribbles yet, Ed. Least of all Ricky's scribbles.' Penny held the marked-up scripts as if to camera. Life imitating art. Rick's hurried scrawl suggested a post-TV life as a family doctor.

I got out of neutral gear belatedly. 'Hey, Ed – shouldn't we be taking an interest in Ricky's notes?'

'Calm down, Nate – Penny's gorrit all in hand, haven't you love?' We all know what Ed would like Penny to have in hand. He made a vertical screen wipe of all five foot seven of his fantasy prompter princess. She affected not to notice.

Calm down? It's T-minus twenty-eight hours before we go to air and Script Ed doesn't seem to think it's our business to read the star-of-the-show's notes. Jesus wept! If

Ed ever had an outbreak of competence it would lead on CNN.

I attempted a smile, halfway between carefree and passive-aggressive. 'Well, the script isn't going to rewrite itself. Do excuse me,' I said, squeezing past the lovebirds.

'Positions please,' boomed Steve the floor manager to crew and artists.

It was like I'd never been away.

59

Harrison summit
An hour later – Ed Sullivan Theater, Manhattan – 30 December 1999

'The reason I've called you all here,' the Colonel said sternly, 'is to talk about the Harrison situation.'

Another pre-production meeting, but only just over twenty-four hours pre the production: Thursday 30th. Ricky wasn't here, but Louise said she believed that was because Colin thought he would have slowed things down.

'Fact of the matter is,' Colin went on, 'for reputational reasons we'll have to drop all Beatles material tomorrow.'

There was a gasp in the room; then I realised I was the sole source of it.

'To be brutal,' said Colin, as if that wasn't his usual MO, 'we can't have George dying on us.' And, lest anyone should think it was out of respect for the gifted musician, or his family, he clarified: 'It'll cast a pall on proceedings and put a downer on the ratings.'

God in Heaven: how do you deal with people like this?

Filling the conspicuous silence that followed Colin's ultimatum, my gasp aside, I observed in what I thought was a neutral way, 'It'll leave quite a big hole to fill.' Code for *You're off your rocker.*

'That's what you're all here for,' Colin replied. 'To discuss what takes its place.'

Estelle, part of Colin's praetorian guard, keeps her own counsel next to her boss; Roger scratches his head, his world-weary side in the ascendant; Louise shoots a quick look at me, which I want to believe is empathic; production manager Steve seems nonplussed; Terry, heading the operational wing of the *Fandango* will adapt to whatever's decided with cheerful fatalism; and Script Ed is, well, Script Ed.

Have I become an accessory to the Colonel's balmy Beatles excision by not resisting it? I desperately need an ally, but I don't think it's coming from this soggy ensemble.

BAM! Straight out of a Batman comic the door opens loudly and our caped crusader – well, he's wearing a grey sweatshirt with a large collar and a short zip – Ricky arrives. 'Sorry I'm late – or I would be sorry and would have been late if I was expected.' Oops. 'I heard you wanted to ditch the Fabs, or their soundalikes? That can't work, Colin.'

Golly. Angels come in strange guises.

Ricky went on, 'Punters won't take kindly to airbrushing George out of the picture. It'll look mean-spirited.' That's something Ricky would know about. 'Plus, there's the Ed Sullivan connection – no other performers are linked with him in people's hearts like The Beatles. Worst case: poor George dies, we do a tribute. We should have that up our sleeves. Nate can write an alternative script.' Of course he can – just like that. 'If George lives, then we wish him well and have the feel-good factor. And make sure one or two of his songs are in the set.' Then Ricky's coup de grâce: 'If The Beatles go, I go.' He looked deadly serious.

This time there was a genuine gasp around the room. And I never had Ricky down as such a Fabs fan.

60

Corridor conversation
**Two hours later – Ed Sullivan Theater, Manhattan –
30 December 1999**

The best meetings take place in corridors. They're eyeball to
eyeball, aren't tied to an agenda and, above all, aren't
minuted. I was having a corridor conflab with Louise
between rehearsals.

'What's it like to be back, Nate?' It reminded me of
my dad's question every birthday: 'What's it like to be nine,
Nate?' Or ten, eleven, ... He stopped asking me at fifteen. It
was simultaneously both a daft and a philosophical question.
Plus it was a bit redundant since he'd been all those ages and
more before I was born. But responding to Louise, as with
Dad years earlier, I fielded it with good grace.

'It's ... emotional. Nothing can prepare you for it,' I
said. 'Other than having been here twenty-four hours before.'
Oh God – did that sound sarky? She smiled – I'd got away
with it. Louise had reapplied make-up since the tears in the
hotel lobby. As my dad would have said, the mascara had
'pulled out her eyes'. Sounds gross but he'd have been talking
as an artist, meaning the cosmetics had accentuated her eyes.

'You've heard about The Beatles compromise?'
asked Louise. 'Re George.'

I'd managed to park the horror of the attack and the
threat of its effect on the show away from the front of my
brain. How could there be a compromise? 'We just have half
the tribute group on?'

I got weary eye-rolling for that.

215

'Colin says if George makes it through the night we go ahead,' said Louise, matter-of-factly.

'Jeez.' The idea of it being an 'if'. 'I'll be lighting a candle anyway. Everything crossed.'

'Oh – and Nate: that, er, stuff we talked about in the hotel. Our ... bedroom arrangement. You won't ... tell anyone here, will you?' She coiled a few of her hairs round an index finger.

'No – of course not. I'll work it into my script but they'll never trace it back to—'

'Nate. I'm serious. Don't become one of those dicks in the biz who are never "off".'

I nearly pointed out I'm never 'on', but seeing her glare it would have gone down like a cup of cold sick. Plus, I knew she knew I knew she was talking figuratively.

Louise had a point – the chirpy cheeky chappie was a routine, like that of a frustrated performer. It was partly a desperate attempt to get noticed by her (with the emphasis on 'desperate'), but since the news about April it had another purpose: blotting out my latest identity crisis. If I was busy thinking about my next witty line to Lou, trying to sparkle like her hazels, I wasn't piecing together the messy jigsaw of my life. Distractions work a treat with a troubled mind.

'Promise me,' she underlined.

'I promise.' I was pretty good at keeping that kind of promise. The only time I'd failed was during The Breakdown – or as Mary might have called it, the breakthrough. Then, I'd betrayed confidences and blabbed things I shouldn't have.

The advantage of doing that while you're mad is no one takes you seriously.

61

nathan.daniels@connectright.co.uk – 30.12.1999

Hi Jane –

Or should I say 'Hi sis'?

I suppose the ball's in my court re a meet. Thanks for giving me the space (now) to work that out for myself.

You can't see it, but there's at least 5 mins between each line here. I've written sketches more quickly.

Elton John (strictly speaking, Bernie Taupin, his wordsmith) got it right about 'sorry'. Not the easiest word. But probably the right one here. Though in my rage I thought I was addressing someone else. In mitigation.

Is that someone – you/not you – still making a show about genealogy? And does that even matter?

Don't know how it fits round my millennial show but we must meet somehow. That's if I sense correctly you want to. I fly back on Sunday so I've really only got New Year's Day (Sat.) to meet up.

You said you're in Boston? So is meeting somewhere round there on the 1st a possibility?

Yours hopefully, N.

62

Studio rehearsal day three – dance
Ed Sullivan Theater, Manhattan – 30 December 1999

Back after the break and the studio goes into dance mode. Now you might think I had nothing to do with this, but who do you think writes the storyline for these sequences? I know that's a redundant question – lots of viewers think these kind of things 'happen'. If they think at all about a dance routine they would credit the dancers, and they might get as far as being aware there's a choreographer involved, but beyond that it's getting into subtleties for the casual viewer. It's possible to see that as the greatest compliment – that the performance is so smooth and natural it seems to have emerged, unbidden, into the ether. As if ...

Weeks ago, back in London at those endless pre-production meetings, others were floating ideas for dance themes like 'shared moments in history between London and New York', and the old George Bernard Shaw chestnut, 'two countries divided by a common language' (how was that going to work as a dance, by the way?). It was then that a certain N. Daniels came up with the idea of a three-pronged approach for the big millennial dance number: past, present and future. Okay – like the best ideas it's simple. And not original, either – I was inspired by Dickens' *A Christmas Carol* ('the Ghost of Christmas Past', etc.). But it gave the dance a natural three-act structure, was easy to grasp, and shouldn't outstay its welcome.

My shadowy secret is that with the Seventies TV variety shows I was brought up on I couldn't wait for the opening production number, invariably a group dance, to finish. It could be because I move like an arthritic penguin, but more likely it was because I wanted to jump-cut to hearing from my favourite friends on those shows: the words. I was far more at home with the sketches and banter between guests than the physical spills and thrills of shimmies and twists; they left me cold. So to finally find in my thirties a marriage between my best friends and those moves feels like a result.

The next question was how to represent those two boundless epochs, past and future, and the transient filling in the sandwich, the present moment? I stopped short of suggesting, say, crumbling back-to-back housing as a backdrop to the historical element, with oppressive working conditions in Blake's 'dark Satanic Mills' – we have to keep our eye on the light-entertainment ball. Human beings cannot bear too much reality. So was there a way to encapsulate the second millennium post-Christ?

With a bit of digging, it turns out 1000AD in Europe is sometimes considered the border between the Early Middle Ages and the High Middle Ages. Cue me writing a gag in the introduction for Ricky about his being in early middle age. We somehow had to get to the more relatable twentieth century we're all in, but I noted that a discovery by a certain Christopher Columbus was virtually bang in the middle of the second Christian millennium; he was, of course, sailing that ocean blue in 1492. Given that we were in the land of the Pilgrims' arrival, that had to be one of the pegs to hang the dance on.

Further research suggested one school of thought is that globalisation began in the late 1970s; another, that it began around 1500. The latter is much more fun and suited to our purposes, handily fitting in with Columbus's discovery. But there's yet another view which places the beginnings of globalisation at the start of the second millennium.

I have half an inch to move in in which to find humour, get the facts right – or at least monkey with them in a way which is obvious – and to not frighten horses, upset history teachers, Christians, Muslims (the latter were in their Golden Age), and adherents to all other faiths and none. It's like trying to escape a straitjacket without wriggling.

I'm always amazed popular TV is ever popular.

So on come the dancing girls and boys. They're the usual array of ne'er-do-wells and misfits (I mean that as a compliment), joking and laughing, and stretching to stay on that optimal physical peak – warmed up and ready to rock. With a 'positions please' from Steve, they were off for another of those TV stagger-throughs. Too aptly named, as it turns out.

Music came off tape for early rehearsals; the live band would only appear for the dress run and the show proper for cost reasons. In the absence of musicians, we hear a keyboard cover of Robbie Williams' 'Millennium' – yes, we took it out of our back pocket. It's arranged, played and recorded for rehearsal by the musical director Ken Storey. Sure, thematically it's a little safe, but then mainstream entertainment is not in the business of alienating large chunks of its audience. Besides, the song made number one in the UK – Robbie's first – and dented the Mainstream Top 40 in the US. I defend the use of the song to myself and anyone who'll listen by saying the creativity is in what we're doing with it: tying it to a whirlwind comedy history of the millennium which is a day and a half from ending, complete with a nod to the present and a tease around the future. And it's only one of a number of songs in this sequence. To me it's like Art of Noise wanting to do avant-garde things in the pop song 'Close to the Edit', such as sampling the sound of a car engine starting. Rather than make everything in the song equally experimental, they built it on the familiar chassis of the twelve-bar blues. Horses calmed, edginess incremental, and – *voilà!* – a hit chalked up.

So the dancers move to the music – actually, they're miming digging and planting and are dressed as farm workers. Yes, I've smuggled an agricultural history lesson into prime-time TV! And the kicker is, I won the battle to include a comedic narration by one Ricky Ryan. I agonised over whether a picture really could tell a thousand words, or whether a thousand years of history needed words and pictures, especially in the pursuit of laughs. It felt for a moment like a defeat for the visual part of the medium, but then I chose to see it more as a victory for those small packets of meaning, Wittgenstein's little helpers, my best chums since childhood: words.

A mention for the choreographer, without whom ... Aiysha Hope, who has a CV as long as her legs, and has created award-winning work for stage and screen. She's African American and known to be particularly good at bringing abstract ideas to life in an accessible way, so she's perfect for this. I'm in constant wonder at the skills both she and her fellow hoofers bring to their work; it probably comes from a wellspring of envy on my part, lacking as I do a strong interface with the physical world. I observe them, anthropologically, as a subculture: obviously tactile, tending to be socially liberal and, unsurprisingly, at ease with their bodies. But while the rest of us dig deep into the denial of death, dancers seem keenly aware the clock's ticking for them professionally as it is, say, for footballers, with both groups likely to have to make major career changes in their thirties. Perhaps that awareness feeds the intensity of dancers' performances: you're only as good as your last pirouette.

Ricky's happy to do the narration live on the night, which is good because he can then tweak timing and intonation in sympathy with how it's going down with the audience in the room. But for reasons best known to himself he doesn't show for this rehearsal, so FM Steve reads for him in a stilted way, which annoys me. A rehearsal's either worth doing with full commitment – and, ideally, the full cast – or it shouldn't take place at all. Sadly, it's an agreed concession to the star that they're routinely excused the rigours of rehearsal we mortals have to go through. So they have the least preparation for a performance on which most hangs. In short, stars show up last, get the most money, and bugger off first. If they get away with it, as Ricky consistently and miraculously does, we mystify it by calling it 'star quality'.

We stagger on, then, rehearsing the dance number, through gags – consistently killed by Steve, of course – relating to significant milestones through the ages, like the invention of the ambulance (a creature of the Crusades), the rocket, and buttons (the latter two from the thirteenth century). Then we move to the printing press (1439) and on to Columbus's critical cruise. You'll forgive us for devoting quite a bit of energy to this latter event given our location, and the fact the show is being carried on the west side of the Atlantic as well as in the UK. We've combined Columbus's three ships – the *Pinta*, *Niña*, and *Santa Maria* – into one. Aiysha does us proud with a figurative representation of the ship – half the dancers form the shape of the vessel and, initially defying all physical limitations, manage to roll smoothly along the raised stage area while the others, employing a trick of perspective, mime being on board. It's not lost on Aiysha, as I know from previous conversations, that she's choreographed a white-leaning history, but as she said to me in a quieter moment with a smile, 'You pick your battleships.'

One dancer's physical limitations do become a bit too apparent in the first camera rehearsal, though: one of the young guys who goes by the riotously showbiz name of Heaven got a bit carried away as the lead at the bow of the ship. He rotated a little too fast, lost his orientation, fell off the riser – the raised part of the stage – and his roll was only stopped when he made contact with his head on the base of a camera pedestal. Of course everything's paused, he's given first aid, the camera operator seems as shaken as Heaven, and Steve encourages us all to take a fifteen-minute break. Aiysha works on as she's got to hurriedly rechoreograph this section.

So much for the stagger-through.

63

Assault

EXT. WOODS – TWILIGHT

This is shot with a handheld Technicolor look suggesting the 1940s or 1950s. We are in some woods on a cloudless evening. The trees have partial leaf growth hinting at springtime. We see over the shoulder of a MAN to a fearful looking late-teens young woman.

MAN

Go on – you'll like it. It's our way of showing God's love to each other. Come on. It won't take long. You wouldn't want to disobey God, now, would you?

YOUNG WOMAN

(quietly, nervously)

It's not right. I don't—

MAN

Stop teasing me like the Devil. Like a little temptress. A little fucking temptress. You put me up to this. Just do what I say and you won't get hurt.

We see from over his shoulder the man grab the young woman and push her down.

YOUNG WOMAN

(anguished screams)

No! No! Help!

The camera pushes into the man's back till his dark clothing fills the frame.

FADE TO BLACK

64

Hotel bedroom – night
Next-to-Lex Hotel, Manhattan – 30 December 1999

'You know the deal, Nate. I'm knackered and we've all got the biggest day of our working lives tomorrow. With a stupidly early start.' Louise sat on the end of her hotel bed and pulled off her boots. 'I've stopped you wandering the streets. So let me sleep. Please?'

It was an interesting deal. A kind of floorspace-for-peace deal. An inverse John and Yoko 'Bed-in for Peace'. More an out-of-bed experience – for me, at least, a few feet from Louise's bed lying on cushions on the floor. They were taken from a sofa in the room, and Louise donated a pillow she hadn't needed from her bed. She also gave me a spare blanket. We'd had the 'We'd make lousy lovers, Nate' conversation earlier. When I'd asked why she said, ''Cos we have to work together.'

'So did Liz Taylor and Richard Burton,' I offered. There'd been a pause.

'I think you're making my point for me.'

Damn. Rotten example.

And now Louise carried on undressing matter-of-factly in the hotel room's dim light. In trying not to look at her, I caught her out of the corner of my eye. Oh my God she's wearing a lacy black bra. I quickly removed myself to the en suite to avoid embarrassing both of us, bidding her goodnight. If this was my Gandhi-esque celibacy test I'd already lost a few marks for arousal.

I couldn't pee, naturally, so I had to make some perfunctory noise with the taps in the basin and bide my time.

The beige tiles by the bath and constellation of warm ceiling lights would have been restful in another situation. I made a mental note of the arrangement of the shower over the bath. If only they could standardise the controls for water flow and temperature for every shower, you'd know which was which without scalding or freezing yourself first.

She must be in bed by now, I thought.

I tiptoed back into the main room. Ironically, I now realised I both could and needed to have a piss. The window of operability might be short. So I tiptoed straight back into the bathroom. I tried to make the tap noise sound different, to cover my previous deceitful use, in case Louise was still awake. If she'd heard my previous tap operations but without the urine outflow sound she might retrospectively reappraise my first entry into the bathroom as, say, the sound of me running the tap to try and get a mark out of my jumper, or some such. The danger for me of that is she might then question why I wouldn't combine urinating (followed, obviously, by handwashing), with jumper-stain removal in one bathroom visit. I decided if she raised the issue, so to speak, in the morning I would have to be honest; ultimately, it doesn't reflect too badly on either of us. Although of the two of us, thinking about it, I come off as slightly more juvenile, and less in control of myself.

Do other guys have these problems? Or trains of thought?

Hands washed – for real, this time – and dried, I re-emerged into the bedroom. The light was now off but stray light from around the curtains guided me to my cushions. Louise seemed to be breathing more slowly and deeply, suggesting she was asleep. 'Are you okay?' she asks quietly. Bugger. Not only is she not asleep, her question implies she's not buying the 'mark on the jumper' version of events.

'Fine, thanks,' I say. 'Just getting used to the plumbing arrangements.' What the hell did that mean? Jeez. Outside, the city was no more asleep than she was. I turned my back to the bed in case Lou could see I was getting engorged again. I'd never heard her voice so sotto and sexy before. And this setting and her closeness were making things worse. Or better.

No, worse.

I stripped off down to T-shirt and boxers, set my alarm on the phone and lay down with my back on the cushions, head on the pillow, and pulled the blanket over me. My feet were facing the window overlooking 55th Street, meaning I was in the same orientation as Louise. It felt wrong for both of us to be lying the same way round with our two bodies parallel, if a few feet apart – not least because I was closer to her breathing and couldn't un-hear it. So after a couple of minutes I got up and turned around, moving the pillow with me. Now my head was closer to the traffic and paid the price.

Big day tomorrow. Not so much the stress on me as on my words.

65

Therapy part three: discovery
Thornton Heath, south London – 5 October 1999

'If you can, tell me about the moment of discovery. When you found your mother.' Mary wore her most solemn expression yet. She also wore sober clothes, a charcoal blouse with a gold broach, a pleated black skirt. Her greying hair was in a bun. (Think I preferred it dyed.) I surmised she'd been to a formal conference, perhaps as a speaker. She sat still in her chair which could rotate, reminding me of our family-doctor's chair. As antique as the pipe he used to stoke while listening to my mother's trauma when I was young. Tough gig for Mary: imagine empathy was your day job. Who can be that compassionate, client after client?

'I have relived it – replayed it – a thousand times. But here we go again. One more time.' I sought to sound factual, not embittered. Deep breath.

'Thank you.' The oddity, and the generosity, of being thanked for adding to Mary's workload.

'I replay it as a movie now.' I looked at my fingernails. 'Mum always said I had a photographic memory. She might as well have said I had a cinematic memory.' I looked up at Mary. 'Perhaps that puts the pain at one remove – seeing everything through a lens.' I was half asking, half stating. Conjecturing.

Mary left those questions hanging.

'I came home from school one November afternoon. I was fifteen. It must have been the last knockings of dusk. Mounted the stairs. And this is where I see over my own shoulder, as if through the camera. The door to my parents' room is open. I see – or the camera sees – my mother, motionless, on the bed. She's propped up on her right hand. There's a strange green quality to her complexion. I don't know why. If anything there should be a hint of the orange of the sodium light outside the window. The curtains are still open. Why would she bother to close them, thinking ahead? It was probably full daylight as she swallowed the pills.'

Mary gave the subtlest of nods.

'There were a few stray, whiteish pills left. On the bedside table. I don't know how many she'd taken. By then things were kicking off. The phone rang: Dad. "Was she breathing?" I felt so foolish saying I'd have to check. Shouldn't that be the most obvious thing to have done?'

'That sounds very self-critical, Nate.' Mary seemed to be wringing her hands. 'You need to cut yourself some slack or this could haunt you forever. Beating yourself up is toxic.'

'I know, I know.' Yet part of me doesn't know. Like an anorexic person staring in the mirror and seeing someone overweight. 'Then the timeline gets shaky. Whether before or after Dad's phone call – or between a first and second call from him at work – Doreen from over the road arrives, all breezy, bless her: "Put your shoes on Nate we'll go to the hospital." I make the motion as if to put my shoes on then another friend arrives. I must have phoned her before or after phoning the ambulance, I don't know. She says to Doreen there's fluid dripping from my mother's nose, and I know that's code for, *She's dead.* Confirming what I already knew deep down. A manic, tragic tableau seen from above. Then the ambulance arrives and they give their verdict. I'm downstairs, shoes half on. I take them off again. Everyone is doing their best ...'

'And that includes you,' adds Mary.

'Oh – and I forgot. The note. Can't remember word for word, but it said something like, "If they bring me round take Nate to see me." And something about wanting depression to be seen as a chronic condition. And about Dad going to his mum's – she was still alive then. But the word that stuck out was "zombie" – she said she hated dying like one.'

The grandfather-clock's tick in the hall moved to the foreground with the hour's chime. 'You're doing well, Nate – confronting your darkest experience.' Mary offered a soft smile.

I wanted to imagine she had limitless reserves of patience and goodwill, the ideal parent every child would want. The slight complication being I was an adult, of course. I fought the urge to be helpless, hopeless, to curl up into a ball and be nurtured.

You've got to grow up sometime.

66

Hotel bedroom – night part two
Next-to-Lex Hotel, Manhattan – 30 December 1999

Need to distract from Lou's breathing. Think, think.

Distraction technique. What to worry about first: work, or April?

Think about tomorrow. And tomorrow. And tomorrow.

Last-minute script tweaks. Will the sketch take the strain? And if I change anything, will that throw the actors – learning new lines at the last minute? Ricky's tied to the prompter – he doesn't learn lines. Don't think the white stuff's helped that side of things – he says his memory's shot. At least he'll read what he's given, albeit with the acting prowess of an ironing board.

But will it satisfy the Colonel?

Oh God. *If it be Thy will – take this cup of suffering away from me.*

Fat sodding chance.

I've sweated blood over this script. The show – and, by extension, the script – will no doubt get crucified by the critics. But Saint Patrick, Paddy, no, Ricky can take the heat. Thank fuck for fame.

Work anxiety quieted I briefly slip away in this Garden of Gethsemane into the hoped-for solace of sleep. In a grainy dream a lighted Catherine wheel, named after an early Christian martyr, starts turning and picking up speed, shooting sparks and spinning ever faster. The sparks then become words spewing randomly at all angles and I start to recognise them as coming from my script. They're all the right words but now necessarily not in the right order.

I wake with a start, briefly relieved I haven't got to gather up the words to reorder them.

Now what?

Breathe in, breathe out ... Louise turns over with a subtle sigh. The city that never sleeps continues its insomniac life. A group of merry premillennial revellers loudly see in the eve of the big day, walking past at processional pace four floors below.

Think April, June. No, Jane: my new sister.

What a phrase, 'new sister'. Okay – half-sister. Sis.

I need to talk to her again. April. Jane. The missing link. It's a head-mangler, suddenly not being an only child after decades.

So if Jane is the last piece of the puzzle, where in God's name does she fit in?

Mum said, 'I can't forgive myself for what I've done.' But her crime seems to have been to bring life, April, into the world, not take it away ... not until her own sad demise. Victim blaming. 'So many chapters left unfinished', as her gravestone reads. Dad's words. Dad knew the weight of words, etched in marble. Mum's gravestone is in the shape of a book. It had a beginning and an end. She bequeathed me this riddle, this April riddle in the middle.

Think positive.

Remember Mum well, not ill. I remember her well. We will remember them. Lift up your hearts. We lift them up unto the Lord. Prayer – response – prayer ... Tension, release. World without end. Amen. Amen.

Amenuensis. Amanuensis. Amaninhavana. Amin. Amas. Amae. Aman. Ama.

I count words instead of sheep. I only hope the words can be herded.

67

Therapy part four: 'I Know Where I'm Going'
Thornton Heath, south London – 12 October 1999

'We sat on the sofa once – Mum and me – to watch a film she was in.' It felt like I'd gone down a memory rabbit hole with Mary. If she felt it too, she hid it well with the sheen of a professional listener. She was back to the grey camo combat fatigues. The grandfather clock provided a sotto but steady heartbeat downstairs. 'She was only an extra, but the world of film was exotic to me as an eleven-year-old. It was pretty exotic to Mum, too, who'd been about the same age during the filming. The exterior of her school – Harrow Grammar School for Girls – was chosen for the opening of a movie by Powell and Pressburger – the Coen brothers of their day. The picture was *I Know Where I'm Going*. She marvelled how they were shooting for a whole day just to get a crowd of kids, herself included, pouring out of the school gates, presumably embracing their futures. The scene was over in seconds. But to watch it together it was one of those mother-son bonding sessions, I guess. The building blocks of shared moments.'

'It's good you remember it as life-affirming, Nate.'

'I sometimes wonder if she was really allowed – allowed herself – to "enjoy" me. There were too many threats, storm clouds gathering, hovering all the time. I mean, Mum was only seven when the war started. The next year her mother stopped her going to ballet lessons as it was too dangerous. Imagine that. Then Mum lost a friend to an oil bomb in the Blitz. And a few years after the war she lost a friend in the Harrow train crash. Her card was marked.'

'She certainly had to contend with a lot. That generation did – but then your mother seems to have been unlucky on top of the shared pain.' Mary's brow was furrowed.

'Then I arrived.' I hadn't meant a comic juxtaposition, but thought I'd exploit it. 'As if she hadn't suffered enough.'

Mary tends to err on the side of seriousness, but she relaxed for a second.

'No one arrives with a clean sheet, do they?' I went on. 'Like when you're born, it might seem you can be anything, do anything, but you're hemmed in by everyone's limitations around you. And your family's situation – if you've got a family. What did the Bard say? "The thousand natural shocks that flesh is heir to." You inherit those whether you like it or not.' The case of *Daniels* v. *Life* continues.

'Are we having an intellectual discussion, Nate? I'm interested in your feelings in all this.' Mary had me bang to rights: if I wanted to weigh these things up academically I could join a debating society.

'Sorry. It makes me so bloody sad.'

'And angry?' Her gaze locked on to mine like a heat-seeker.

I squirmed. Why are all therapists obsessed with anger? Is it a projection of their own rage?

'Sometimes therapists can appear to be saying contradictory things to different clients. Some clients need to dial down their anger.' Mary touched her nose for a second, like an experienced bidder at an auction. 'But I sensed that you needed to *find* yours – in the jargon, to be "in touch" with your anger.'

'The thing is, it exhausts me. I don't find anger an energising life force – it's a pain in the arse.'

'Perhaps you need to take a more positive view of it, Nate.' Mary laid her hands serenely in her lap.

I took a moment to absorb the painting of a poppy over her shoulder. A thin, light-coloured wooden frame encased a white mount around the picture proper. So many poppy associations. Blood red, ephemera, war, delicate beauty. Heroin.

Mary leaned in subtly. 'Where've you gone to?'

I couldn't say, 'To the killing fields of Afghanistan.' So I said, 'The poppy on your wall. It's the right colour for anger. Red mist – red with rage ...'

'The thing is not to see red ...' She smiled at her misstep. 'I mean, in a picture. The challenge is to see the anger in ourselves and to express it in civilised ways.'

'Knocking seven bells out of a punchbag at the gym, you mean?' I needed a real-world example.

'That's one way. Another is more domestic and workaday – hitting one pillow against another on your bed. Sounds silly but can be effective.' Mary made the humdrum sublime.

'Okay.'

'Just mind you don't hit the table lamps!' she said with a rare laugh.

That session was illuminating.

68

Bevan's baby
Psychiatric Unit, Watford General Hospital – January 1983

I'm trying to get off to sleep in my own room. An afternoon nap. The apricot blanket would be cheery if it wasn't standard issue to every room in the psychiatric unit. That and every wall slapped with melancholia magnolia. Plus we all get a bedside table with a cupboardy bit for our personal effects. Strange term, 'effects'. (And what are impersonal effects?) Is the bedside table a gift from Nye Bevan, father of the health service? Bevan's bedside bonanza. A little bit of luxury to take the edge off the meds.

Still, the mini locker at the bottom of the unit doesn't prevent stuff from getting nicked. A few friends bought me what my English teacher would have called 'a sizeable bar of chocolate' (of the sort she awarded me and classmate Neville for producing the best pretend newspaper in the class). Maybe the very size of this hospitalised chocolate made it more desirable and more nickable. I say 'hospitalised', but was it discharged that day or was the crime an inside job and the choc stayed – and was consumed – on-site? I should set up an identity parade of suspects. Only a few people knew about the existence of the confectionery so the parade would be short. Or was it a random theft – empty room/nobody about/fishing expedition to see if anything worth having? And so should the parade be widened to all those who could have had access to my room (not locked like the one at the asylum)? That could be a massive number. It would have to include cleaners, nurses, , doctors, patients, maintenance people. And visitors. Maybe it was stolen back by the mates who brought it. They had the knowledge, the motive and the opportunity. Bastards.

Strange you're rewarded with your own room here just as you go a bit saner. On a clear day you can see the car park. At least I don't have to hear the stories of holiday excess from the trainee gas engineer like I did on the ward. Less a ward, more a ditsy dormitory. There's no justice. He's on a hundred quid a week telling us his dad calls him a cunt and there's me with a loving father on six quid a week in-hospital benefit. Here's that sick squid I owe you. An old joke I can't remember the build-up to. There's a lot I can't remember.

Like how I ended up with a drawing in my room from an old school friend. Or why he depicts the world the way he does. It's all haunted-Munch's *The Scream* faces clashed with, I dunno, spindly art or whatever you'd call it. Weird, disturbing images of a broadcaster connected via an old gramophone needle and a cable directly to the world. (Inspired by me in voluntary radio.) But the DJ has a hawk's head and spooky eyes and a skinny body. If you could call it a body. And all in black pen and ink on white cartridge paper. My shrink Dr Samuels showed an uncommon interest in it on his ward round today. I thought he was going to ask me to get my mate Ewan, who drew it, committed. Or to commission a work from him for his office at the hospital. It was art as a cry for help. Seems touch-and-go with some of my friends why I should end up inside and they stay on the outside. It's said Ewan comes from a dysfunctional family. Is there any other sort? He has issues with his dad. Deffo.

So this day I'm in my room and there's a strange disembodied sound. Not a cry and certainly not a laugh. More a keening – like a wolf howling atop a hill. First, I have to check it's not inside my head. I rule that out – when I turn my head it doesn't move with me. Then I establish it's from outside my room. Maybe the corridor? My door leads immediately on to that, so I pop my head out but it's not there. It's coming from the women's dorm to the left. I skulk along the left-hand wall from my door to the edge of the dorm's doorway so as to not be too obvious. The door's open and through it I recognise Magda from the community meetings. She has long, mostly dark, wiry hair streaked with a brilliant white. Her knitted cardigan's also white but with pink bobbles above the bustline, and she's wearing a white top underneath. Clasped with a black plastic belt she's got a pleated non-matching red tartan skirt. Her surname's Mc-something but she's not Scottish, she's Canadian. She sounds American to me when she's talking in the meetings – she has a drawl that barely leaves her mouth and she doesn't make eye contact with anyone as she speaks. Here she's pacing up and down while emitting this strange noise. She doesn't clock me, but Sue from the Fabs does – she was trying to nap, too – and she comes over, flitting her eye between me and Magda.

'What are you doing here?' whispers Sue. 'You know it's a woman's ward.' Her ever-stressed forehead looked like it was buckling under years of being ruched.

'Yeah, but I wondered what the noise was.'

Sue beckoned me to the empty nurses' station outside my room and spoke a bit more normally. 'Magda's had a letter from her daughter. Evelyn. She's not coming to visit after all.' Ah, this is the daughter left behind in Canada. Montreal, or thereabouts. Not a young girl but late teens, I think. Big old place, Canada. And a long way from Watford. 'She's devastated.' Sue would know pretty much what that feels like, having lost access to her son, her little angel. Though he's only five, or was when he was taken from her.

A memory of Dr Samuels' line about 'so many disturbed women' drifts across my brain. Parenthood looks like hard work; being deprived access to a child seems worse. Don't want my future kids visiting me in the loony bin. Or taken away.

Think I'll give having kids a miss.

69

The Open Suitcase: a Play

I come from a long line of performers. At the height of her yearly distress, Mum would theatrically lay an open suitcase on the floor of the bedroom she shared with Dad and put items in it, one by one. It was all for the coming day when she would leave him as a punishment for his supposed crimes and inadequacies, his sins of commission and omission.

Except that day never came.

She got as far as finding a boarding house in west Watford, an address with which to taunt Dad (who bore it with a mix of good humour, resignation, and despair), but she never occupied it. I could imagine the situation as a one-woman play, *The Open Suitcase*, garnering rave reviews from a world of disenchanted housewives. But would it have a satisfactory ending? Mum got better and the suitcase was returned to the wardrobe, only to reappear for the next year's anguish. Case closed. Or perhaps, as Mum was half-Scottish, case not proven.

The case against my Dad was certainly suspect. It was a proxy for my mother's inner war, she acting out, as they say, rather than resolving internal conflicts. And casting him as the Bad Guy was never going to fly: he was a sweetie. Out of his depth, like the rest of us, like society at that time, but definitely not a pantomime villain. So they were doomed to play this uneven two-hander, she acting opposite the wrong guy, he desperately trying to do the right thing, and in that very process managing to do the wrong thing. Trying not to rock the boat, yet the boat was rocking anyway, and being a neutral actor wasn't going to steady it. I guess he has to be an off-stage character in this one-woman play, and it's for the audience to deduce that the on-stage character – let's call her Barbara – is a classic unreliable narrator.

But how does this drama end? I don't mean the one where the protagonist is propped up on her right hand, an empty pill bottle beside her. I mean our adaptation as a one-woman play. Does our leading lady see through her own conceit, the scales falling from her eyes: she's only trying to run from herself? Or is there some outside intervention, from a health professional or otherwise, which forces a dénouement? The audience expects to go away with some satisfaction, some resolution. This is not the messy stuff of real life, with unpalatably tragic endings. The ticket buyers need some takeaway to quaff port over in the large-mirrored salons near the theatre afterwards: 'I think the auteur was trying to show compassion for a woman's lot whilst apportioning blame to no one.' Or perhaps we go for the fringe, a sweaty room above a pub with a rent-a-gob slugging real ale while rolling a ciggie. 'I reckon it's all about female emancipation – women's lib, they used to call it. An urgent cry to put the female centre stage – literally – and release her from her chains.' Cut back to the bourgie salon and our public-school slimeball is warming to his theme: 'I think the suitcase is a metaphor for escape, the longing for an alternative existence.'

Metaphor it might be, but it's still an effing suitcase. Beaten up, a knackered off-white, its faux leather cracking through years of use and mishandling. It bore the legend 'Mrs Daniels' in biro, inscribed by a receptionist or nurse checking her into the local psychiatric institution. I was four or five when I was first aware of the suitcase filling up with clothes by the day. Later I learned it was also packed with unfulfilled promise.

70

jane.butterworth@altavista.com – 1999.12.30

Hi Nathan -Bro!

Thanks for your message. Would LOVE to meet up!! Genealogy? Yes & no. I"m interested in yours (ours) for sure, but there's no TV show. i'm a speech therapsit. [I guessed she wasn't a proofreader.] I found you via marital reocrds on the net, More when we meet. (LOVE that phrase). I live in Boston but am on vacation is Cape Cod. Will think where we could meet. Ciao for now

    Jane x(April)

71

Show day – morning
Ed Sullivan Theater, Manhattan – 31 December 1999

Louise looks like she's in shock. I know she might be sleep-deprived but this is something else.

It's the morning of show day in the production office and photocopiers and printers are doing their thing, phones are ringing and being answered, researchers are picking up clipboards and headsets, and there's a constant flow of traffic in and out of the two doors of this open-plan space. Yet all is not well with the kingdom. I become aware of a raised but oddly muted voice in some hard-to-place area, which I eventually locate as the Colonel's domain. It's a transparent box at one end of the office. It's been likened to the glass coffin of yore, but this one contains no beauty, sleeping or otherwise, although there are plenty of curses emanating from there.

'Ricky's done a runner,' Louise says plaintively, standing by her desk, three rows back from the Colonel's dugout. Ah – haunted look accounted for. She seems suddenly fragile in her pastel blue turtle neck and black trousers.

I surprise myself by not panicking. Is that because I feel there's some straightforward explanation, or he can't have gone far and/or be gone long, or is it I simply haven't got the energy to fret? I could have done with more than the few hours' restive sleep I got last night. Perhaps I'm in denial. It's too colossal to absorb. No wonder the Colonel's voice is raised. I ask what I think is a reasonable question. 'How do we know he's not just late for work?'

'He's not late for work. He's not due in till this afternoon.' Of course – for the dress run. 'But Jacqui said he didn't go back to their room last night, and this morning she found a note from him saying sorry for letting everyone down.'

Cripes. I'm starting to find the energy to panic. I lower the zip on my charcoal sweater. 'So what's the action plan, Lou?'

'Colin's been on the phone to Ricky's agent, Mike. That's gone nowhere. Now he's trying to find a backup presenter.'

'Backup? Bloody hell. But it's *Ricky Ryan's Millennial Special* ...' The clue is in the title.

'We can't take the risk. We've got hours of live TV to fill.' Louise sounded borderline tearful.

'Sure, sure.' If only the network, instead of taking away half an hour, had taken away four hours.

'You haven't got any ideas, have you? Where he might be? You're his mate.' Louise touched my wrist lightly. Electricity shot through me.

'Mate' is a debatable term, I thought. And do I spill the beans about Paddy's fondness for the white stuff? Would be harder to keep a lid on it, so to speak. But was that even relevant to his disappearance? Then I remembered that freaky conversation. 'Before I came back to the show – after he booted me off – we spoke on the phone. He mentioned The Men ...'

'Men?' Louise's brow was etched with stress.

'It was a thing we made up as kids. Pretend people who lived under rocks.'

'I haven't got time for stories, Nate.' Louise ran her fingers spread like a coarse comb through her hair.

'All I mean is it might be a clue. To where he's gone.' I didn't quite know myself what I meant, but Louise's forehead relaxed for a moment, which was probably the point.

Or had Paddy followed through on his 'If they go, I go' threat about The Beatles act? Please God, no; given Colin's compromise of keeping the tribute band on the show if George survived the night, that would mean Paddy had heard Harrison had died.

I quickly asked a keen-as-mustard researcher sitting at his desk to check *The Guardian's* website wasn't flashing the next Beatles death. A fresh-faced graduate – think Dustin Hoffman as believably young – turned from his PC screen and gave the glad tidings. Phew. Thank the Lord. Then Hoffman Jr. picked up a copy of *The New York Times* next to him. From it he read, 'Harrison said his attacker wasn't auditioning for the Traveling Wilburys.' Sounds like 'the quiet Beatle' isn't falling silent any time soon. Or turning humourless.

Minutes later I was on the phone to Jacqui; Louise had given me her number. I'd found a discreet corridor in the theatre where I could call her on my mobile, undisturbed. 'Apart from the note, was there anything Ricky gave away – clues to where he was going?' I asked. Jacqui always used Paddy's stage name. Had she fallen for the star, not the man? The analysis would have to wait.

'He said he wanted to get away from it all. All the noise. He has not even taken his phone.' Jacqui's endearing French accent added to her mystique. I pictured her black bouffant and highly-coloured eye shadow flashing as she blinked with concentration.

'Has he done this before? Is there somewhere he goes at times like these?'

'He sometimes goes to art galleries to clear his head. Or somewhere in the nature ...' I resisted an image of a naked Paddy. Jacqui meant well, but on a landmass of over three million square miles holding 280 million people she hadn't narrowed the search much.

I had a thought, though: could she see if the hotel had recorded any unusual requests – say, a different newspaper, or had Ricky made any calls from the room's landline?

'You want me to flag up he's not here? The news could get out.'

I could almost see the Gallic shrug. 'Fair point,' I conceded. But my dad was a great believer you had to ask a silly question en route to a sensible answer.

'I suppose I could see if I can trace any spending on the credit card.' The thought seemed to cheer her.

I didn't know how far she'd get with that, but I didn't want to rule out any lines of enquiry. Hark at me: 'lines of enquiry'. I was becoming some two-bit rerun TV detective – Columbo meets Barlow.

The name's: Columbarlow.

72

Leaving the asylum
Napsbury Hospital, London Colney – October 1982

Time for another escape from Alcatraz. Third time lucky, I hope. The first go at leaving the asylum went a bit wonky, to be honest. Or never got off the ground. Remember that guy who said you could eat your way out? I had a weird dream about that, though waking hours are generally more weird than sleeping ones round here. I began nibbling at skirting boards in the dream and worked up to plaster board and sash windows. The wood was chewy and my tongue was spiked with splinters but I guess nothing you really want comes without pain. Not sure if that counts as an attempt as I wasn't awake, but since going sane, the firewall between dreams and what's laughably known as the real world has crumbled.

This window thing has come round again. My second go at escaping was when I was on the production line in the Rubber Room – pens and all. There was a high-up openable window where I went to the loo. I was on my own at last in a locked cubicle. For a mo it seemed too good to be true. I thought, Are they testing me? Like they'd have someone on sentry duty outside the window. Checking if I can resist temptation. After flushing I yanked myself up by the pipe which led up to the cistern. You gotta beat the cistern. It groaned a bit and started to pull away from the wall. That wasn't gonna matter though as I'd leave it all behind. Who cares if the fuckers got flooded?

I could leave in victory: 'Guy who revolutionised the nuthouse workplace breaks free'.

I managed to kneel on the deep windowsill and look out the glass. It was raining – I could see it on the evergreen leaves.

Then the knock at the door. It was nurse John. 'You okay in there, Nate?' I froze.

Damn.

Damn him and damn my cowardice. My hair's grazing the ceiling as I fiddle desperately with the handle. Yes this window's designed to open (the handle uselessly swings on its pivot) but it's also been nailed shut for years. 'I'm fine thanks, John.' Fuck.

Time for The Dunkirk Spirit – retreat in the face of adversity.

So now, two weeks later, attempt number three: I'm leaving with full military honours and a ticker-tape parade. Ish. It's not a full escape; since it's official this time, it's a discharge from the dark satanic asylum back to the psych unit of the general hospital. A nice social worker/doctor/nurse/occupational hazard with a tight blonde perm and a wide smile took me into the Big Boss's office at the psych hospital. She said to him what progress I'd made and could I now leave and he smiled and she said could I tell the Boss what progress I'd made and she made a play of encouraging me to say the right thing and so I said the right thing and he smiled and she smiled and I wasn't quite sure what game I was playing and which of us were actors.

Whatever it was, it did the trick. With three bounds I was free.

In my passing-out parade Bert the cleaner with the tight voice I cruelly mimicked told me it's now down to me to do the work to get better. Was he a psychiatrist in disguise? He was tall, grey, muscular and ancient – probably forties or even fifties – and I repeated him back but with the send-up tones of another Bert, Ernie's partner in the Muppets. Resisting the urge to deck me, cleaner Bert was standing in the entrance of the lounge, the morning light streaming through the tall bay windows catching the left side of his face.

He was leaning against his mop that he'd propped up in a red bucket with Charge Nurse Jo-Anne alongside him. 'Don't even think of coming back here, Nate,' she said. Her crisp white uniform gave her the air of an angel.

Angel air.

Behind them, snoozing in a chair, was Business Man Matt, the besuited middle-aged company guy: slicked-back red hair, oily skin, pouting expression. Because I thought he might use computers, I used to tell him, as I had been told in computing lessons, 'Don't leave dangling pointers.' The arcane code of computer science.

I felt the need to anoint Matt as I left so I said, as St Paul did in the Bible, with a rhythmic pulse, 'Awake O sleeper from the dead and Christ will give you light.' Far from taking up his pallet and walking, and thanking me for the enlightenment, he grumped: 'Aww – I was having such a good nap then, you sod. Piss off back to the General and stay there.'

73

Show day part two – Ricky intel
Ed Sullivan Theater, Manhattan – 31 December 1999

My little Nokia rings again – it's getting a lot of use recently. Could become habit-forming. Much of the office bubble seemed to be bouncing along with its own nervous energy, as if unaware there was a vacuum at its heart where the star performer should be.

It's Jacqui phoning with some progress. 'I've found out Ricky's hired a car. From Alamo.'

On any other day I might have thrown in a quick comeback about Texas, battles, reinforcements ... You could weep. Sadly, I knew she was referring to a car-hire company. 'Where did he pick it up?'

'Midtown – Broadway area. A blue Oldsmobile Aurora.'

Ah – a suitably grand sedan for the star. 'How do you know all this?'

Jacqui paused. 'I'll tell you later. I cannot discuss it over the phone.' Was that the famous mystique, or a bit of calculation? I let it go. 'But you haven't heard the worst of it yet.'

'Oh, Lord ...'

'The thing is he has hired it for a week.'

'A WEEK? Jeepers. He really doesn't want to do the show, does he?' I said. 'Any clues where he plans to go?'

'Nothing as yet. *Rien.* I will let you know as soon as I hear anything.'

'Yes – soon as. Please.' I looked at the office clock: 8.13am. In a few hours we'd have dipped into the last pm of this one thousand years. EST, of course. And it was already afternoon in my home city. Thank God for the extended lunch break to rest. If we all got that far.

Got to be time for coffee, I thought, mourning being away from my homely grinder and machine. I caught Louise's eye on the other side of the office. She looked under the cosh as she was on the phone, but smiled as I mimed coffee-bean grinding and pouring – the international sign language of caffeine addiction. I headed for the kitchen as the Nokia rang again. What now – wasn't even a coffee break sacrosanct?

'Hi, Nate – it's Jane.'

Lummy. 'Oh. Hi.' I'd reached the galley kitchen and was aware of other listeners. 'I've been meaning to call. Except we have a little local difficulty ...' Me and my mouth.

'Shoot. Anything you can talk about? Is this a bad time?'

'Yes and no. Well, no and yes. Don't go, though. How can I help? I mean – briefly.' Behold, the Master of the Mixed Message.

Jane chuckled. 'I was thinking it would be good to meet. We got kinda cut off last time – which was also our first time!' Very diplomatic. I'd put the phone down on her – literally. I placed it on the table as I absorbed the bombshell. She must have enjoyed a couple of minutes of the sound of a busy Big Apple diner before I said a fazed farewell.

'We should meet – definitely,' I agreed. 'I'm a bit tied up with the show, though, Jane ...'

'Sure. And I've got millennial drinks with friends tonight.'

'Then I fly back to London in a couple of days.' My brain was simultaneously trying to pour two coffees from the machine and compute scenarios with Paddy having the hire car for a week; did that mean delaying my return flight?

'Let's cut to the chase,' said Jane. 'How about tomorrow?'

Gulp. 'Um – why not?' I didn't have enough processing power to stall her. 'You're in Boston – is that right?'

'Cape Cod right now. But you're busy. I'll text you a couple ideas where we could meet. OK?'

Louise had entered the kitchen and was miming something inscrutable to me. She can't have been that much in a rush for her coffee? 'Er – fine,' I replied to Jane. 'Do text. [Yuck.] Listen – I've got to go. Bye – sorry – bye.'

If there's a facial expression for small talk Louise wasn't wearing it. She then uttered five of the most frightening words in the English language. 'Colin wants to see you.'

Kill me now.

'Was that Jacqui on the phone?'

'No – it was Jane.'

Louise looked puzzled.

'The genealogy woman,' I fleshed out, for want of a better term. 'Jacqui called earlier, though. Ricky's hired a car.' I thought I'd drip-feed the words 'for a week' later.

'Balls. Tell me more once you've seen Colin. I wouldn't keep him waiting.'

'Which of us would?' I said, handing Lou her coffee. I resigned myself to mine going cold.

74

Total eclipse part one
Falmouth, Cornwall – 11 August 1999

The last total solar eclipse of the millennium. It was only to
be visible in the UK in the south-west corner of England. I
was still with Sam, or 'wifey' as we'd both ironically referred
to her, especially in the early days of our marriage. Looking
back, the nickname was a way of distancing ourselves from
actually admitting we'd surrendered to this 'honourable
estate', as the Book of Common Prayer has it. Forever is a
long time. Over time the irony of the name decomposed into
sarcasm: Sam would begin sentences with 'Speaking as your
wifey ...', which she'd utter through clenched jaws. We
waited for someone to send in the clowns. Sam had chosen
to marry a kind of clown – I was already writing jokes for
Ricky on his Wednesday show for Irish TV when Sam and I
met in '95. I'd fax the opening monologue to Paddy on a
Monday. He'd circle bits he wasn't happy with, and I'd work
on them on Tuesday, as well pressing on with other material
– links, sketches, etc., as required. Wednesday was reserved
for last-minute tweaks and inserting topical gags: the latest
political pratfalls, pop-star infidelities, and sending up soap
storylines, preferably from rival networks.

With hindsight I should have read the runes on first
meeting Sam. She was a primary-school teacher in a deprived
London borough. We got chatting at a local art gallery for the
launch of a new exhibition centring on social realism in
photography; we'd been invited by mutual friends. Sam had
contributed a few shots of her kids on field trips and the like.
I showed interest in her photographs, and in the day job

which inspired them. When I told her about my work she laughed and said, 'Is that actually a job?' I forgave her dismissiveness at the time because of how sweetly she delivered it, and because of the way those piercing blue eyes looked up at me through her striking blonde fringe. To say nothing of her celestial body. The clincher was when she laughed again – this time on my terms – when I deadpanned, in answer to her question about my job, 'No – writing gags isn't a job. Thirty-seven monkeys bash away on typewriters for me till they come up with something funny.' Point made; dinner date agreed.

Cut to half a decade later: numerous contretemps weeks in advance of the eclipse over whether Sam would indulge my obsession with it and join me in Falmouth on that fateful day. I was baffled as to why, for her, it was worth the fight; if she didn't want to go, she didn't have to. Lord knows by then we were doing loads on our own. I could only rationalise it down to two reasons why she should make a fuss: either she really saw it as the last chance for our marriage, or she secretly shared a fascination for the event that dared not speak its name.

Because we'd ummed and ahhed for so long about whether to go, our options boiled down to a handful of B & Bs in the Cornish town. Far from speeding us up to secure an ever more scarce resource, this slowed us down, as we applied a forensic analysis of each one, arguing over the merits and demerits of each place's proximity to main roads and to the coastal common land we were going to use as our viewing point, and of the range of times breakfast would be served and what variety of options each establishment had for it. The narcissism of small menu differences. Whether a place served a continental breakfast and/or a full English vegetarian became a proxy for whether we had any compatibility left, and the signs weren't good.

Somehow, we were organised enough to slouch towards Falmouth from London the day before, check into a nondescript B & B by early evening, get up in time for an inoffensive breakfast the following day, and to get to the site, joining the crowds on the hill with a quarter of an hour to spare.

75

Mortification – 10am EST
Ed Sullivan Theater, Manhattan – 31 December 1999

I resisted the temptation to salute the Colonel. And I just suppressed an urge to click my heels. Plus, Script Ed was in attendance. Marvellous: I would be fighting a war on two fronts.

That Colin would have a glass box in the middle of the open-plan office was entirely appropriate; a hothouse in which he would cultivate his plants and have them twist towards the sun for their very existence. His nicknamesake, Elvis's manager Tom Parker, had his roots in fairgrounds as a barker who lost no sleep putting chickens on a hot plate to make them 'dance'. I was starting to feel the heat before sitting down, but I drew the line at dancing. Colin beckoned me to join Script Ed on a puce-coloured two-seater sofa.

The Colonel was in his high-backed black leather swivel chair looking down at Ed and me across an immaculate charcoal glass desk. His clipped tones were straight outta Sandhurst. 'Clearly we're up against the clock, Nathan – it's T-minus six hours.' Or in English, it was 10am local time; six hours from transmission. 'I would've loved to have flown in an established UK star, but we don't have time. This situation's far from perfect and we've got to improvise. If that shit Ricky can't fulfil his contract then I've found some local talent who can: it's not a name, but they're competent and they can read a bloody prompter. It's a local TV news magazine presenter, Morton Silus. He's a regular on the channel that's taking us in the States – NYTV. I've decided he's the kind of person we need at short notice: a no-

nonsense pro who won't get ruffled; he'll let the stars around him shine, he'll be sober and he'll turn up on time and fuck off home when he's finished.'

Script Ed shifted next to me on the retro sofa and piped up: 'You see, Nate, this guy doesn't do gags. Mort's more of a journalist.' Lest Ed should sound insubordinate next to his Lord and Master he added, 'I-I mean as Colin says he's perfectly competent. And he's got a little sparkle in his eye. He's not a humourless war reporter. He "gets" showbiz, but – er – from a discreet distance.'

'What Ed's trying to say is we need you to cut out the gags – they're not going to work. Silus won't have the timing or delivery. But we need everything else around him to pick up the slack and be funnier. Is that clear?'

As mud. 'Yes, of course,' said the survivor in me. Sure – I'll just snap my fingers and everything minus the presenter will be funnier. Why, I deliberately make scripts less funny than they could be for this sort of occasion.

I've been delivered my most impossible assignment ever, but I'm not alone; so has Ed and poor, tragic Mort.

Colin took off his glasses and leaned in as far as a desk the size of Sweden would allow. He looked suddenly fatigued, as if a career on the front line of multiple battles – with networks, artistes, agents, and the press – was catching up with him. The lines etched on his face were so deep they resembled trenches, and his tan, wiry hair was increasingly diluted with rebel white stragglers. These could only increase in number till they overran the incumbents and a truce would have to be declared. Unless he summoned the cavalry, bottle-hardened. But I felt he'd never say dye.

'What I need from you, Nathan,' the Colonel could be uncomfortable with the familiarity of shortened names, 'is a constant feed of script rewrites submitted to Edwin, who will then box them into some sort of shape ...' Charming. '...And pass them on to me. I suggest we simply start from the top and work our way through the show. That way if it's not all ready for the dress run, Nathan can work on through the rehearsal, and if he's not ready for the end of that we've still got the first part of the live show to catch up. That's why I've got an old trouper from live news to front this thing 'cos he'll be used to winging it. Make sense?'

'Sir yes sir!' I didn't say, but thought.

Script Ed managed a grunt of consent, but with the ease of someone signing their own death warrant. I fell into line with a quiet 'Sure' to appease the firing squad. But they would be standing by, guns cocked.

76

Total eclipse part two
Falmouth, Cornwall – 11 August 1999

Superficially, Sam and I were standing together on a patch of
grass in a place we didn't know miles from home with a load
of strangers gathering to see an absence of something for a
couple of minutes: light. But that would be to downplay the
experience. It was the first such eclipse in the UK for
decades, and the next one isn't due there until 2090. I don't
see myself schlepping to the Arctic for 2021 and, short of
stem-cell tech mastering immortality, I don't see myself
anywhere by 2090. So there was a certain unique intensity to
the morning of Wednesday, 11 August 1999.

I'm too urban an animal to have felt at one with the
druids who seemed to be congregating to our left. And not
quite urban enough to feel particularly comfortable wearing
my free heavily-tinted mirrored specs, courtesy of a special
souvenir book. But accepting mortality means accepting the
limitations of your eyesight in the face of a roaring fireball,
even if it is due to be dimmed shortly, so I overcame my
resistance to the specs and wore them with pride, or at least
not too much shame, and joined the throng looking
skywards. There was a burble of anticipation from the crowd.
Young, old, and middle-aged were gathered as if waiting for
the Sermon on the Mount, or a secular Second Coming.

I couldn't help looking at Sam to gauge whether she
shared my excitement. Her smile was equivocal. But more
than that I was struck by the fact that, with our mirrored
shades, I was looking at two reflections of myself. That seems
appropriate; being partnered with someone is like dating a

half-silvered mirror where, as well as your partner themselves, you see yourself reflected in them, for good and ill. No surprise, then, that splitting up with someone hurts, partly because you lose a part of yourself.

Sam and I were still theoretically still an item; she didn't hit the nuclear button until a few weeks later. But all the signs were there that this would be our final break together before the final break. It was in her language, tone, weariness with me, and in our physicality (or lack of) with each other, and had been for weeks, if not months. How much of this is using the perfect science of hindsight is a bit of a blur.

There we were duly gathered on a grassy knoll with hundreds of expectants, our worst fears about heavy cloud cover – which would have made a mockery of our travelling hundreds of miles here – not realised, though we'd have to tolerate some on/off obscuring of the sun. My LCD watch beeped the hour for 11am: a matter of minutes to go. To our right a mile or so away, a peninsula with rocky cliffs dramatically fell away to the sea. To the left the postmodern druids were getting 'in the zone' and their priest was moving deosil, casting the magic circle in a sunwise direction, as one of them explained to us afterwards. I kind of admired they had something to believe in at this time, even if many people would see them as a bit bonkers. Who was I, a writer of telly gags and a veteran of psychiatric institutions, to call anyone bonkers?

I determined to remember everything that happened next. As the eclipse began and morning darkness fell, scores of flashbulbs popped pointlessly for amateur photographers' pictures of artificially lit darkness. Then, more surprising than the birdsong going quiet, than the temperature falling, than fading light giving way to mast lights on the promontory, for ninety intense seconds Sam took my hand, squeezed it, and for the last time in public we were one under the sun.

77

Desperately seeking Paddy
Ed Sullivan Theater, Manhattan – 31 December 1999

'There has been a sighting of Ricky's hire car an hour away from Manhattan.' Jacqui sounded genuinely relieved on the phone; this was no performance. 'A place called Bridgeport.'

'Great news – but how the hell did you get it?' I was heading down the corridor to my dressing room. 'You promised me you'd reveal your sources.' At least she wasn't a journo.

'I cannot do it now, Nathan. Some other time. Maybe when we meet next.' There's such a thing as English reserve, but was this French reserve?

'Ok. I've now got a lot on my plate with rewriting. You're free to trail Ricky, no?' If I talk to Jacqui for any length of time I end up speaking pidgin English.

'It is not that straightforward, I am sorry to say. I am indisposed.' I could feel the stress hormone squirt through my system like squid ink. Indisposed? Thanks for your help, Jacqui – not. Jeez.

'I can't be in two places at once.' I tried, and failed, not to sound too worked up. 'I've got to rewrite the entire show so I can't go chasing after yer man.' Now I was trying to sound quasi-Irish. To soften the harshness I added, 'Sorry.'

'Who is going to do it then? Who will find your friend Ricky?' Damn her eyes. She knew what she was doing using the F-word 'friend'. I had a flashback to Paddy lying in that stream one summer holiday, concussed by the stones those bastard boys hurled at him. I saw the blood issuing from his nostrils. These days he has nosebleeds for different reasons.

If I took Jacqui's question at face value, who else could possibly seek out Ricky? Louise was tied up on the show – rehearsals go on. Script Ed had the time, but not the inclination. The Colonel's too angry with Ricky, plus it would involve getting his white ceremonial gloves dirty. Maybe one half of the Jenni-Penny prompting double act could be spared, but I couldn't see them digging into detective work. Besides, they were hired in as service providers with a limited remit. Oh, crap – it all came back to me. Again. 'We-ell ... Looks like I'm going to have to do it somehow, Jacqui. As well as the scripting.' More oral treachery. Dear gob.

'Thank you, thank you, Nate.' So good she thanked me twice.

'I need all the information you've got, though. We haven't a moment to lose. And I need a picture of the car. Buzz me back when you have everything. And you're going to have to tell me how you got it. Please.'

'*Bien sûr.*' Moments of high drama clearly require the French language. Of course.

78

Therapy part eight: Jane
Thornton Heath, south London – 18 January 2000

Periodically I need a therapy top-up. It's either that or go to Lourdes, to paraphrase Woody Allen. When I got back to the UK, as well as the trunk and large backpack, I was carrying a lot of other baggage. Jane wasn't with me, but she weighed heavily on me. The whys and wherefores of her coming into being, why she was a secret, the shame that implies, how things might have been different had I known about her as a child ...

So I arranged a one-off visit to Mary to discuss these things. My head was whirring. She showed no shock on hearing I had a half-sister. Is that the training making Mary impassive, or has she heard it so many times before? Or a bit of both? One comfort of working with her is she's never blown off course by anything I say. She's unshockable. Which makes everything I bring to her seem commonplace, and therefore tolerable. On a good day.

'Did your mother give any clues about Jane?' Mary had dyed her hair since we last met – probably more than once. It was bible-black with a professional sheen; I found myself picturing her with a shock of lustrous white hair.

Focus.

'Mum knew Jane as April – I don't know if that was her choice of name. But for some reason she'd put "April" on what was otherwise a shopping list. Ours was an eccentric household! It only clicked into place – the word "April", written next to my mother's maiden name – once I'd spoken to Jane. She became Jane after she was adopted.'

'I see.' Mary smoothed her black-and-white, large-patterned skirt. She was dressed soberly: a black cardigan over a grey silk chemise and black earrings.

'Something else has come back to me since I returned ...' I needed a cue to elaborate.

'Go on.'

'In Mum's last, dark days she'd had contact with a depression charity, the High Street Saints. One night I was woken by her being on the phone to them. My bedroom was above the phone. I was drifting in and out of sleep. Her voice didn't disguise her illness: a monotonous and sleepy drawl. That made it easier to disconnect from.'

'So you would have been mid-teens then?'

'Yes – fifteen. This was within weeks of her suicide. And she referred on the phone to having had "two beautiful children". At least, for a moment that's what I thought I'd heard. Then I remember consciously telling myself I hadn't heard it – that I was dreaming it. That's weird, isn't it?'

'Well, at the age you were then, your parents would have created your world – although you were approaching puberty. That's the stage where you'd normally start to challenge received "truths". But with the stress you were under, you probably couldn't take more shocks to your system. So it's ... not that unusual, no.' She dropped her eyes for a moment, then raised them again to add, 'Certainly nothing to beat yourself up about.' Her eyes glinted as she offered a half-smile.

'I'm left with a hell of a lot of unanswered questions. Was Jane conceived through rape? Speaking to her, she believes our mother – that's a strange term to use ... She actually uses the ugly term "birth mother", as if Mum was a biological breeder. Like a sow in pig.' I found myself picking at the leaves of a rubber plant next to the chaise longue I was on in Mary's consulting room. Her eyes registered it, then looked back to me. 'Anyway, Jane doesn't know for sure, but she thinks she was conceived on a church camp in Easter 1949. Of all pure escapades. Clearly the Holy Spirit was hard at work there. Jane thinks she knows the surname of the father ... Biological bloody father, excuse me ...'

'It's okay to be angry about this, Nate.'

One sentence guaranteed to make me angrier. Ta for the fucking permission. 'I'm angry into a void though. I don't know if Dad knew. If he did, I'm furious with him. Crazy, since he's dead. If he didn't know, where does that fury go? How do humans live with themselves? We know enough to know we don't know enough. What kind of headfuck is that?'

'There's nothing wrong being angry with your father. Over time, though, there has to be a process of forgiveness. Acceptance.' Mary kept her immaculate posture under fire. 'That might sound odd given he's deceased. But above all, forgiveness is about freeing the forgiver.'

I saw myself with fists clenched against the cosmos. I want to say, 'I defy you stars', like Romeo on finding Juliet has died. Instead, I say, 'That's a lot to digest.'

'You have a lot on your plate.' We both smile at Mary's poetry. 'But you're not going to win against the human condition. We all have to work within our limitations.'

'The human condition is incurable, then,' I said, wistfully.

'I might not put it like that. But what about your mother in all this? Women I've worked with who've given a child away tend to feel they've lost a part of themselves.'

'That side of things all seems to fit now.' I leaned in. 'Giving a child away – a baby, when Mum was only eighteen – is the missing link for me.' I felt I could chalk 'QED' up on a board. Case proven.

Mary pursed her lips and paused, before saying, 'Bear in mind, most women who give a child away – pained though they are – live with that pain. They find a way to steer round it. They don't inevitably blame themselves. Most don't kill themselves.'

I shifted to look round directly at Mary, feeling a swell of adrenaline. 'Is this some pecking order? Coping and not coping?' I snapped. I was fighting for the honour of my dead mother.

'I'm not making a judgment on any woman, Nate. I'm saying different people react differently. And suicide is not the inevitable result of giving up a child for adoption. Suicide is rarely about one thing. In the jargon, a lot of mothers "integrate" their experience of giving a child away. They weave it into their life story. It's a tragedy your mother couldn't do that.'

79

Desperately seeking Paddy part two
New York State – 31 December 1999

My driver turns on to the Interstate to Boston – the I-95. In the back of the Lincoln Town Car I have reams of paper, a selection of pens and highlighters, and a combined VHS player and TV. The last gasp of the analogue age! Plus, my fully charged-up, humble Nokia 3210 and Ricky's fancy Nokia 9000 he's left behind. The 9000 is a souped-up phone with e-mail. The workflow is for me to e-mail rescripted material (typed laboriously into the 9000) to Script Ed who then kicks it upstairs to the Colonel if he's content with it, or he bounces it back to me if not. If Colin approves it, it goes to Louise and a team of researchers, while I and the driver are making progress – hopefully – in finding Paddy. If we find him, the writing is redundant, and no one will be happier than me. If the star of the show remains elusive, we have no option but to fall back on our local TV news anchor, Mort Silus. (Did I slip a certain assumption past you there? That to find Paddy is to coax him back to the show. Optimism isn't my strong suit, but I'm trying it out for size.)

     Louise took some persuading she should sign off the expense for a car and driver. Before that, she was digging in on a budget self-drive hire car for me, until I pointed out I couldn't simultaneously write and drive in a strange country on the opposite side of the road to the norm, while looking out for a needle in a haystack with a Lincoln lookalike (the person, not the car) in it. But even the hire car seemed to be a step too far when I first discussed the plan with Louise, given the Colonel sees all programme expenses and has to approve them. She reached a deal with the car-hire firm for a delay in billing to circumvent that elephant trap.

We also had fun and games finding a battery VHS-TV combo so I could watch tapes of our man Mort fronting the news magazine on NYTV. Mort writes his own scripts linking items on the show, as I found out during our brief phone call before I hit the road. He was courteous and professional but, entirely as Ed and the Colonel said, doesn't really do jokes – or not as light-entertainment types know 'em. So if I can get used to his cadences and phrasing – any quirks and tics he has – I can make him sound more natural.

Another conversation I had before jumping in the car was with Jacqui – in person, as she insisted. We met a block or two away from Ricky's and her hotel. The black bouffant was obvious from twenty feet, but I only clocked her equally dark poncho closer up. We exchanged quick '*bonjour*'s, and only then would she reveal the source of her information on Ricky's car and the sighting: a private investigator. She'd hired them after having suspicions Ricky was seeing other women. (Frankly I think Ricky would sue anyone who accused him of *not* seeing other women; it could harm his brand.) I feigned my best surprised look. But it also explained why Jacqui wouldn't reveal anything substantial over the phone; she was too aware of the PI's use of telephone intercepts. She said she nearly hired that rarest of beasts, a female private detective, but thought better of it, having worried Ricky might have an affair with her, too. Jacqui thrust a hire-car leaflet into my hand, pointing to a photo of an Oldsmobile like Paddy's, so I knew what I was looking for. Very sleek, very limo-like, very A-lister. With that, she kissed me on both cheeks and bade me well.

Now in the car, and five minutes into the tape, I'm quietly despairing: Mort's self-scripted links are, to put it kindly, linear. But I could tell in his head he thinks he's creative. If a report begins with a close-up of wheels or cogs, buckle up for a line about 'the wheels of government ...' or 'it gets the cogs whirring ...'.

And then the phone goes. Louise.

'They've found out,' she says. She sounds unusually panicky.

'Who? What?' Have I been found out as a writer? The high-rises of Manhattan recede at speed to my left.

'News outlets. In Britain. They're leading on Ricky deserting the show. The *Evening Standard* got it first in London, now radio and TV bulls are running with it. It's a disaster.'

Man alive. 'How'd they get hold of it?'

'Dunno. Does it matter? It's out there. And we're screwed.'

We're screwed anyway, I thought. 'Look – keep calm,' I said, having been infected by her anxiety. And breathe. Think, think. 'Get Publicity back home to agree a line with Roger and Colin and bat off any enquiries back to London. If anyone asks say, "There'll be no more comment at this stage." Should shut it down.' I nearly believed it.

'Okay – thanks, Nate. We could do without this, eh?'

Lack of sleep can't have helped her. It wasn't helping me, either. At the mere thought of the S-word I wanted to stretch out on the back seat. A stretch limo. I suppressed a yawn while saying, 'One day we'll laugh about this.'

Louise did a near-titter through sniffs. A tiffer. A snitter. Concentrate, tired brain. 'Bye, Nate.'

'Adios.' *Adiós* – I leave her to God. Till the next phone call.

The speed limit on Interstates feels slow right now. And I can't believe trucks out here still haven't got guards round them to stop cars being dragged under. Would just be my luck ...

Back to scripting. I play more of the news-magazine tape. Mort seems to like alliteration – we have that in common, at least. But what works for Ricky won't necessarily work for Mort. I flick through the printout of the old script Louise ran off for me. I'd already departed from the usual

'Won't you do the *Friday Fandango*?' line I've been copying and pasting for Ricky for three years now. For tonight I'd gone for: 'It's Friday, it's 9 o'clock across the UK, but it's a *Friday Fandango* like no other.' I'd fleshed that out to create a scene-set: 'We're in New York City [pause for cheer]. It's a once-in-a-thousand-years kinda show. And the Millennium's so good the Big Apple's celebrating it twice! Once in three hours when we hook up with London for Big Ben's chimes. And then again, five hours after that, when this *Millennial Special*'s shown on New York TV station NYTV. So happy new millennium, whether you're watching in the UK or the US. And if you're not sure where you are, you've hit the bubbly big time!'

Don't forget that, thanks to our warm-up man northern English stand-up Bob Bell – aka Bobbles – if Ricky ever gets to deliver the above, the audience will have been worked into a frenzy – appropriately with help from some bubbles. (The work it took to prise Colin's fingers from the moneybags to provide cheap champers in paper cups for the crowd.)

But how to translate Ricky's opener to Silus-speak? Don't think Mort can carry off the bubbly line. With the Town Car's suspension smoothing most bumps, I write in a steadyish hand: 'Ladies and gentlemen, you don't know me, but I'm Mort ...' Oh, great, Nate – start with alienation. Take two: 'Ladies and gentlemen, time to change your partner for the fandango ...' Hmm. Assumes too much knowledge about this dance, and the show (we'll have plenty of first-time viewers). Plus it sounds promiscuous. Family unfriendly. Kids'll be staying up later than usual. Think, think ...

Ah ...

Mort's a journo so he likes facts and figures. And we need to make him relatable, reaching out across the Atlantic. How about, 'Over thirty-five years ago four lads from Liverpool were introduced to over seventy million Americans by an Irish American ...' Christ, no! We can't remind the viewers of a missing Irishman. Not yet. But the stats might work. And the 'lads/Liverpool' alliteration can stay. How about, 'Over thirty-five years ago four Liverpool lads were introduced to over seventy million Americans by a fellow American. He was called Ed Sullivan, they were, of course, called The Beatles. And why am I telling you this? Because tonight – for one night only, the most special night in a thousand years – we're coming live from the Ed Sullivan Theater on Broadway!' [Pause for applause/whoops of delight, etc., etc.]

'What are you watching there?' Oh, God. I'm hearing voices. Then I catch the searching eyes in the rear-view. I'm hearing one voice: the driver's. 'You seem interested in the TV, then you go someplace else.' His leather jacket creaked with his energetic arm movements. He has a disturbing habit of looking over his shoulder, which is to say he takes his eyes off the road.

'Oh – it's nothing. Just Mort Silus. I'm writing his script—'

'Morty?' Oh bugger. 'You write for Morty? Get outta here! He's a star.' Jesus. I'll never get anything done. And he's not a star, he's a journalist. On a local station.

'Yeah, well, it's a little gig. You know, a bit different to his usual ...' STFU, Nate – don't fan the flames.

'I watched him since I was a kid. The voice of reason. You wouldn't trust your parents, but you'd trust Morty. My ... In my car ...'

Actually, no – Mort's not in your car, just his new scribbler. But they say you shouldn't wake sleepwalkers.

80

Back to the General
Psychiatric Unit, Watford General Hospital – November 1982

I remember more about coming back from the psychiatric hospital – the forbidding Edwardian asylum – than being driven to it. But, even so, there are plenty of gaps. Who would have accompanied me back to the general hospital in the ambulance? Could it really have been one of the two ambulance men in the back with me? Surely not – there must have been a nurse. If so, I have no memory of them. Neither do I remember getting into the ambulance, or anything about the journey; not even blurry visions of passing trees at speed.

I have a recollection of having to sign back into the psychiatric unit, helping the charge nurse keep a tally of my worldly goods: some keys and cash, the clothes I wore, and a beat-up, off-white suitcase; not much more. A kindly young female nurse helping with the signing-in process expressed shock at seeing me in something other than jeans (I'd acquired a pair of unexciting grey slacks). A bearded trainee doctor was alongside her. I think my irony sensors were flicking because there was a hint of a smile at the edges of his mouth as he uttered a welcome. It felt like winter approaching as it was starting to get dark earlier.

Then I looked out the window and something clicked: the new hospital wing under construction, floodlit for the workers and still windowless, was suddenly an ordinary half-finished building. In that manner of soulless modern constructions it was growing apace without growing prettier. It resembled a multi-storey car park. And yet I saw it anew.

As I'd left to go to the psychiatric hospital this section was being built for me, a prince, the Son of God. And now it was just a building. I struggled to let the delusion go; I felt a hollowness resembling the new block's empty shell.

Looking back, this feeling was the beginning of something better; more grounded. But recovery was months, years off. For sure, it had felt good to have a building created just for me. And that wasn't all: even the names of my anti-depressants became significant in my maddest phase. Imipramine became I'm a Prime, another endorsement of my new omnipotence. Why wouldn't I have a hospital wing built especially for me? That was before going to the more acute institution, to a locked ward. But now I was The Man Who Fell to Earth.

Only then did I find some of my compatriots at the general hospital's psych unit had been convinced I wasn't coming back. Polythene Pam, so called by me I think because she wore a plastic pinafore, perhaps for a therapeutic pottery class, thought the best I could hope for was supported living – what was known as a halfway house. God, that would have been death for me: a sense of never quite getting well. Of course, it could have been temporary; that's what 'halfway' implies. But I would have worried I'd never leave it. I could get forgotten there by the medics.

So what kind of reception did I get on my return, the prodigal patient? I hadn't spent a fortune like the wayward son in the Bible, but had I exhausted people's compassion? One male nurse, Tony, was quick to say on my return, 'We'll mark you down as a success'. It was meant to be tongue-in-cheek – I think – but at this distance I feel his pain in the humour; with so many inmates falling off the wagon, or off a building or a station platform, for someone merely to survive is something to celebrate.

As an outpatient months later I went back to the unit to visit a former fellow inpatient, Neal. It transpired he'd OD'd and died. Death was such a frequent visitor to the unit Tony felt able to joke in my hearing with a colleague, 'Did he take the blue ones or the red ones?' Life was cheap and so were the meds. Neal had worked on oil rigs in the North Sea. He should have been the picture of health with that physical lifestyle and all the sea air. He talked of three weeks on and maybe a week off, and exotic add-ons, like taking helicopters from the rig back to Aberdeen, and generous paydays and dating girls. I once met his parents in the side room where Neal lay in bed; they were visiting him at the same time I was, and were very pleasant and cultured. I couldn't work out what ailed their son. In group therapy he'd talked of wanting to emulate a literary figure who combed his pubic hair; something intrigued Neal about living such a squeaky-clean existence that even parts of you that weren't on show were just so. Was that the key to his misery: the idea he could never attain that degree of perfection? You'd look at him with his blow-dried, brushed-back chestnut hair and matinee-idol looks and you'd have laid much safer odds on him making it than me. All these years later I wonder if he died of cynicism.

I wonder, too, if the mortician, when laying Neal on the slab, tidied his pubic hair?

81

Desperately seeking Paddy part three
New York State – 31 December 1999

'I have just spoken to Ricky – it is not good.' Jacqui was in tears on the phone. 'He rang from a call box. He talked about futility, about how it was all meaningless. Hollow fame, he said – again and again.' Oh brother. Sounded like a coke comedown. My car was at a virtual standstill due to some hold-up ahead. Never rains but it pours.

I put my scripting on hold – again. 'Did you ask where he was?'

'I ask but he was not precise. He talked about the sea. I could hear the gulls in the background. He said he might go for a walk and join the fishes.' She sniffed.

One of us had to remain in control. 'Did he ring your mobile?'

'No – it was the hotel phone in my room. Our room.'

I was processing, processing. 'If he calls again, your private detective could put a trace on him.' I hoped that was true.

'I think he already has. But David – the private investigator – says it conflict with what we had before: a sighting in Bridgeport. The trace now points to Norwalk.'

'Man alive – isn't that California?' Blind panic. I had visions of a night flight and Ricky at LAX.

'No, no, Nate. I do not know about California. But this Norwalk is in New England.' Jacqui veered at times between stiff learned English and the vernacular.

He was within reach of New York, in other words. 'Phew. That's better news. I have to head there, then.' I was about to give the driver new instructions when I saw the tailbacks stretching ahead and realised it could wait till the end of the call.

I'd thought there was hope for Paddy's mental state in that he'd hired the car for a week, not simply twenty-four hours, but that cocoon seemed to be unravelling. By the sound of things, we might need the coastguard as well as David the PI.

'Don't worry, Jacqui, we'll find him.'

'I hope so, Nate. I do hope so.' The line went dead.

'Bye,' I said to the silence. I hung up and switched my attention to the driver. 'I'm sorry – I should have asked your name before?' I had a feeling I was going to need it.

'Tony, sir. Italian American. Right outta Brooklyn.'

'*Molto bene.*' I saw his smile in the driving mirror. I wasn't going to tell him I'd used up most of my Italian in one go. 'We need to reroute, Tony. Our man Paddy has been traced to Norwalk.'

'Paddy? I thought we're looking for—'

'Ricky? One and the same guy. Ricky's a stage name.' Though technically, under my own internal rules – the star was off-duty – I was looking for Paddy.

'Ok Mr ....?'

'Call me Nate.'

'Gotcha, Nate. But first I gotta check with the Big Man. My controller.' Oh God – bureaucracy, even in a cab.

The traffic started to move as Tony got on the radio to clear his new orders. Then he began the more alarming process of leafing through his book of maps to fathom his new route: one hand turning pages while the other simultaneously gripped the mic and the steering wheel. The mic's black coiled cable stretched and gyrated like an angry cobra. The hiss of the radio when the controller spoke completed the effect.

An all-clear was eventually given. 'OK we'll stick with the '95 then come off left by the river.'

He might as well have been speaking Italian. 'Ok – I must get back to scripting.' I was trying to get the hang of typing an e-mail, if you can call it typing, on the 9000. I learnt to touch-type many moons ago but you have to kiss goodbye to speed and technique on a miniature keyboard. And Script Ed would have to get used to typos as a trade-off for haste.

Following the intro, the opening monologue I'd written for Ricky on being an Irish-Brit alien in New York was hardly going to fly for Mort. I'd taken a leaf out of the American-evening-chat-shows' handbook: I'd beefed up what was normally a minute or so's riffing at the top of the weekly London-based show to make it more Letterman-esque at about three minutes. I still had to bear in mind Ricky didn't have a grounding as a stand-up, so he didn't have the licence to depart from his script in the same way as a Leno or a Letterman. Neither could he be so fluid with his delivery. I'd long since learnt in TV that while you keep people within the limits of their competence, the audience can project all kinds of additional feats on to them; the moment you push the performer beyond those boundaries, though, the camera widens out to reveal their feet of clay.

I needed to help Mort and his slightly bemused audience into the show as soon as possible. They would have some awareness of Ricky's disappearance through the press, and now other broadcasters, but they wouldn't have any context.

I thought of how Cilla Black invited her viewers to 'step inside' her own Saturday-night live fandango, topped and tailed with a musical invite written by her friend ... Paul McCartney. I mused where all that footage went from those eight years of smash-hit shows. I don't mean the tapes; I mean the impact it made on the viewers. Are those of us who hung on her every word at the time carrying around a little piece of *Cilla* – her TV show – with us? If so, for me it's an ever-diminishing piece, sadly. I'd be hard-pressed to detail anything substantial from all the hours I watched. I do remember the surprise sprung on a different household each week as a live crew landed on their doorstep, barging into the lounge where the family were hopefully watching the show. One week, from the comfort of her studio in Shepherds Bush, Cilla asked the lady of the house in the impromptu outside broadcast to change channels, and she switched to a rival commercial station, much to Ms Black's apparent horror; probably, as I now suspect as an adult in the biz, it was confected. Cilla appeared to mean a change of channel within the same family of channels, but the lady had switched to what was euphemistically referred to as 'the other side'. I recall that scene, like many others, in black and white, because that's what our TV was at that point. How many others of the millions who saw that are reliving it right now, decades on? A vanishingly small number, I'd guess. So does that make popular broadcasting disposable: here today, gone tomorrow? And does that matter?

It doesn't do to think too much about the flimsiness of our medium and the public's relationship with it; you could end up thinking it doesn't matter what you write because almost no one will remember it years from now.

As Barbara Windsor said when a fellow actor was agonising over a lame script in rehearsal, 'Oh, get on with it – it's not fucking Chekhov.'

82

Losing Nana
London – April 1971

My first major bereavement was the loss of Nana, my mother's mother. I remember dreaming about her a few days after her death. She appeared in my dream as being on a huge TV screen, a screen so big they barely existed in those days, the early Seventies. In pre-industrialised countries the deceased might appear as bats or mythical creatures with significance to that culture; trust the guy who becomes a TV writer to see his dead grandmother on telly. What inspired it, I think, was a dubious TV ad *The Sun* newspaper used to run around that time, recalled by me in black and white: a pretty, young model is in the studio wearing a short dress; she is full-length in a wide shot. But a really tight shot on the hem of what's she's wearing is blown-up big time on the large screen next to her, with the voiceover selling some exposé in the paper about how dresses are creeping up the thigh. I remember as a kid having what Ben Elton calls a 'trouser tingle' at what was effectively soft porn. It's perverse my subconscious has reworked that profanity into something more sacred featuring my deceased Nan, who in that image was comforting me in her physical absence. It was as if she had left this life and passed on to immortality on the screen, passing over to the other side. My dreamy subconscious had linked sex and death in a way that years later has become the calling card of the youthful TV station Channel 5. As a seven-year-old I had related this dream (minus any reference to *The Sun*'s ad) the day after to my dad as we walked over the road to the recreation park to exercise the dog. I remember telling him Nan was not dead but asleep. This was an example of what, later, a therapist called 'a child parenting the parent'. I would have liked Dad to say something consoling at the time, and he was not usually lacking in empathy or compassion, but on this occasion he was emotionally absent, perhaps with his own grief or Mum's at second-hand, or just at a loss as to what to say.

I found out after my mother died that *her* mother had left her husband, Mum's dad, at one point; I was shocked. That kind of thing hadn't happened in my experience in the Seventies, and the further back from that it was it would have been proportionately a harder move and more scandalous. More questions were raised than were answered by knowing my grandmother had walked out: What year was it? What was the trigger? What brought her back: resolving her differences or penury? If the latter, it could have accounted for what appeared to be her passivity and rumination. Maybe she strongly disagreed with my grandfather's decision – and in a male-dominated house he would have had the last word – to send my mother to a convent in Godshill at the age of eighteen to give up her baby, born out of wedlock. But if that was the case Nana would have had the weight of society's expectations at that time against her; she would have been swimming against the tide of 'respectability'.

In a more church-dominated age people around me were taking their moral cues from religious leaders. These days I see vicars as branch managers and bishops as area managers for the C of E brand, but in my youth their edicts could get under the skin. When we attended the local branch, St Stephen's, as a young family just having moved to the area, I would say the liturgy along with my parents; I'd trot out phrases such as, 'We have strayed from your ways like lost sheep ... and there is no health in us'. As a five-year-old, I queried with my dad how negative that last phrase sounded, particularly as I felt none of us Daniels were that bad. I also questioned the use of incense, apparently asking if it made you live longer. Dad was amused, more than anything, about this, but still had no answers. Religious rites are hard to explain to a child.

In my teens I developed my own rituals, including what is known by evangelicals as a 'quiet time'. That means a daily period of reflection, including reading the Bible. I managed it for years, and it was so ingrained and part of the texture of my day that the morning after my mother had killed herself, I sat as usual at the table in my bedroom and opened my Bible, an Authorised Version. But I sat there with the extended seismic shock of the previous day and felt such a lump in my throat – possibly repressed rage against the Almighty for what had happened – that after a minute or so I silently shut the book again, not to open it again for years. Mum died, then God died the following day. Except you can never really escape the religious mindset; at primary school we sang a hymn 'God Be in My Head' and He – the patriarchy ran through everything – really was in our heads and world view, entangled with the double helix. I always wanted to write a response to Mary O'Malley's play *Once a Catholic*. Of course, it had to be called *Once a Protestant*, and it would demonstrate that 'RC's (as Roman Catholics were 'othered' then) didn't have the monopoly on being tied to the faith for life, nor in being throttled by acute guilt. We – Protestants and Catholics alike – were fellow sufferers, doomed to be locked inside our own minds where the Godhead lived, so the least we could do was to find common cause in our suffering.

83

Desperately seeking Paddy part four
New York State – 31 December 1999

I was starting to get on a roll with the script. And to get used to the fiddly 9000 keyboard, despite the odd bump on the Interstate. It helped that the opening monologue for Mort was much shorter than for Ricky. In fact, it was so short it wasn't worthy of the name 'monologue'. More a slightly enlarged opener. The sleight of hand I was performing was to get Mort quickly on to the first dance/music number to kick-start the energy levels so viewers wouldn't notice he wasn't too charismatic. Plus, the audience would associate him with the feel-good factor and good times, which again would compensate for any sluggishness on his part. Ultimately, you can only get people to play to their strengths. Mort's strength was to stolidly move between items, not to raise the roof. I knew it was a doomed quest when I floated the idea but I tried to get Colin to find a more upbeat sidekick for Mort. The answer, accompanied by a withering look that could fell the enemy at fifty paces, was, 'Nathan – if I could find such a person they'd be presenting the bloody show instead of Morton.' He had a point, but he could have been less brutal about it. Or perhaps he couldn't.

My Nokia went: Louise. 'How's it going?' I grunted a response – she wasn't ringing to make small talk. 'Script Ed says your e-mail's all garbled.' I was tempted to say that's how I write, but now was not the time. That smug new species the e-mailer may sneer about 'snail mail', but when the letter gets there the words do too.

'Can you ask someone in IT to look at it?' I said.

'This is a theatre, Nate, not a college computer lab.'

'Oh, come on! They transmit live pictures round the world; the place is crawling with geeks. There must be someone in a Crimplene shirt with BO who takes PCs apart in their spare time.'

Louise laughed, a sound I hadn't heard in a while. 'You're terrible.' No stereotyping there.

'Look – I could try sending that section again.' If in doubt with computers, switch off and switch on again. Perhaps that could work for me and Louise.

'Resend it anyway and I'll follow the scent of a super-nerd. Otherwise, standby with quill and parchment.'

I had a couple of biros and a chunk of A4 printer paper as backup. I risked darkening the mood. 'How's the press thing about Ricky?'

'London's on to it. But I don't think they can shut it down. The bloody network itself is leading with it.'

'Christ. Talk about shooting yourself in the foot.'

'And Jacqui's getting loads of calls. She doesn't need that.'

'No. And neither do we.' An inchoate thought gurgled somewhere in my brain. 'What if ...? No. Doesn't matter.' I should have waited till it was fully formed. Fatigue was taking lumps out of me.

'Say it, Nate. What if ... what ...?'

'A mad idea but I've got to work on it. Will let you know later.'

'Eughh! You're such a tease – but not in a good way.'

'Gee, thanks Louise. Speak in a bit.'

She signed off and I resent the e-mail.

'You got a problem, buddy?' Jesus. Now Tony had come out of hibernation.

'I have a problem alright. Well, several problems now. Perhaps you can help me think through one of them.'

'Oh yeah? Try me.'

'The press in Britain have got hold of the story of Ricky's disappearance. It's all over the papers. Sounds crazy ...'

'I like crazy!' Tony's eyes lit up in the driving mirror as he caught my gaze.

'But ... I was wondering if we could get them onside to help in the search. The papers, I mean.'

'Hey, look – I'm just a regular guy. I drive a car for a living. What do I know? These Limey press guys, though – they're all in London, right? So how do they get here in time? Sure, Concorde's quick, but it's not that quick.'

'The papers' HQs are in London, yeah. But they have people called stringers all over the world. They help with stories – freelancers on the ground. They can be phoned up at the drop of a hat.'

'Ah, I get ya. Seems to me the more people we have looking for Paddy, Ricky – whatever – the better. Long as they don't run me off the road!' He laughed, then got into a hacking fit so bad I thought he was going to run us both off the road.

Emboldened by Tony's approval, I rang Louise. It went to answerphone (I can't be doing with that 'voicemail' label. It's either voice or mail – not both.) I had immediate pictures of her being chatted up by another guy. I tried hard to replace them with images of her at work. That ought to have been easy, given how busy she was. I even saw her being smooched by Colin. And then it was time to speak into the void. 'Hi, Lou – this is Nate. That idea – it's a mad idea, but it could just work. The press want stories to sell papers. We want to find Ricky. What say we help the press help us to find Ricky? They get the ultimate scoop – first on the scene as we find him. We get our star back. Win-win!' I hung up.

The I-95's down to two lanes each way now, framed by fragile-looking wintry trees on either side. Tree after tree after tree, soaking up our exhaust. The road's parallel to the rails – the railroad – for a while. To my right, a train heads in the opposite direction, gone in a flash.

I replay my answerphone message to Louise in my fatigued head. What worked talking out loud to Tony – who says we're passing through Greenwich, Connecticut – now seems madder than ever. Again and again. Win-win. Win-win. Like the ghost sirens I used to hear on sleepless nights. winwinwinwinwin ... Repetition is Hell.

If only I could suck that message back, never to have left it. Like the gentlemen of the press are pussycats who want only the best for me and Paddy and the team. What sodding planet was I on? I look such a dick.

I ring her answerphone again. I hear the ringing tone and rehearse what I'm about to record. Louise: Please ignore my last message. Don't even listen—

'Hello?'

Shit – she's back. In real time. Improvise. 'Er – hi. Only me.' Full marks so far. 'That last message ...'

'I heard it.' Bollocks. 'Sorry I missed you – I was with Colin.' Course you fucking were. Loosening his army fatigues. Falling on his ceremonial sword. Your skirt concertinaed ready to blow air over his bellows. What's it like – Louie, Louie – to be a fallen woman? 'He thinks it's a good idea. Get the press involved.'

God Almighty.

'But with strict red lines.'

'Oh yeah? Well, of course,' I said. 'We can't have anarchy.'

''Course not. So Colin's drawing up a protocol. It's being legalled right now.'

Am I dreaming this? A mess of stiff dicks and loose accordions are cascading through my conscious unconscious. Or unconscious conscious. Who needs Class A capers when you're seriously tired and stressed?

I see a council flat with grapefruit wallpaper and three porcelain ducks ready for take-off. In front of my fatigued mind's eye the grapefruits turn into busts; not one, but a thousand effigies of Saul Bellows.

'Are you alright, Nate? You seem to be groaning.'

84

Tears

I never saw my dad cry – not once – until the day my mother died. My mother said she only saw him cry once in their entire time together. But she wouldn't tell me what the occasion was. I assume now it was after one of her suicide attempts. He must have cried after the other one, too, but maybe she wasn't conscious to see it, whether asleep or out for the count.

Mum was going to explain everything to me one day: girls, women, sex, my father's tears. I'd ask her about life's mysteries and imponderables, and the answer was always something like, 'I'll tell you when you're older', 'Not now Nate', or 'I'll tell you when you're sixteen'. She killed herself when I was fifteen.

There was a guy in the office at the first radio station I worked in, Joel who, whenever you asked him how he was, always said, 'Surviving through this vale of tears.' The first time I asked this response was unexpected and darkly amusing. The second or third time it had the quality of a running gag. But the tenth time I swore to myself I would never ask him how he was ever again. By mistake I asked him once more – you try never asking after someone's health and you'll see how hard it is: it's a polite reflex on seeing a colleague – but I quickly wrong-footed him by adding, 'And is your valley still moist?'

He cracked a smile for the first time in my presence.

James Joyce said Christ wasn't ever really tested because he never lived with a woman, but Joel seemed to pass the test; he only stopped wading through his vale of tears when he discovered sex at the age of forty-two and moved in with Margaret. He called her his 'new love' ('first love', the office unanimously demurred). I started asking Joel how he was again, and he declared variations on a theme of, 'Never better, Nate, never better.'

I find myself replaying the first time I saw Dad's eyes full of tears again and again, even as an adult, decades after the event. I don't know what it is: something mournful about the light grey winter coat he wore, the look he gave me as I sat on the sofa when he entered the lounge, a look combining his trademark hesitancy with utter desolation (he'd got on the first train out of London once he knew Mum wasn't breathing) ... No – as I consider it now it's the way he virtually landed on me with a tight hug and said in my ear as he wept, 'This is going to take some faith.'

He wasn't to know then my faith was about to leak away into the cold earth to rest by my mother's body, never to return. Or not in a recognisable form.

Ironically, my mother died thinking I wanted to be a minister of religion. She'd seen me talk at the grand old age of fourteen at some kind of local non-conformist Sunday service, and she expressed surprise at my do such a thing. But I'd got a buzz from it and told her that's what I wanted to do for a living. At the time I might have claimed some kind of divine gift but after my loss of faith it was easier to analyse what Mum had witnessed in terms of presentational skills, ego, a desire to belong and a need to be heard. It all started to make far more sense when I heard that my radio idol, Kenny Everett, a manic showman, disc jockey, writer, technician, television and theatre performer and – lest we forget – fellow Liverpudlian friend of The Beatles, at one point started training for the priesthood.

I met Kenny briefly once. Or should I say I met Maurice Cole ('Ev''s real name). Several years after his death it's a shame I'm never going to update the 'little boy lost' look of his I witnessed that one time. He was sitting next to his dresser in the TV studio where he was making a sketch show.

I'd like to substitute that memorised look for something more upbeat. It was early in my career, and I think I hadn't yet got used to seeing the lack of animation in the face of stars when they were off-stage. So he might not have felt lost at all at that moment; he merely wasn't required to provide humungous amounts of energy until the evening's show. Having said that, I don't think at that time I appreciated how normal it was for performers to have such a wide mood and energy range between their 'on' and 'off' lives, even though I knew what it meant from a personal perspective. I'd experienced manic depression (as it was then known – bipolar disorder as it became) in my teens, but it somehow never occurred to me that these outwardly solid, successful-looking stars could be struggling internally in that way as I had. Not until I made the connection with Paddy.

After that incident near Paddy's Irish home one summer when the bullies landed him in the stream, I started to observe a more irascible side to him. I'm not blaming the physical blow to his head for the increase in his rage. Rather the humiliation of the event seemed to lower the threshold at which he'd lose his cool; it was a blow to his pride more than anything. And it was his bad luck it coincided with the tumult that is adolescence.

Things at home were getting difficult in his teens, a time which is fraught with enough grief – hormonal, societal, psychological – without needing further complications. His parents' marriage was wobbling, and his father was leaning too heavily on the booze, though which was cause and which was effect wasn't always clear. Suffice to say voices were frequently raised and many doors slammed in the Ryan household, as I witnessed myself. Paddy's older brother Jim, far from being a help, was often goading Paddy into greater flights of frustration. Ah, the healing power of testosterone. And whereas my rage would get sublimated into swotting or introspection, Paddy's would burst out with explosive force into his world, embedding emotional shrapnel into teachers, girlfriends, relatives – anyone who tried to get or couldn't avoid being near. I still bear the scars as a close friend.

As Ricky – as he became publicly known – got sucked into the fame game, far from being more content he became less so. With every pound of extra pressure piled on him, he added two pounds on himself. In his head ratings were never sufficient, production support was always lacking, and as to privacy, to paraphrase Dylan, you could sell it, but you couldn't buy it back. Ricky's public image was ever more shiny and alluring, even as his inner world turned darker and more threatened and threatening. He was like a man with a foot in two boats drifting apart, and instead of the solace of safe harbour, he was heading for the high seas, facing ever higher waves. While performing the splits.

Crunch time followed another sweat-drenched show in London. The studio was being derigged by the techies, and the circus of production staff had moved on – to bars, parties, or the refuge of their beds. As I put my jacket on, Louise asked where Paddy was; his then girlfriend Candida had phoned the gallery to say he hadn't appeared at the meal with friends in Chelsea. It had been arranged for weeks. I'd only been in Paddy's dressing room minutes before (one of the corollaries of a long friendship with him was I'd always have a copy of his dressing room key for scooping up scripts and so on). He was nowhere to be seen then, but Louise persuaded me to have another look. I was more scrupulous the second time and loitered. After a bit I detected a whimpering sound which appeared to be coming from the en suite. There I found him crumpled and clothed in the bottom of the shower, with water dripping on his head. (Which performer said, 'You're a king on-stage and a pauper off it?') Through Paddy's pathetic tears I could just make out he said he was trying to cleanse his soul with 'holy water, Nate.' Subsequent conversation hinted at a possible church-related abuse when he was an altar boy, but details were sketchy then and, in any case, he subsequently denied he'd said it. Which, in the slippery world of non-denial denials, is not the same as saying the abuse didn't happen.

85

Desperately seeking Paddy part five
Connecticut – 31 December 1999

'Nathan. We have the *Mail*, the *Express*, and the *Mirror* on the case. They've all got stringers driving around Bridgeport and Norwalk looking for Ryan.' The Colonel sounded in his element: at last he got to plan a battle. I pictured him pushing military effigies around a contoured map like Churchill in the Cabinet War Rooms. I was desperate, though, for him not to hear the engine noise. I was meant to be diligently writing for Mort in a quiet dressing room, not bouncing around on a noisy Interstate.

A truck blasts its forte horn next to the Town Car. 'What in Heaven's name was that?' asks Colin. Quick as a flare I said, 'It's a news report on VHS. I'm watching Mort – Morton's show on NYTV. Trying to get a handle on his writing style. Story about road haulage.' Road haulage?

'Thank Christ for that. Put it on pause, there's a good chap.' Ruddy hell – being on manoeuvres has softened Colin. Now we have a common target. He clearly savours saving the not-so-private Ryan. It's not driven by love for the star presenter – it's all about ratings. An unknown face on your screen, even a funny one, let alone a Mort-type character, is a massive telly turn-off. Colin knows this and, having calmed down, has worked out his self-interest in getting Ricky back. 'Now we've got the stringers out in Connecticut: you know Ricky – where's he likely to be?'

If I had the answer to that, Colin you total tosspot, I'd've found him by now, wouldn't I? Wanker. 'Mmm, let me see, sir.' Jacqui had sworn me to secrecy about the private detective; it would raise too many questions. 'He likes loitering in cafés. Rehearsing his material meticulously.' You owe me, Paddy. Rehearse, my arse – he's leching at the female clientele.

'Roger that. There must be a plethora to choose from.' I remind myself the Colonel's talking about cafés. 'Any favourite genres? Styles?'

'Crikey. Let me think. Maybe art deco?' Hang on – it's wherever the totty is. 'Actually, I think he gravitates towards areas with colleges. Hoping to find research libraries.' Can't get an image of Monica Lewinsky out of my head. Talk about a hand on the lever of power. Polishing off the presidential pecker. Once you pop you can't ...

Another truck horn sprays decibels over the Colonel's words. Think my driver was pushing his luck cutting in under the cab's nose. Pre-emptive strike with the head honcho needed.

'Sorry, Colin – the VHS dropped out of pause. What were you saying?' Another of my nine lives lost.

'I must have been talking too long. Thanks for the intel. I'll disseminate.' An unfortunate choice of pay-off, just when I'd cleared my head of Lewinsky.

Colin said his farewells and I was left fazed by his niceness.

'You not meant to be on the road then, Nate?' Driver Tony's tongue was loosened again. 'All this talk of trucks on tape when I can see 'em and hear 'em for real!'

'What my mother would have called a "white lie". A little untruth. I'm meant to be holed up back at base scribbling away, not cruising on the I-95. How long to go?'

'Till the centre of Norwalk? We're in the outskirts of Stamford. Lemme see. With this traffic ... I reckon about a half hour. If you're lucky, twenty minutes.'

'That's progress.' A large green road sign guided drivers to the delightfully named Mianus off to the left, and, yes, Norwalk was signposted straight ahead. I looked left in the vain hope of seeing Mianus. So to speak. 'FUCKING HELLFIRE.'

'Jesus, Nate! What's the problem? You frightened the life outta me.'

'It's Paddy.' I leaned forward into the gap between the front seats, my right elbow against the passenger headrest. 'Ricky. Overtaking us. There! The blue Aurora.' I pointed diagonally left.

'How d' you know it's him?' Tony threw a quick look back at me.

'I saw him. That slicked-back hair. I know that profile from behind. Put your motherfucking boot down. We've got to go for it.' I could smell the leather of Tony's jacket close up.

'Hey – I got my licence to think about. I thought we was going to pull up ocean side. Some quiet car park.'

'Look – I've got this shitting show to think about.' No more Mr Nice Nate. 'The production'll bail you out. Name your price. Chrissakes. Just DO IT.'

I saw Tony concentrating hard in the mirror. He seemed to do a quick calculation. 'If that's what you want, buddy ...'

I heard his foot hit the floor. The V8 roared like a roused lion and I was pushed back into my seat. Then I was thrust to the right and my head glanced the glass in the rear door – 'POW!' like a Lichtenstein – and the car lurched left as Tony scooted round a bright-red pickup truck in front of us. We were now in the same lane as Paddy, but there was a dirty white station wagon, a gleaming motor bike, and an SUV between us and him. You could just about make out the sky-blue bodywork and the wall of red lights and reflectors at the back of Paddy's hire car. Plus, every now and then, teasingly through the rear window, the silhouette of Britain's number-one TV entertainer.

86

Paddy cornered
Stamford, Connecticut – 31 December 1999

It'll take some time to get over the memory of that chase. The dodgem spirit of weaving between vehicles, the red and blue flashing lights which terrified my driver Tony, then turned out to be the cops chasing someone else, the eventual clocking by Paddy that I was in the back of this (to him) anonymous cab. After depositing me, shaken and stirred, Tony said he learned his craft as a getaway driver for the Mafia. I wasn't sure how serious he was being.

Tony did indeed get his 'quiet car park' where Paddy eventually painted himself into a corner. Our quarry took a right towards the sea where the only options were to park up or get soaked.

Sounds daft but I never rehearsed the possibility Paddy didn't want to get caught, or at least, caught up with. He'd found a parking slot for the Aurora in this still spot by the water in Stamford, Connecticut. He shot me a fleeting look of utter despair, which surprised me. But this is the star of the show who couldn't stand the heat, is having substance-abuse problems, thinks he's jumped the stable door only to find his colleague and supposed friend blocking the paddock gate. What did I expect: the *Hallelujah* chorus?

With Paddy looking on, Tony had pulled up alongside the Aurora facing the water. I removed my writing gear and the video machine from the Town Car and told Tony to head back and his office would worry about (delayed) billing; I'd thought his presence looked too threatening in this delicate situation. I walked over to the driver's side of Paddy's car and motioned that I'd put my clutter in his boot. Returning to Paddy, without looking at me he held the button to lower his window. I sought to defuse the tension as soon as I could. I found the perfect foil in an intriguing view over the water: ten or so leafless saplings planted into the ocean bed, with the nearest one fifty feet or so from us. Forming an S-shape working their way out into deeper water, they struck me as a natural artwork: too neat to be random, too organic to be manufactured. I drew Paddy's attention to them.

'Do you think a lone person wandered out at low tide to stick those in? Are they even alive?' I looked across to my right waiting for Paddy's reaction. In the winter sun, and without his TV make-up on and the studio lights boring into his facial lines, Paddy was showing all of his thirty-six years. I hoped he was taking in the trees, even if he was looking through them, not at them. But in a way it didn't matter too much whether he saw them at all. It was about taking him out of himself; a distraction.

'The Men ...' he said after a while, still staring out to sea.

'Ah yes, The Men.' Not my preferred topic as it took us into 'screw loose' territory. But it was something – a callback to those hazy, lazy days in Ireland in our summer holidays, skimming stones on the lough near his home.

Paddy suddenly opened the car door, nearly bowling me over. 'C'mon Nate!' He was already halfway towards the tree artwork and raised his voice, while I looked on bemused. 'Last one to find a stone's a cissy!'

Paddy knows anything competitive is a red rag to me. For years I had to swallow that drive as his showbiz stock rose. Here among the stones and The Men under them we were equals, though I wanted to be more equal than him. I rummaged around the pebbly beach urgently for the perfect specimen: it had to be smooth and round with a low profile, like a 1950s idea of a UFO. Stone after stone failed the test, while I suffered the humiliation of Paddy already getting ahead in the skimming race.

'Three bounces – no, four!' he cried triumphantly.

Sod it. If only I could compromise. More scrabbling, more let-downs.

The brine on the bracing December air gave me an energy boost. Gulls shrieked overhead as if suggesting places for me to look.

And then ... the One. A shiny, black beauty with white veins, product of a billion years of seismic activity, climate catastrophe, wind erosion, the Big Bang, and big and little waves ... I limber up with my cosmic gift and flick an arc several times, my left hand gripping the perfect stone, but without letting go. And then I run to join Paddy. 'Watch this, you old bastard!' I yell. I spin the stone with such ferocity it bounces four, five, six times before yielding to its watery home, a soul returning to itself, dust to dust, rock to rock.

'Best of three.' Paddy had cast his silver weatherproof jacket aside away from the water line, and was rolling up the sleeves of his cedar-green sweatshirt. 'And that one doesn't count, Napster.' He'd been picking up a reserve of stones while I was focussing on the One.

'You're on, Padre.'

He reached in a front pocket of his ripped jeans and yanked out a packet of Park Drives. He coaxed one cigarette to stand proud of the pack, fed it straight into his mouth, and flashed up a brushed-metal lighter.

'Time-wasting!' I shout like a hoarse umpire, as Paddy luxuriates in the first draw of smoke, hollowing out his stubbly cheeks. He smoothes back his unwashed hair.

He enjoyed an early lead as my first official turn was half-arsed. 'Six-three,' he declared. 'You can retire now if you want?'

'No way, Padster. That was a tax loss.' I waited for him to concentrate again, then added, as he tensed for the spin: 'After you, my friend.'

'Fucker!' he said, and relaxed his skimming arm. A couple more puffs and then a refocus, like a Wimbledon champ bouncing the ball before serving. 'Get yer goggles round this.'

Paddy's second stone, which had a hint of ruddiness to it, left his hand like it was on a mission. Its first contact with the surface created a crown of spray and splash, then came the aftershock, as if from a depth charge. It repeated this pattern on an ever-smaller scale, but still managed eight, then – at a pinch – nine bounces.

No pressure.

I rolled up my sleeves, too, hypocritically buying time. I could hear my inner TV commentator intone quietly for the audience, 'Like every sport it has its physicality, but ultimately skimming's a mental game. Daniels to skim next. Ryan on fifteen after two goes. Nate needs twelve to equal at this point.'

Paddy was staring out to sea. He stubbed out his cigarette on a stone. Rain clouds on the horizon threatened to roll in.

I warmed up my left wrist with a few flicks, without letting go of the projectile: a light-grey stone this time, flat as a discus. I adopted the stance with my legs: right thigh forward with the lower leg making a 120-degree angle at the knee; the left leg stretched out nearly straight behind, as if about to kneel in lopsided prayer. I did, in fact, bend down, but not before the Almighty; it was to moisten the stone, to reduce friction. Paddy missed that trick.

And here goes: the stone gets up some serious angular momentum on the spin; I don't so much let go of it as it fights to leave my grip.

The straightness of the line created by its bounces, which I count one by one, is to die for. 'Ten!' I cry.

Paddy demurred, turning back to me. 'No – nine, Nate.'

'It was ten – on my mother's life.'

'Nine, and no mistake. And is that your mother walking on water over there ...?' Paddy turned seawards and pointed to the middle distance.

'You little shit!' I gallop towards him, jump on his back before he can turn round again, and lock my right arm around his neck, squeezing his windpipe. He throws me off then we scrap and scrabble on the shore, half in play, half in rage built up in our pressure cooker over the years. I enjoy a moment's supremacy with my knee on his back while he's prostrated. 'I'm the king of the castle!' I exclaim, then make lip-smacking sounds, moving ever closer to his ear, and plant a big wet stagey kiss on his cheek. 'Mwaah!'

In reaction he rears up like a bucking bronco and throws me off, saying, 'Get down yer dirty rascal,' making great play of wiping his cheek where I'd made contact.

I wiped my lips likewise, saying 'Euugghh – my stubble catching yours. It's like bloody Velcro.'

Paddy dusted himself down. 'As I was saying, you scored nine.'

I stared at the trees snaking into the water and had an idea. 'It was ten, but I'll call it nine on one condition.'

Paddy looked at me, eyebrows raising slightly. He's too cool ever to be in my thrall. 'Yes ...?'

'You see the trees in the water? On the final go, we have to skim between the third and fourth trees, and the bouncing must go cleanly through them.' I stood there, wondering whether he'd take the bait. He seemed to be doing a geometric calculation, moving his head side to side.

'Okay – you're on.' He made a curious composite move, his left arm chasing his throwing arm as both described a rainbow arc over his head. His upper body then twisted from upright to stretched back to the right, while his left arm rapidly cleared the way for his right arm's power swing, as if bowling underarm. But then his knees bent, and his right upper arm stayed horizontal for the final approach, as if throwing a frisbee. The stone whizzed from his hand with a slight tilt, making one, two, three hops before finding a route through the prescribed gap between the trees. Then it continued its hops, four to seven. Paddy willed it on, rooted to the spot, then half-whispered, 'Yesss!'

My announcer spoke out loud again, in spite of myself. 'Ryan on fifteen plus seven, so twenty-two total. Daniels on twelve after two goes, allowing for one disputed bounce. Minimum eleven required for a win.'

I had to go for the kill. I shifted left to right to view the tolerance I had between the third and fourth trees of this mysterious installation. I found an especially flat stone, cream in colour with jagged edges making five sides, two of which happened to be parallel. It looked like a chunk of broken-off naan bread.

I dipped it in the water. Paddy tutted at what he clearly saw as a superstitious act. I toyed with the idea of aping his unconventional throwing technique but dismissed it as too risky without a rehearsal.

I was left with my normal approach. But how to put a winning twist on it? I imagined I had to slay a seabird bobbing in the distance. First, some pre-emptive flicks of the wrist, then the real thing: the release. The weapon left my grip with plenty of power – too much, in fact. Too much in the wrong direction, that is. Three bounces, then it clipped the fourth tree just above the water line and ricocheted off diagonally to the left. It managed a further desultory two and a half bounces, died a death, and was buried at sea.

87

Film script 1 – scene 3

EXT. HOUSE – DUSK

The handheld camera starts very tight on a key going into a Yale lock. Widen out and track back to reveal a **BOY** in his teens, school bag over his shoulder, going through an apricot-coloured front door with a stained-glass inset. We hear a swish accompany the door opening. The boy looks down, motivating a pan down to reveal three letters on the mat which have been jammed under the door, and so have moved with it. We hear the door shut and see the boy's hand enter frame as he picks the letters up. They appear to be nondescript bills and corporate promotions. The camera pans up with the boy's hand holding the letters, then lets him walk to the end of the short hall. It's gloomy inside with most of the light reaching the interior coming from outside: a sodium lamp is casting an orange glow over the walls and fixtures on them, including a barometer on the left. The boy walks out of sight past a wall to the left. We hear a click and a light goes on out of shot. We see some of the reflected light at the end of the hall. It catches a plate which appears to have an African-style folk design on it, hanging on the wall. We hear the boy's footsteps go up the stairs.

88

Paddy talks
Stamford, Connecticut – 31 December 1999

'You complete and utter knob. Nay, borderline eejit!' Paddy was on his back like a flipped beetle, limbs flailing, laughing his nuts off (if beetles have nuts).

A tad histrionic, methinks. 'Steady on, old chap,' I said in English self-parody. 'That's not cricket.'

Crickets, beetles ...

'No it's not – but if you were bowling instead of skimming, you'd-a got the wicket alright. Did you think those are willow trees?'

'Oh, fuck off, Paddy.'

Oops.

Swearing at the boss can give you a limited shelf life. Not usually a good career move. My P45 flashes before my eyes.

An anxious pause.

'As it's the millennium, I'll let you off.' That Abe Lincoln stare. Praise be. 'On one condition ... you go skinny dipping. In and out the trusty tree trunks. With no trunks.'

In December? In the Atlantic? In public? 'I'll meet you halfway,' I say. 'We go half-naked, trousers hoicked up, weaving through the trees. One goes out first, and as soon as they see the other one reach the last tree then the first, no, the second one goes, er ...' The conviction in my voice drains into the slate-coloured sea.

I summoned up the blood.

'...Or we could both stop this pissing contest and you could tell me why the hell you absconded from the biggest gig of your life?' Shocked at myself, I met the Lincoln glare head on.

Paddy, if anything, looked more shocked. For someone who uses his gift of the gab professionally, he went very quiet.

We stood six feet apart. My hands, which had been open in a pleading way, now found my pockets. 'We need to talk,' I said, stating the obvious. Paddy didn't dissent.

Half a dozen sunloungers formed a sad off-season squad near us at the foot of the brick wall which edged the car park. Someone had forgotten to store them for the winter, or not deemed them worthy of protection. They were inviting in the way only cheap white plastic with last night's rainwater on it can be. I beckoned to Paddy to join me.

His Oldsmobile Aurora, or rather Alamo's Aurora, was parked up to the edge of the wall, overhanging slightly. Between the raked headlights, a block of slanted blue bodywork formed the snout. The fender, forgive my American, bore a central 'Mass plate', a term that intrigued me when used by the PI in a message earlier. He translated it for me as a Massachusetts number plate.

I'd shaken the rainwater from the two least decrepit loungers while Paddy tried to find something from the Olds for us to sit on. I angled our loungers in on themselves a bit; not parallel, but half facing out to sea, half facing each other. Then I hastily randomised the angles – they looked too symmetrical. The rhythmic music of lapping waves made for a calming soundtrack. For now.

Paddy came down the grey slabbed steps with a black floor mat in each hand. He'd put his jacket back on. Offering me a mat he said, 'Here – get yer English arse on this.'

As we sat beneath the hire car, it seemed to dominate proceedings, sticking its proud nose into our business. And we had no shortage of that.

I placed a mat centrally on my chosen lounger and sat side-on, facing Paddy's lounger. He placed his mat askew on the white plastic. I thought he'd sit transversely like me, but he reclined back with his left leg in front, his right leg splayed out, foot anchored on the ground, away from the lounger. He was like an old Hollywood Lothario obliged to keep one foot on the floor. Paddy looked out to sea where a container ship slowly headed north. He reached into his jacket and pulled out a much-squashed packet of fags. Selecting one, he lit up, took that first long drag, and I got the only attractive smell there is for a passive smoker like me: from the first puff. Like the initial hit of coke (they say), or the first tea of the day, nothing ever matches it.

'So how did you know which direction to find me in?' Paddy asked, still looking out to sea.

'I asked first. What were you running from?'

He readjusted his position on the recliner, mumbling a variation of 'fuckssakes' ostensibly to himself, but for me to overhear. 'It's complicated, right? There're things you know about, things you don't.'

'Yeah, well how about we don't waste time on what I already know? Big gig, big coke habit, fragile ego ...' Crikey, my mouth had gone for UDI.

Paddy stroked his speckled stubble. 'It's Jacqui. She's – she's *torrach*.'

'Torah? She's Jewish?'

'No – *torrach*.' Him and his passive-aggressive Irish words. 'Up the pole.' I could guess, but didn't want to say it out loud. Paddy sighed. 'She's pregnant. Preggers, as you Brits say. I'm going to be a daddy.'

'Bloody hell. The pregnancy bit I understand. It's the daddy bit I struggle with,' I said.

He shot me a look. '*You* struggle with it? How do you think I feel, Nate?' He thumped the heel of his hand on his sternum. 'No more partying, no more dodgy doogu doogu.' He got that term off me, and I got it off a Jamaican friend in London: patois for sex. What else?

This is where my 'learned optimism' came in – my brave attempt to force myself to think positively. Or should that be futile attempt? This time, though, I was putting it to use for Paddy. 'What you're forgetting is the upside of fatherhood: you're not factoring in feeling a greater love for your child than anything you've ever known. A unique bond for life.'

'If I wanted a bond for life I'd speak to a financial adviser. Look, I'm just not cut out for it and that's that.' He took another drag and his cheeks hollowed out like he was seventy.

'You may be right. In the sense that no new dads are cut out for it. But you can learn. My therapist says babies teach their mums how to be mothers. Must be the same for dads. Trust your instincts. Keep your eyes and ears – and your mind – open.' God – what did I sound like? Kitsch Me Quick.

Paddy stubbed out his ciggie on a pebble, emitting one last belch of smoke. '...Says the non-parent Nate.'

'That doesn't invalidate it. I mean, I've never flown a rocket, but I know it'd be a good idea to lift off with the pointy end at the top.'

'It's not the fathering bit – it's all the crap that comes with it: nannies, nurseries, keeping the press away, being forced to put the little wretch through posh school 'cos Daddy's famous. Then the kid turns out a proper little madam. Or little Lord fucking Fauntleroy.'

It was news to me poshness might be a problem: I thought Ricky was building a power base on the Thames, like a latter-day Tudor king. 'Any son or daughter of yours is likely to have a classy English accent, that's true. You might want to make your peace with that. They'll also be rather good at French, thanks to *maman*.' But with the waves twenty feet away I felt we were ignoring the sea elephant in the vicinity. 'Isn't this really about your old man, though? Playing the fame game as a ruse to win his love.' Shazam! Amateur Therapist Hits Nail on Head.

'Spare me the sub-Freudian psychobollocks, Nate. Me da hit the juice young to cope with the stress of being in your hostile fucked-up country. Who could blame him? In the Seventies anyone in London with an Irish accent was The Enemy. The Met had him up against the wall more than once in the middle of the rush hour 'cos of his Irish number plate. Humiliated him. Crushed him. And, tired of being treated like a terrorist when he was trying to earn an English crust, he took us back to the old country. I wasn't rivalling Dad to shag me ma, sorry. So much for your Oedipal Sigmund gobshite. 'Fraid the truth's more mundane.'

Wow. Touched a nerve there. Quod Erat – I think – Demonstrandum. The more he digs in against my analysis, the more I think I'm right. But how to get through to a resistant client? 'I'm sure your father had a good side you might want to copy? For the bairn.'

'Yeah – I plan to be like Dad in one respect: an old soak. Numbs the pain and takes the edge off those broken nights.'

Well, that worked.

'I keep having this vision of booties and mobiles.' Paddy had suddenly become wistful. 'Not those frigging phones that rule our lives. I mean those floaty things the child looks up to in wonder above the crib.' Paddy sat himself up and faced me for a moment. Then he looked away. A milky sun peered through wispy contrails. I thought I saw a tear form in his eye but dismissed it. His palm brushed whatever it was away roughly, as if in irritation. Then he looked back to me and, yes, both eyes had filled up. 'How can that ever be enough, Nat? After the highs of performing, being on fire, the buzz of big ratings, the laughter, the cheers, the applause, and – yes – the freaking coke highs? How can I ever take an interest in a snotty, cacky child who won't sleep?' Those deep-set eyes exaggerated his isolation, as if he was seeing everything from an extra, recessed distance.

'Do you want to be with Jacqui?' I thought I'd spare us the L-word – love – this time.

'Course I do. Uniquely among women she seems to give a fuck.' He lit up another fag and looked out to sea. Foreboding signs warned of dangers in the deep.

Could this really be the end of Ricky – not Paddy – bumping and grinding from bed to bed?

I leaned in, resting my head on my hands, elbows anchored on my thighs. 'Children change us.' So now I'm making the case for kids. How did that happen? I never made it convincingly to myself. The body in the bed killed my children. 'It won't be "a child". It'll be your child. You'll have a bond with it. It's a mystery, but it's ... real. You can't see it, like you can't see gravity. But you sure can feel it.'

Poor Millie visits me briefly, as if in a film as short as a blipvert. Scratchy Super 8 bumps through the gate like a home movie. She's in a tight shot, smiling to camera. All innocent, her life – and new life – before her.

Don't mention how the bond can fail. Or how a parent *feels* it's failed.

89

Film script 1 – scene 4

INT. GREEN ROOM – NIGHT

RICKY RYAN is watching himself back on a TV in the corner of the green room. We see him from behind in long shot, framed with the large screen over his left shoulder. It's the show he's just finished fronting, live from London to the nation. Colleagues who've also worked on the show are huddling in groups, camera right [i.e. on the right side of the viewer's screen], half in shadow, away from him. They are laughing and joking among themselves and piling food on to plates at the buffet. Two hospitality assistants are refilling glasses at an adjacent table. No one else is watching the TV or, for now, registers Ricky.

Slowly, smoothly the camera starts to track anticlockwise around Ricky. The TV sound is mostly drowned out by the chatter in the room, but audience laughter cuts through in reaction to a comic monologue Ricky is delivering in the recording. We see the real-time Ricky's shoulders in the foreground shake in time with the laughter coming from the TV. A background artist in the green room flicks their eyes across to Ricky, but continues their conversation. The person they are talking to quickly looks behind themselves at Ricky, and then immediately back again.

The huddles of studio staff are now framed out by the tracking move as the camera sees Ricky in profile, with the TV also in profile now on the right of frame. He is holding a plate with some uneaten buffet food on it, as well as a near-empty glass streaked with red-wine legs.

The camera finally settles with the TV Ricky is watching seen from behind in the foreground, and we are virtually in Ricky's eyeline. We hear a little more of the TV sound relative to the chatter in the room, and catch the odd line, including the apparent end to a gag, '...it's no laughing matter!' followed by an audience laugh. We can see Ricky's shoulders are shaking because he is crying.

90

Paddy talks part two
Stamford, Connecticut – 31 December 1999

Paddy, reclining on the lounger, was quoting from a regional guidebook that came with the hire car. '"Stamford, a city in the state of Connecticut, boasts a number of Baptist churches ..." Plenty to immerse yourself in, if you want to get wet, Nate.'

'I never got what's so threatening to your lot about total immersion?' I shot back. 'It works for my hot water system. St Paul was plunging people fully under from the year dot to wash away their sins. None of yer timid sprinkles on the forehead.'

'Nate – would you ever listen? My "lot", as you elegantly call them, from the earliest times practised triple immersion. That's three times as many as your people.'

'Triple immersion? What was that in aid of? I know troubles come in threes ..."

'In the name of the Father, Son and Holy Ghost. Forever three-in-one. Like the oil.'

'It's not about one-upmanship, Pads. Or even two-upmanship. The point is being completely dunked is a bit of theatre – you'd understand that, as a showman. It worked for me in my teens – for about five minutes. Then I had my first doubts during the tea and biscuits afterwards.'

'Should have taken a leaf out of the Catholic playbook and gone to confession. Say what you like about the little box with the curtain, it gets things off your chest.'

'First time I set foot in a Catholic church I thought the confessional was a fancy photo booth. I guess either box has flashes.' Ouch. It was out my gob before it could even be run past the censor. Too close to the mark?

Paddy swung round to face me. 'You know, boy, the Church of England has its own skeletons in the vestry. Has done for years. And here we are on opposite sides of the fence, but at least we're not pointing guns at each other. Eighty years ago, it would have been a different story.' His gravitas had extra gravitas because of the contrast with his chirpy public persona. '"A terrible beauty", and all that.'

'More terrible than beautiful,' I said. 'One thing I'm with Bono on. In that U2 film he says "fuck the revolution". Amen to that. And I speak with the bombing of Harrods still ringing in my ears after sixteen years. Working there as a porter in '83. Doing my civic duty, checking the stock room for suspect devices after a coded warning over the tannoy. Found nothing, went to lunch late.' I paused. 'Then that sickening dull boom from the other end of the building. The deadly sound of failed politics. Set to the shrill music of screams.'

'Violence became the voice of the voiceless. You were never denied a job or a home because you were Protestant. Both things happened to Catholics. It was the norm in the north. Second-class citizens.'

'I couldn't bear to look out the window,' I said. 'And I didn't need to. It was enough to watch a colleague do it for me, to see her revulsion. And tears. Absentee revolutionaries never had to look out that window, to face what happened with the coins they put in the collection pot, in New York or old Kilburn. The miracle of turning silver into shrapnel. Praise the Lord and pass the Semtex.'

'It was born of despair.' Paddy shifted on the recliner. 'Your government wouldn't listen till the bombs were on their doorstep.'

'"*Dulce et decorum est.* It is a sweet and noble thing to die for one's country." Nothing sweet or noble about six dead at Harrods, from whichever side of the divide. Or 600 dead – or 3,000. Could have been your nieces. Or your brother. Or Jacqui and your unborn child.'

Paddy lit up again and looked out to sea with a thousand-yard stare. The water mirrored the greyscale of the sky. But there was just enough blue to make a pair of sailor's trousers, as my mother used to say. Queen of the Aphorisms.

'I visited you in hospital,' said Paddy, sharing that lovely transgressive smell of the first puff. 'At the nuthouse.'

'Hey – only I'm allowed to call it the nuthouse. I don't remember you being there.'

Paddy tried out his best London East End accent. 'You was out for the count.' Then, defaulting to his native Cork lilt, he added, 'Der. Off your tits on drugs.'

'Legal ones.'

'Still drugs. And still an altered state of consciousness.'

'Chlorpromazine. Largactyl. Imipramine. Lithium. Ah, no – that came later. Anti-depressants were the gateway.'

'You were a bigger junkie than me.'

'I didn't choose those drugs.'

'Don't tell me, fellah: they chose you?'

'Are you sure you were there?'

'I was there alright. Pity you weren't. I brought you a book.'

Curiouser and curiouser.

'Your da gave it to me to give to you. *The Custard Stops at Enfield.*'

'Not Enfield – Hatfield. By Kenny Everett.'

'Cuddly Ken!' we said in unison.

'Our radio hero.' Paddy drew again on his ciggie.

'I wondered how it got into my room,' I said. 'Fancy that – I had a celebrity postboy. Well, a future celeb.'

'You probably constructed some fantasy tale of how it flew there. Or how Ken brought it round in person.'

'He served time in the nuthouse. Or, at least, he did a stretch in the hell of his own head. I remember as a kid listener him bunking off his breakfast shows 'cos of "ill health", shall we say. There was that photo in the *Evening Standard*. Of him looking into the lens like a lost soul. The same look I saw years later as he sat next to his dresser in the TV studio. Don't meet your heroes.'

'Does that apply to you? And me?' Paddy turned to face me. His skin looked weathered.

'It applies to everyone.' And then I got it. 'Do you think you're my hero?'

'I didn't say that,' Paddy snapped back, adding, 'I asked if it applied to you as well.'

I laughed a brief, mocking laugh. 'Jeez! Do you think that's how it works? I stay on the show 'cos I worship you? Christ, that coke's strong. It's true what they say: it fucks with your ego.'

In for a penny ...

Paddy squirmed in his seat. 'I shouldn't meet my heroes, neither.' Another punctuating puff. ''Specially when they're in the nuthouse.' A seagull squawked an awkward refrain. 'Your mate Millie said what strength of character you must have had to survive that. It haunts me.'

'Did she really say that?'

'What are you – some kind of lie detector?' Paddy sounded irritated.

'Blimey. You wouldn't have put money on me surviving this shit and her not. She died days after Diana. You'd expect them both to make the millennium. And miles beyond.'

'Stop with your survivor guilt, Nate. You've a right to your life.'

'And Millie did hers, too. Where's the justice? I used to think life's like a relay race where one generation hands on the baton to the next. But Millie dropped hers early – before she'd finished the lap.'

'As did your mother. But the ones left behind adapt. They have to. You picked up the baton before you were ready ...'

'Flunked it. Dropped it.'

'Picked it up again.'

While I was briefly in credit, I thought I'd stay with the seriousness. Deep breath. 'So any further thoughts about easing back on the coke?'

'No. No further thoughts.'

Bugger.

'...'Cos I've already had the big thought.' Paddy exhaled a ciggie coda then stubbed the fag out between us. 'A man should be master of his desires, not slave to them. Though it pains me to say it, Nate, I think it's time to knock that habit on the head. New millennium, new parenthood ... New me.'

Bloody hell. 'Nice one.' Paddy never tires of wrong-footing me.

'In fact, I'm thinking of writing a book about kicking the habit: I'd call it *Ciao, Charlie.* My manifesto for the new era.' He pronounced that last word 'Eire'.

'Cool.'

'You should write a book, too.'

'Nah, mate. You're the star. No one wants to read about Jack Shit from the Shires. The follow spot follows you, not me. I wait discreetly in the wings.'

'You might have a point. It's all about me, after all.'

'Hang on – I was being modest. English reserve.'

'Haha! Gotcha. That's the thing about Brits – polite till you get found out. Proud to be humble.'

My Uriah Heep moment. 'So how did we ever run an empire being so shy?'

'Don't start me ... Point was you *couldn't* run an empire. And it was nowhere run worse than in your own backyard, so it was.'

'Hey – I'm not a colonialist.' He loves tarring us all with the Brit brush. Time to address another elephant. 'So if you've become a reformed coke fiend, Paddy, can I coax you back to the show?'

Coax you. Or coke's you?

91

Film script 1 - scene 5

INT. HOUSE - DUSK

A handheld camera is in close up above a 1960s wooden bedside table with an indistinct handwritten note on it, blue biro on a small scrap of lined paper. A hand - the boy's - comes into frame and picks up the note and moves it closer to camera, which is unsteady. A post-production effect makes certain phrases come into prominence and focus then move out again, while defocussing other phrases. Thus we see snatches of sentences hove into view, like 'if they bring me round', 'dying like a zombie', 'depression as a chronic condition', 'live at your mother's', 'bring Nathan to see me'. A tear seems to fall on this last sentence and smudge the words.

92

Paddy talks part three
Stamford, Connecticut – 31 December 1999

I needed another layer against the eastern seaboard's chill.
Paddy tossed me the keys to the hire car. I went to the boot
to get my fleece to be reminded it was Comms Central – both
Nokias were in the pockets. And – jeepers – they had four
messages on them apiece. I started to work through the ones
on my phone, then Paddy appeared. He'd decided on
layering up himself as well. I offered him his phone back, but
on seeing the number of messages sitting on it he declined.
'I've got enough ball-aches without that,' he said, poetically.
Before heading back for the white recliner, I readied myself
to ring Louise for the precis. Not such a bad idea; my phone
showed the time as 10.48am.

Dear God.

Quick mental calculation: we've got to get back to
the theatre for the dress run at 1pm. For a long show like this
it's more a 'topping and tailing' of sections – links between
acts – which has to be finished by 3, and then there'll be
director's notes. Audience in 3.15pm. Technicians back
3.30. Warm-up for fifteen minutes from 3.45, Ricky talks as
if confidentially to the audience, then we hit the air at 4pm
Eastern Time (9.00pm UK time) for three hours up to the
UK's midnight, then another hour for the post-UK midnight
segment. Then a 'post-record' to get a few special links for
the US edition in the can.

I was about to ring Louise when the phone rang first.
'Where are you Nate? Any word on Ricky?' It was Louise
sounding jumpy, even by jumpy standards. 'We've ploughed

on rehearsing with Mort.' I sat on the back seat of the Olds. Icy calm. Keep breathing.

I don't leave any further room for admonition. 'Sorry sorry sorry. Yes I've found Paddy. Ricky.' Get the good news in first – classic PR trick. 'He's alive and well – and coming back to the show.' Silence. I wasn't expecting 'Oh bliss, oh rapture', but surely that would buy her off?

'You haven't seen my messages, have you?' I got told off anyway. Louise's tone darkened.

This wasn't going to be pretty.

'My last message said Colin had decided on a cut-off. He wanted Ricky tracked down by 10.30 or he needn't bother coming in.'

Oh fuck.

I mentally rewound the morning furiously. All that time I was fannying around with Paddy, skimming stones and male bonding, thinking I was doing the show a favour, to the Colonel we were running down the clock. Bollocks.

'I guess that's it, then,' I said.

'I'm sorry, Nate.' It's not that she didn't sound genuine. But I hated her for being Her Master's Voice. We wrapped the call up.

Got to tell Ricky. Paddy. It's Game Over.

Wait.

Do I *have* to tell Paddy? Isn't it kinder to feed his delusions that, as he returns to the fold, he'll be Jesus on Palm Sunday, cheering crowds throwing fronds before him, his donkey showing he comes in peace and not on a war horse? And that there'll be rejoicing in Heaven at one sinner who repents: the return of the prodigal presenter?

Or is that actually crueller – a time-limited reprieve signifying nothing, a chimera which vanishes with the morning dew?

My mental wrestling was cut short with the return of the big man himself. Paddy went to open the driver's door but was interrupted by 'noises off': female squeals of delight.

'Is it Ricky? No – can't be. It *is* Ricky. You're Ricky Ryan, aren't you?'

Intrigued, I got out of the car to see two women, early twenties or so, one with a blonde bob, the other a brushed-back brunette, rushing over to the Olds, intercepting Paddy before he got in to drive. They'd dressed for December, at least: both wearing thick synthetic fur coats which were nearly as blonde as the first woman, the acrylic fibres carrying an unlikely sheen, as if from a fake sun.

'We love the show, Ricky,' said the blonde one, her accent placing her somewhere in the south of England, and somewhere south of middle class.

'Yes,' added the brunette, with a carbon-copy accent. 'We can't get enough of the *Farrago*.'

'*Fandango*,' corrected Ricky, his annoyance suppressed by charm. He smiled generously, looking from the first woman to her companion and back again.

'Could we get your autograph?' said Pretty Woman One.

'Yes,' cajoled Pretty Woman Two. 'We're massive fans of yours.'

'Sure,' said a newly suave Ricky, adjusting his collar, his exclusive watch and the dark thatch of his forearm partially revealed under his shirt sleeve. 'Do you have pen and paper?'

'I've got this,' said Pretty Woman One, proffering a black felt pen to her hero. 'You got paper, Ruthie?'

''Fraid not, Nicky.'

'I guess you could sign these,' said Nicky. And with that she flung open her fur coat to reveal all she had between her and the elements was skimpy red and black lingerie.

'I'm next, Ricky!' yelped Ruthie, parading fulsome breasts barely held in check by an emerald basque.

Ricky didn't drop a stitch and boldly found the flesh above Nicky's half cups, powering through any self-consciousness with the line: 'Not sure how steady my handwriting'll be, ladies.'

His handwriting was indeed unsteadied as a cacophony of high-revving engines blasted the crisp air. A trinity of muscle cars sped into the car park. Ricky's head turn to take the scene in truncated his autograph as 'Ricky Ry_____'

'GOTCHA!' came a cry from the opposite direction across the bonnet, accompanied by popping flashbulbs.

'Over here, Mr Ryan,' came another call from a red sports car with white Starsky and Hutch stripes. As it screeched to a halt two more paps had piled out, snapping images like a machine gun expends bullets. 'Shoot first, ask questions later!' quipped one.

I began to flash forwards, as it were, to the first British tabloids' front pages of the new millennium; I imagined an arresting image of Ricky's phallic pen captured in the cleavage of one of two models beaming big crimson-lipsticked smiles. They look lasciviously at the nation's top television performer apparently unable to complete his own name. You can write your own headlines, but I pictured variations on the theme, 'RICKY'S BOOBED'.

93

Caught martially – 12.37pm EST
Ed Sullivan Theater, Manhattan – 31 December 1999

'What the bloody hell were you thinking of, man?' The Colonel's war-worn features were more contorted than ever. Those steely blue eyes, which had seen action across the wastelands of British light entertainment for too long, now pierced Ricky's defensiveness as we stood in Colin's office-within-an-office. He would have waved the white showbiz flag long ago, but he had too much alimony, too many leaching children (born of demanding mothers various), and a folly in Esher with life-size battlements to support. Rumour had it his disposable income barely covered his sandwich budget, though as the source of that rumour was Ricky, it should be taken with a sachet of salt.

I'd put off looking at the messages on Ricky's phone on the journey back as they were likely to be higher stakes, but I couldn't delay it any longer. The Colonel had left a message – which Louise had primed me for – angrily drawing a line in the sand, like Monty at El Alamein: 10.30am local was indeed his strict cut-off. Speeding along the Interstate, what I didn't expect to see was Jacqui's message describing in graphic detail, and with an urgency matching only that of her early reaction to Ricky's disappearance, how she was bleeding. She went on to say she was going to lose the baby and what was she to do being away from home and family, etc., etc.?

I decided that for Paddy ignorance was bliss. Common decency demanded I spoke to Jacqui urgently from the car, though. But what could I say that wouldn't panic Paddy, who would overhear? And if I said the wrong thing to Jacqui, that could lead to her making the wrong decision. I'm clearly not a medic, and even medics don't like diagnosing diseases remotely, so I wasn't going to play amateur obstetrician over the phone. But I had to say something. She needs urgent attention, I thought, but I can't use loaded words in front of Paddy like 'hospital', 'emergency', 'bleeding', etc.

Paddy and I had been silent as I mulled this over and he seemed to be in a motorway-induced trance, with some disposable pop on the radio at low level, so I rang Jacqui's hotel room phone number with some trepidation. The phone rang, and rang ...

Oh God, she's on the floor ...

...And rang ...

Or she's in hospital ...?

Finally, Jacqui picked up. 'Allô?' she said hesitantly.

'Oh – hi, love – it's Nate. I ...'

'Ah, Nate. I was in the closet. I am sorry for the delay.'

'No problem. I was just wondering, er, how you ... are?' I held Paddy in my peripheral vision, furiously monitoring him for any reaction. I self-edited my words carefully.

'I'm fine.'

Lummy.

'That's good,' I responded. 'No – er ...?'

'No, what ...? Ah, the bleeding. No, that stopped nearly as soon as I had messaged you.'

Ah. 'Good.' But it would have been nice to have been told. 'We're on our way back to the studio.'

'Yes – I know.'

Crikey – how? Oh, yes ...

'The PI told me.'

Of course he did.

'He saw you leave the car park.'

Big Brother was watching us.

Meanwhile, back in Room 101, The Colonel is carpeting Ricky. We stand in his office like two scolded schoolboys, taking the heat, but without a textbook between us to shove down our trousers.

'Give me one good reason why I should let you back on my show?' Colin locked his heat-seeking gaze on to the fallen star to my left. 'One bloody good reason.' Ouch – the idea the Colonel had reappropriated the show as his own must have hurt Ricky. Great tactic, though.

There was a silence as in the Book of Revelations when the Lamb opened the seventh seal. Certainly it felt like 'about half an hour'. Only instead of an angel's trumpet, it was me who piped up, breaking the silence. It was shit or bust. 'As we headed back here, Ricky got papped, Colin. A couple of, er ... photogenic fans sought Ricky's autograph. I think it'll make the press, and I think it'll be good for the show – for when we pick up in London. T-taking the long view.'

'Don't you worry – I was going to get to that,' said Colin, leaning far back in the swivel chair behind his desk. He lit one of his torpedo-shaped Cuban specials with the silver flip-topped lighter that lived by his blotting pad. 'Hanson's already been on the blower.' That would be Cliff Hanson, aka Cliff Hanger, Fleet Street's most loved and loathed publicist, depending on whether you were newspaper client or target. 'The autograph hunters – page-three girls, he called them – are the least of our concerns. He says as well as them, he's got a photo of Ricky here enjoying a Sherbet Fountain. Or some other white powder that's not too good for you.' At that, the Colonel opened a drawer next to him and produced a 10" x 8" print of Ricky caught hook, line and mirror. 'Cliff asked me which story I'd prefer to buy.' Knowing Hanson's method, the story you buy is the one that *doesn't* get printed. Some people call it blackmail. 'So which story do you want to see in *The Sun*?'

94

Film script 1 – scene 6

INT. VICTORIAN ASYLUM – DAY

The camera takes in the white-painted brick of a side room off the main dining and visitors' area. We hear the patient, a **YOUNG MAN**, before we see him. We are aware of some sound of teeth chattering and rustling of clothes. The camera slowly and smoothly pans left while also tracking left across the white space to reveal corners of posters held in place by sticky tape on the brick. Eventually the camera reveals two particular posters ripped, but leaving enough detail to register firstly a U2 poster promoting the *October* album, and next to it the photo from the front cover of the *Beatles for Sale* album. We can just see George on the left and Paul on the right, with John and Ringo missing.

The camera pans slowly down diagonally left to reveal the patient lying on a bed. He is involuntarily shaking, as if his muscles have gone into spasm. **A MALE NURSE** in casual clothes is on a chair next to the bed, leaning in to be closer to the patient. The nurse looks concerned.

NURSE

If you carry on like this, you'll kill yourself. I don't mean deliberately. It's that your body won't be able to take this much longer.

95

Less is more – 12.41pm EST
Ed Sullivan Theater, Manhattan – 31 December 1999

Colin drew on his cigar for so long I thought he'd turn blue.

'I don't need to tell you how many wannabes are queuing up for the *Fandango*'s juicy time slot, once we get into the new year,' said the Colonel. 'Or perhaps I do? And, being a new millennium, we could freshen things up. With a female lead, perhaps? Or there's always a Premiership footballer coming to the end of their sporting career looking for a new direction. Gift of the gab, high-profile, ready-made fan base. What's not to like, as they say over here? We could even have a troupe – the latest Footlights high-fliers. Or we could trawl the alternative circuit. The world's moving on, Ricky.'

I was reminded of those war myths in which the enemy's penises were cut off and shoved in their mouths. That was kind of what the Colonel was doing to Ricky as the torture continued in his office. I could only guess how this was going down with El Ryan, who stood impassively next to me. The build-up of smoke was starting to make me weep, and I didn't want Colin to see that as a sign of weakness. Worse, I might cough at any moment.

Outside our glass cage, the office went about its business with a muted soundtrack as the door was shut. Keyboards were pounded, filing-cabinet drawers opened and closed, photocopiers kept hot with hyperactivity.

'But there's one thing that might redeem you in the short-term, Ryan.' The Colonel leant back at forty-five degrees. 'You might say it's paradoxical.'

'Yes?' Blimey; Ricky had found his tongue again.

'Take a seat.' Colin beckoned us on to one of the sofas that nestled in the shadow of his desk. We duly sat. 'You'll be familiar with the phrase "less is more". It seems the less you're around, Ricky, the more people want to talk about you. Speaking to London in the last hour, according to high powers at the network, your disappearance led every UK news bulletin going. TV and radio. Pop, rock, classical, speech stations – top story. And now you've been found, the angle's changed from "Where's Ricky?" to "Why, Ricky? What was your disappearance about?" The phone-ins are full of speculation. Every Poundland dingbat wants their say. Conspiracy theories abound. Is Ricky involved in a new moonshot? Has he been spotted in Area 51? I exaggerate, of course, but it's only a question of degree. The chatter's there, for sure. Rolling news is fixated, too. They're looping footage of you from rehearsals with cultural commentators voicing over, for Christ's sake – adding their twopenn'orth about your "societal significance". It's a bloody master stroke. You should disappear more often, dear boy. Oh, and by the way, we have our half hour back – so you're doing a full four hours again. And it's only a matter of time before we get "Ricky Ryan Ate My Hamster".'

Colin then offered us his equivalent of 'trebles all round' – tea from a machine in the adjoining office – but we both politely declined; that would have felt tasteless in more than one sense. Besides, the clock was ticking. Though at least Ricky was granted a reprieve for tonight's show.

He wanted a shower before final rehearsals so I left Paddy ensconced in his star dressing room.

96

Corridor conversation two
Ed Sullivan Theater, Manhattan – 31 December 1999

Back in the studio, Ricky looked supremely at home – as if he'd never been away. How could it be otherwise with the consummate showman? One of the demands of the job is to be able to compartmentalise to a pathological degree. In fact, the worse things were off-screen, the wittier, smarter, and smoother he seemed on-screen.

We'd been here before. When the unpaid tax became an issue for him and had the potential to sink his career, Ricky seemed to return with extra stature, and he stood tall enough as it was.

Watching him now standing coolly in a pool of light, looking sharp in an immaculately ironed black suit and his crisp 'television white' (i.e. off-white) shirt, with a slightly bigger collar than was fashionable for the end of the century, you wouldn't have guessed we were only hours away from transmission. And a good chunk of the nominal 'rehearsal' time would be taken up with the finishing touches to Ricky's make-up, re-batterying of his radio mic, and one final wardrobe check. A tweak here, a tuck there. Plus any last-minute notes from director Roger.

Observing him from the gloom at the foot of the audience rostrum I was reminded of the loneliness of the long-distance presenter. Northern comedian Les Dawson, a staple of light-entertainment TV in the Seventies and Eighties, described the lot of the stand-up as the 'loneliest job in the world'. Ricky's more an MC than a comic, but seeing him in the cone of light carved out by his follow spot his role looks plenty isolated to me. Many's the person who would clamber over the competition to claim Ricky's crown, but most of them are chasing a mirage. They're running after a myth of their own making, but they won't see it for the flimsy construct it is: they'll never be good enough (or, one could add, lucky enough) to get a chance to prove themselves. They'll have to settle for the label 'also-ran'.

From my vantage point, Ricky's spotlight catches the numerous scars in the floor surface, the only evidence of the countless shows which have preceded this one. Elsewhere in the building corridors are lined with photos of past productions, grins fixed through time, artists' fame faded even if the print hasn't. And then, in some remote location, countless rows of tightly-wound tape carry the invisible intricacies of recording: a million TV shows – and the collective pain experienced in making them – reduced to the precarious memory of magnetism.

Ricky seems to rise above the ephemeral nature of this game. He says he embraces entertainment's short shelf-life. At least, he says that to me, not to lifestyle-column interviewers. 'The alternative, Nate,' he says, 'is to go mad.' But is he really reconciled to being a footnote in the history of his craft? Can any of us cope with our loss of significance that blithely?

Still, that's not anything he's got to worry about today. The show must, of course, go on.

Dress run over (such as it was), as I walked from the studio to my dressing room I heard muffled chanting from the street at the front of the building. I thought it was expectant audience members – assorted Ricky and *Fandango* fans. As my ear zoomed in on the noise, I twigged that these chanters weren't on Team Ryan: they were angry and hostile. What could be causing their rage?

After listening for a moment I shrugged to no one and moved on; my preferred poison, that pre-show G & T, wasn't going to drink itself.

Making the perfect gin and tonic: rub a slice of lime around the rim of a chilled glass, squeeze a little into a good measure of gin and ice, throw in the remaining carcass of the fruit, then add tonic at the last minute and stir with a swizzle stick for maximum effervescence.

I learnt to prep this aperitif from Sam, my estranged wife. In the early days we'd sing, 'Now I know my ABCs', but with the letters replaced by 'G & T'. Cutesie, homespun stuff for sure, but there are worse ways to relate. We learnt those later.

I went round the corner, propelled by visions of fizz and muzz to settle into my dressing room, past the white-painted brick of the corridor, but something in my peripheral vision wasn't right. It was like my weird gift of flicking my eyes across a script and having an intuitive sense there's a typo, without even knowing what or where it is. I'd registered a flash of gold somewhere indeterminate while lost in thought. Now I realised the shiny stuff was on my dressing-room door. Or, rather, what had been my dressing-room door. Brushed gold was the background to a name-plate with 'Mort Silus' etched in black on it. Bugger my old boots, I thought – they've moved me. The fuckers have moved me.

A star-spangled cheerleader passed me randomly in the corridor, looking slightly lost and taking in the names on the dressing-room doors. Despite her displacement she still managed an all-American smile. And then Louise sidled up. 'Welcome back – glad you could make it.' She smiled, but my sarcasm detector was flashing. She'd partly changed since earlier in the day and was wearing a dark-blue-and-black-checked chemise, still with the sober black trousers.

'Yeah – we thought we'd drop by for the show. Anyone good on?' Now I didn't know how sarcastic I was being.

'There's at least one really good person on.' Louise pursed her lips slightly, as if containing her amusement at her own hilarity. The effort created cute dimples complementing her subtle freckles.

I swear her eyes scooted past me to look at Mort's nameplate. It wasn't funny. But it was all the encouragement I needed to raise the issue.

I went sotto voce in case Mort was in residence. 'Why does Mr. Silus need to be around now Ricky's returned?'

Louise's gaze briefly moved away as if looking down the corridor, then settled on me again. 'That's something you might want to take up with Colin.'

Was this the same woman who'd been so charming at other times? What's the female form of Judas: Judiths? Judath? Sounds lisp-like.

Then the piece of silver dropped. 'I get it,' I said. 'It's *pour encourager les autres*. It'll concentrate Ricky's mind.'

'I think that's a bit cynical ...'

Butter wouldn't melt. I hope to God Ricky doesn't see it before we go to air.

'Look, Louise: I'm used to being made homeless, but dare I ask if there's any alternative accommodation for me?'

'Yes.'

'Great.'

'Yes – you dare ask. And the answer's no.' More dimpling, less cute this time. Had Louise gone native?

'Referee ...'

'If it's football analogies you're after,' she offered, 'the star player's not performing well and the team has slipped down a league. So the facilities aren't as good.'

'Even the lower leagues have dressing rooms.'

'I think you'll find they don't get individual ones.'

Damn and blast. One-nil to her.

Louise looped a wodge of curlicues behind her left ear. 'It always was a bit of a luxury to give the writer his own room, I'm afraid Nate. Or even to send him abroad in the first place. Not standard practice. But then, it's not normal for the writer to be old buddies with the star.'

'Only fair there should be some compensation for a lifetime of putting up with Paddy,' I countered. 'That said, I wouldn't mind having somewhere to write those last-minute tweaks, Lou.'.

Was that 'Lou' overfamiliar under the circumstances?

'I'll see what I can do.'

Oh, the power. Briefly, again. 'Thanks,' I said.

I watched as the blue and black of Louise's top dissolved into the shadows of the adjoining corridor. The colours made me think of bruises.

97

Film script 1 – scene 7

INT. HOUSE – DAY

A middle-aged WOMAN is sitting smoking at a table, a green-cabled phone beside her. A BOY sits opposite her, but she doesn't acknowledge him. She is too distracted by writing on a small pad. The phone goes and she picks it up. The camera slowly, smoothly tracks anticlockwise in a circle continually, starting in an over-the-shoulder two shot favouring the woman.

WOMAN
(Abruptly to the caller)
Who is it?
(pause)
Be brief – I need to make an urgent call. I've got to phone the doctor.

She draws on her cigarette and passes the phone to the boy. She carries on writing. As the camera continues tracking we are now nearly front on to the boy in an over-the-shoulder two shot with the woman's back to us. The writing pad drops out of frame as the camera gently tightens on the boy.

BOY
Jules? I have to be quick.
(pause)
No, nothing. It's all fine. See you later then?
(pause)
Confirmed. Yup. Thanks – bye.

He hands back the phone to the woman, who doesn't look up. He attempts to catch her eye with a faint smile which soon fades. The camera continues its circular track back round behind the woman, then it cranes up and over her to reveal, not so much the words on the writing pad, as their shape: her handwriting has a large margin which slopes diagonally to the right, becoming larger with every line. And each line itself drifts downwards as it travels from left to right. The woman appears not to have seen the breakdown in her script. Her hand comes into frame in the overhead shot; she picks up the phone and starts dialling.

98

Script Ed flaps – 13.55pm EST
Ed Sullivan Theater, Manhattan – 31 December 1999

'Nate, Nate – quick. We've got two new sections to write.'

Script Ed had put on his cravat as he always did near showtime, as if it would lend him sudden clarity of thought. I noted the royal 'we'. He'd found me chatting to Jenni (or was it Penny?) at the prompter position. I'd had my back to him while facing Jenni(?), who was now in a white chemise with a gold necklace and emerald centrepiece. She clocked my eyes rolling upwards before I turned to face him. Pulsing, cheery music was playing through the PA as the audience arrived. A bass speaker under the audience rostrum belted out the low notes. Hundreds of heels shuffled above our heads, blending with excited chatter. I tried to assess how tipsy they might be, and hence how well my gags might go down.

'What is it?' I asked Ed. I couldn't work out if he was vexed or elated. He tended to shift his weight from side to side whatever his mood. Not sure the cravat worked with the fifty-something man's V-neck pully he wore over a pink-collared shirt.

'What is what?' he asked.

Lord, give me strength. 'What are the new sections?' I asked with infinite patience.

'Well, you know ...' The warmth of his northern accent provided succour. (One born every minute.) But it covered his ignorance. 'Those meetings we held earlier today, like. Against the odds they went for your ideas.' He dragged his hand over his face, as if to reset it. 'No accounting for taste.' Touchez.

Suffice to say in timing the elements of the show in their respective last rehearsals, given the half hour had been restored, Louise calculated we were 'a bit light'. What she hadn't explained was trampoline act Daemon & Fiske were dropped when the half hour was first lost and, when the time was awarded back to the show, and a junior producer rang the guys' agent to reinstate them, the answer came back from the artists, 'Nuts!' Hence the call to plug the gap with a few more minutes' material. Writing the accompanying scripts wasn't the problem, but – denuded of my dressing room – finding a quiet place in which to do so was. And I didn't want to be too far from the studio floor as Ricky liked having me on hand.

I made the mistake of airing my dilemma to Ed.

'You could stop in my dressing room for a bit,' he said, wiping his face.

Blimey O'Reilly. Everything in me that was good screamed 'No' at the very thought. 'That's very kind, thanks Ed,' I said. My mouth, my traitor.

Ed threw me the key to his room, saying, 'Make yourself a nice cuppa – I've proper Yorkshire Tea'.

I made my way there, laptop under my arm, just as the dance troupe emerged from being dressed and made up. They flaunted feather boas and sleek black headdresses like humanoid crows, chattering excitedly down the corridor, pumped up on the greatest drug of all: adrenaline. The show had expanded beyond the confines of the studio due to its vast scale. The dancers had spilled out of an overflow area which became a production line, preparing the various ensembles for the camera in strict show order, in lockstep with the clock.

Our script editor's dressing-room door bore his name, as exciting as the man himself: Ed Smith.

Once inside, I thought I'd stepped into a 1950s bungalow in the 'burbs. Ed had tried to make it homely in the only way he knew: by putting a photo of his wife Edna on the side table, draping a few horse brasses on the trouser press, and arranging some alabaster figurines of cats by the kettle.

I wasn't sure I could concentrate in this stifling space. The priority was to get the studio output on so I could see the show as it aired. Or it was before I spotted the teabags. I was tired of having lame nearly-tea made with lukewarm water and hot milk in this teaforsaken country. They even tried to palm me off with salted water once. Jeez! You shouldn't have to say, 'Can I have hot tea with cold milk and unsalted water?' anywhere. It's enough to make anyone a cultural relativist.

I powered up the TV (standard size – Ed didn't qualify for a widescreen) and on came a documentary channel with a fascinating study of traction engines. Turn on, tune in, drop off. I flicked through outlets of rolling news, soaps, comedies, porn (scrambled, like the brains of those who watch it), and shopping channels – shitloads of them. Every niche catered for in this nation of shoppers. I finally find the familiar form of our warm-up man, Bob Bell, known affectionately as 'Bobbles'. That meant I was on the right channel to get 'Studio Out' – that is, the output of the studio, which would eventually be the show beamed both sides of the Atlantic, albeit at different times. Bobbles spoke in gags and was never 'off'. You'd fear asking him a question because the answer invariably included a punchline. The only way out was to try and beat him to the punch, though that was largely a lost cause. Your punchline would invite yet another punchline (or 'tag', as we call it) from him.

I left Bob riffing on supermarkets in the background. I had work to do.

And then, the knock on the door.

The voice couldn't wait for me to open the door. 'Nate – quick! Ricky's got a problem.' The unmistakeable panicky tones of everyone's favourite script editor.

Now what?

I flung open the door. The cravat hung round Ed's neck limply. His remaining hair was ruffled. 'He's got an urgent mission for you, like. We're on-air in five minutes.'

Der. I kinda knew that. 'What's he want?'

'It's his jacket. It's the wrong kind of black. He needs the spangly one. He picked up the matte one by mistake. The right one's in his dressing room.' Thank God it wasn't anything trivial. In the small world of showbiz, style was a big deal, especially for Ricky. I knew he wouldn't settle without every 'i' dotted. Bobbles' one-liners were hitting home on the monitor high up on a corner shelf. 'He's in make-up. I said you'd gerrit for him. There's a good lad.'

Jeepers. Fifteen years as a broadcast writer and now I'm a bloody runner.

I scoot out of Script Ed's home from home and round the maze of corridors to Ricky's dressing room. En route I catch a bit of Bobbles booming out of the bass bins as someone opens a studio door.

I wave the room-key card over the sensor and it goes red. Another go: red. Calm down. Try again more slowly. Green: third time lucky. This being a star dressing room there are two sofas. And the jacket's not on either of them. So where could it be? I search his clothes rack. 'Spangly, spangly ...' I mumble psychotically, while riffling through his collection of denim, cotton, and fur jackets. Nothing fits the bill. Nothing's even dark. His shirts are all to the right of the rail – no jackets spirited away there, either.

Back of the door? Nope – just a dressing gown. I look at my watch: under three minutes to air.

En suite? Must be. Last place to look. I push open the door with too much force and it bounces off the doorstop. I catch it on the rebound. 'Jacket, jacket ...', I intone like a mad meditation, while looking for the damn thing. Shower, bath, floor ... Of course it's not there. But something catches my eye the other side of the soap from the basin's mixer tap. A small mirror with a trace of a white dusting, and a razor blade ... NO. Can't be. And I decide it isn't. *Ciao Charlie*, my arse. They say 'ciao' can mean hello as well as goodbye.

I turn to leave, doubly dejected, and there it is: a spangly black jacket skulking on the back of the en-suite door.

99

Film script 1 – scene 8

INT. HOUSE – BEDROOM – DAY

The handheld camera – not a Steadicam this time, but apparently shooting amateur-style Super 8 low-quality film with a sepia effect, with scratches and occasional bump cuts, as if poorly edited – follows a middle-aged MAN up the stairs heading straight into a bedroom. He fills most of the frame as he arrives at the foot of the bed. We can just see some feet on the bed past him to the right of frame. The camera then moves with urgency past him to his right, panning left to contain him on the left of frame. He looks from the pills on the bedside table now on the right of frame – quickly reading the label on the bottle – to the person lying on the bed, propped up on their right arm next to the bedside table. The MAN hurriedly shakes the person on the bed, who only responds sluggishly, as if barely conscious. We see it is the BOY, now as an older teenager.

100

nathan.daniels@connectright.co.uk – 31.12.1999

Got to be brief, sorry – we've just hit the air.

Ta for getting back April. Jane!

Best to message me from now on as won't be on e-mail.

Glad re meet. Looking forward.

Wish me luck.

N.

101

The wrong jacket - 3.58pm EST
Ed Sullivan Theater, Manhattan - 31 December 1999

I need to retrace my steps from Ricky's dressing room - and fast. Round to the left then off to the right, and as I approach, I see red lights flashing: we're now into two minutes to transmission. Touch and go whether I can deliver the jacket for the top of the show. Plus Ricky won't be in wardrobe now, he'll be in position.

But oh God there's a burly security guard on the door, and in the rush to leave Ed's dressing room I've left my pass in it. Shit a brick. I can't afford the time to go back to Ed's hang-out, so I approach the guard and show him the jacket and explain it's the star of the show's and how Ricky has picked up the wrong dark jacket and how this spangly one is the right one and how he won't be comfortable starting the show with the wrong one. And I look at the guard with his 'no dice, baby' expression and he looks like he's seen action in Iraq or perhaps Panama or, given he's black and his skin's defying the ageing process, maybe he was in El Salvador or even Vietnam. And he gives me a look which seems to say, 'Do you think I'd of risked having my balls blown off for a spangly jacket?' And I wonder if over here security guards are routinely armed - or if he has his own personal-issue weapon. Then what he actually says is, 'Sorry, my man, but no ID, no entry. You dig?'

The guys on the doors were letting us through during rehearsal, but they won't with red lights on. Or on and off. Oh crap oh crap I think, in sync with the lights flashing. I wander away from the gaze of the guard and wonder if there's time to go back to Ed's room? Trouble is, I don't know how far into those two minutes we are – plus, what's our exact on-air time? My watch is useless with that question – it's in the gift of the network 3,000 miles away. For one insane moment I think I can ring Louise (a) assuming I've got my phone, (b) it has a signal in here, and (c) she's got time to answer at the most stressful moment of the broadcast. It's like phoning a pilot during take-off.

Light-bulb moment: the show opens with a VT (videotape) of a sketch set in Ricky's dressing room, so we don't come live to the studio till after that and the opening music and titles. The titles are just under a minute – same duration they've been for years, albeit with an adapted and remixed version of the music, and different visuals for our New York special. How long's the sketch, though? I wrote the darn thing, but I couldn't tell you. Louise would know (but see problems (a) to (c) above). Hey, wait: I can visualise how many pages it was. I've always had a photographic memory, as my mother said. So I picture page 1 of the sketch, page 2, turn over and it dribbles into a third page. Running time is a minute a page. So I think it's just under 2½ minutes long. Eureka! I've got time to take an alternative route. So I go up the adjacent stairs to the gallery, which isn't guarded. And I sail past Roger and Louise and Co. who are concentrating so intently they don't even see me, and I take the nearest door leading down to the studio floor. And I hear Ricky's familiar words from the dressing-room sketch booming on the PA ('I've had a thousand years to prep for this and I still haven't learnt my lines!' – it gets a laugh in context, thank goodness), and I head down the spiral staircase to the fire lane to one side of the audience rostrum, and I power-walk on behind the set to find Ricky.

He's standing, jacketless, by costume designer Jan, who's holding the other jacket (presumably as an insurance). On seeing me – or rather, on seeing the jacket – his face lights up, and he eagerly dons the spangly number, and as the sig tune strikes up, against the odds, he gives me a big hug and a wet kiss on my cheek, sniffs a sniff I ignore and says, 'I love you, man.' I can't quite reciprocate, but I manage the old adage, 'Break a leg.'

To end the revised theme tune, the musical director has snuck in a quick quote from 'New York, New York' on the brass, the drummer goes mental like Animal from the Muppets, Bobbles starts the applause, and a spangly Ricky steps forward, out of my sight, occluded by the curtain nearer to me, to deliver the first line from my script.

Waving, Drowning

Part Four

Waving, Drowning

102

Show on-air part one – 9.04pm UK time (GMT)
Ed Sullivan Theater, Manhattan – 31 December 1999

Ricky has got us smoothly on to our first pre-recorded 'package', a collection of images, graphics, ambient sound, speech, and music built around him and the streets of Manhattan. The studio audience's reaction to the first live sequence lowered my blood pressure; they obediently followed the unwritten code, meeting Ricky's hunger for reaction speedily (Bobbles warmed them well). They were the lively congregation to his preacher; the shepherd is in charge of his flock.

The VT package was recorded on Tuesday afternoon – a lifetime ago. It still shocks me how the presence of a camera alters people's reactions, and most folks move up a gear to provide a performance; the observer affects the observed. They also match Ricky's infectious energy, and his performance enhances theirs.

So a small crew – Ricky, me, camera, and sound operators, plus an assistant producer – were collecting vox pops – the voice of the people – to get a feel for what New York residents and passers-through were going to get up to for the millennium. We collected a range of responses, from those spending more traditional family time in NYC for a sort of Thanksgiving 2.0, to those flying off to foreign climes by the end of the week, many within the States, but some to places as far away as Finland, Kazakhstan, Japan, and, yes, the UK. The winner in terms of air miles we think was a tourist heading home to Xining in western China.

To get a little under the skin of the Big Apple, or at least, what's doable within the confines of an entertainment show, we tried to flesh things out with mini-interviews. We asked people about their roots and their home countries' customs and traditions in this melting-pot city. Ricky queried what people were going to eat, were they going to have fireworks, how were they going to record events (photos? video camera?), how many friends and family they were going to have round, or gather with, and so on. The video editor, guided by the producer, naturally selected the funniest or most poignant answers. And pepping things up was a guy performing close-up magic, apparently one of the passers-by, dropped in periodically in the piece. Except that that itself was a sleight of hand. He was hired by the show and directed to provide the best bang for its buck on-screen.

So we were a bit economical with the *vérité* about the magician. Can I square a little TV trickery like that with what's left of my conscience, after a decade and a half in the biz? Well, the imperative in entertainment is to entertain, so that aces everything, including telling the whole truth, in my view. Ricky had been impressed by David Blaine's street magic in his earlier incarnation, before Blaine moved more into endurance feats like Buried Alive near Trump Place back in April. Plus, Ricky had hired a NY-based magician, Phil Stewart, for the reception at his second wedding, and liked his chutzpah: in front of the newlyweds, and the mingling crowd, Stewart had said to Ricky, 'And for an encore, I'm going to make your first wife disappear!'

Apart from being agog at what our illusionist, that same Mr Stewart, conjured up for the camera, Ricky tried to do a bit of magic himself while we were rolling – the fashionable, so-called 'immersive' presentational technique – under Stewart's coaching. It was Ricky's attempt to reprise his mentor's trick of changing some Iraqi currency (with 'Uncle' Saddam's face on it) into dollars, featuring Uncle Sam – well, George Washington's visage. It worked flawlessly for the pro, naturally, but Ricky stumbled, threw the cards over his shoulder on 54th Street, and gurned into the lens. He mimicked a clapperboard with his hands, indicating 'cut' (I think he nicked that off Kenny Everett), giving Nick the VT editor an 'out'. The punters seemed to like it, laughing approvingly.

We'd had two other locations to record at on Tuesday: the ever-moving vantage point of the Circle Line ferry around Manhattan Island, and the World Trade Center. The ferry provided a hospitable place to shoot from. The coordinator, Simon, was a genial host, ever eager to oblige. When our sound recordist questioned the level of the PA, Simon reduced it immediately. I felt slightly guilty we might be spoiling it for the passengers, but then they'd been offered a rebate, or a later cruise, as compensation for having to slum it with TV types. Our guide apologised for it being a misty day, too, but that seemed fair game to me – circumstances beyond their control. In any case, I could see the murk being an aesthetic plus, giving the footage that naturally grainy look and washing out the colours. As we went under Brooklyn Bridge, I prayed what we shot would be reminiscent of the opening sequence of Woody Allen's transcendentally powerful monochrome movie *Manhattan*. Having been out on manoeuvres skimming stones and more for most of the day, I'd missed seeing the finished article until now; I was viewing it, like a member of the audience, for the first time. And when the opening clarinet glissando of Gershwin's *Rhapsody in Blue* struck up over our desaturated pictures, I wonder if any of the crew saw I appeared to have some grit in my eye.

The shooting schedule for the World Trade Center was tight. I don't think the production manager had factored in the time taken to go up and down 110 floors in the lift. At least we didn't have to queue like mere mortals. It would be hard not to get dramatic shots of such vast skyscrapers, the iconic twin towers of the WTC, looking up at them from street level. It was harder, perhaps, to do justice to the scale of this landmark, and to the view, from within. But I remember quietly appreciating, for myself, the surreality of looking through a glass tile in the top floor directly down to the pavement below. I was surveying the human ants scurrying frenetically in this city which architect Le Corbusier described as a 'beautiful catastrophe'.

Looking towards the Hudson from the North Tower we were in, I pointed out to the cameraman next to me a light aircraft flying hundreds of feet below us. 'Wow,' he said. 'You know you're high up when the planes are flying below you.'

Wow, indeed.

103

Therapy part five – karma
Thornton Heath, south London – 21 September 1999

'Sam's leaving seems like karma.'

'Karma for what?' Mary could be relied upon for the feed line. Sometimes we were like an old-school double act. She had her hair dark and down today.

'For me doing the same to Kelly. A six-year relationship up in smoke – and I was the arsonist. One cowardly phone call.' Keeping my head in my hands I swivelled slightly to the right to look out the window at Mary's kempt back garden, and to the fertile allotments beyond. 'Me at my worst.'

'There seems to be a lot of self-flagellation in the air today, Nate.' Mary was floating a little above the fray, as if touching the earth was sordid.

'Yeah? Well maybe it's spot on sometimes,' I snapped. 'Punishment can be right. 'Specially when you've wronged someone so close.' I brought my gaze back into the room. 'Someone you claim to care for.'

Mary seemed to be calculating. 'But can you recall a time when self-punishment was constructive?'

'That's not the measure of it. It's about doing the right thing. For the situation.'

'Perhaps you can hear how addictive it is?'

I had a flashback to the hospital, to inmate Janet wanting to be 'beaten up'. Janet who shat 'on the group'.

Mary went on: 'To assuage your guilt for the "sin" you think you've committed, you make yourself feel worse. Then you punish yourself for feeling bad.' She described a circle in the air with her hand. Her thin gold bangles jangled. 'Have you got depression, or has it got you?' When I don't reply she lowers her head to try and make eye contact. 'Where have you gone?' It's done with a little more softness than usual.

'Off with Kelly into the sunset. It was only after our split she talked about having wanted a rose cottage in some rural idyll. Another dream slips from my grasp.' I realised I was pressing my right thumb into my left palm. For a moment I saw it bloodied and stigmatised from trying to cling on to those rose thorns.

'It helps us make peace with ourselves if we can learn to let go of might-have-beens.'

Kiss them goodbye. 'Kiss from a Rose'. Seal-ed with a kiss. 'I handed Kelly a ticking time bomb. She was an innocent in all this. I was playing pass the parcel with pain.'

'But you'd had pain visited on you.' Mary leant on the 'you'.

'That doesn't justify it. Are you letting me off the hook?' I could hear my own anguish. God knows how whiny it sounded outside my head.

'Nate, you know it's not for me to stand in judgment over you.'

I was testing Mary's patience, I could tell. 'Aren't you meant to be the modern confessor-priestess? Can't you grant me absolution?'

'It's not always clear when you're joking.'

'This isn't a bloody joke. I gave Kelly a nervous breakdown.'

My voice ricocheted off the lemon-painted walls. A crow sounded an alarm in the garden. People pottered on their allotments.

'She threatened to kill herself. As if I didn't feel bad enough. That wretched recurring theme.' Could I ever escape from death's black hole?

'I'm sorry,' said Mary, softly. 'There's no pain-free way to part from someone who wants to stay with you.' Those eyes. 'But I'm not sure it's helpful to think of yourself as having "given" Kelly a breakdown.'

'It wouldn't have happened without me. She didn't give herself one.' I wanted to row back on my rage but had too much forward momentum.

'Are you still in contact with her?'

'No – this is some time ago. Five years plus. Last time I saw her she said a very pointed, "I don't want to go out with you." I felt the whole meeting was engineered by her so she could say that.' I sat up a bit straighter.

'Perhaps she needed to say that. For her own reasons. It might actually be a sign of some healing.'

A sign of fuckloads of therapy, more like.

Mary interlaced her fingers on her lap. 'It could be a resolution of sorts.'

My hand covered my mouth of its own volition. I removed it to say, 'I-I'm not telling the whole truth. Or nothing but.' In my head I was calling Mary 'Mother Superior'. I went on: 'I was a bit unfaithful ... Sort of.'

Pause. 'Go on.'

Big breath. 'Someone at work – on the show. Someone, anyone. It happened to be Bethany. Beth. Part of the production team. Standard nonsense – working long hours together, seeking refuge from stress by wisecracking, getting closer. Safe harbour. Both of us having relationship wobbles.' So clichéd.

'It's always tempting when things are going awry to seek out newness. Humans love novelty.'

'Maybe. But I always saw Beth – as I told Kelly – as a symptom, not a cause. A distraction from things going pear-shaped with her. And Beth happened to be in the frame, poor sod.' I clocked Mary's blouse with a white bow at this point. It reminded me of one Louise sometimes wore. 'I mentioned Beth to Kelly when we were on holiday in Cuba, and she said, "You've brought me to a paradise island to say you're dumping me for her?"'

Mary's laser look stayed locked on.

'Could have done without the adolescent word "dumping", but the gloves are off at these times. Nothing happened between me and Beth. Nothing. But just thinking about it ... I felt I was in moral free fall. I chose not to tell Kelly that Beth invited me up to her hotel room. Before the Cuban holiday. The network paid for her room, between a late and an early shift. Tangled web, eh?'

'We're complex creatures,' said Mary, diplomatically. 'Certain actions can make things harder for ourselves. The ideal is to have compassion for ourselves and others.'

I bet she was longing to say, Serves you right, mate.

What she did say was, 'We have to fight snap judgments.'

'So, can you?' I asked, plaintively.

'Can I fight snap judgments?' Mary looked thrown for a moment.

'No – can you grant me absolution? Absolve me of my sins? Make me pure as the driven?'

The clock ticked downstairs in the gap between question and answer.

Mary looked pensive. 'I haven't taken holy orders, Nate,' she said, subtly smiling.

I would just have to say ten Hail Marys on my own.

104

Show on-air part two – 9.13pm GMT
Ed Sullivan Theater, Manhattan – 31 December 1999

Ah, the monologue.

It took me thirty-one years to give up biting my nails, and five minutes into the live transmission I've resumed. I pace up and down like a football manager with fleas, nervously watching their side play from the touchlines. And, like the manager, I can't get on the pitch myself, and I can't give coded instructions using hand signals. I'm powerless now. I stay way out of Ricky's eyeline.

He was described in a press preview of the *Millennial Special* the other day, or so I heard from London, as 'Wogan on acid'. Wrong drug, obviously: Ryan prefers coke to LSD. But there's a kernel (no pun intended) of truth there. Being of a younger generation – Ricky is thirty-six to Terry's sixty-one – our man can be a bit more dangerous and less deferential than the Limerick star. Wogan started ceding the Anglo-Irish crown to Ricky on an edition of Gay Byrne's chat show from Dublin a few years ago. (The British tabloids couldn't resist variations of 'Gay News: Ryan Byrnes Wogan.') The mere fact of the two UK-based presenters appearing on the same bill – to say nothing of the same sofa – was a sign of mutual respect, and they tried to outdo each other in acknowledging the other's track record.

So Ricky steps forward as the curtain rises on the four-hour *Special*, finds his mark (a crucifix of tape on the floor) and acknowledges the huge applause. He motions with his hands outstretched for calm, starts talking once, twice (still they applaud), he stops, he laughs, they laugh, and the third time he's committed, so they quieten, realising their self-interest in shutting up and letting the turn do the work. He talks over the remaining stray whoops and whistles, and occupies that self-contradictory space where to plough on implies humility (from not wringing every last laugh out of the audience), and egotism (in attempting to ride roughshod over the crowd in the first place).

When eventually we spoke during the car ride back from the coast, Paddy and I had agreed we had to acknowledge his disappearance. Hence, my rewrite to kick Ricky off with, 'Do I get extra for showing up?' Thank God it gets a laugh; the implied greed, when many of his fans are in laborious, low-paid jobs, could have bombed. But such is their loyalty and devotion. I follow up with the surreal but strategic deflection, 'A guy disappears into a corner store for a snack, and there's a national manhunt!' A discreet low-angle camera behind Ricky provided the odd reverse shot, revealing the smiling crowd, and the 'starburst' filter on the lens showed off the sequins of our man's reunited suit.

'Now, this is a very special edition of the *Friday Fandango,* and have we got a show for you ...?' Interrupting the flow he repeats, but without the rhetorical flourish, 'Have we got a show for them?' The bastard only goes and turns his head over ninety degrees to look straight at me, off-shot, finding me instantly; he'd obviously prepared. All I can do is beam positively and nod. It's the eternal showbiz law that the person with the mic always wins. But I knew Louise upstairs would be saying on talkback that phrase every writer – and director – dreads, 'He's gone off-script.'

To be fair, mixed in with my dread was an uplift from seeing Ricky was sufficiently comfortable to ad lib.

And then he went back on-script. 'Of course, we try to make every edition of the *Fandango* special, coming as we do normally live from London each week. Or London, England, as they say over here. But then, it's no ordinary Friday, is it?' Assorted oral reactions. 'It's New Year's ...' He deliberately underpowers it, leaving himself somewhere to go. So the audience reaction is real, but restrained. 'We're not just at the threshold of a new year, though ... Or a new century.' Building reaction. Then Ricky fires on all six cylinders: 'We stand at the gate of ... the new millennium!' The crowd goes wild. Plenty sound like they've gone native. I'm all for that quasi-American expressiveness – it makes the jokes seem funnier at home. And it's not often an allusion to an obscure 1908 poem by a female LSE tutor gets a massive cheer in prime time. But who knows how many got the 'gate' reference to King George VI's speech, given at the beginning of the war in Christmas 1939? Sixty years ago almost to the day. I'm not sure even Ricky got the reference; and I wasn't going to point it out to him, for fear he'd scratch it on imperial grounds. But it got past the censor: Script Ed's a massive monarchist.

Ricky then takes the energy of his delivery down, making it a bit more conversational. 'Of course, there was an amazing act that took this place by storm on the Ed Sullivan Show on February 9th, 1964. Without a doubt it changed the course of their career. You know who that was, don't you? '

A good chunk of the audience reply in unison, 'The Beatles'. (I made sure Bobbles worked it into his warm-up routine, though without saying we were going to allude to it in the show.) Ricky affects not to have quite heard: he's obeying my direction on the prompter in square brackets [CUP HAND ROUND EAR]. One or two extroverts repeat 'The Beatles'. The sound mixer was primed in rehearsal to amp up the audience mics generously at this point so the audience responses could be heard more clearly at home. 'Yes, that's right,' says Ricky, 'Charlie Brill and Mitzi McCall.' Laugh. 'The well-known husband-and-wife comedy act.' Joy all round – and both the audience and the presenter are correct with their different answers.

Ricky went on, 'We all know how showbiz marriages can be put under incredible strain. Few survive.' He looks mournfully into the camera that's quietly eased its way in, and raises his eyebrows. It gets an empathic 'Ahhh' from the audience, followed by their (delayed) knowing laugh as the penny drops. Given he's regular tabloid fodder, millions of the viewers at home, too, would know Ricky's got through two marriages. 'And so it is with great sadness I announce that Charlie Brill and Mitzi McCall ... are still together.' Over the tail of the ensuing laugh he corrects his faux stumble. 'Er – I mean, we're *delighted* to say they're still together ... And you'll be able to see them for yourselves, as the couple who shared a bill with ... The Beatles!' The delayed acknowledgement gets an overdue cheer and whoop, helped by alliteration and the bilabial plosive punch of the letter 'B'. 'Mitzi and Charlie are joining us later!'

The show's bill of fare continued ricocheting round the room, courtesy of the strident PA. And then, emerging from the fire lane's shadows away from the cameras, with his trademark clipboard, cravat, and lumpen gait, comes the one-man warrior against understanding, Script Ed. 'How's the new stuff going? Colin needs it in half an hour.'

Sweet Jesus.

Distracted by the greasepaint and the crowd, I'd forgotten the millennial clock ticked remorselessly on. Or I'd buried my head in displacement activity as inspiration failed me.

History will decide.

105

Show on-air part three – 10.02pm GMT
Ed Sullivan Theater, Manhattan – 31 December 1999

You have to laugh.

It's taken me the last few days to align my body clock with Eastern Standard Time and, an hour into the show, I'm having to tell my internal timekeeper that 5pm in New York is 10pm, so I'm realigned with Blighty. But that's probably nothing compared to my serious sleep deprivation from last night.

The latest boy band to grace the charts, Elam (pronounced EE-lamm – stress on the first syllable), have just taken their bows at the Ed Sullivan Theater at the end of their Christmas hit, 'Snow Joke'. Nice enough guys, but not my musical *tasse de thé*. There's only one boy band for me and they weren't thrown together by an A & R guy. Plus, they grew up. God, Elam's man must have worn through some shoe leather scouring London's gyms, dance halls, and gay clubs. His mission was to find guys with the best physiques, dance moves and dentition.

This band's name, the press release lovingly explains, is simply 'male' backwards. Oh, to have been at the meeting when they were named. I think they should have gone for an anagram: Lame. Might have gone with their gold lamé suits. Or they could have used back slang for boy: Yob. Not only was their name backwards, so was their creation. Rather than start as talented mates who go out and create a following like The Beatles, Elam were borne of a flip-chart fuckfest to plug a gap in the market.

While the fulsome applause for the band sounds, with a few excited squawks (mostly female), Ricky walks out, smiling, applauding, and looking over his shoulder at the band. (He can't stand them musically either.) He eventually comes to rest centre stage at the mic stand as the plush red velvet curtain lowers behind him. His job now is much the same as the curtain's: to cover for the resetting of the stage ready for the dance number. The art of the scriptwriter here is to fill without it seeming like a fill. So I've tried to weave this mini-monologue into the flow of the show: Ricky throws forward to some of the items coming up in the next hour or so, teases with a reference to a big man with a message towards the end of the show, then tells a 'funny thing happened to me'-type of story.

He starts this sequence by explaining some of the cultural differences between where he was raised in sleepy rural Ireland (we airbrush the bit when he lived on the outskirts of London, for fear of tainting his Irish roots) and the mania of Manhattan where he's been staying for the past week. Except he's interrupted by a guy with a lighting pole reversing into him mid-sentence. The lighting man acknowledges Ricky without apology, explains his name's Troy, he's from New Jersey, and he's got to adjust the lighting for the star of the show.

'I hear he's a real douchebag,' deadpans Troy – actually an actor called Chase – apparently unconscious of the crowd or the camera. Or of who he's talking to. It gets a good laugh of recognition. He covers the laugh by adjusting his curly hair. The light catches the odd white hair among the black. ('Douchebag' went via Script Ed and Colin right up to network level to get cleared. I underplayed its original association and we got away with it.)

'You don't say,' says Ricky, shooting a knowing look to the audience in the room, and then to the viewer. He's got a couple of prompter screens off to the side, as well as several others on all the cameras, apart from the handheld.

'No kidding,' Troy went on. 'Works his staff like servants – he even has them slaving over New Year's.'

'Is that so?'

'Sure. Plus, it's the millennium.'

'So it is – I'd forgotten.' Ricky seems to have settled into the show. He throws a conspiratorial look at the audience again and gets a big laugh. It helps having some of Ricky's fan club in tonight.

'Hey, buddy,' Troy taps Ricky's breast bone with the back of his hand. 'We're having a protest tonight – you wanna join us?'

'Wh-what kind of protest?'

'Here – hold this, bud.' Troy passes his lighting pole to Ricky, who looks it up and down, bemused. Then to keep the focus on the action, he looks to his left where the lighting guy – or 'sparks' – has freed his hand to rummage inside his jacket. Our actor then produces a folded and crumpled leaflet. 'Me and the boys are calling it ... ' here, Troy unfolds then reads from the leaflet: '"Lights Out – Walk Out."' The audience gives a reassuring 'woo' – they're keeping up. 'We're saying enough's enough.'

'You're switching off, then, er ... going off?' Ricky hints at editing an oath in the gap, and stokes the crowd with another look.

'Pretty much, yeah. We figure if the star's that good – what's his name, Nicky? – he can twinkle on his own.' The audience reacts again, some in mock horror. 'Here – have a flyer.'

'Thank you, my friend,' says Ricky, taking the leaflet, and screwing it into a ball with his opposite hand so the Troy character can't see it but, in the wide shot, the viewers can.

BLACKOUT

APPLAUSE

106

Therapy part six: EMDR
Thornton Heath, south London – 28 September 1999

Mary has assessed me as suitable for EMDR – eye movement desensitisation and reprocessing. It's a treatment for PTSD – post-traumatic stress disorder or, as I would call it, heavy shit. As a therapy it's all a bit weird, and after ten years or so is tiptoeing into the mainstream. It turns out, though, that the bilateral stimulation I was promised is not as much fun as it sounds. Each hand holds a 'paddle', like the handle of a skipping rope, and the paddles pulse alternately left and right. It suggests hypnotism to me, but Mary insists that's an entirely different discipline.

And, yes, I have to trawl through the trauma, that much-loved old friend, one more time, only on this occasion with a throb switching between palms which is meant to help heal 'unprocessed' memories. These supposedly have got stuck, backed up as in a traffic jam, in a rush for the entrance.

Mary had encouraged me to bring a milder memory to begin with, a gentler test case by way of an introduction to the treatment, before digging deeper within. I oblige, naturally happy to do anything to defer the evil hour. So I dig up a recollection of being troubled at infant school by my mother not showing up to take me home one day.

I'm aware there's a hint of dark comedy to it – your own mother seemingly managing to forget to pick up her kid. But it was taken sufficiently seriously at the time (when I was four or five) for the teacher to give me a lift home. In the process of being steered through the memory by Mary, I recalled the teacher's car as a Ford Anglia with two-tone paintwork, pastel yellow with a white roof, and shiny chrome-plated hub caps. The car has been reborn as cool, as the kids would say now, thanks to a certain Harry Potter.

Mary guided me through the scenario, and I tried to recall the events unfolding, starting in the classroom, where I must have told my form teacher my mother hadn't arrived, after everyone else had gone home. I could see the teacher looking concerned, and I remembered her going away briefly to make a call in the school office, then coming back and saying decisively, 'Right – let's get you home, love.'

Being a boy fascinated by the motor car, and coming from a carless family, the journey itself was a treat, but the feeling of abandonment, as I would now label it, was tough for a sensitive child. We left that part of the memory (as an exercise) outside my then home, but the complication was that in reality my mother wasn't in; it later transpired she'd been readmitted to psychiatric hospital. Still holding those paddles, I felt the pulses start up again as Mary talked me through an alternative scene which resolved itself more kindly. When the pulsing stopped, she asked me to revisit the classroom in my mind's eye, and I saw this strange segment of a bubble intruding from the bottom of the frame (my brain was operating in widescreen). I remember thinking, even at the time, it would have made more sense if I'd been looking through it – it could have been some healing viewfinder through which to see a less disturbing version of the scene. Equally I realised I could, by an act of will, have got rid of the bubble altogether, but I felt content to let it sit there, as the rewritten scene played itself out. In the event I saw an infant version of myself quietly crayoning in a colouring-in book on the right side of frame, where the pupils' desks were, while the teacher remained, self-contained, on the left pottering about near her table. And then my eyes looking on the scene became my father's eyes and, for a moment, I felt a strange paternal pride looking at myself as a youngster, like an out-of-body experience with a generational gap.

So what was the bubble all about? Search me – you'd have to ask my subconscious. That's the bit that generated it! But my conscious take on it is that it was some kind of filter which took the sting out of the separation from my mother, although it still strikes me as odd that I was looking over and past it, rather than through it.

But then, what my subconscious throws up *is* odd.

107

Hanging with Colin – 11.18pm GMT
Ed Sullivan Theater, Manhattan – 31 December 1999

Having got my latest opuses past Script Ed I was steeling myself for the Colonel to view my work, trash it, and tell me to redo it.

I wasn't expecting to see Ricky standing having a ding-dong with his boss as the show was going out live. Our hero had slipped out during a VT, internally referred to as 'Wonderful Town Montage', about the history of entertainment in the Big Apple. It was playing quietly to itself on the TV suspended from the ceiling in the Colonel's sepulchral office.

Ricky was so loud I could hear him a few feet away in the open-plan. Oh, and could it be coincidence – or passive aggression – that he hadn't fully closed the door behind him? 'It's one thing to clip my wings after I'd flown the nest,' he said at gale-force ten, leaning into Colin, 'it's quite another to put that fucker next to me and rub my nose in the shit.'

I watched the spectacle, amazed and appalled in equal measure. For a moment an insecure part of my psyche, the enemy within, thought Ricky was talking about me. Perhaps it was egotism. Then I twigged it was his newer dressing-room neighbour vexing him. To put it mildly.

'What's his bloody name? Mort. What's that short for: mortician? Don't they usually wait for the feckin' body to go cold?'

Colin leaned in. 'Ricky, love ...'

Love? I've never heard the Colonel use that word – I didn't know he knew it. Still less what it meant.

'Don't you "Ricky, love" me. And your Mort Silly-Ass has been hanging around the studio like a spare part. I want that fucker off the show and out of his dressing room. And he can stick his journo's nose up his journo's arse.'

While Ricky snarled at his exec producer, his knuckles on Colin's desk whitening as his claws dug in, thirty tap dancers from *42nd Street* smiled the brightest smiles on the TV above Colin's head.

Just then a young woman with cans and a clipboard knocked on Colin's door. Ricky turned round and opened the door wider, his expression the very picture of solicitousness for the brunette beauty before him. She announced, 'Five minutes, please, Mr Ryan.' She looked relieved to have found him. Ricky gave her the subtlest of nods and stared into her eyes twelve frames too long. I saw her smile decay as she turned towards me, leading Ricky, who barely acknowledged me, out of the glass cage.

I'd been using our presenter as a human shield between me and the Colonel. Now the star of the show had headed off with Clipboard Colette (for want of a name), I was in Colin's sights, clutching my script printout.

He beckoned me in with all the warmth of a hangman.

108

Show on-air part four – 11.26pm GMT
Ed Sullivan Theater, Manhattan – 31 December 1999

Floor manager Steve was chewing gum at his most furious rate yet. A succession of clipboard carriers were speaking close to his ear, defying the loudspeakers. His features seemed more ashen with each approach.

'Three minutes on VT, studio,' he barked to the crew. In another time and place I would have loved to savour the sounds and images being beamed around New York State and back home in Blighty in this 'Wonderful Town Montage'; we'd reached Cole Porter, and I never tire of hearing his sassy lyrics and their unbelievably cheeky rhymes. And he wrote the tunes, too. But the elephant in the room was the elephant had left the room: bizarrely – despite being chaperoned by Clipboard Colette from the office – Ricky was absent. Again.

I'd walked back with Colin from his glass tomb to the studio, as he sensed, rightly, he needed to be nearer the action. If there was one advantage to the crisis it was that a distracted Colonel had OK'd my new scripting with barely a glance at it; he didn't have the resources to fight a war on two fronts. Once at the studio he made his way up the stairs to his booth just off the control room, and I headed for the floor, having recovered my pass from Script Ed's dressing room.

How I hadn't missed the bone-rattling PA. Ricky's 'voice of God' narration, pre-recorded on the VT, impressed itself on my skull as I diverted past Penny and Jenni's dugout under the audience rostrum. I passed over another floppy disk with my latest opus on to one of the prompter twins, then took up my position again beyond the edge of the stage; I stood in a gap between the drapes which separated the set from the fire-lane perimeter.

Steve was closer to the stage. I saw in his face a mental lever being pulled, and he buzzed up to the gallery that we were missing our presenter, none of the floor assistants could track him down, and could Roger sanction Mort being substituted for Ricky?

I leaned into a nearby floor assistant's headphones to try and hear the 'cans spill' – the sound leaking – but the FA drew back. 'Why don't you get your own headphones?' she said.

I told her I didn't know there were any spare, but she pointed me back to the prompter redoubt. I picked up the last talkback set secreted under the table where Jenni/Penny pointed, and donned the headphones and clipped the box to my belt. Knowledge is power, and I now knew what was going on in the gallery.

I heard Roger tell Steve on talkback he couldn't put Mort on without Colin's say-so. Steve bellowed 'Two minutes' to the crew. Roger buzzed through to Colin in his booth overlooking the control room and asked him to clear Mort to go on. There followed twenty seconds of huff, puff, and bluster from the Colonel, who eventually announced, 'I'll go downstairs.'

The Colonel entered the theatre of war as if he'd been made up to Commander-in-Chief. His cold grey-blue eyes indicated he took no prisoners.

'I Happen to Like New York' boomed over the audience's head with Ricky's pre-recorded voice telling Porter's tale.

The Colonel made a beeline for Steve, who straightened himself up on seeing him.

'What's all this nonsense, then?' the Colonel barked, irked at being in a space where TV is actually made, like a vegan stumbling into an abattoir.

'Sir, we have a presenter problem,' said Steve. His American accent made that 'sir' seem less deferential. 'Or a *lack*-of-presenter problem. Ricky disappeared once we got on the tape. Do you think Mort, as a journalist, would be well-placed to get us off that and into the interview with the charity woman?'

Good ploy: a suggestion disguised as a question, phrased to make Colin think he'd come up with the idea. The Colonel went pensive for a moment, but Steve's, 'One minute on tape,' forced the issue.

'That bloody Ryan,' said Colin, expiring through clenched teeth. Then, mysteriously, he added something like, 'Run the fowss tape.' With that, he disappeared. I imagined him being hurried to a helipad and flown off base under cover of darkness.

Internally, I questioned what I'd heard: 'fowss tape'? I thought I had a pretty good handle on TV lingo from fifteen years in the trade, but that one beat me. Steve passed the instruction upstairs, and no one queried it; clearly Louise, Roger, and vision mixer Hilary all knew what it meant. I mouthed 'fowss tape' with a questioning look to a nearby researcher, but she shrugged; she seemed as clueless as me. Steve, however, didn't flinch at the term. It seemed cognisance was strictly on a need-to-know basis. So why was I locked out of this knowledge, as if blackballed from a secret society? I felt betrayed by Louise; surely she should have kept me in the loop?

Steve went over to Bobbles and had a word in his ear, and the warm-up man nodded vigorously. Bobbles then walked to the foot of the audience rostrum. His dichroic suit shimmered as it caught the lights, veering between navy and fawn. As the 'Wonderful Town' tape was ending, Bob offered a UV-friendly showbiz smile to the crowd in front of him, and pointed up to the monitors without saying anything, indicating the audience needed to continue watching the screens above their heads. As 'New York, New York' played over aerial pictures of Manhattan at the end of the VT, he mimed applauding over his head, and the audience duly clapped.

On the floor monitor near me, with Minelli belting out the last transcendent note of the Seventies classic, I saw the mix-through from Fifties monochrome footage of Broadway traffic to a pre-recorded Ricky – our once-again truant star – centre stage in mid shot, in continuity clothes, also applauding. You could say he was 'off-script', but was there a script to be on? Certainly it was nothing I'd written.

'...And now, ladies and gentlemen,' said the pre-rec Ricky, 'I want to introduce you to a proper New Yorker, a local star whose every word comes with a copper-bottomed guarantee ...' The audience goes 'ooh' in response, being willingly guided by Bobbles with his extravagant hand signals. Ricky, master of the art of leaving a gap for audience response during pre-records, nodded in apparent reaction to the audience. His black ear stud sparkled as he tilted his head.

'Thirty seconds on VT,' said Louise on talkback. Yikes. 'Coming out to a wide of the stairs on 5. Standby Mort. Standby applause. Standby sting.' ('Sting' refers to a brief fanfare-style musical punctuation; music director Ken would have raised his hands ready to conduct it live as he heard Louise's call to, er, arms on his headphones.) Fingers crossed Mort was ready at the foot of the stairs at the back of the set.

Ricky's graven image on the screen went on: 'Not only is Mort a chat-show charmer, a great interviewer and a great personal friend [I choked at this point], he's also a rock-solid newsman.' Did I detect the dead hand of Script Ed scribing this dog-eat-doggerel? Holding his left hand out straight, beckoning his colleague (who wasn't there at the time of recording), Ricky says, 'I want you to meet him right now. Please welcome the star of *New York Tonight* on NYTV, Mr Mort Silus!'

I try and work out when it was recorded. It must have been tagged on to the end of the dress run, when I was made homeless – dressing-roomless. I know the game being played, doubtless to Colin's rules: viewers need Mort to be endorsed by Ricky so they give the new boy a chance. Otherwise, if Mort just sauntered on without introduction, a baffled nation back home would put the kettle on – and/or channel-hop. But when this section was recorded, they couldn't have known Ricky was going to disappear, or that this segment would even be needed. Strange. Sinister, even. A just-in-case insurance policy? It certainly put Ricky's recent contretemps with Colin in perspective. Ricky will have fought tooth and nail to avoid doing it. No wonder he didn't mention it to me.

On talkback, Roger had quickly given notes to cameras, reassigning 3 to Mort instead of Ricky. Camera 4 was for the interviewee, and 5 had the wide. The handheld was dispatched to give shots of the audience on merit – that is, its use depended on how gripped they looked. While the Colonel had been making his mind up about Mort, the props guys had rebuilt a mini chat-show set-up, fashioned weeks before by the designer, and built to plan as rehearsed earlier, with marks on the floor to steer in the scenery and furniture. This comprised a cream sofa for the guest, a matching swivel chair for Mort, a cappuccino-coloured backdrop, and a low-level coffee table with a pot plant on it. The guest had been steered away from the personal politics by being brought in from the other side and quietly sat down on the sofa. I tried to catch her eye as she looked my way: it was my sometime hostess, refuge provider, and sleeping partner Elsa, fresh from Midtown. She winked irreverently. I beamed in reflex. Still couldn't believe my idea for her to be interviewed was adopted.

The audience by now had offered up a great swell of appreciation for someone most of them had never heard of. And then Mort appeared, steadily walking down the steps, clipboard under his right arm, wearing a dark suit and a bold yellow-ochre shirt, with his tie a mix of canary yellow and overlaid dark filigree. He was around five-seven, five-eight, with a wedge of mostly night-black hair swooping over his forehead, follicle-perfect, with the rest lying obediently about a side parting, and only the vaguest hint of errant sproutlings at the crown, largely invisible to the viewer. There was a hint, too, of Mother Nature's highlights – grey – as befits one of his slightly greater age than mine. I'd put him at thirty-eight, thirty-nine. Such naturalness is embraced in TV news, suggesting as it does experience, maturity, and authority. It's anathema, though, in entertainment; hence Ricky's clandestine capers with the Clairol.

Elsa had made a similar sartorial effort to Mort. She sat proudly on the sofa, her uprightness belying her seventy-plus years, and her teal dress likewise signalling a youthful energy, with its vivid, superimposed crimson pattern. The repeating shapes looked like something cell-based and organic. Make-up had accentuated Elsa's lips, and her skin had been powdered a warmer tone than when I'd stayed with her. I assume she'd given her consent for the makeover; I can't imagine her being docile in the controlling world of TV. And she wore plenty of what rappers call 'bling': her earrings matched the rings on her fingers, which also matched her brooch; the effect was of a glazed, rich-coloured look, all indigos and emeralds and pigeon-blood reds. The brooch was fashioned in a salamander motif. Elsa smiled sweetly, and her eyes came alive as Mort joined her and she briefly stood. He shook her hand before they both sat in sync, Mort settling in the swivel chair.

He deftly slips into presentation mode, his educated New York tones taking me back to those VHS tapes I watched in the cab earlier today. It feels like an age ago; it's been A Hard Night's Day.

'Hi there, and if you've just joined us, I'm very definitely not Ricky Ryan,' said Mort. He trod on the laughter, despite my written steers; he isn't used to waiting for audience reaction. 'But this sure is Ricky's *Millennial Special* ...' He quickly learnt to wait for a response, giving space for a gratifying cheer. Unlike Ricky, Mort's happy to read from a printout, his eyes flicking economically down to the clipboard, topping up his buffer of words. 'Thanks to Ricky for that flattering introduction. We've got a ton of entertainment for you again later, but let's take the energy down a little first as we head toward our charity appeal. I want to introduce you to a very special guest: Elsa Meyeroff. Elsa was a child back in the Second World War and, as a Jew in what became occupied Paris, she was extremely vulnerable as the Nazis increased their stranglehold on the French capital. So, Elsa, can you paint a picture of your life up to that moment, because you were born in Germany, weren't you?'

Elsa steeled herself, took a big breath, and dived deep into past pain. For that, despite all of her rattiness with me in the morning when I'd stayed over with her, she was my hero.

109

Therapy part seven: post-EMDR
Thornton Heath, south London – 2 November 1999

Mary shifted in her seat as she crossed her legs. The potted
plant by her had an elegance and nobility lent by its highly
polished leaves. I presumed the gloss was the work of her
cleaner, not Mary herself. We were in her downstairs front
lounge; there was work going on in her upstairs counselling
room for a few weeks.

'Where are you?' Her gaze could pierce steel at a
hundred paces.

I resisted saying I'd been imagining her on all fours
scrubbing with the Baby Bio. 'I'm trying to picture life
without you.'

The slats of the beige blind caught the morning sun.
I took in the louvred image of the elegant Edwardian houses
opposite. In the bay window Mary had a large white vase
holding some pink chrysanths.

'Endings can be painful,' she replied. 'But they also
offer opportunities – new beginnings.' She saw I looked
hesitant.

When I first floated the idea that I was thinking of
bringing our sessions to an end some weeks ago, she did that
infuriating therapist thing of pretending not to have a view. I
should have known better than to ask her opinion; my
soliciting it was met with an economical, 'You're asking me
to sit in judgment,' not for the first time. And then, after
another armour-piercing look of ten seconds, 'Why do you
think our work should end?'

I'd explained I felt ambivalent. Whilst we obviously couldn't go on forever, I said I worried my desire to finish could itself be another sign of depression. I might be pulling the rug from under my own feet. 'Denying myself something good that works,' is how I put it.

'You could make the argument either way,' she'd observed after a pause. 'But with the stage you're at, I'd tend towards recommending you go with your hunches. It's not as if you would be ruling out our working together in future. Barring a crisis, it might be useful for you to have a break – it would give you a chance to put some of the techniques you've learnt into practice. And to give the EMDR a chance to settle.' Mary laid her hands in her lap and breathed through her nose. Her posture said 'former ballerina'. 'The job of the parent is to make themselves redundant; that's how therapists should work, too, I believe.'

That was then, but here in my last session with her an anxious part of me wants to hit pause, to say it's all been a terrible mistake, I still need her and can't face the big, bad world alone. Even her blouse under her cream gilet makes me anxious: all delicate Laura Ashley flowers which would be buffeted by the slightest breeze. Life's so bloody fragile, and here I am planning to make it harder for myself.

I treat her to the shortened version of this thought process or, rather, feeling process. 'You know we talked about the reptilian brain?'

'Yes – the fight or flight part.'

'Well, I want to take flight.' I pictured a wrinkly pterodactyl trying to get off the ground.

'A degree of fear is okay, Nate – it's natural. The thing is to not be immobilised by it.'

Natural it may have been, but it's also nuts. How could I be safe in the bosom of Mary and run away from her at the same time?

She had a way of giving visual cues that she'd only paused temporarily. 'Therapy doesn't exist to quash all your fears – indeed, it can't. But two things are important about nerves: one is, they're a sign you're alive. And the second is they hold within them the possibility of change. They can be transformative.'

To live is to worry, to worry is to live, she seemed to be saying.

'The nerves have changed you in our time together. Remember when you first came here you would sit mute in some sessions?'

I nodded and sighed as a wave of past ennui crashed over my head. Terrible times. Like having an ingrowing personality. Having nothing to say because the current crushing low undermined everything that had gone before.

Mary adjusted her gilet over those fragile flowers. '...Now I can't shut you up!' Her eyes carried a mischievous glint.

I laughed. Mary could be an entertainment scriptwriter if only she'd up her gag rate. During the period I was working with her I'd consolidated my position as Ricky's default wordsmith. And I'd shared with Mary in the last fortnight how my contract had been extended for another series of the *Fandango*. She seemed to see that as an endorsement of our work together.

'We need to finish there, Nate.' It had taken me two years, but I finally worked out how she knew when the hour was up: she'd planted a small clock buried among the books over her client's shoulder – including here downstairs – so she never had to break her eyeline to check the time. Genius.

She led me into her hall as usual. For our last session I wanted to do more than the normal perfunctory handshake. Professional ethics forbad a hug. Instinctively, as well as my right hand shaking hers, my left hand gripped Mary's forearm and squeezed it. I risked crushing a few Ashley flowers in the process.

'Thanks for everything,' I said, trying to suppress the lump in my throat.

'Thank you – and go well. Don't forget, you can always come back if you need to.'

I acknowledged with a nod. Mary opened the front door wide, and the morning light gushed in over the slate roofs opposite.

I headed down the path without looking back.

110

Show on-air part five: sofa, so good – 11.31pm GMT
Ed Sullivan Theater, Manhattan – 31 December 1999

What kind of person would put a philosopher on a sofa on prime-time TV – and then suspend him, or rather the sofa, from the rafters?

Pleased to meet you.

The hardest part was trying to track him down again. (Louise, bless her, holds the full story of the wild goose chase I sent her on, confusing Cornell and Columbia universities.) Remember the professor from the Irish pub, when I was on walkabout? Peter, unlike Elsa, didn't slip his calling card into my mitt.

That's it: Larry David! I'd been trying to think who Peter reminds me of, and it's only as I see him suspended on a sofa, hung on scene hoists high up in the Ed Sullivan Theater 'in front of a live studio audience' it comes to me. The sticking point was the height difference. He's a bloody tall Larry bloody David!

I'm not going to match David's *Seinfeld* slickness in my scripting around Peter (that's a group effort in any case, and I'm solo, held back by Script Ed). Worse, I've written it for Ricky to present, as I only crafted it a couple of hours before going to air, and thought by then he was safe from the chill winds of the Colonel's ambivalence. I didn't plan on Mr Silus to be depping. Mind you, I doubt it was in Mort's career plan to be fronting an audience show, starting an interview with a philosopher on a sofa suspended several feet above his head.

Mort might have thought – hoped, even – his turn was over after what was generally agreed to be a very moving interview with Elsa. He'd triangulated deftly between Elsa's answers and gentle prompts in his earpiece from the director. Roger quite liked to be able to talk, unmediated by Steve, directly to his presenter for a change; Ricky's always refused talkback. But if Mort thought Ricky would return shortly to take back the reins, he was mistaken. I was aware of an ongoing buzz of nervous activity as assistants with clipboards and headphones continued the search for our star, and whispered updates – or lack of – to each other in the fire lane.

Forgive us telly types: we're programmed to make a spectacle out of everything we lay hands on, especially in entertainment. It's like a media Midas touch. But it's all to engage you, the viewer. Sliding a philosopher into peak time required a hook. Actually, four hooks – one on each corner of the sofa. Yes, it's a gimmick, but it's the opportunity cost of getting some serious thought into a light-hearted show.

So Mort finished the interview with Elsa, and the vision mixer, Hilary, cut up a full-screen graphic which included the number of Elsa's Todd Myeroff Tolerance Foundation, which she'd formed in memory of her late husband. Mort read the number live – twice, to buy time – OOV (out of vision). Straight off the back of that was meant to be an 'internal trail', thirty seconds or so of video pointing viewers to the musical finale of the show in the next hour, after the midnight chimes of Big Ben. But the trailer featured Ricky, and since nobody knew if he was going to complete the show Roger dropped it, and asked Mort to voice a quick live scripted trail over video of the musical act. I knocked up the words for it hastily during Elsa's interview; for speed, I entered it straight on to Jenni's/Penny's PC. And thanks to my mum for encouraging me to learn to touch-type, as her mother had done. That sped things up in the prompter lair with the seconds ticking.

The camera now shot from the left from the audience's perspective so the last of the chat-show set used for Elsa can be struck to the left without crossing shot. Roger has to shush the scenic ops for being too noisy. Mort now explains into camera, 'After hearing from the amazing Elsa, what we have for you next can only be lighter. Though if I tell you it involves philosophy ... [Mort stops for the audience's "Oooh" he's learnt to expect.] ...you might think it's a bit above your head.' The audience laughs because, as Mort has been walking downstage (i.e. towards them), the camera has craned down, widened out, and panned up a bit to reveal the sofa, while still containing Mort in the foreground. In 2-D screen terms both furniture and philosopher appear to be above his head. Bobbles had trained the studio audience to frequently look to the monitors above their heads to see what viewers would see, especially if their direct view was blocked. Many of them wouldn't have been able to see Peter up in the air from their seats, obscured as he was by numerous lights.

And then the sofa gets so far ... and gets stuck.

I look to Steve the floor manager; he's looking nervously at the guy on the hoist panel, who's catching the eye of his scenic colleague. He, in turn, goes round the back of the set to check on his colleagues working the pulleys which should have lowered the sofa gently to the studio floor.

Meanwhile Mort has to accept the new facts on the ground. Or, rather, not on the ground. He adjusts his tie's knot and launches straight into my intro.

'Please welcome your friendly neighbourhood philosopher, from Columbia University here in New York City, Professor Peter Laud!'

The audience reaction was energised and, thrillingly, applause morphed into laughter as Peter affected a royal wave from his lofty position. I wasn't sure if they'd cottoned on he wasn't meant to stay at that height. Mort moved upstage as was intended, so he could look up to Peter, but 'favouring' the audience – that is, more turned towards them. The cameras could then get their close-ups. Peter looked very stylish in a beige, collared shirt with a grey jacket.

Mort continued, 'Now as a philosopher you think for a living, don't you, Peter? What do you think of how we're presenting you: suspended on soft furnishings?'

Peter smiled widely, as he had at O'Riordan's. With his warm East Coast-intellectual tones he came back with: 'I think I just reached a career high!'

As well as laughs that earned him one or two whistles, despite Bobbles cautioning against such crudeness.

Staying in the prompter den I could see what was coming next. I'd written it, of course, so it was familiar. Looking over one of the teleprompt twin's shoulder at my words on her prompter screen, I was reminded of two assumptions I'd made:

RICKY
So Peter, now you're on solid ground ...

The Penny-Jenni prompter complex had a couple of other monitors: one was always switched to Mort's close-up, so they could see any hand signals or other indications he might be giving them when he wasn't on shot; the other was Studio Out – what the viewers would see at home. So at times, both monitors would be carrying the same shot. While Mort was on the wide shot – which, because of the suspended sofa was really wide, to contain both Mort and Peter above him – I caught his eyes momentarily flick to his close-up camera to look at the script on the prompter. We could see locally, but it was barely perceptible in the wide shot, Mort seemed to slightly grimace, doubtless clocking the redundant reference on the prompter to 'solid ground'. Without dropping a stitch he quickly looked at his clipboard then back to Peter and said, 'Things don't always happen the way we plan in life.' Nice. Proper pro. The crowd were following his train of thought – they'd clued into something having gone wrong with the sofa – and a knowing ripple of recognition passed through the audience above our heads. 'Can any of the philosophers help us with the bumps in the road – unexpected things life throws at us?'

Peter laughed. '"Life is contingent," as the novelist Iris Murdoch said. She was also a philosopher. By "contingent" she meant "subject to chance" – or, as we might say, "stuff happens". And, sadly, her life provided more evidence that "stuff happens" towards the end, and we lost her earlier this year.'

Hilary cut to Mort's close-up as he nodded at this point.

'Iris might have thought a good word for this situation I'm in is "absurd",' Peter continued. 'We use it day-to-day to mean "crazy", "nuts", and so on. Like, "This one-way system is absurd, honey". But the French philosopher Albert Camus used the term "the Absurd" to mean something else: the clash between our longing for meaning in our lives, versus the fact the universe doesn't always seem to want to serve it up on a plate to us.'

'So does Camus think we should all pack up and go home?' asked Mort. 'Is it all meaningless? We need to know, as the new millennium is breathing down our necks!' I listen to the audience perched on the raked rostrum above my head; they seem engaged, so the viewers should be, too.

Peter had nestled himself into the corner of the sofa, arms spread wide over the top of its cushions. 'The good news is Camus says we should embrace life and live it with passion. Even if we're stuck in the air in prime time. [Laugh.] I added that bit. [Laugh.] That philosophy should serve us well for the next thousand years.'

Result: I feel vindicated for recommending Peter. He's great box office.

But where the hell is Ricky?

111

Protest – 11.36pm GMT
Ed Sullivan Theater, Manhattan – 31 December 1999

Time to trudge through the labyrinthine corridors to Paddy's dressing room. I'd left the talkback unit in the prompter lair as it wouldn't work that far away from the studio. I told one of Steve's floor assistants where I was going to be, in case of a further studio crisis; I didn't want to alert anyone too high up the food chain, though, in case it worried people at the Roger/Colonel level. Colette (not her real name) said she'd knocked on the dressing room door three times but hadn't got an answer.

I was rounding the corner past Mort's base when my phone vibrated in my pocket. I worried I was being summoned back to the studio, so I stopped to check who it was. A message had appeared on the mobile's mini screen.

'R u ok 2 meet at provincetown mcmillan pier 2.30 tmrw? Happy new years! Jane x'

I replied hastily 'AOK. Ditto! x'. (Actually I first wrote 'Titto!' by mistake and spent far too long correcting it.) I'd have to work out where the pier was, but I'm sure I could ask someone in Provincetown, or plan ahead and Ask Jeeves.

Hanging a sharp right after Mort's dressing room I knocked on the door of Star Dressing Room One and said in a raised voice, 'Paddy, it's Nate.'

Paddy opened the door, but only a sliver. He was being oddly cagey and looked troubled.

'Is everything OK?' I asked.

'Yeah, sure.' He pulled on his black ear piercing. 'It's a bit ... complicated.' He opened the door wider.

Then the shock: there must have been thirty or forty people cross-legged and crammed on to the floor behind Paddy. All seemed petite and dressed in identical silver jumpsuits with a central metallic zip, and all sported face masks covering their features. The character, whose photo was on all the masks, was unmistakeable: Yoko Ono. The Yokos unnervingly all seemed to be looking my way, like a living Antony Gormley work.

I mouthed to Paddy 'What the fff ...?'

Paddy bowed to the inevitable and introduced me, while walking away from the door to his built-in dressing table opposite. 'Please meet the man who puts words into my mouth.' Gosh – it must have been serious; finally I'm credited as a writer. 'My good friend from England: Nate Daniels,' he said with false bonhomie.

'Well,' I said to the Yokos, 'it's, um, a group effort, but someone's got to type it up.' There was a general vibe of indifference. But I had to ask, 'How did you get past security?'

'First of all, we're not "you" – we're Yokos,' said one, angrily.

'Second of all, we're not gonna give our tactics away,' said another, equally fiercely.

A third piped up, 'Let's just say distraction techniques work real good!' There was group laughter at this. Their accents sounded more American than Japanese.

'We're situationists. We're good at creating situations.' I think that was the first Yoko again. She provoked more laughter, but it wasn't easy to see which Yoko was talking.

'Situationists?' I queried. It had a vaguely hippyish connection for me, but little more.

Paddy seemed to feel the burden to explain. 'It's a kind of socio-political critique of advanced capitalism, built on libertarian Marxism with a dash of Dada.' Blimey. He sounded like he'd been captured by a cult. 'Our Yoko friends here—'

'We're not your friends,' said one Yoko.

'I'm hoping you might become my friends,' Paddy came back.

'We're here to split up The Beatles,' said another Yoko. 'Again.'

I wanted to point out technically it was John who broke up the band, although you could argue Yoko was a catalyst. But now wasn't the time.

'We're tired of male hegemony.' Thus spake another Yoko clone. 'The Beatles are yet another band of brothers. Grow up and move over, boys!'

'Yeah – split up The Beatles,' a third Yoko said, the first to sound, to my ear at least, authentically Japanese.

'Split up The Beatles! Split up The Beatles!' the group repeated en masse. The phrase had the lilt and repetition of the Eighties hit 'Pump Up the Volume'. It was loud in the confined space.

'Smash the patriarchy!' offered another, though this didn't catch on. I couldn't tell if this was for want of collective passion or because of poor scansion.

I didn't have a good feeling about this, and couldn't help blurting out to Paddy, 'I'll call security.'

'Don't,' snapped Paddy, a little too urgently.

'I wouldn't do that unless you want to be front-page news for the wrong reason,' said the Japanese-sounding Yoko. 'One of the sisters caught your mate Ricky, er, rehearsing his lines,' she added, 'while looking in the mirror. With a straw.' More laughter followed with some of the sisters closing one nostril and inhaling with the other. The penny dropped: they had Paddy by the nadgers.

It transpired they'd been in the middle of a debate about the mass media. Paddy sat in his swivel chair by the main mirrors, the Yokos in a crescent at his feet, as if he was Jesus suffering the little children. 'As I was saying, I don't have to justify my job. There's a place for escapist entertainment in people's tough, busy lives.'

'They wouldn't need escapism if they had less shitty lives,' said one of the Yokos, a little shrilly.

'Yeah – give them something to live for, not escape from,' offered another.

'Right on, sister – start with curing the alienation.' This Yoko made it sound like 'alien nation'. Was that deliberate?

Paddy didn't look comfortable with the direction of travel. 'What are your demands, then?' he asked. For a spiritual leader, he seemed on the back foot. 'What will it take for you to let me get back on set?'

'I think we can have a conversation about that,' said one Yoko.

'We got a real situation here!' said another.

112

Colin and the Yokos - 11.43pm GMT
Ed Sullivan Theater, Manhattan - 31st December 1999

I had to find my inner negotiator - and fast. I'd beetled it
back to the editor's booth to explain to the Colonel his star
presenter was in his dressing room 'being held by the Yokos'.
(That phrase tickled me. I could hear Kenneth Williams say
it if they'd ever made Carry On Broadcasting.) How to
persuade the Colonel to let thirty or so Yokos on to the set,
with a promise of good behaviour, as the price for restoring
Ricky to his rightful place in front of the camera? In this,
Ricky was a victim of Mort's success: Colin might think life's
easier with the new guy - the newsier guy.

So I had to try an oblique approach here by the
control room. I could see Roger and his posse hard at work
through the glass, and could hear on Colin's talkback speaker
Roger and Louise's calm voices steering the whole TV tribe
through the miasma. If there was a Venn diagram of me and
my comfort zone they'd be on separate sheets.

And there was Mort in the corner of the booth, on a
TV in front of Colin. The sound was low, but I could just
make out the deputy presenter interviewing Charlie Brill and
Mitzi McCall. They'd shared an Ed Sullivan bill with The
Beatles on that fateful day in '64. Day of my birth.

As a friend said to me years ago, you can never
appeal to someone on your values; you can only appeal to
them on theirs. Here goes ... 'Think of the kudos for you,
Colin: a satisfying view for the folks at home. Ricky returns
in triumph with the climax regular viewers would expect -
only bigger. They'd find it baffling if the show ends with Mort

paying off.' I pointed to the screen. 'Plus, he doesn't have the pizzazz to carry off the finale.' Then I remembered Colin cast Mort, albeit in desperation. 'Er – fine, consummate journalist and presenter that Mort is.'

Apart from one grudging look away from the monitor, Colin failed to meet my gaze. While I was talking, he lit one of his Cuban specials, whether to smoke me out, intimidate me, or to give his hands something to do. Perhaps it was compensation for his smaller space here lacking status props like his swivel chair. He got up from his seat and started wandering around me, staking out his territory.

The Colonel's cogs were whirring. 'We could remove the Yokos by force – easily.' He could hardly disguise his excitement: finally, a military operation he could spearhead with real violence.

'...And they would go to the press,' I pointed out dispassionately. I obliged my voice to keep on through the fog. 'They seem well-organised and media-savvy.'

'We have to face them down, Nathan.'

'It's ... complicated. Some of them saw Ricky use his, um, paraphernalia.'

'His what?'

'His ... kit.' Then, seeing the Colonel's ongoing blank expression, I fleshed it out to, 'His drug kit. Bolivian brain food.'

'Dear God. We must quash this. Take me to them.' Colin beckoned me to go first through the door. I'm sure his geography was up to finding Ricky, but he seemed to want me as his aide-de-camp.

As I approached the star dressing room with the Colonel a few paces behind me, I saw security had arrived. A few motley guards in white shirts and grey trousers stood there, armed with scratchy walkie-talkies. I recognised the Vietnam vet, as I'd now decided he was – the one who'd been guarding the studio door earlier. Ricky was standing him down. 'It's cool, Bill.' Ricky on first-name terms with a security guard? That's a turn-up. 'Our friends ... um, these performers are fine.' The guards had assumed an at-ease posture, but tensed up again on spotting Colin. 'The Yokos just want their voice heard.'

'We don't appreciate being patronised, Ryan,' said a contralto-voiced Yoko.

'Oh no? Well maybe I don't appreciate being referred to by my surname.' Ricky didn't seem to realise he'd unwittingly used their surname, too (he missed the homophone, 'Oh, no = Ono'). Then he clocked the Colonel. 'Ah, Colin – good to see you. Meet these ... performers. I'd introduce you by name, but ...'

'Yoko will do,' said one.

'Ok?' Ricky had a mischievous catchlight in his eye. Pointing to them in turn he began, 'Well this is Yoko, this is Yoko, this is Yoko ...'

The Colonel was not amused. 'Look – we've got to get you back on-air pronto.' Then he added, 'before the audience falls irrevocably in love with Mort.'

Ricky moved like he'd been ejected from his seat. He made his way through the Onos, occasionally steadying himself with a gentle hand on the odd head (with predictable recoiling and sour expressions in response). The Yokos started to follow him but Colin blocked their exit, helped by the security guards. He cast a quick look over his shoulder to ask Bill to accompany Ricky back to the studio, explaining, 'We could do without another kidnapping.' The Colonel then raised his Sandhurst tones to the intruders, saying, 'Not so fast ladies. I'm Colin Ward-Clemens, executive producer of the show. We need to talk.'

113

Show on-air part six – sketch intro – 11.50pm GMT
Ed Sullivan Theater, Manhattan – 31 December 1999

Keeping a big TV show on time is like piloting a vast cruise liner into harbour without scraping the sides. Louise must have been doing some serious calculations, known ominously as The Sum, to keep Mort and all contributors on track. It's not like the midnight bongs of Big Ben back in London would wait for the presenter's bon mots (really my bon mots, of course) before ringing in the new era.

I'd run after Ricky after he left his former hostage-takers in his dressing room. Bill was flanking him, and they appeared to be in conversation fifty feet away in one of the theatre's long corridors. I needed to discuss options as to how we got Ricky back on the show. The apartment sketch preceded the midnight toll from Westminster, but we'd built in a time buffer. All told, there was a spare minute allowed for ad libbery, before going to pictures from the UK at 23.59 local time (18.59 Eastern Standard Time).

'Sorry to butt in Bill,' I interjected. Close up I saw he looked older than I'd thought. His eyes carried the woes of the world, but his deference was so sweet.

'Sure thing, sir.'

'I need to ask Ricky something: how are you planning to pick up from the Brill and McCall interview?' I left it as an open question for PR purposes, but what I really wanted to ask was whether Ricky could wrap up with Mort on camera to neatly dovetail that sequence. That would provide a more satisfying punctuation point for the viewer.

But words like 'neat' and 'satisfying' didn't always do it for our star turn.

'I'm not propping up that pissing pipsqueak, if that's what you mean.' Oh, I get it: forget the nice guy who introduces me as his writer to a bunch of strangers, this is Ricky Ryan version 2.0. After the Fall.

You can't appeal to someone on your values ...

It's bad enough when people can't see beyond their own interests, but when they can't even see as far as their self-interest in letting someone try to help, that's when it does my head in. There's a potency for me about going from hero to zero, some ancient childhood resonance with the bipolarity of feeling secure with a friend, then something cuts the ground from under your feet. There's a part of me that thinks 'Sod Ricky – let him flounder,' but then something akin to professionalism intervenes, and I bite my tongue for the greater good of the programme.

'As you wish,' I said, trying not to sound sarcastic or sulky. Then I'm left wondering how he's going to insinuate himself back on to the show. We get to the studio floor and Bill melts away again, while Ricky checks in with floor manager Steve. They seem to be swapping notes. Mort is keeping the ship afloat interviewing Charlie Brill and Mitzi McCall the other side of the flat. Ricky adjusts his collar, then he's attended to by make-up and wardrobe off-set.

Mort wraps up his interview with the question, 'What's the one memory of being on *The Ed Sullivan Show* with The Beatles that stays with you most?' The item producer wrote the questions, but that wasn't a bad way to go out. Brill, who tends to dominate the conversation over his wife comes back with the tale of a meeting with Lennon in the dressing room. Ricky would have paid off with a sparkier comeback, but Mort issues a serviceable 'out', the interview is given a healthy dose of applause, and our stand-in does the gentlemanly thing of letting the reaction breathe. But then in a headfucking New York second, from nowhere Ricky bounces in front of camera, overtaking and stunning Mort, and carries on as if nothing untoward has happened. In Ricky's mind nothing untoward probably has happened; he's merely taking his rightful place back in the spotlight. The follow-spot operator was as stunned as Mort for a moment, then went with her instincts to follow Ricky, literally leaving Mr Silus in the shade. Ricky unironically thanks his 'good friend Mort' for his contribution, then prepares to intro the loft apartment sketch.

There's a great term in telly called 'hammocking'. This isn't, as you might think, a budget version of the casting couch for minor roles. It's the scheduling of a weaker show between two strong ones; the stronger shows have, by definition, higher ratings, which means more eyeballs are available to sample the show in the middle. That's at least partly because the eyeballs' owners have too much inertia to change the channel; they know they want to catch the later show. Admittedly, with the proliferation of channels in the late twentieth century, this has been breaking down as a strategy. But it can work within a show, too, such as *Ricky Ryan's Friday Fandango: The Millennial Special*. If people know they want to stick around for a feature that's coming up, we might smuggle past them a slightly more pedestrian item – which often translates as a cheaper one. And that leads to another way in which a show can ape a channel: the *Fandango* has 'internal trails' which mimic the network's trailers, but which, as the prefix implies, only 'point' viewers to other items internal to the show, not to other programmes. Why would we want to help them?

But within programmes, the same as between programmes, trails can be a bore, and a cue to put on the kettle. So after the carpeting from the Colonel over my original sketch – a play on two cultures divided by a common language – I thought, What if a stronger, more lavishly resourced item could also smuggle in an internal trail? Around 23.52 GMT viewers got a chance to decide whether it worked.

114

Show on-air part seven – the sketch – 11.52pm GMT
Ed Sullivan Theater, Manhattan – 31 December 1999

With less than ten minutes to go of the old millennium, Ricky looked at his very best friend, the lens, exuded all the love and warmth you can offer a piece of glass, and intoned, 'You know some of the finest shows on TV feature New York loft apartments: *Friends*, *Seinfeld*, and the one making the big noise now, *Sex and the City*. I asked our top producer if we could have a loft apartment, too. To my great surprise he said yes. But then he immediately suggested a cost-cutting measure with the cast. See if you can spot what it is ... Ladies and gentlemen, welcome to a not-so humble abode ...'

LUCY and TOM are a thirty-something couple; LUCY is American, TOM is British. We find them in their loft apartment, TOM at his laptop against the wall at the back of the wide shot, and LUCY trying to get his attention from the kitchen.
LIVE MUSIC CUE: Breezy sting ending on a sense of anticipation ...

INT. NEW YORK LOFT APARTMENT –
EVENING

LUCY

Haven't you finished yet? It's time to hit the town for
New Year's.

TOM

(tapping at his keyboard)

I'm still writing. You can have as much fun here.
With the TV.

LUCY

(sarcastically)

Sure. Marking the next thousand years by staring at
a screen. You Brits sure know how to party. Whoop-de-do.

TOM

(turns round to face Lucy)

Don't be so negative. It's not staring at a screen – it's
enjoying a show. That *Millennial Special*. Beats being
crushed by a crowd.

LUCY

Who's being negative? I wanna be where the action
is – Times Square at midnight. I wanna see the famous ball
drop on One Times Square. Most people can't get there.
We're real lucky – for us it's a couple blocks away.

TOM

I know I'm a Brit, but lovey I'm trying to write the
Great American Novel. I can't do that while being jostled by
a million drunks belching in my ear.

LUCY

If it wasn't for me, you'd be living in a Great
American Hovel. You've been washing dishes and serving in
bars ever since I've known you – when you're not writing.
Some career progression.

TOM

That's not true. Things have moved on since we met.

LUCY

How?

TOM

They trust me with the dishwasher now. Plus, I've got the keys to the cellar.

(he takes the keys from his desk and dangles them in front of her)

LUCY

Oh – you drive me crazy. We never go anywhere nice. For my 30th you took me to a cut-price store.

TOM

We got some good deals, love.

LUCY

...On bed linen. And *I* ended up paying for it.

(Lucy goes to the kitchen area. She's about to pour herself a drink, but pauses. She catches herself and becomes more tender)

LUCY (contd.)

Do you want anything to drink, honey?

TOM

(turning back to his work)

Twenty Tequilas please. It's not going well.

LUCY

Aww – sweetie. Take some time off. Tonight of all nights.

TOM

I wish I could – but the book won't write itself.

ENTRY BUZZER SOUNDS

LUCY

Expecting someone?

TOM

Only the boss of Penguin.

BUZZER SOUNDS AGAIN

LUCY

Don't get up – oh, you haven't.

(she goes to the entryphone)

LUCY (contd.)

Who is it?

VOICE (WITH AMERICAN ACCENT) FROM
THE ENTRYPHONE

Delivery for Tom and Lucy.

LUCY

(into the entryphone)

Delivery?

VOICE

It's a surprise – for the millennium.

LUCY

Mmm ... I guess you should come on up.

(to Tom)

Are we expecting a delivery?

TOM

(still working at the table)

Not that I know.

DOORBELL RINGS

(Lucy goes to their front door, and opens it, to reveal
RICKY RYAN holding a box)

RICKY

(effusively, in the American accent he's just used)

Well, hi there!

(relaxing into his native Irish accent)

I mean – hey. What's the craic?

LUCY

(unsure – doesn't recognise him)

No cracks here ...

RICKY

I meant, "Whassup?"! Happy new year – nearly.

LUCY

We say 'New year's'. But I guess you ain't from
round these parts?

RICKY

No – I'm from further east.

LUCY

Brooklyn?

RICKY

Cork. My ancestors helped build your fine city.

LUCY

I'm sure we're very grateful.

(Tom has been listening in and has slowly twigged who the visitor is. Tom abandons his laptop and walks round a partition wall to see Ricky in the doorway.)

TOM

Oh my God! It's you – Ricky!

(to Lucy)

Lucy – this is the star of the show – the *Millennial Special*.

RICKY

...Of *Ricky Ryan's Friday Fandango*.

LUCY

(slightly at a loss how to react)

Gr-reat ....?

RICKY

It's a little ... TV thing I do. Don't you want me to open the box?

TOM

I'd rather 'take the money'!

RICKY

(sees Lucy looking confused)

I'll explain later.

(he rips open the box)

I've got a selection of party poppers, streamers, hats ...

(throws one out, ostensibly to the audience)

...And party blowers.

(demonstrates)

LUCY

What are these for?

RICKY

Tonight.

LUCY

We won't be needing them. Thank you.

(she tries to shut the door, but Ricky has his foot in it)

RICKY

Ah, you will, you will ... To accompany the show.

LUCY

But—

RICKY

We've got some great features: 'The Millennial Quiz' – with big cash prizes. We bring you the midnight celebrations live. Plus a fabulous music act in the last hour. Oh, and the odd sketch.

(looks straight down the lens)

That's a bit meta.

LUCY

It's a shame we'll miss it. We'll be in Times Square.

(she tries to shut the door again – Ricky's polite but persistent)

RICKY

Ah – but so will we. We have our cameras there – in the heart of New York City. We've got the build-up for everyone, then our British viewers get to start the millennium with Big Ben in London, and the American gang gets to enjoy the Times Square experience at midnight Eastern Time.

TOM

Cool!

(catches himself after a filthy look from Lucy – he has 'betrayed' her)

RICKY

I promise you a night to remember. Plus we get our cameras closer to the famous ball on One Times Square that descends at midnight – closer than you could ever get if you were there! And you can cuddle up on the sofa with Tom and a nightcap – no worries about getting home.

TOM

Or getting crushed ...

LUCY

It's tempting ...

(she sounds like she's being swayed)

But my mind's made up. I'm a New Yorker.

TOM

How about I stop writing before midnight ..?

RICKY

Good move, Tom. Oh, and I forgot.

(to Lucy)

About Tom's writing. You wouldn't want to be like the guy who turned down The Beatles? I've got a hunch Tom's book's going to be a big hit ...

TOM

(flattered and enthused, but needing reassurance)

Really?

LUCY

(sarcastically)

Really?

RICKY

(confirmatory)

Really! I may even feature it on the show when it's done. For our millions of viewers.

TOM

(to Ricky)

Wow. And that's funny – 'cos my book features you!

RICKY

Great subject.

(to Lucy)

Then he can keep you in the style to which you'd like to become accustomed. And whatever happens, you can both go for a walk in Central Park on New Year's Day – and it won't be crammed to the gills like tonight. What do you say ...?

LUCY

Where's that party blower?

(Lucy and Tom rummage through the box and find and blow party blowers, wear hats, throw streamers at each other, etc.)

RICKY
(straight to camera)
Have a happier millennium when you 'Relate with Ricky'!

APPLAUSE

115

Show on-air part eight – 11.57pm GMT
Ed Sullivan Theater, Manhattan – 31 December 1999

The montage before midnight UK time was designed to give regular viewers to the show reminders of some golden moments in the *Fandango*'s four-year history. For opportunist, millennial newcomers it's meant to excite the sense of having missed out, leading to their acquiring a new viewing habit for the new year. For me it's a reminder of the plethora of pain-in-the-ass times we've gone through to get something on the air.

In three minutes of VT journeying backwards in time we collectively enjoy/get retraumatised by Ricky helping 'build' the Millennium Dome and the London Eye (a tabloid critic suggested Ricky may have jinxed the cables which snapped in the attempt to raise the world's largest Ferris wheel); Ricky introducing Gwyneth Paltrow live on the show, and the sliding doors installed specially at the top of the stairs for her walk-on got 'accidentally' stuck (prompting memories of the back-and-forth with the movie publicists who didn't share our sense of humour); Ricky emerging from a giant lemon and monkeying around with Bono on the launch of U2's album *Pop* (the frontman was surprisingly unprecious, but management as ever wanted all spontaneity scripted). And then the climax of the piece was the start of the very first *Fandango* back in '95: Ricky attempting to rope 'his' luggage on to a donkey on the car-free Greek island of Hydra (it dovetailed with a romantic holiday for two we had to give away, but didn't dovetail with Leonard Cohen, who has a house on the island, being publicly available; an army of researchers weren't to know Cohen was in splendid isolation on an LA mountaintop until spring '99). The montage ended with a tease to the music act which rounds off the show after the Big Ben bongs.

During the VT, Ricky gives the nod to warm-up man Bobbles, who quickly reminds the audience how they're going to help with a countdown into the new millennium.

Yer man Ryan then has a luxuriant golden minute, the last sixty seconds of the second post-Christian thousand years, to do with as he sees fit. There's material of mine sitting there on the prompter ready to rock, but you just know he's going to go off-script and let his ego do the talking. It's why I love him and it's why I hate him.

He riffs around 'new beginnings with old friends, daring to dream dreams and to banish nightmares, to give and not to count the cost, to reach out to the future and clasp it with courage ...' He flirts with incoherence and then, as he seems to be about to crash land, he comes back on script, on to *my* script and says, 'But, let's face it, we'll all be so hungover tomorrow you won't remember a word I've said. [Laugh] So let's be bold, and sashay shamelessly into the next thousand years!' We'd spent fifteen minutes discussing whether he'd be able to say 'sashay shamelessly' under the pressure of the moment, looked at alternatives, and he assured us he wouldn't need them. And he didn't.

Then vision mixer Hilary in the control room presses a button which cuts up a live shot of Big Ben (OK, the Palace of Westminster's St Stephen's Tower) from London on the big Eidophor screens on either side of the stage, while Bobbles, standing at the foot of the rostrum to one side, keeps the punters on track and prompts the crowd to chant '10 ... 9 ... 8 ...' Ricky has manically run round to the back of the set and up the cheap, out-of-vision wooden steps, making it in time to appear at the top of the glitzy showbiz stairs for '5 ... 4 ...' And, in true Hollywood style, as he lands on each step it lights up, with chasers giving the semblance of red and orange lights playing tag with each other along the outer edge of each tread. Then he spends the last three seconds of the old millennium with alternate feet touching down on the final trinity of steps as the crowd belts out '3 ... 2 ... 1!'

His whooped-up theatre audience cheers, the young, the old, those going through midlife crises (is there any other sort of middle age?), fans from our radio days, planeloads of the faithful from The Ryanistas fan club, New Yorkers who couldn't get into the Broadway musicals they'd wanted to, tourists who happened to be in town and fancied a freebie, the lame, the lithe, believers, unbelievers, everyone in the room was united in that millennial moment. And, further afield, on another shore, thanks to electromagnetic waves and cathode rays, scintillation, luminescence, liquid crystal displays, satellites in orbit, pipelines under the ocean and synchronously thrumming acoustic cones, viewers could see and hear us in the land of my birth. The viewing millions tuned in, generations united, grandmothers with little ones wriggling or snoozing in their laps, young lovers made merry by booze, snug on sofas in each other's arms, nursing mothers grateful for the distraction, for the warm, familiar flicker of those fire-like twenty-five frames a second, care homes and second homes were united in their focus, lonely retirees finding solace in the nonsense, four- and five-year-olds allowed to stay up extra late 'just this once' by indulgent parents and carers with an eye to posterity. And in workplaces across the UK knackered retailers at all-night stores with ten-inch TVs perched above serried cigarette cartons, kebab shops keeping faith with the *Fandango* on a suspended screen, firefighters in crew rooms praying not to be interrupted by a shout at this, of all moments, nurses at their stations huddling around sotto tellies to see in the new year, flight attendants eking out the last of their ground-based breaks before preparing to take off again, beefy transmitter engineers shinning up an errant Eiffel-lookalike transmitter tower to get the show back on the air, willing the signal to scythe through hedgerows and high-rises, darting across lakes, and delving needlessly into unoccupied caves, cutting across curvy rail tracks and multi-lane highways, taking transverse paths cross-country, bonding city and hamlet, parking lots and patchwork fields, beaming into palaces and paupers' places, thatched cottages, starter homes, women's refuges, council-run care centres for teens, packed pubs with extended hours, and echoey corridors of political power with on-call comms teams smoothing their sound bites ... And all making up that great mongrel mass – 'the mainstream viewers' – who keep us TV types in work.

As Big Ben chimes, '1 ... 2 ... 3 ...' the audience in the Ed Sullivan see the fireworks around Big Ben answer the bells, '...6 ... 7 ... 8', and then viewers at home and 3,000 miles away in Manhattan see the aerial shots of central London's landmarks – '...9 ... 10 ... 11 ...' – from Barry and Pugin's Parliament to the new London Eye, and somewhere a smudge of light which is the River of Fire tearing along the Thames. And at the strike of twelve Hilary cuts back to the studio and Ricky doesn't need to add much for the crowd to go wild: 'Time to wish you a stonking, great, HAPPY-NEW-MILLENNIUM ...!' He bends backwards with outstretched arms for emphasis. With that, confetti-and-glitter cannons explode rainbow-and-foil-fillet showers over the stage, flambeaus spontaneously light on either side with a mighty whoosh, a deafening cheer becomes one with the sound of the CO_2 jets, dry ice starts to steal its slippery way down the steps, clouding the chasers, and Ricky looks so high on life he could burst.

And as I look on from the side of the stage, mesmerised by the spectacle in the studio and the helicopter shots on-screen from the city of my birth – where I went on to the world's stage thirty-five, going on thirty-six years ago – I can't help thinking of one sultry summer's day in '82, when a palmful of pills nearly shuffled me off-stage prematurely, and almost made me miss this millennial moment, and all the moments in-between.

116

The gift of time
Oxhey, Hertfordshire – Christmas Day, 1972

It's around five in the morning on my ninth Christmas Day. Mum and Dad are upstairs asleep. I can't sleep, because I'm too excited at what the day might bring, including presents. I'm in the music room, so called because it's home to the piano and any other instruments we might drag into it to bash, blow, or twang. On the piano stool is a gift bearing a tag reading, 'To Nate with love from Mummy and Daddy xx' in my mother's rounded handwriting. The parcel is slim and rectangular, nearly as long as an octave on the piano – fifteen centimetres or so. Time has dulled the memory of the wrapping paper, whether it had an age-appropriate design from, say, *Just William*, or *Thunderbirds*, or was plain and stylish. Or perhaps it had a Cliff Richard visual pop reference. But I do know with my artist Dad's love of detail and penchant for presentation it would have been double-wrapped, with coloured tissue paper at its core. The extra layer meant more delayed gratification, especially with the Daniels' 'no peeking' policy, even when down to the inner wrapping.

I know, too, I will have delicately unwrapped the item layer by layer, trying to peel the clear sticky tape – or, if my Dad had had a good year, special sparkly Christmas sticky tape – from the wrapping paper, so as to leave it reusable for another year.

Now I'm sliding what feels like a box from its outer gift-wrapping shell and unfastening the tissue paper fashioned with Dad's trademark V-shaped overfolds. I now see, yes, it's a box, but it gives little away about its contents: it's plain white. I shake it to see if there are any percussive clues, any loose contents, but there aren't. The package is light, with the weight distributed evenly. I slowly open the hinged lid and, emerging from the cardboard's shade, is a watch – a Timex boy's watch. In one sense it's not particularly fancy: no date function, it's not waterproof, not battery- or quartz-powered. The strap is plain black plastic, not leather, and the body isn't particularly chunky. Virtually the only visual extra is a red second hand. But in another sense, it's almost unspeakably special: it's my first watch, it was bought for me by my parents who, while they're not broke, don't have, in that dread phrase, much 'disposable income'. Also, it's an entry point into the adult world of appointments, commitments, and marking the passage of time.

I take it out of its box and slip it on my left wrist.

'It suits you, love,' says a voice from behind me. My mother has quietly crept into the room; I don't know how long she's been looking over my shoulder. She wears a bright red dressing gown with white piping on its edges. The thing about Christmas Day is it falls right in the middle of her worst months psychologically, but a combination of my not being fully aware of that at this age, and her working hard to disguise how wretched she feels, means the season is not without joy. And she looks as pleased as Punch to be able to afford this gift for her little boy, using hard-earned money, as I later find out, from her festive work in a shop.

117

Show on-air part nine – dance – 00.01am GMT
Ed Sullivan Theater, Manhattan – 31 December 1999

We come off the Big Ben bongs without any words, straight on to a futuristic dance number.

Music director Ken Storey has fashioned something led by electronica, but with space for bass, guitar, horns, and drums. He's moved up a gear from a Gary Numan/'Are "Friends" Electric?' template; to my young ear, that sounded like it had landed from another planet, but now it reads like a big synthesiser has been grafted on to a conventional pop/rock band, and the graft has taken. Ken has doubled up the synths, and uses the latest textures; he's folded in some drum-and-bass grooves with a frenetic snare picking out offbeats along with a driving ride cymbal, but he's softened it with an 1980s-effect sweet, slow-moving keyboard melody gliding over it; eventually in rehearsals I identified it as the tune from the Human League's 'We're Only Human'.

The boys in the dance troupe are pushing at their physical limits with cutting-edge robotic gyrations in their metallic onesies, while the girls move at the more sedate pace of the top-line tune. They're wearing black leggings cut off at the knee with a cheeky classical white tutu on top.

Lighting director Mark Short stirs strobes into the mix for brief bursts. In-between, robotic Vari-Lite programming 'walks' tight beams like long legs along the back of the set in cool, contemporary blue. It reminds me of the animated marching hammers in the video for Pink Floyd's 'Another Brick in the Wall', albeit less oppressive.

The ultimate visual ace is the scrapbook-style video backdrop carrying chopped-up visions of the future from the past; most powerfully (and unintentionally witty), is a scratchy 1930s monochrome dystopian vision of New York City, with hover-pods and monorails, and people appearing to fly between skyscrapers with jetpacks against a fearsome sky. Vorsprung durch Technik, Gawd 'elp us.

Our first post-millennial dance number gets a great reaction in the room, and Ricky walks on from camera left and stays to the left of frame, pseudo-graciously steering the rousing applause with his outstretched left hand to the dancers who hold their positions while discreetly taking replenishing breaths a few paces back.

They then exit symmetrically in four different directions while Ricky moves centre stage, and beams like a Cheshire cat as the clapping continues. There's a palpable sense of expectation.

Except Ricky stands.

And stands.

Takes in the audience again, and looks into the camera.

Come on, man. I know you want to surf the wave of audience approval, but ...

Jesus.

What the ...?

And then he goes off-script.

I look to the nearest person with talkback – a Clipboard Colette. I mouth 'What's up ...?' She leans into my ear, removing one earphone so she can hear me, but still hear the director with her other ear.

'Prompter's failed,' she stage-whispers against the PA.

'You're kidding,' I say, needlessly. TV folk like a laugh, but we pick our moments. This is not one of them.

Fuck a duck.

Scenarios race through my head at the speed of thought:

Ricky doesn't learn lines.

Ricky doesn't like printouts.

Thinks they look amateurish if you hold them when you don't need them.

And he'd hate to consult one even if he did need it.

We need to go to VT.

I can hear an amplified Ricky talking about what's coming up, but ad-libbing it. He's checking in with the crowd they're alright. They respond faithfully; they're still upbeat.

Prompter twins.

Yes.

I must get to Penny. Jenni. Both and.

Urgently.

I leg it round the fire lane to their position.

Hell's breaking loose.

Jenni (or Penny) at the keyboard, furiously trying different keystrokes.

Three engineers clustered around, checking cable connections, consulting a manual, steering Jenni(?) through different options.

Penny/the other one is on the phone; sounds like a call to Prompter HQ.

And then I see it. Before my eyes, on the prompter monitor, the words I've lovingly crafted start sliding down the screen and   display   wi th   ran-

dom   spac   ing
        and   gather ing   in
                                                                                        a
heap with rand0m
            char@c   ters !!* *&c
                                                        at   the

                        bottom   of the $$
            screen.

And then summarily disappea

My mind's racing in a blind, fade-to-white panic. An eternity's gone already – how are we going to get through the next, crucial hour without a prompter?

One engineer turns and says to the others, 'StalagByte 2.0.' The other engineers, arms folded, nod in agreement.

I ask for a translation. One freckled guy says, 'Y2K.'

My brain can't compute. My expression must be as blank as my internal screen.

Another engineer elaborates: 'The Millennium Bug.'

I start to process this when I think I've heard something odd on the PA. I'm about to rewind the last three seconds in my head to check the buffer, when it happens again: yes, Ricky's said my name on-air.

I zone in to what he's saying ...

'...when I started out in radio ...'

A New York second later a Clipboard Colette careers round the corner and beckons me to follow her. She's leading me towards the stage, explaining oh-so-briefly, 'Ricky seems to want you to help fill till the prompter's fixed. Good luck.'

'...Ladies and gentlemen, please welcome programme associate extraordinaire, Mr Nate Daniels!'

Colette virtually pushes me on and then I'm blinded and can't work out why.

Oh my God, the follow spot's following me.

Gulp.

More speed-of-thoughts:

What am I wearing?

Will it do?

Are my flies done up?

Keep smiling.

Can I pretend to adjust my trousers while sneakily checking the zip's at the top of its travel?

This applause is loud. I've never had applause like this or a spotlight before ...

Mouth dry.

Heartbeat. Heartbeat. Heartbeat.

Follow his lead. Don't upstage.

Christ – I'm alive. This is really happening.

Ricky's smiling a million-dollar-showbiz smile and reaches out to shake my hand.

Wing it.

I take his hand, smiling with so much effort I think my face will crack.

'We go back a long way, don't we, Nate?'

I rein in my smile enough to regain the use of my lips. 'Sure do.' Sure do? Bugger. Am I trying to sound American? 'Memories of long summer holidays in Ireland with you, Pad – er – Ricky.' Bollocks. Unforced error. The association with childhood pal Paddy before he became Ricky. Like returning from abroad and driving on the wrong side of the road.

Ricky's unfazed. He immediately picks up, 'I'd love to say we enjoyed Californian-style sunshine, but most days it rained, didn't it?' Warm audience laugh – they're with us.

'That's the price you pay for Ireland being so green!' Call yourself a gag writer, Nate? You'll be doing warm-ups at wakes.

There's an extra intensity in Ricky's features as he looks at me now, but at first I discount it, never having been in this sort of live TV situation with him, eyeball to eyeball. He seems to want something from me, but I can't discern what it is. He starts reminiscing on his – our – radio roots but something's not quite right with his eyes. As he talks about our early days in local radio, I become aware of his blinking; it's very pronounced. I must keep listening in case he throws in a curveball, but now I wonder if he's got some nervous thing I've never noticed before. Or perhaps it's surfaced at this time of high stakes? Or is it some eye irritation? But that all seems unlikely, going on impossible. Then I start to see a pattern: three short blinks then three longer blinks then three shorter blinks again.

Dot-dot-dot dash-dash-dash dot-dot-dot ... SOS. Emergency. And Ricky's doing what that American serviceman we heard about as kids did. Jeremiah Denton had been captured by the North Vietnamese and was being interviewed on TV. He was saying one thing but blinking another: the word 'T-O-R-T-U-R-E' in Morse code. 'Blinking Morse code,' as Paddy and I used to say, hilariously. Ah, Samuel Morse: ushering in digital transmission, circa 1837! I worry the viewers will spot Ricky's blinking, but looking over his shoulder I can see the floor monitor, and Hilary has cut up the wide shot and seems to be holding on it, making Ricky's eyes less prominent to the punters.

So as Ricky tells an anecdote about how he was set up live on-air one April Fool's Day, I'm trying to work out how to subtly let him know I've cracked the SOS code. Nodding won't cut it as I'm already nodding to acknowledge his story. Then I recall a pop act that, as a superannuated disc jockey, he'd remember playing. As he relates how I got the engineers as a prank to pitch up his voice in his headphones so he was less Orson Welles, more Minnie Mouse, I found my moment to say to Ricky, 'And I remember you saying to the engineers, 'Just Be Good to Me' – like the SOS Band sang – and sort my headphones out!'

Ricky nods and stops transmitting SOS. Then I see on the TV showing the studio output they've found some archive of Ricky in the radio studio – brilliant. We're both free from being in-vision – for now – but between us we've got to keep filling until the prompter bug's fixed, or till we can find an alternative.

Steve will have pointed to the floor monitor in Ricky's eyeline on the other side, so he'll know we're visually free for the moment; the viewers can't see us live, they're seeing that old footage of a pre-TV radio star. I give Ricky the thumbs up as he references what the viewer's now seeing; he knows he's off-camera. He can't learn lines, but he's lost none of his radio ad-libbing skills, thank God. Liberated from the lens, Ricky now blinks more deliberately as he talks about the road from radio to the *Fandango*. I'm now looking out for his next transmission.

OMG – I've got to trawl through my memory bank to decode his message. It starts with four short blinks, ie., four dots: .... I remember the most common letter, E, is one dot. But surely he can't mean four Es? (Four Es a jolly good fellow? How encoded is this?) I decide the four dots must apply to one letter – he hasn't put enough of a gap between the dots for them to be different letters. Think, think ... From my sketchy memory, I have that first letter as K. Gap. Second letter easy – one dot = E. Gap. Third letter: a dot, a dash, and two more dots. That rings a bell as Y. No – Y is a dash, a dot, and two dashes – the very negative of what he's blinking. Then it comes back to me: it's the letter L. Gap. Fourth letter: one short blink, two longer blinks, then one shorter one. While I process this, I have to keep engaging with what he's saying, fleshing out the story of the donkey in the first *Fandango* over video of the Greek island of Hydra. The gallery's now playing the latter part of the montage – the *Fandango*'s greatest hits, first used before midnight UK time – with the sound kept low. Dot-dash-dash-dot. God, what is that? R? No, that's one dot and one dash then another dot. Ah – it's P, not R. So Ricky's spelt out 'K-E-L-P'. Kelp.

What's seaweed got to do with the *Fandango*? Now Ricky, while talking about our show's ratings success in the run-up to the millennium, is (while still off-camera) drawing a vertical line in the air, and putting a dot under it. A dash and a dot? But a vertical dash?

I mentally spell out K-E-L-P with what he's drawing. I twig it's an exclamation mark: KELP!

You idiot, Nate – he's spelling out *HELP!* Four dots is H.

But surely SOS Help! is a tautology? SOS means 'help', of sorts. So he must mean something else. And the exclamation mark changes everything: it has to be a Beatles connection. Their song, album, and film *Help!* As Ricky brings viewers up to date with the *Fandango*, I'm going to take a gamble: he knows we've got something Beatly coming up, but he's not sure how we get on to it. I think he's forgotten Macca's on before the band. So I stick my neck out and pick up from his pay-off, 'And that's how we got here!' I can see Hilary has cut off the archive video to a two-shot on us.

I start to speak, but my words are lost under colossal applause; I hadn't allowed for the old sod having worked his magic with the crowd while my brain was on overload keeping up with him. I let the clapping subside, then I restart my question: 'You know we promised our friends a *night* to remember?'

'Ah, yes – that we did,' said Ricky. His demanding look has settled.

'Well, I think it's time to deliver on that, don't you, Ricky?' Got his name right this time.

'Certainly is, Nate. You wouldn't be thinking of a *knight* of the realm, by any chance, would you?'

Ricky's back on track, thank Christ. I've got to give him some space now. I feed him a leading question: 'A certain Sir ...?'

'...Sir Paul McCartney,' he picks up, effortlessly. He's got his mojo back: a sparkle in his eyes instead of blinking. And I can see on the TV over his shoulder, Ricky's on a single shot; the gallery's confident they can go in close again.

But something's nagging at me.

The writer of 'Something''s nagging at me. We can't wish his predicament away. I took a deep breath and said, 'We should point out this was recorded before the terrible attack on George Harrison yesterday ...'

'Thank you – yes.' God, Ricky thanking me live on-air? How the world's changed. 'So obviously Paul doesn't reference that – this was recorded beforehand. But I know he's sent all his love to George and his wife Olivia. And so do we.' Ricky ends on the 'we' in the ascendant.

More fulsome applause. I let Ricky do the rest. 'So without further ado, let's hear from the one, the only: Sir – Paul – McCartneeeeey ...!!'

Yet more applause. So proud to have one of the biggest musicians of all time on the show, even if he isn't here in person.

We've now got two and a half minutes to think while the Macca VT's on-air. And I think I've witnessed the end of my TV presenting ambitions. I look into the lens now we're not on shot and it's ominously black: the prompter's still dead.

Ricky doesn't waste a moment to go to Steve, the floor manager, standing by camera 3. Our star turn is careful to turn his back to the audience, so they can't see he's fuming. Or read his lips. 'Get fucking Mort out here again. Pronto.'

Steve looks bemused. 'But you're here, Ricky?'

'Not for much longer. This whole Prêt à Prompter thing's a fucking farce. I'm going to Millennium Bug-ger off till it's sorted. If you've a problem with me taking a break, get that dozy-shit director down.'

Steve looked like he'd been slapped across the cheek by a cricket bat. His index finger hovered over the button to speak to the gallery. But first he took a deep breath while he thought how to translate Ricky's tirade for consumption by Roger.

118

Show on-air part ten – two's a crowd – 12.14am GMT
Ed Sullivan Theater, Manhattan – 31 December 1999

They're an unlikely pairing on screen: Ricky, lithe and lanky, not quite matching his lookalike Lincoln's six feet four, but only a couple of inches behind; Mort, a little portly and a good few inches shorter. But that's the least of Roger's woes right now. To say there's a problem with chemistry is like calling World War II a little skirmish.

Individually they can each connect with the lens, but between them is ice. To be fair, Mort is at least looking to Ricky periodically and smiling, but the effort is asymmetric. As if by magic, Ricky now, like Mort, has a clipboard (this one being commandeered during the McCartney VT from a passing Colette).

With the prompter still playing up, Colin had decreed to Roger in the control room that Ricky couldn't just slope off until it was repaired; viewers would have been confused enough by his earlier disappearance. And who knew how long the Millennium Bug might bite for? What stopped Ricky doing the *Fandango* flounce was Colin's threat to pull the plugs on the show for good. The Colonel also felt that the audience had warmed to Mort and would be baffled if he now disappeared.

And so TV's latest Odd Couple stagger on to the concert part of the show. Under strictures from Colin, Ricky has been told he'll get to introduce the band, but only if he gives space to Mort to deliver a newsflash.

'We're getting reports from the hospital where George Harrison's being treated in Berk-shire, England ...' starts Mort.

'It's pronounced "Bark-shire",' corrects Ricky, half turning to his impromptu partner.

Mort says, 'Excuse me,' and continues, 'Mr Harrison said he felt his attacker wasn't a burglar but that he – quote unquote – "wasn't auditioning for the Traveling Wilburys"'.

There's an audience laugh, if slightly guilty sounding, with some people adding a sympathetic sigh and tut.

I know Ricky won't have liked Mort provoking laughter – 'a hack fancying himself as a bloody entertainer,' I could imagine my old mate saying. So Ricky takes the moral high ground and repeats good wishes from the show to the Harrisons, then picks up the energy up to explain, 'We were racking our brains to think what act could possibly do justice to us kicking off the next thousand years. And we all need a party, right? [Reaction.] And then we thought – we're in the Ed Sullivan Theater on Broadway [cheers for the building again], famous not only for Irish-American presenter Ed Sullivan, but also for a certain four-piece "beat" group [more cheers] he welcomed to this very stage in the last century.'

A kind of Lotterby cloth – named after sitcom director Sidney Lotterby, who liked to hide visual plot spoilers from the studio audience till the last moment – obscures the band, but gives a strong hint as to what might be behind it: a huge black-and-white still from the Sullivan show starring the mop tops fills the entire giant cloth. (A Lotterby cloth would normally be plain.) It's frozen a seminal moment in popular culture which the new millennium would find hard to eclipse. Ed divides the band by standing between John and Paul, and George and Ringo. And then there's an audio clue: the opening guitar riff to 'Twist and Shout' plays loud, proud, and live on the PA, with Ringo-esque alternating double and single beats on the snare as part of a repeated phrase before the vocal comes in.

The band hold down the volume as Ricky returns to his radio roots and talks over the intro like a DJ:

'Ladies and gentleman, we decided we had to try and recapture something of the magic of the night a wee quartet captured the heart of this great nation,' rang out those much-loved Cork tones. Ricky was riding the waves of crowd reaction, like his smooth stones bouncing off the surface of the Atlantic earlier.

But then the undulations were cruelly interrupted by cries of 'Break up The Beatles, Break up The Beatles ...!' The many Yokos, heard but not seen at first, had broken through whatever cordon had penned them in on the studio floor, and they'd smashed through the undertakings they'd given of good behaviour. 'End male dominance – end dominant males!' they chanted.

And now they were in vision, appearing from the back of the set at the top of the stairs. As I stood at the foot of the audience rostrum, I heard a collective gasp from the ticket holders. There was a different kind of surprise for me: the gang had removed their uniform silver jumpsuits and now wore highly-coloured jumpsuits with a silky sheen, top to toe, one person's cloth being glistering gold, another bright lemon, another rich vermillion, and so on. I could now register their Mary Quant wet-look white wellies, and many of them now had props: placards reinforcing their slogans about splitting up The Beatles and bringing down the patriarchy. It was that Miss World/Bob Hope moment from 1970, the disruption of the beauty pageant in London; or as the lascivious showman had labelled it, perhaps a little too honestly, the 'cattle market'. But here it was being played out a generation later as avant-garde art: situationism.

The band behind the Lotterby cloth had stopped playing; all eyes were on Ricky to see how the ultimate showman would cope with literally being upstaged. I'd heard what the Colonel what had agreed with the Yokos, so I knew what had been meant to happen. Ricky being the mercurial artist he was, though, and the Yokos having jumped the gun, it was anybody's guess what would *actually* happen.

'I'm so sorry ladies and gentlemen, boys and girls for this interruption.' He looked solemnly into the lens, but I could hear the sound of Ricky's forked tongue waggling. Acres of forest would be felled discussing this moment in print for years to come, and already electrons were being excited to cross the Atlantic in both directions with the news, like digital smoke signals. How 'sorry' was Ricky really to have a career-defining moment that would guarantee him lecture spots on cruise ships into his dotage? 'We'll get on with the show as soon as we can. But I think it's only fair to hear these ladies' concerns.'

The Yoko I recognised as Japanese-sounding seemed to be the one who put herself forward to talk to Ricky now. 'We're not ladies,' she said pointedly. 'We're women.' Oops.

'I'm sorry,' said Ricky. 'Perhaps you could explain your fellow *women*'s concerns. Why are you here today?'

'We heard you were having a Beatles-themed party and we felt we couldn't start the new millennium with an all-male bastion. We're sick of male dominance and oppression, and we want something different.'

'But the Fab Four only ever sang about love,' Ricky countered. 'As Paul said, "We weren't encouraging our fans to leave their parents."' Good retort. I wish I'd written that one. It's as if he's been taken lessons on journalistic balance from Mort, who'd stepped back a little.

Yoko Uno, as I now thought of the premier Yoko, came back with: '"The Fab Four" – your term, not mine – were the first truly commodified group. The clue was in the album title: *Beatles for Sale*. Pop as product.'

'Nonsense,' shouted someone from the back of the stalls. The studio audience was getting restive and Ricky knew it.

'Bollocks,' bawled another. He seemed portly with a white shirt and a bald, shiny head. We had to hope he wasn't under an audience mic.

Ricky couldn't afford to lose control of his big gig. How was he going handle this one?

'Millions of people have heard what you've had to say,' said Ricky, 'And they'll be able to make their own minds up – er ....? What name do I give you – Yoko?'

'Yoko 23.' Shame. I preferred Uno.

'But I know our audience work very hard in their lives away from watching the *Fandango*, and they want to hear our fine band now.' And addressing the people in their seats directly he asked, 'Don't you?' He stoked their reaction with a beckoning move of his right hand, palm upwards and arm outstretched.

'Yes!' they shout as one. Good move to have them demonstrably onside – stops lone hecklers.

'And,' Ricky went on, 'We may just have a surprise up our sleeves for all of yous: Yokos and people watching and all ...!'

119

Show on-air part eleven – 12.25am GMT
Ed Sullivan Theater, Manhattan – 31 December 1999

Our Beatles tribute act were going down a storm. I've always thought of 'Ticket to Ride' as a drum song. Although we hear George's line first – the jingle-jangle, and rhythms which tilt at a slight angle to true – it's Ringo's roll which thwacks it all off for real. Then snare and tom flams slice through the air, extending Harrison's syncopation with a sophistication few get right; the guy at the back is on the money yet again, and it's taken for granted. Victim of his own success. Ringo's a left-handed drummer on a right-hander's kit – maybe that's the secret of the tilt, the oblique approach. And did I mention a certain doe-eyed bassist's underpinning, in lock-step with Ringo's kick drum? More precision mechanics; McCartney's playing is taken for granted, too. Then everything's beautifully set up for Lennon's vocal entry. John's reference to sadness in the first line pulls against the jollity of the jangles; for me, it's the creative tension built into the song. Plus, the tribute act takes 'Ticket' at a lick about ten per cent faster than the record. No wonder the crowd cry out for more!

Ricky piggy-backs off the applause to steal some for himself, and he beams broadly like he's the fifth Beatle. The players bow as one, a nod (sorry) to the parent band's early, disciplined days, then Ricky – standing centre stage – motions for them to come over. 'Folks,' he hollers, 'please show your appreciation for the She-tles!' Another surge of support. 'Keep your applause coming for Jean, Paula, Georgia and, er, Ringola!' Laughter followed by revived clapping. The foursome march in a line towards Ricky, their beige round-neck Shea Stadium-era suits giving a coordinated quasi-military look.

The Yokos, who've had the wind taken out of their sails – where's the oppressive male conspiracy now with this all-female tribute? – melt away to the camera-left side of the stage, guarded by an assistant floor manager and security.

'So, let's speak first to Jean, and I'm told you want to talk about your vital statistics?' fed Ricky, to an ambivalent reaction. He points a mic in her direction.

Jean's not far off six feet, meeting Ricky virtually eye-to-eye, and she leans in slightly to the mic. She has a slightly faltering German accent as she says, 'My statistics are 153, 37,000 and 1,500.' Endearingly, 'statistics' comes out closer to 'sadistics'.

Taking a deep breath at a moment of career jeopardy, and shooting a deliberately nervy smile into the lens, Ricky asks, 'Would you ever explain that to us?'

'Yes of course,' she obliges, flicking back her auburn hair, which is about the same length as John's, c.1968. 'It's my IQ, my earnings last year in dollars, and the amount I paid for this guitar.' She shows her Epiphone out front, to the odd cheer, laugh and wolf whistle. A pair of brown-checked boxer shorts are hurled on to the stage to her obvious amusement. (Don't ask if that was scripted.) But camera 3 offers a close-up of said underwear, swiftly snapped up by vision mixer Hilary – the shot, not the pants. Ricky then picks up the boxers and holds them at his waist, earning another laugh from the crowd. He then throws them 'off' in my direction.

He works his way down the line with the other three and, true to our previous long deliberations, delicately takes down the mood for the Georgia/George axis, given Harrison's condition. Sure enough, Georgia, resplendent in blonde curls, her right arm resting sexily on the upper side of her Rickenbacker's body, unbuttons her light khaki tunic to reveal a T-shirt underneath saying, in a groovy late-'60s multi-line font, 'Get Well Soon, George!' Hearty applause and further whistles follow.

Nearly halfway through the finale yer man has one more stunt to offer. He sends the She-tles back to their split-level podium to 'sit quietly for a moment' while he shares a bit of 'good news'. He beckons his partner, Jacqui, to come out of the audience and join him on-stage. She swishes on in her swirly red taffeta ball gown, as if she's about to dance a spectacular tango. Or fandango? Her glossy dark hair is piled high, apart from the ringlets which have broken free and are finding common cause with her gold dangly earrings. Complete with Audrey Hepburn eyes and supermodel's neck she looks every bit showbiz royalty; nay, she *is* showbiz royalty, the more so when her prince has something to ask of her in front of the adoring millions.

Going down on one glossy, black-trousered knee he asks plaintively, 'Jacqui – will you marry me?'

Things went quiet suddenly, apart from the Vari-Lite cooling fans. '*Mais oui* – yes!' she replied, sounding quite emotional. The studio erupted.

Cynics would say she was never going to refuse live on-air, and that Ricky exploited that. Others, ascribing darker motives to Jacqui, would say she'd sunk her much-manicured talons into her A-lister man's flesh, and got what she wanted. But the truth didn't seem to be at either extreme.

Ricky sounded a little choked as he said, both to his belle and to the audience, 'You may know I haven't always lived the life of a saint.' The audience murmur in a way that suggests, 'You can say that again.' 'In fact,' Ricky continued, 'it's often been a case of "halo – goodbye."' The audience laughter grows with the spreading realisation of the Beatles reference, and follows up with a good-natured groan. Who writes this stuff? Ringola, who's snuck back behind her kit, caps things off with a snare thwack and a kick-drum beat. 'But the new millennium will see me face the ultimate test of my humanity, and whether I can be redeemed. Jacqui and I are going to have our first child.' The audience spontaneously bursts into applause, with whoops and whistles. But Jacqui looks pregnant with a thought she wants to air.

She helps herself to the handheld mic her future husband holds by his side. The sound mixer, appropriately called Mike, is sufficiently on the ball to fade it out while she's handling it, then fades it up once she's settled. With her *exotique* French lilt Jacqui says, looking out to the audience, then into the lens, and then to Ricky himself, 'I have to tell you Monsieur Ryan [she pronounces his surname as 'ree-ann']: we are expecting our first *and second* child. I am having the twins!'

The crowd goes wild and Ricky smiles for a second, then Hilary cuts off the two-shot with him and his future bride a little earlier than she might have wanted. She goes instead for a wide shot of the band on camera 1, whose operator's framing excludes the camera-left side of the drum kit. The studio audience can see what viewers at home have been denied by Hilary's sharp reflexes: Ricky has involuntarily reversed on to Ringola's Ludwig floor tom and Georgia's Vox amp in a looks-like-he's-seen-a-ghost full-fat faint.

120

Show on-air part twelve - 00.48am GMT
Ed Sullivan Theater, Manhattan - 31 December 1999

If you were expecting Ricky to be revived by a fan - by which I mean a device for cooling, originally from Old English *fann*, a contraption for separating wheat from chaff - I'm going to disappoint. Neither were smelling salts involved. Nor a light dusting to the nostrils of coke, or a blow job from a fan - as in 'fanatic' - or a transfusion of neat alcohol. These were some of the theories doing the rounds after the show on those diabolical bulletin boards the Internet has spawned.

In fact, it was the sheer primal noise of 'She Loves You' that brought Ricky round when Ringola (or Lynda Rutt, to give her her real name) played an opening salvo on the snare. It should have been on the floor tom, but Ricky's fall had also felled Linda's second largest drum. No matter; jazz drummer Buddy Rich routinely used a floor tom just to put his sweat-drenched towel on, and pros are used to improvising. Director Roger protected his star and the scenic guys righting the floor tom by ripping up his plans and avoiding wide shots. The She-tles' roadies were tied up restoring Georgia's amp to its upright position. Roger directed his crack camera crew to go in close on the faces of our ersatz Beatles and on their fingers or sticks on their instruments, variously strumming, picking, singing, and thwacking. Keen students of television might have found the direction a bit claustrophobic at first, but ninety seconds in both Ricky and the floor tom were upright, the latter memorably thanks to Lynda shouting instructions to the scenic ops away from the mics without missing a beat.

Ricky pulled himself together in double-quick time for his penultimate link in this fourth hour of the show. He had to: 'She Loves You' is less than 2½ minutes long. Make-up and wardrobe swooped in at speed to check he was presentable, then our hero was steered by floor manager Steve on to the correct mark. The closing chord was swamped by applause and cheers. Over its tail, summoning up his numinous powers, Ricky looked straight down the barrel and said, 'We're not quite done – we've got time for one more song. [Audience cheer.] We need an anthem to send us out on a high. Give it up again for the She-tles!' More high-energy applause. Ricky then looked across to the band, asking rhetorically, 'Paula? Jean? Any ideas?' Those two rested their arms on their bass and electric guitars respectively and feigned a lack of inspiration. Georgia and Ringola shook their heads, too. Ricky looked to the audience: 'You lot?!' They reacted warmly to being called a 'lot'.

"Fixing a Hole',' cried one portly guy in a tank top.

'That's a bit niche!' says Ricky with a quizzical look.

"Yesterday',' calls out a woman with what you're meant to call mousy brown hair. I think it gives women – and mice – a bad rap.

'Gorgeous song, but too slow, love,' Ricky replies.

Mouse Woman looks dejected – or is she play-acting? She seems to mouth the word 'love' to the guy she's with, possibly in disdain. Ricky can, at times, be defiantly old school.

'Hey you – I got an idea,' says a male voice with a New Jersey accent. It was actor Chase, playing the part of a lighting engineer. He was standing centre stage with a pole, adjusting a light which was pointing down at him. Since the light was coming from above it emphasised his jowls and the bags under his eyes, as did the make-up. His curly black hair was flecked with white. The lighting director – the character's notional boss – then dimmed every other light so the 'spark' was standing in a pool of his own light, supplemented by a follow spot.

You could have heard a pin drop. I'd scripted to bring down the manic energy at this point. Ricky, lit by his own follow spot , and with his footsteps being the only sound, walks across to the actor.

'Oh, yeah?' says Ricky. 'What's your name?'

'It's Troy, sir.'

'Ah, yes – we may have met earlier. And which Beatles song are you suggesting, Troy?'

'It needs to stay true to the original,' the electrician responds.

'That's not a song.' Our star plays baffled.

'It kinda is, sir.'

Paula plays a major chord spread with a flourish across the keyboard of an upright piano. She's been steered not to show her musical hand too soon, so the chord comes disguised.

'I'm not following you, Troy.'

'Oh – you will, Ricky, you will ... It *is* Ricky, ain't it?'

Ricky smiles. 'You recognise me now, is it?' The audience gets the callback to the earlier sketch with Troy, union agitator, and laughs.

The follow spot on Troy and the luminaire above him fade to black.

The light now comes up on Paula at the piano. She looks straight down the barrel of the lens, her face in tight close-up, and starts to sing 'Hey Jude'.

Jean has moved to bass playing, and the band follow the gentle build of the original recording, the only Fabs song I was familiar with at the time it was in the charts (even though there were later hits), and one of my first childhood memories. I recall someone having it on a transistor radio when Mum, Dad and I were on a narrow boat on the Grand Union Canal. At this distance of time, it seems like the memory of a memory, but I sense Mum was next to me on that glorious late August day, as we glided along the glistening water. You might say it's hindsight, or rewriting history, but I have a feeling that even at the age of four, I was aware things were starting to turn for Mum as they did every August, and that she was about to pay for a summer of fragile 'good' mental health by heading into a dank, dark tunnel.

The audience has spontaneously broken into applause after the first line of the song. It's accompanied visually by back-projections, initially of Beatlemania and of *The Ed Sullivan Show*, then it moves through the 1960s with images of Mary Quant fashion, anti-Vietnam protests, the Mini car juxtaposed with the miniskirt, DJ Tony Blackburn kicking off Radio 1, then a shot of the vinyl single of 'Hey Jude' showing The Beatles' Apple label, which starts rotating, then the picture mixes through to a rotating newspaper headline which, when it slows down, can be read as 'Prague Spring turns to Winter', mixing through to a Soviet tank on fire next to protestors carrying the Czechoslovakian flag. This in turn melts into footage from the 1969 investiture of the Prince of Wales, followed by footage from the television documentary *Royal Family*, then the first moon landing and performances from Woodstock, including Santana, Janis Joplin, and Jimi Hendrix.

As the coda begins with loads of 'na-na-na's, which Ricky encourages the crowd to join in on, the stage starts to fill. First he beckons on Mort Silus, and thrusts his sidekick's hand – whether he likes it or not – into the air, while saying Mort's name. The crowd accompanies each name with a swell of applause. Next to take their bow are the actors from the sketch, Rich and Sophia, then, as Ricky says, 'What they lack in profile they make up for in numbers – the backroom boys and girls' and, en masse, scenic operatives, Clipboard Colettes (researchers) and assistant floor managers all crowd the stage. Steve runs on at the last minute and leads the others to lower their heads in sync. There's an interesting conundrum we thrashed out in interminable meetings about these bows: namely, that we were still on-air, and people had jobs to do. We decided to make a virtue of this, and – to take the example of the camera operators – Ricky says, 'Now, there's the small matter of people too busy to take a bow, including most of our talented camera crew, so please welcome, acknowledging your applause on behalf of all nine cameramen and -women, our supremo of the small screen, supervisor Rod Spencer.' A healthy roar accompanied – people understand that TV needs cameras, and cameras need operating. At that point the on-air camera itself – operated by Rod – takes a gentle bow, panning down on a wide shot to the assembled company's feet and up again. Some departments – for instance, the real, not thespian sparks – had a revolving door of bowees who'd emerge from the back of the stage, fold from the waist down, rise then walk straight off to resume their roles.

And, lest the viewer lose faith with anonymous faces, despite Ricky's best efforts to sell the featured individuals' skills, to the continuing accompaniment of the She-tles' and the audience's 'na-na-na's, the backdrop keeps moving through time, reaching the 1970s with the extra-hirsute McCartney chopping wood, post-Beatles split, on his Scottish farm; industrial strife at Grunwick's photo processors and at coal mines; a family in moody candlelight during a power cut; prime minister Ted Heath asking, in a party political broadcast, the suicidal question 'Who governs Britain?'; John Lennon at Madison Square Gardens singing alongside Elton John, then a standpipe and a poster exhorting the reader to 'Save Water' in the hazy summer of '76; the Queen arriving at Heathrow Central tube station on the newly-opened Jubilee Line dissolving into the Sex Pistols' single label for 'God Save the Queen'; a 'Sorry No Petrol' sign on a garage forecourt; Margaret Thatcher standing outside No. 10 Downing Street for the first time; and Ronald Reagan on the campaign trail in November '79.

The timeline rolled on into the 1980s, from the Royal Marines yomping over the unforgiving terrain of the Falklands, to excessive use of hair gel at Wembley Stadium during Live Aid; and on into the 1990s, including a still of a mural referencing David Bowie's 'Heroes' on one end of a siege-damaged building in Sarajevo; a shot of the Windows 95 boot-up screen; Tony Blair walking with his wife Cherie into Downing Street through a thicket of Union Jacks; and a shot of the Millennium Dome – due to open in a matter of hours – with its twelve distinctive yellow masts protruding from the roof. That was to have been the culmination of the sequence of images of our shared pleasure and pain in the modern world. But, at my suggestion, one more was added at the last minute: a beautiful portrait of the best-looking Beatle facing the lens square on, *c.*1976, George's cheekbones rising majestically above the summit of his beard, his auburn hair and dark-brown eyes blending with the classic 1970s colour scheme of his orange-brown shirt-and-jumper combo, something in his serious expression hinting at frailty or melancholy – or both. It brought the house down.

And then the bastard Colonel emerged at the peak of that stolen adulation, holding Roger's hand high, two complete unknowns to the watching millions, only given context by Ricky introducing our 'award-winning executive producer and director', both then hurriedly returning upstairs to their powerful obscurity. Then the star of the show motioned the quartet to take it down a little, while still going round the 'na-na-na' chords. They immediately obliged, with Paula singing sotto, and playing the piano *piano*, Georgia dropped out from acoustic strumming, and Jean took down her level, but took up her sophistication, moving to funky octaves, picking, or even slapping like Mark King in Level 42, and throwing in the odd blue note. Ringola remained solid but moved from a four-to-the-floor rock beat to gently swinging, moving from the hi-hat to the ride cymbal.

As soon as the players had settled into this new groove Ricky announced, 'A special occasion deserves a special response, and to celebrate moving into the year 2000 we have a new verse to sing to the tune of 'Hey Jude'.'

The crowd were wooed by this.

'That's the good news,' said Ricky. 'The even better news is you get to sing it!' [Laugh.] And, looking straight into the bottle, Ricky emotes, 'That includes you, as well, gentle viewer.' The photos on the big screens and on the backdrop behind the band gave way to these new lyrics.

The She-tles sing it in unison along with Ricky who, it turns out, doesn't have a bad little singing voice. Take-up in the audience is sporadic, but that's fine on the first time through as it leaves somewhere to go:

> *Stay true*
> *Don't feel no fear,*
> *It's a new year, and new millennium,*
> *A great chance*
> *To start all over again,*
> *I'll be your friend*
> *Forever and ever ...*

There's something between a laugh and polite applause at the end of this world premiere. Ricky follows the age-old showbiz imperative not to accept the first attempt as sufficient, yet not to slate it too much, either. The band quietly continues to play the three-chord pattern that accompanies the 'na's repeatedly under Ricky.

'That was good – but you can do better, can't you?' Ricky looked out pleadingly while mumbled assent rippled through the audience like a Mexican sound wave. 'I'll take that as a yes,' he deadpanned straight into camera, the familiar hungry look in his eye. That prompted a laugh. 'And this time we need the "ever" of "forever and ever" to go on and on – like the Lord's Prayer without the Amen.'

Ringola went from holding back to full-tilt loudness with a 'shut up and listen' roll around the kit.

This time my new verse – yes, mine – went down so much better, massively helped by the assembled crowd still on-stage joining in. During the first couple of lines, the Yokos sidled on singing along, then Ken brought in the house-band's horns and percussion, adding his synth. The vocalists added the icing.

At the repeated 'ever, ever, ever ...'s, Paula let rip like her near namesake, showing a similar touch of the Little Richards, too. I feared for her larynx, but her only concern was to give it 150 per cent.

On a prearranged cue, apart from anything so Mike the mixer had a fighting chance of pushing Ricky's projected words through above the extended chorus, Ricky said his farewells before the stroke of 1.00am GMT. The Yokos pulled one last stunt by removing their masks, and revealing their composition was pretty much 50/50 male and female, but they'd only put forward spokeswomen. Doh. Bloody situationists.

'Thanks for watching,' says Ricky, as the vast credits roll. 'And enjoy the next thousand years!'

Part Five

Waving, Drowning

121

Crystal ball gazing
Times Square, Manhattan – 31 December 1999-1 January 2000 EST

Hitchcock understood the value of suspense. We all felt it, being roundly jostled in Times Square with two and a half minutes to go till the new millennium: pauper Paddy, fresh from being King Ricky, sporting a Cossack hat and a dark greatcoat, and wearing his newly revealed dark-framed glasses, having not put his contacts back in; Jacqui – technically plus two – resplendent in a mustard wet-look Quant-like mac; Louise modelling a candyfloss pink furry cap the same colour as her stole; and yours truly, concealing a black polo-necked woollen top under a high-collared black winter coat. Bet mine was the only gear from a second-hand store.

Being with a million intimate strangers, crammed from Central Park to 42nd Street, was a surreal experience. There were a few too many party hats for my liking, among other oddball headgear, and a few too many decibels. It might be the closest I'll get to Beatlemania, and while The Beatles weren't there, the mania definitely was.

The animated billboards seemed more hyperactive than ever. And only New Yorkers could get excited about a ball dropping down a pole at midnight on New Year's Eve in the middle of the world's densest concrete forest. I blame the media: as my guidebook pointed out, the boss of the *New York Times* – which gave its name to Times Square – kicked off the ball-dropping fetish in 1907, and people have been getting more unhinged about it ever since. Quite apart from that, I was trying to fathom the much-celebrated ball's colour sequence, thanks to its ever-changing lighting, but no sooner had I got as far as blue-green, er, red-purple ... then there'd be a distraction: some quip from Paddy, someone pointing to a fantabulous array of balloons, or fancy dress, or a suspected pickpocket. How to appreciate this moment? It became increasingly impossible the more I thought about it. To experience something so intensely is to risk not experiencing it at all; if you have to work so hard at it, does it really have substance? I was trying to make it special, yet haven't I been in packed crowds before? And seen in a few new years? And Times Square has become familiar these last few days. It's all so arbitrary, like the timing itself. No Christ, no millennium. But I don't know anyone – not even ardent believers – who think the baby Jesus was born on 1st January AD 0. Also, why are we going to town on this new year? Because, by some accident of counting in base ten, the new year arrives gift-wrapped with a whole load of noughts. And why do we count in base ten? Because that's the number of digits nature's endowed us with. Again, arbitrary.

These thoughts are all displacement activity for me getting upset about Louise being here under sufferance. She wanted to go clubbing, not watching a lump of Waterford Crystal make its way down a greasy pole. She's been a bit stand-offish since whatever did or didn't happen between us last night. Christ, what a long twenty-four hours. Like that artwork showing Hitchcock's *Psycho* at two instead of twenty-five frames a second, every moment painfully drawn out beyond its elastic limit. And the fatigue. God, the fatigue ...

Getting here was a feat in itself. The city's yeomanry were being very inelastic about entry to this area. Strictly by ID, and only up to 11pm at that. We had to play a sort of TV Top Trumps and make special pleading; or, as others might call it, privileged whining. I was carrying a Polaroid of Ricky and Mort side-by-side from earlier. The sentry didn't recognise Ricky, but at least he was with us in person. I tried to protect Ricky's feelings but of course it was Mort's likeness in the photo which got us into to this pen; Mort, the local news hero of the New York patch.

Hospitality after the show had been kinda spirited. Celebrations began in two green rooms soon after we came off the air, but that was a stopgap while they reset the studio to make it party-friendly.

Jacqui had been radiant in the repurposed studio. I think she's going to be one of those women who bloom in pregnancy. She was wearing a white cotton wrap-around dress with a gold chain belt. Sadly I didn't know her well enough to remark, 'I didn't get the memo it was a toga party.' So perhaps I shouldn't have said it.

Paddy was later than her, his hair still stylishly wet from the shower. He wore a slightly incongruous black baseball cap, topping off a relaxed look of man about yacht: navy blue cotton jacket; a gold, black and white striped shirt; and beige Oxford bags. Overcompensation for not having gone to Oxford?

'Nate – thank you so much for the chance to reach a wider audience,' beamed Peter the philosopher, approaching me from a table groaning with victuals. He was performing a delicate balancing act with a thin-stemmed glass of white, perched on a plate of smoked-salmon blinis. He'd swapped his collared shirt for a brilliant white grandad shirt, buttoned to the hilt. Larry David would be proud.

'No – thank *you*,' I said, with more sincerity on the inside than I could convey. 'I was going to dub you "the armchair philosopher" on-air. But any mention of soft furnishings now might bring back the trauma.'

He raised his eyebrows quizzically while taking a sip. 'Trauma?'

'Of keeping you, er, in suspense. The old hoists jamming.'

'Oh – the sofa not moving, you mean? I did wonder if that was intentional. Glad they got me down the ladder, though,' he said with a smile.

'Good of you to be so philosophical about it.' We laughed about my unconscious use of the P-word.

Just then the Prêt-à-Prompter twins passed by en route to topping up. I flagged them down. 'Peter – I want you to meet the ladies of letters, Jenni and Penny – though not necessarily in that order. They make my words reality on what you Americans call the teleprompter.'

'Ah – the teleprompt twins! Delighted,' said Peter, holding out his hand. 'So, which is which?'

The one I was sure was Jenni said, 'I'm Penny.'

'Hold on.' I said to 'Penny', wanting to resolve this for all time. 'How is it Script Ed always gets you the right way round, yet I'm always wrong? You do look slightly different – something in the eyes. But I thought I'd sussed the difference.' I apologised to Peter for cutting into the intros, but I was perplexed.

The twins looked at each other and burst out laughing, possibly fuelled by on-tap cava. 'Are you going to tell him, or shall I?' said one twin to the other.

'We had a bet with Script Ed,' said twin two, 'that you wouldn't notice if we treated him like he always got it right and you always got it wrong.'

'I'm really Penny ...' said the first one.

I was inclined now to believe her.

'And I'm really not,' giggled her twin.

Infantile in the extreme, but they were both demob happy, and who could take offence to giggles? Peter laughed along with the whole absurd scene. I imagined it appearing in an academic textbook by him some day.

Elsa was swapping notes and, it seemed, contacts with Jacqui – in French – at a nearby settee. I caught the odd '*Enchanté*', so they seemed to be getting along okay.

Noise levels escalated as the booze flowed, and the arms race of turning up Earth, Wind & Fire's superb Beatles cover, 'Got to Get You into My Life', by a person or persons unknown (shhhh ...) only made them louder.

The sketch actors were huddling with our sparks thesp, bitching about a variety of casting and creative directors interchangeably. Then Mort sidled over to Ricky to show 'no hard feelings', but it turned out our star *did* harbour hard feelings, and the newshound backed away, crestfallen.

The prompter twins moved on and I retreated back to a safe haven with Peter. 'You weren't telling the whole story with your reference on-air to Albert Camus, were you?' I put it to him, trying not to sound too finger-pointy. 'It's like that quote about people not being able to bear too much reality?'

'Ah, yes. I feel prime-time TV is not a natural home for a discussion of anarcho-syndicalism, even if your friend John Lennon sang 'Power to the People'.

'How do you know he's my friend?' I asked.

'I saw your intense absorption in the female Beatles – what were they, the Femme-fatales?'

'She-tles,' I corrected, wondering if he was dicking with me. 'It's a fair cop, as we say in Britain. But that's not quite what I meant.' I swirled my second G & T of the night. 'I was thinking of Camus' opening question in *The Myth of Sisyphus* ...'

'The "one truly serious philosophical problem" of suicide?' Peter scrunched up his forehead as he said the S-word.

'Got it in one!' It actually took two goes, but I was feeling generous. 'It's an arresting first sentence. It demands we find a reason to live. So sad Camus died young – same age as my mother, in fact. Oh, and I have to ask: since most philosophers are miserable bastards, how come you're so happy?'

'Ha!' He put a knuckle to the dimple below his lips and looked down for a moment. 'My philosophy can be summed up in the profound insight of my Jewish grandmother. He looked back at me. '"Life is short. So have another piece of chocolate cake."'

On cue Peter ate his last blini.

Two sofas away one of the make-up artists was taking a photo of the twins on either side of Jacqui, each with a hand on her fecund belly. Smiles all round. Then Lynda, aka Ringola, sauntered past carrying a quartet of lagers. With the Shea suit and drum kit packed away she was free to wear a kaftan and copious bangles, together with bishop sleeves and – be still, my beating heart – a black velvet bejewelled choker round her neck. Selica lives! 'Excuse me, Larr— Peter.' I turned to the She-tle. 'Lynda – I loved the band. Really. Pass on our massive thanks.'

She smiled, but looked very self-effacing. 'Thanks. Will do. Though The Beatles are the real stars.'

Damn. How do I get her to take a compliment? 'I'm not sure Ringo had to contend with a fainting presenter. I loved your ad lib on the snare.'

'It was a case of having to. I was down to a choice of that or the rack tom. I've already been lectured by a couple of chumps who thought I played it wrong 'cos I'm female.'

'Bloody hell. Chalk that up to envy. But who are your heroes – apart from the Fabs?'

'Mmm ...' Lynda scratched her nose and thought carefully. 'It would have to be Filipino-Californian rockers Fanny.'

'Fanny?' I suppressed a schoolboy snigger. I also had to think quickly as to whether I should confess to not knowing them. I decided to wait and see whether Peter would plead ignorance first. He did.

'Not on my cultural radar. Who they?' Peter's eyes were as engaged as ever. His glass was now empty.

Lynda was on a mission. 'An all-girl band who "played like motherfuckers", as Bowie said. Did a great version of the Fabs' 'Hey Bulldog' and worked with Beatles engineer Geoff Emerick. Then, of course, I adore Karen Carpenter.'

'Yeah – an amazing voice,' observed Peter, moving closer.

'Great voice – but an even greater drummer,' said Lynda. She'd put down the tray and took a swig from one of the glasses. 'Moving out from behind her cocoon of the kit might just have killed her. So sad.' Lynda had a faraway look in her eyes. And I went back briefly in my mind to the Funny Farm where I was when I heard of Karen's demise. The cold, cold winter of '83.

Somebody spoke and I emerged from my dream. I was back as part of the Gang of Four in Times Square.

'Aren't you going to watch the ball drop, Nate?' It was Louise, large as life in my face: big grin, perfect dentition, with that pink hat the source of her cascades of corkscrews. 'Get ready to count!'

Paddy and Jacqui were canoodling a few feet away. Perhaps Paddy, in allowing himself to be crushed up close with the hoi polloi, was finally acknowledging he was unknown in America. He was unlikely to be happy with that for long, though. He saw his fame stateside as a work in progress. I think Jacqui saw her future husband as a WIP, too.

As Jacqui flattered Louise about her couture, something was bugging me regarding Paddy. I had to ask him: 'Pads – you know when they ran in the tape of you intro-ing Mort?'

He grunted some kind of acknowledgement.

'Why,' I asked, 'was it called the "fowss tape"?'

'Fowss?' For a moment Paddy was perplexed. The spirited crowd carried on cavorting. 'Ah, you mean the Faust Tape. Poor diction by the English. I called it that 'cos I felt I was doing a deal with the Devil – selling my soul so that Silus fellah could walk on to warm applause. The audience would've rejected him without me bigging him up. And the feckin' Colonel worried he wouldn't have had a show without me doing the tape. Thought I was gonna do a runner. I had him over a barrel.' He spat those last words out then wore a self-satisfied smile.

Mmm ... I suspect Colin had said, 'You'll record this link, mate, or else ...' If there was a barrel, it wasn't the Colonel over it. But, hey, I didn't want to spoil the moment.

Paddy moved quickly on. 'There she goes!' he cried, looking at the crystal finally heading south for the last minute of the old millennium, as we came back together as a foursome. Only Jacqui out of our gang was sober, safeguarding the next generation. The twins wouldn't remember this moment, of course, but they'd be heirs to it for the rest of their lives: children of the millennium, forever as old as the century, just like my grandfather was for the twentieth century. Let's hope that, unlike Grandad, they only spend time in Flanders Fields as a holiday choice.

'10 ... 9 ... 8 ... 7 ...' The mass of humanity counted as one – or tried to.

I had a distinct feeling of déjà vu, having lived through the millennium already, five hours before. Perhaps that's why TV folk age twice as quickly as normal people.

'...6 ... 5 ... 4 ...' The crystal continued on its downward journey.

Camus urged living intensely. I tried to live these seconds fully, especially as this millennium, unlike the one hours before, was going to be my last.

Paddy enveloped us all in a group hug, as we shouted, together with the numberless celebrants, '...3 ... 2 ...1!!' The Waterford Crystal ball reached the end of its travel, disappearing behind a huge illuminated '2000' on top of One Times Square.

A roar went up like the biggest goal ever had been scored. My eardrums struggled to contain the sound. From nowhere Paddy produced a bottle of Champagne and three plastic cups, stacked inside each other. He handed us each a cup, filled them all, then took the one from Jacqui for himself. He produced a soft drink for her as a substitute.

Jacqui landed a quick kiss on my cheek. Above the din I could just make out her say, 'Thank you for finding him.' Her last word had the gorgeous Parisian edge of 'eem'.

'*De rien,*' I said, and she giggled. 'It was nothing.' I added, '"*Santé!* We all toasted each other. 'Good health!'

Then Louise planted a great big smacker on my lips without so much as a written warning. Her eyes flared closer to mine than I could focus on, as a cheeky tongue darted in my mouth, carrying the effervescence of the champers she'd just swigged. Our tongues did the do-si-do for a moment, yielding to a fleshy play-fight for a few delicious seconds.

She pulled away without fanfare, throwing over her shoulder, 'See you round the clubs.' And she was gone, folding into the vast mass of revellers as if she'd never existed.

Paddy and Jacqui had missed this, being absorbed in another pre-conjugal clinch.

Finally unloosed from his bride-to-be Paddy fist-bumped me like a baseball ace, and locked those Lincolnian eyes on mine, saying:

'Happy new year, mate. And remember The Men. Remember ... The Men.'

122

Sister act
Provincetown, Massachusetts – 1 January 2000

I parked up the blue hired Oldsmobile, sublet from Paddy, next to MacMillan Pier in Provincetown. At first the car felt too big a beast for me, but I could get used to the luxury. The Wedgwood sea churned under sculpted grey clouds. A biting cold made my jacket feel like paper. I looked at my watch: 14.23. A bit early for half-past. Did it look neurotic to be early? I suppose, though only if Jane was early by the same amount.

Phew. It cancels out.

What if she was late? Well, (a) she wouldn't know I was early, and (b) I would have the moral high ground. Oh, come on – you do know I'm joking, don't you? What kind of person stakes out the moral high ground for their first meeting with a long-lost sister?

But then, what kind of person thinks they're morally superior for not doing that?

I may be overthinking. Wish I didn't have the time. 14.25.

Should have arranged to meet at 16.20 – 1620 being the year of the Pilgrim Fathers landing here. Then my first line could have been about meeting at *Mayflower*-o'clock.

Hilarious.

Reminder to self: I don't have to play the funny man here. And it's not a date.

But then ... what is it? A solemn social occasion? No kisses, obviously – respectful handshaking required. Polite language only. Avoid overfamiliarity.

14.27. Still time for more thinking. OK. Change of tack: observe the fishing boats moored up alongside. Their rigging beats out a random rhythm inspired by the chill North Atlantic wind.

14.32. She's late. Sloppy. Or lack of enthusiasm? More time filling ...

I look at the cute names for craft: Hailee James, Idle Hour, Jersey Princess ...

'Do you always read out loud? That might take some getting used to.' The voice with its cool, all-American burr, came from over my shoulder with a short laugh.

I spun around. The woman from the photo was suddenly made flesh in front of me. 'Bloody hell, Jane – you're in 3-D!' She gave me a huge hug. With my nose and lips squashed against her left cheek, technically I suppose I kissed her.

'Thank the Lord it was you, Nate,' she said. 'Could have been some other English eccentric talking to himself. But I took the risk you'd be underdressed.'

'Too scruffy?' I asked. 'Sorry.'

'No, no – I meant, not enough layers for our New England winter. We're a bit exposed here. Turn right over there,' she pointed east into the water, 'and it's 3,000 miles before the first wind break.'

'Or as I call it: home. So how about we take shelter?' I suggested. 'As the local, you can choose where.'

'Sure. There's this nice little place I know ... An Italian. Real old.'

'Gosh – you mean pre-Elvis?'

'About the same time his career took off.' We'd have to see if she got my humour and was meeting irony with irony. 'It dates from the Fifties. Ciro & Sal's. Just to the right.'

'Not 3,000 miles away? Or down a long and winding road?'

'Ha, no – ten minutes' walk! D'you think you can manage?'

'You're the American here. How many car lengths is that?'

Jane purses her lips as if calculating, then relaxes into a grin. Wisps of dun and white hair poke out of her grey woolly hat and dance in the wind. We start walking.

As we turn right into Commercial Street, she loops her arm in mine.

123

Film script 1 – final scene

INT. HOUSE – BEDROOM – DUSK
It is mid-afternoon. The winter light is failing.

We see part of a bed over the shoulder of a fifteen-year-old **BOY** who is looking away from the camera. He is obstructing the camera-left side of the bed.

The camera, which is on a jib, cranes up to reveal the body of a middle-aged woman beyond the boy, propped up on her right arm. It is the boy's **MOTHER**. There are a few white pills by a bottle on the bedside table nearest her. Her face is drawn and lifeless. Her eyes are shut; she doesn't appear to be breathing. There is a hint of green in the light on her face.

The camera then slowly cranes down, swings left on its arm, and pans right on its pivot point as the lights dim on the mother. She is then framed out as the camera slowly rotates 180 degrees to reveal an adult **FIGURE** in shadow, a couple of paces behind the boy, who is himself in a pool of light. The figure is facing the same direction as the boy; the boy is unaware of him. Both characters are facing the camera, though looking beyond it.

The taller figure steps into the light and we see it is the **WRITER**. He gently places his left hand on the left shoulder of his younger self.

The boy bends his left forearm back to touch the older hand on his shoulder.

WRITER:
She's ...

I shut my laptop. I feel the catch click into place through the lid. The fan stops whirring. New York burbles outside my hotel window.

I don't need the words in front of me – I know what comes next.

I say out loud, 'She's at peace now. Let her die. Her war is over. You'll get through this – I know you will.'

FADE TO WHITE

Other titles by BLKDOG Publishing for your consideration:

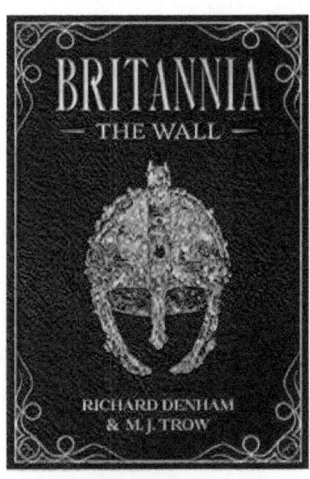

Britannia: The Wall
By Richard Denham & M. J. Trow

THE END OF ROMAN BRITAIN BEGINS.

The story opens in 367 AD. Four soldiers - Justinus, Paternus, Leocadius and Vitalis - are out hunting for food supplies at an outpost of Hadrian's Wall, when the Wall comes under attack.

The four find their fort destroyed, their comrades killed, and Paternus is unable to find his wife and son. As they run south to Eboracum, they realize that this is no ordinary border raid. Ranged against the Romans at the edge of the world are four different peoples, and they have banded together under a mysterious leader who wears a silver mask and uses the name Valentinus - man of Valentia, the turbulent area north of the Wall.

Faced with questions they are hard-pressed to answer, Leocadius blurts out a story that makes the men Heroes of the Wall. Their lives change not only when Valentinus begins his lethal sweep across Britannia but as soon as Leo's lie is out in the world, growing and changing as it goes.

Goblin Market
By Maryanne Coleman

Have you ever wondered what happened to the faeries you used to believe in? They lived at the bottom of the garden and left rings in the grass and sparkling glamour in the air to remind you where they were. But that was then – now you might find them in places you might not think to look. They might be stacking shelves, delivering milk or weighing babies at the clinic. Open your eyes and keep your wits about you and you might see them.

But no one is looking any more and that is hard for a Faerie Queen to bear and Titania has had enough. When Titania stamps her foot, everyone in Faerieland jumps; publicity is what they need. Television, magazines. But that sort of thing is much more the remit of the bad boys of the Unseelie Court, the ones who weave a new kind of magic; the World Wide Web. Here is Puck re-learning how to fly; Leanne the agent who really is a vampire; Oberon's Boys playing cards behind the wainscoting; Black Annis, the bag-lady from Hainault, all gathered in a Restoration comedy that is strictly twenty-first century.

Fade
By Bethan White

There is nothing extraordinary about Chris Rowan. Each day he wakes to the same faces, has the same breakfast, the same commute, the same sort of homes he tries to rent out to unsuspecting tenants.

There is nothing extraordinary about Chris Rowan. That is apart from the black dog that haunts his nightmares and an unexpected encounter with a long forgotten demon from his past. A nudge that will send Chris on his own downward spiral, from which there may be no escape.

There is nothing extraordinary about Chris Rowan...

www.blkdogpublishing.com

www.ingramcontent.com/pod-product-compliance
Lightning Source LLC
Chambersburg PA
CBHW020827030726
47496CB00001B/123